W9-BLN-158

Benevolence

Benevolence

A Novel

Julie Janson

HARPERVIA

An Imprint of HarperCollins*Publishers*

BENEVOLENCE. Copyright © 2022 by Julie Janson. All rights reserved. Printed in the United States of America. No part of this book may be used or reproduced in any manner whatsoever without written permission except in the case of brief quotations embodied in critical articles and reviews. For information, address HarperCollins Publishers, 195 Broadway, New York, NY 10007.

HarperCollins books may be purchased for educational, business, or sales promotional use. For information, please email the Special Markets Department at SPsales@harpercollins.com.

Originally published as Benevolence in Australia in 2020 by Magabala Books.

FIRST HARPERVIA HARDCOVER PUBLISHED IN AUGUST 2022

FIRST EDITION

Designed by Terry McGrath
Map courtesy of Magabala Books

Library of Congress Cataloging-in-Publication Data is available upon request.

ISBN 978-0-06-314095-0

22 23 24 25 26 LSC 10 9 8 7 6 5 4 3 2 1

Dedicated to the memory of my great-great-grandmother
Mary Ann Thomas of Blacktown Road, Freeman's Reach

FOREWORD

In Darug Australian Aboriginal language, I greet you: "*Quai bidja, jumna paialla jannawi*—come here, we speak together."

I am of the Burruberongal clan of Darug nation, Hawkesbury River, New South Wales. I pay respect to the local Aboriginal Elders past and present and to the ancestors and spirits of the land, the knowledge and culture.

There is archaeological evidence about the ancestors of Indigenous Aboriginal Australians landing in the north of Australia some 65,000 years ago. The most important human remains ever found in Australia are Mungo Lady and Mungo Man at Lake Mungo, New South Wales. These 42,000-year-old ritual burial sites give us evidence of some of the oldest modern human remains (Homo sapiens) yet found outside of Africa.

Indonesian traders bought trepang and pearl shell from Yolngu Aboriginal people in the north of Australia from the early 1600s. Dutch explorers made the first recorded European sightings of Western Australia in 1606; they called it New Holland. Other Europeans followed, until in 1770 Captain James Cook charted the east coast of Australia for Great Britain.

With the loss of American colonies in the American Revolutionary War (1775–1783) the British looked to find replacement colonies. The First Fleet of British ships landed to establish a penal colony in Botany Bay (now Sydney) on January 26, 1788. Indigenous Australians call that day "Invasion Day" or "Survival Day"; other Australians refer to it as "Australia Day."

The British invaded and established colonies while declaring our continent to be Terra Nullius, empty land. Indigenous Australians fought back with long battles that became known as the "Killing Times." This colonization impacted Indigenous Australians by reducing the land, food, and water resources. Many people died from smallpox and other introduced diseases. Our hero Pemulwuy led his Bidjigal clan in a guerrilla war and was killed by the British in 1802, and his head was preserved and sent to England. Countless massacres were carried out by British soldiers, settlers, and police between 1788 and the 1930s. The country is dotted with memorials for British colonizers, but none for the people they massacred. Indigenous children were forcibly taken from their families to be raised in cruel institutions; these people are called the Stolen Generation.

We as a country are not in the post-colonial era; colonization is ongoing, until there is an Indigenous Voice to Parliament and a National Truth and Reconciliation Commission.

Recovery from losing one's country is a long process; 238 years of colonial domination over Australia's First Nation peoples has led to an Indigenous "writing back" of our history: the interpretation of shared events through Aboriginal and Torres Strait Islander eyes. Protest in the form of the arts has long been a method of Indigenous people fighting for recognition. We did not die out; there was no dying pillow to soothe.

Restoring faith in Australian fairness and democracy in relation to Indigenous history begins with restoring the right to be heard. We are often from families who were denied education and lived in poverty; many are landless in our own land. For Indigenous Australians, there was no treaty and no ceding of the land to the British Crown. A "Makarrata," or compact, is a document of reconciliation demanded by many Indigenous Australians. There is now a request for constitutional recognition; we are still waiting.

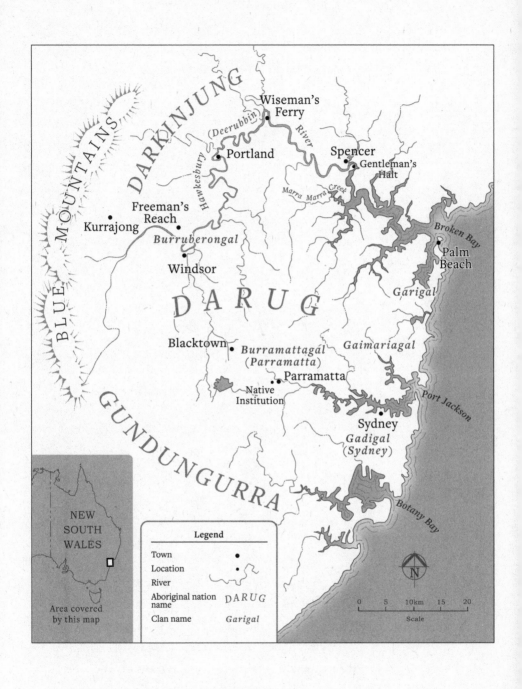

Author's Note on Darug Language Use in *Benevolence*

I have used one main source for the Darug language, J. L. Kohen's *A Dictionary of the Dharug Language: the Inland Dialect*, Blacktown and District Historical Society, 1990. I am grateful to researchers and the Darug community for their invaluable language work.

Some Darug words may have spelling that differs from other sources. I apologize for any misspelling or unsure meaning but assure the reader that the intent is to render Darug language as I have heard it spoken and as I have studied over some years. Please forgive my poetic license.

CHAPTER ONE

1816: Muraging Is Given Away in Parramatta

The gray-green eucalypts clatter with the sound of cicadas. Magpies and currawongs warble across the early morning sky as the sun's heat streams down. It is eaglehawk time, the season of *burumurring*, when the land is dry and these birds fly after small game. Muraging's clan, the Burruberongal of the Darug people, gather their dillybags and coolamon dishes and prepare for the long walk to Burramatta, the land of eels, and Parramatta town. The old women stamp out a fire, and one gathers the baby boy in her arms and ties him onto her possum-skin cloak.

Muraging hears rattling carts full of *waibala*, whitefella, and the sound of pots against iron wheels. She looks back and sees the deep wheel marks, like huge snake tracks, and hurries after her father, Berringingy. He gives her a *waibala* coat of red wool. So, he loves her. He turns away and she watches the boy take her place. She can see the love between man and boy.

She doesn't understand what is about to happen, but she knows she must try to have courage. There is loud talk around her. She is limp with the heat and imagines herself floating in a deep, cool creek. But her father is speaking to her and what he is saying brings her back. He tells her he met some men in Parramatta town who offered to teach Aboriginal children to read and write. She is to be an important part of helping their people and she must learn their language and their ways. She must be brave and remember that he loves her and one day he will come back for her. He reminds her that the sky god, Baiame, and his son, Daramulam, will watch over and protect her. She panics and grips his hand. Alarm rises and her aunt mothers look away.

Her father lifts her up and holds his head with her body pressed against his black curls. She longs for food and chews wattle gum to ease her thirst. The red coat is dropped along the track.

———

They walk for many days before they arrive at Parramatta, where carriages and bullock wagons churn mud—and the horses are terrifyingly big. She quivers at the sharp hooves and the whinnying, like the sound of monsters. A wooden stage rises near the church, where soldiers stand in formation, rifles by their sides. Musicians play on the stage and a juggler tosses balls in the air while a boy raps on his drum. Men in black coats and women in long dresses hold parasols as they gather. Roses bloom behind picket fences.

Today is the Annual Native Feast—a day when blankets and food are distributed to the Deerubbin Aborigines of the Hawkesbury River area. Families sit in groups on the lawn, passing roast meats and swigging at jugs of *bool*, rum. Different clans sit next to each other, some dressed in rags and others resplendent in possum-skin cloaks. They gather in front of the veranda, where the governor's wife, Lady Macquarie, hands out blankets.

Berringingy pushes through the melee searching for the man in a black coat. Muraging's head turns back and forth staring at men in red with sabers. She is startled by the noise and loud music. She sees a tall wooden box covered with striped material, surrounded by small children who shout and laugh. Tiny people in bright colored clothes are trapped in the box hitting each other. One has a hooked nose and a red pointed hat with jingling bells. Muraging pulls urgently on her father's arm to get him to look at this spectacle.

Her father places her down and hands her over to the government men of the Parramatta Native Institution to be a school pupil. She is shown where the big fella boss stands—Governor Lachlan Macquarie. He gives a speech about his feelings of benevolence toward native people and how he accepts their gift. This word *nguyangun*—gift—can't be correct.

Muraging wants to scream but she can't move or speak. Berringingy is standing in the sunlight and the boy now clings to his shoulders. The longed-for boy. She wishes they had left him in the bush for the ants.

Her father stands, places his knuckles together on the top of his woomera spear thrower, and leans forward, listening. A captain in red wool is talking slowly as if her father is stupid. The English words sound like the rattle of sticks.

Berringingy looks over at her and wipes away a tear.

Muraging stares at him. She has seen this look of confusion on his face before, when he was first given a bag of flour. He made a joke—had they given him white dust or ocher paint? He mimed spitting it out as he tasted it. He threw it away and the bag burst and produced a white cloud. They had all laughed. The tribe had kept their eyes on him to see what to do about these ghost men with fire sticks that killed. Her father was their star and moon. But then the soldiers had laughed at him. She had been dismayed to see him, their leader, ridiculed. They produced damper bread from a saddlebag, and the terrible horse had whinnied, frightening them all except her father. Berringingy stood tall, turned his back, and, with a flick of a hand, the whole mob walked away. Proud. They didn't need white dust from dead people.

Only later would Muraging know what it is to beg for just one scoop of *waibala* flour.

Now she is naked in front of these ghost men, their ghost-blue eyes glowing as she pulls a cotton shift over her head.

Governor Lachlan Macquarie stands next to Berringingy. Macquarie is dressed in a red coat with gold buttons and braid and a hat of bright green feathers. The men beside him also wear red coats and gold braid; swords hang from their belts. Indian ceremonial daggers in silver scabbards glint in the sun. Muraging squints at the governor as he delivers his speech:

"We are aware of many Darug clans inhabiting the area around our newfound settlement. The Gadigal of Botany Bay are responsible for many incursions. In Prospect, new farmers are undergoing terrible afflictions as a consequence of these incursions. Other woods tribes are the Bidjigal at Castle Hill; the Burruberongal on the Deerubbin, the Hawkesbury River; the Cannemegal near Parramatta; and the Cabrogal at Liverpool. They are often reported to gather together for catching eels and what have you. We must endeavor to bring a civilizing influence on these natives, who possibly number up to five thousand in this area alone. Today, I bring good tidings: we shall, with the enthusiastic aid of my good wife, add some pupils to our Native School, including this rather untidy child."

He points to Muraging and she is shocked to see people stare and laugh at her. The crowd cheers and the governor smiles at Muraging. The *waibala* ghosts in their long black shiny boots laugh a lot with snorting pink noses.

Macquarie puts out his hand to his wife, Elizabeth, who stands in front of a line of scrubbed Parramatta Native Institution children, like trees in white shifts. She leans down to Muraging and shows her a gold frame with a dead child locked inside. The child stares back at her, trapped in a gold stone.

Muraging feels the edge of the lady's dress as it brushes her face.

Perhaps if she keeps still, she will not be eaten. It is a relief when she is not eaten. Still her guts turn to liquid and she thinks she might wet herself as she is pulled along with the other children. Scissors snip at her hair and she grits her teeth as her curls drift down into the dirt. She wants to show she is strong.

Her chest pounds and she thinks it will burst. For the first time she looks at the newly arrived schoolchildren. One little girl cries and wets herself, but nobody seems to notice. Muraging is terrified but stands very quietly. She wills herself to withstand this moment. She must be brave and stay ready to escape. Her granny's spirit is standing by her side, as always. She imagines she is biting the white people, screaming and punching and running as she leaves the *waibala* empty-handed. But for now the sun is hot as she crouches to watch ants moving a crumb of bread. She puts a twig in their way, and they climb over it.

She looks around the square, surrounded with big stone buildings, to see a whole bullock cooking and turning on a stick. Juice sizzles and her mouth drools. The smell attracts stray dogs and a white one runs off with some meat. She wants to chase it and grab the food. She watches her father feeding the boy some delicious, chewed meat. Her meat.

She looks toward the edge of town and the great gray gum trees are full of spirits watching them. A white cockatoo drops from the sky and sits beside her. It speaks to her about its need for some seeds or bread and she agrees; life is hard.

The children have been taught to curtsy and told to do so to the fat men and ladies; this makes them giggle nervously. But Muraging refuses and kicks the nearest *waibala*. She stands tall while a big sweaty man with a red nose introduces himself as Reverend Masters. He is wearing dark clothes with a white collar that seems to be choking him. He's a minister and a magistrate. He wears a gold ring embossed with a black cross. He smells of perfume and pipe smoke. She cringes before this man's cruel eyes.

Two tall people, dressed like crows in long black gowns, push through the crowd. They stand in front of the line of Aboriginal children and bow to Reverend Masters.

"Dear Reverend, I hope our other charges from the Parramatta Native Institution show you how we are successful in taming the natives in becoming useful members of society," says one. "Thank you for Muraging. I will be like a father to her."

She is startled to hear her name.

"Mrs. Shelley, Mr. Shelley, I am pleased to see you take on these native charges on behalf of the Colonial Missionary Society," says Reverend Masters. "Teach these children of God to see into their souls. God's will endures. We hope that you can provide for the young natives so that they can learn English and become interpreters for their savage cousins. We can hope that they may marry and breed a better type of native. The full bloods will naturally die out. These innocents will be more respectful of our ways and desires. There will be no corruption of souls here. We can save them from damnation."

"Yes, our sole motive is the conversion of souls, and for this we have come so far from our missionary activities in Tahiti," says Mr. Shelley while Mrs. Shelley nods. "My wife and I desire to do much wonderful work and trust our little school will be a beacon of hope for these poor innocent children."

Reverend Masters puts his glasses on and peers closely at Muraging. "She seems to be about twelve years old. She has features that are close to the African. I feel little hesitancy to classify these Aborigines with the progeny of Canaan who was cursed by Noah. They are cursed to be servants of servants."

"Surely not. Jesus will love them, as shall we, and we will bring them improvement and civilization," says Mrs. Shelley.

"Madam, we are the civilizers of heathens," says Governor Macquarie.

"Perhaps you are not equal to the exertions required. We do not wish the natives to languish in ignorance of the Lord," says Reverend Masters.

"Governor, if you wish to enumerate any difficulties, we shall attend to them with no hesitance. The Negroes in other new worlds are said to be ready for emancipation. Who knows what may eventuate with our humble endeavors," says Mr. Shelley. But no one seems to be looking at him. Masters picks his teeth and examines the contents. He rubs Muraging's head and tickles her ears in an awful way as she squirms. He is greasy and hideous with a huge shadow in the sun, like a Hairy Man.

Mr. and Mrs. Shelley smile and beckon to her. She thinks at that moment that she might be eaten.

"Now take care that the females remain ignorant of all but sewing, cleaning, and prayers—all the better to serve husbands," says Masters, as he grabs Muraging's ear and peers into it.

"We will call her Mary James, after my old housekeeper," says Masters, as his hand creeps across Mary's skull; he then wipes his palm with a silk scarf.

"Say your new name, Mary," says Masters.

"Muraging," she says.

She shivers and tries to rub his smell off her head.

"Mary! She will grow used to it," says Masters.

Berringingy appears and walks up to the governor. Has he changed his mind? Muraging smiles at him hopefully while the governor bows before him.

"Greetings, Chief Berringingy. This is an unheralded visit but a most welcome one. I remember that Governor Phillip met your esteemed leaders, Nurrugingy and Yarramundi—or is it Yellowmunday?" says the governor.

He continues: "On the Richmond Creek. They exchanged gifts. Two stone hatchets in return for two metal ones. Very good to see you all here with us in peace. We offer you breakfast. We will present you with a breastplate and take your child for the school," Governor

Macquarie continues. He is holding out a brass gorget for the chief to wear.

"You teach my daughter, no *whu karndi*," says Berringingy.

"I hereby name you chief of the South Creek tribe. I have already promised your countrymen Nurrugingy and Colebee a grant of thirty acres on South Creek as an additional reward for fidelity to our government with their roles as guides. You may be next," says the governor. Her father bows his head, and the shiny metal crescent hangs from his neck like a noose. He nods. He will not look at his daughter as he swings the boy onto his shoulders and walks away.

———

Lady Macquarie leans forward and kindness pours out of her face as she nods to Mr. and Mrs. Shelley.

"Please allow me the indulgence of speaking," she says. "I can see the other children assembled and you say they have made progress in their studies that is equal with English children of the same age—and they can read the Testament or Bible. Marvelous, seeing as they were only rescued from the Appin punitive expedition last year. A terrible event, with many natives perishing, but it was necessary to bring peace. We have two boys and two girls for the school, and they will join your charges. How is that naughty girl, Mercy?"

The tall girl next to Muraging smiles and pokes her tongue out at her.

"You Mary?" asks Mercy.

"Muraging," she says.

"No more," laughs Mercy.

Muraging shoves Mercy away and stares with fury.

"She achieves adequate reading skills," Mr. Shelley replies to Lady Macquarie.

The feasting begins in the marketplace. Muraging and the children are given meat and bread, and they gulp it down. Mrs. Shelley hands her a striped lollipop. She crunches and sucks the red-and-white peppermint stick, and it dribbles down her chin. The world is still.

Muraging watches her father and her aunts as the feast is finished. She rushes toward her family but is captured by a soldier, flung over his back, and returned to the schoolmaster. The children are marshaled back into line and Muraging trails behind.

Mrs. Shelley tries to take Muraging's hand, but she struggles out of the woman's grip and runs away to stand by the grand sandstone church, feeling lost. Saint John's spire is the tallest building in the town. Muraging hears an eerie wailing in the distance, like someone has died. *Mulbari.* She wonders if the wailing is for her. She picks her nose and examines the contents, but a white hand smacks it and drags her back. Muraging tries out a smile, hoping it will make her more appealing. She hopes they won't put her on a big white bird ship to disappear over the edge of the sea.

"*Biana, biana!*" cries Muraging when she sees Berringingy moving away. But the bargain has been made. Eyes gleam at the sight of bags of food and her hungry family shambles away into dust. Her people laugh and drink and are having a grand old time on *bool.* She watches her father trying on a blue coat from the governor. He strokes the braid and pulls off a button for his son to play with.

Then he looks back at her and calls, "*Nogra whu karndi, waibala.*" Be brave and do not run away. He smiles at her and turns his back.

There are ashes in her mouth. She tries to uncurl the pink fingers around her own. She could bite Mrs. Shelley and run. She can almost taste the salty blood. She wants to rip and tear the hand like a dingo feasting on a bone.

"Governor, she will settle; they all struggle at first. But under my tutelage she will learn to be like the English. Why, under the dirt she is quite pretty," says Mrs. Shelley.

Mrs. Shelley has a high, white choking collar and her hands flap like frightened birds when she speaks. She grins at Mary with scary intensity; her yellow devil-devil teeth are sharp.

"Are you still hungry, Mary?"

"*Karndo. Jumna gorai.*"

"We will give you all the meat you want at our home," says Mrs. Shelley.

Mrs. Shelley squeezes her hand and from a bag she produces a white hand-spun pinafore, which she puts over Muraging's head. She smooths the large garment and it hangs nearly to the ground. It smells of yams. Mrs. Shelley drags Muraging's arms through the arm holes as big tears roll down her cheek. The girl blows her nose with her fingers, but Mrs. Shelley wipes it with a perfumed handkerchief.

As Muraging leaves the square she crosses her legs and wiggles. She needs to pee. Mrs. Shelley takes her to a tree and squats down. They pee, *yilabil*, and Muraging sees that Mrs. Shelley is a girl like her. Her soft black dress is hitched up and she giggles at her new pupil.

CHAPTER TWO

1817–18: Life at School

The Native Institution, which doubles as a home for the Shelleys, is on the edge of Parramatta town, on a street made of earth and stones. It is next to a convict workers' camp on one side and a church on the other. The church has a tall steeple and a sign that says, "Thou shalt love thy neighbor as thyself."

The school is white wattle and daub with thick, pale clay walls and glass in some windows. English gardens surround the building and a lean-to kitchen with hanging pots and pans and a huge iron wood fuel stove stands at the back. A picket fence surrounds the school, and its English gardens include a vegetable patch and chicken enclosures.

Muraging sleeps her first night on a pallet bed. She will learn to read and write, and to eat with cutlery. She will learn to sit up straight with a stiff back and arms pressed to her sides. She will become like the English. She stares at the whitewashed walls but only wants the sky. Breathing this air is unbearable. Muraging dreams of milk spray from her mother's breast, but her mother is dead, long ago, from *waibala* influenza. She curls up and holds her arms around herself in a hug.

On the first morning Mrs. Shelley calls the thirteen polished Aboriginal children to stand in line and introduce themselves to the new pupils. Mrs. Shelley leaves Mercy in charge of the class and walks to the kitchen to give orders for lunch.

The other pupils exude confidence, but Mary is afraid of shadows and tries to see out of the small windows by jumping up and peeking over the window ledge. Mercy takes hold of her arm.

"You called Mary now. Say your name," says Mercy.

"*Naiya Darug! Whu karndi!*" says Mary.

"You not run away! You Mary now! *Paialla* Mary," says Mercy.

Muraging charges out of the classroom and climbs the picket fence onto the road, but she does not know where to run. Mercy chases her and drags her, kicking, back into the schoolroom.

"*Mudjevu werowi,*" says Mercy and pats her to show her where to sit down on a chair.

"*Naiya* Muraging, no Mary."

"*Paialla* English, you learn English and you *budjery werowi*, good girl," says Mercy.

The girls laugh at Mary's matted hair full of casuarina pods and she hides behind Mercy. There are two older boys at the school who help in the garden, and they do not tease her. Most of the children can speak English and are smacked if they speak anything else. But now that Mrs. Shelley is not in the room the little girls in pinafores keep together and chatter quietly in their language—their precious secret. Each child has a wooden doll on her lap that has been made by Mercy. Each doll has a costume fashioned from rags. One little girl holds up her doll and smiles at Mercy.

Mercy has been at the school for two years and is the same age as Mary but is tall with a maturing figure and wavy pigtails. Her face has big, grand features with wide nostrils and huge black eyes. Her mouth is pink under full brown lips that never stop moving. Mary watches her running her fingers through her golden curls and thinks her parents must be from some gold clan. But Mercy is from mountain people, Gundungurra. She has total power over the other children—even the boys look to her as the leader. Laughing loudly is what she likes best, her head thrown back as she gives cheek or plays tricks that are not meant to hurt but sometimes do. A rubber band is her talisman, and she flicks the girls' ears with paper pellets when they are writing in the schoolroom.

Mrs. Shelley comes into the room. It is bath time, and she takes Mary outdoors by the hand and plunges her into a metal claw-foot bath filled with kettles of water from the fire. Mary screams but the other children laugh. She is scrubbed and left to huddle with others. Overhead a carrion-eating bird, *wargan*, flies by. Mary flaps her arms at him.

"That crow is bad fella," says Mercy. "He want to steal all eagle-hawk wives. He chase them all along rivers."

━━━

Days go by and Mary hears other children's stories whispered in the night. Many have seen, and still see, the bodies of their parents shot and hung on trees with corn cobs in their mouths. They watched in horror as crows pecked out living eyes and black beaks picked brains. The white men rushed with swords at natives, who fought back with *nulla nulla* clubs. One of the boys saw his pretty aunty crying as ten soldier men took turns to jump on her; he heard her last sad wail as a man with a dagger killed her. Some tasted blood in rivers and witnessed the burning of farms by warriors and their heroes, Branch Jack and Musquito.

Mary blocks her ears. These stories steal her sleep. Mary tosses next to other hot little girls, also tossing to and fro in the night. Mercy holds Mary's hand and tells her how she had been caught setting fire to a farmer's house on the outskirts of Ebenezer. Her

family had come with her tribe, the Gundungurra mountain warriors, and she had helped to attack a house with firebrands made
with *mootin* spears, but the family had escaped. Mercy is no longer
the laughing and silly girl to Mary. This story is whispered because
such a tale would terrify the Shelleys and perhaps Mercy would be
imprisoned.

"You not tell. You never tell my secret here in your heart," says
Mercy.

It is a secret between these girls, now closest friends.

Mary is pushed, each day, into a scratchy, shapeless shift, like the
shroud of a dead white person. Mr. Shelley bends her head over a
stinking kerosene bath to kill nits, lice, and all manner of "crawly
vermin," so Mr. Shelley says. Mary is getting used to being smacked
for no reason and she is getting used to pining for her father.

Every day the boys close and latch the gate to keep out marauding pigs that snuffle and grunt at the fence. These hogs escaped from
the ship *Perseverance* and have bred. They have short black bristles,
horrible yellow teeth, and razor-sharp tusks.

One day there is a terrible noise outside the school and Mercy
huddles the children together to watch from the window a parade
of starving Aboriginal people running by. *Dyins* grab at their rags
to hold their bouncing breasts. They are in tatters, like spiders that
have scattered before a fire, with big hungry eyes. Men on horses
chase them down like dogs. Why are they being chased? No one
can say. Mercy shakes her head. She doesn't know why this is happening, and the smaller children hold on to her dress in fear. Mary
sees that the running women might fall and be eaten by the hogs.
Her panic is complete. She falls to the floor and cannot speak for
days.

When Mary is better, Mercy explains that at night the wooden
door is closed with a heavy beam used as a latch. Mary asks with her
eyes why the latch will be closed.

"*Tuabilli were waibala.* To keep out bad men," Mercy replies.

"*Karama kurung?*" says Mary.

They hear from the teachers that bad men are waiting on the street to grab them—to push them to the ground and hurt them. She hears the tapping of wooden shoes on the flagstones; she looks out the window and sees men in chains digging in the school garden, rattling metal against shovels.

The door opens and the room is alive with sparkling sun. Mary looks out at the garden and gasps as a convict man watches her from the other side of the gate. Panic runs through her.

The convict's hairy neck shines with sweat. He is thin and white. He touches his palm to his mouth, asking for bread. His eyes beg and she feels sorry for him. She sneaks into the kitchen and takes a piece from a crusty white loaf and hides it under her pinafore. She knows the punishment for stealing is a beating with a wooden cane, but she is valiant and walks calmly out of the gate.

"You, man, eat! *Patama*, bread," says Mary as he looks up. He wolfs it down with a guzzling sound. Then he bows and creeps back to work on the road.

Next day, she throws a bread morsel from the window and the man wolfs it down again, nodding his thank-you. Mary throws the whole loaf and doesn't care if she is punished.

"Thank you, little girl. You will go to heaven. And I will run away to Arcadia over the mountains," the convict yells.

The next day she sees the man huddled by the fire. He seems invisible to all except Mary. He smiles. She watches in horror as he is flogged by the overseers and dragged away to a pillory.

———

Mary begins to learn in the schoolroom and sits with her legs dangling from a wobbly chair with hard edges. The children crowd into one room, sitting along rough benches. A cane hangs from a hook and Mary can see the boys cower as their eyes dart up to watch flies circle the implement. One boy punches another and then clenched fists are up and ready to strike. Mr. Shelley looks at them and they crumple into a docile heap. The fight will keep.

Mr. Shelley walks up and down and studies the green writing slates with their wooden edges and sponge rubbers. All the pupils have been given these writing implements. Mary's has lots of spit where she has smeared the chalk in an effort to copy the marks from the board—the alphabet.

"This slate is an abomination," says Mr. Shelley as he wipes it down. He takes Mary's hand and forces her to hold the gray chalk. She looks at his clean pink nails, as pale as grubs. She pulls her hand away and presses it between her legs as he picks up a ruler and bangs it down on her other hand. Her lip trembles and she feels a rising panic. Mercy nods to her to be still—she must learn to show no resistance. Mr. Shelley scratches his nose with the end of the ruler; Mercy pokes her tongue out and rolls her eyes behind his back.

"Dear child, you tire me out. I am trying to train you to write your letters and speak English. We are inured to this work of toil and cannot recognize fatigue. You will display some respect for your writing!" says Mr. Shelley.

"*Bulala naiya*. Outside," says Mary as she points to the sunlight streaming on the trees; the children cheer.

"No, you cannot go outside!" says Mr. Shelley.

Mary sees a snake eating him from the head down, its creeping throat sucking this *waibala* up. She hopes it will suck up the king of England, too, whose picture hangs above the blackboard. The teacher's wooden ruler is a tiny weapon like a woomera, but this man uses it and his cane to beat children, not hunt kangaroo. She squeezes her eyes shut and makes her body tight.

Mrs. Shelley walks into the room, wafting a perfume of flowers behind her. She strokes Mary's cheek, and Mr. Shelley moves to his wife's side and takes hold of her arm, saying, "Don't touch their hair; vermin live in it."

"Mary will learn with our love, and she will settle," says Mrs. Shelley.

Mrs. Shelley removes her hand and rubs it on her apron, but she smiles at Mary. She sighs and, astonishingly, bursts into song. The children laugh and clap.

"Build on the rock and not upon the sand. You are safe forevermore, if you build on the rock!" she sings.

She dances around the room and lifts her skirt a little to point her black-stockinged foot. She seems so blithe and happy that it is contagious.

When they leave the room, Mercy puts on Mr. Shelley's top hat and mimics his walk. The children scream with laughter.

———

One dark night Mercy and Mary hide in a hall cupboard eating stolen jam pudding. If Cook finds them, they will be hit with a wooden spoon. Mary sucks the sweet sauce and Mercy licks a bowl, still part full of yellow custard. They take turns to taste the mixture on the spoon. A noise stops them and they freeze with spoons in their mouths, worried it might be a *goong*. But it is Mr. Shelley leaning against the door, whispering some love words to Mrs. Shelley. The girls cannot move as they clutch each other. No movement. Now the Shelleys are leaning against the door, breathing hard. He is panting and talking softly. They are fucking!

"Dearest Eliza," he croons, whining like a lost animal. The girls wonder if they should burst out of the cupboard to save the mistress from *nguttatha*; they have heard these noises many times. But the puffing and groaning is tender and not a bad or a frightening thing. Mercy sniggers with her hand against her mouth.

Weeks pass and Mary watches the shadows grow long. The view from her window changes from green to dry yellow grass along the road where the new sandstone road is being built by convicts. Mary hears the click, clicking of hammers. She still plans to run away but somehow cannot make the move. She has become used to being called Mary and practices her words and writing. She learns to speak English and is one of the quickest in class. She speaks to Mercy in her newly acquired language.

"Why *waibala* got big house when our people live like slaves in that Bible and Black servant kept in shed? Why they got picture with dead people? Why they want look at dead men with long beard and them *baletti* dead ladies and dead children? *Bimung garai* stupid. They trapped in glass. Where that place, Tahiti? They talk about flower and coconut tree. Why that?"

"They got big house because they rich," says Mercy. "One day we might get rich. *Wallawa* stay here, marry big fella, rich fella."

"*Beal*, no. Not for me *ngubaty*. Find *biana*. You see."

Mercy shakes her head. "Your father, he gone long time," says Mercy. Mary punches her.

"Not say that thing. *Naiya*, no forget, no *bulala*."

Late in the night, Mary takes one of the orphan children to comfort and climbs into bed with Mercy.

"I heard a story about Barrangaroo, she is wife of Bennelong and she invited for a big dinner, big *karndo*, by that Governor Phillip," says Mercy. "He sent her a new dress and petticoat, really pretty, for her to wear. But that Barrangaroo, she not want that dress. So, she knocked on that governor's door at dinnertime and she was naked. *Nabung* all hung out. She sat down with the fine ladies with fur and jewel. She wore Black skin. She was beautiful already. That governor couldn't stop lookin' at her *nabung*."

Mercy pauses and then says, "I got *nabung*."

"You got *nabung* titty nothing."

———

On the wall of the dormitory hangs a framed picture of Jesus. He is surrounded by a crowd of smiling white children. Mary traces the Jesus head with her finger. Then she finds that she can scrape at the stone wall in this room and after a long bit of crunching with a trusty stick, she has carved a kangaroo around the Jesus picture.

"What did you do that for?" asks Mercy.

"*Buru* is my totem, and my name is *muraging*, native cat," says Mary.

"I'm *wirriga*, goanna."

The afternoon stretches on and Mary eats some cabbage and bean soup, which looks like *waiali*, possum poo.

"I catch *waiali*, a lot. With *bobbina*, we climb up tree with big one rope to make me go up," says Mary.

"He finish up now? He *baletti* dead?" asks Mercy.

"He die influenza. *Biana* real sad," Mary replies.

"I cut them with boomerang, get lotta *waiali*. Good tucker," says Mercy.

"Aunty *Wirawi*, throw for me to take out guts," says Mary.

"Make a pillow too."

Mary mouths the words, "Brush tail possum, *waiali;* glider possum, *bangu;* that ringtail possum, *chubbi.* We won't forget our mother tongue, eh?"

"Not forget. You know I see inside your *kobbera* head, like fire. You real strong," Mercy tells Mary.

All the girls huddle together in the day and pick at each other's hair. It feels good to lie down in a lap and have a caressing hand in their hair. They lean on each other and do everything together and are, in some ways, a tribe. Sometimes, they all follow Mercy during the day, and she scolds them for not doing any work such as cleaning the room with brush brooms. Mary feels alive when she is all tangled up with children.

———

One day Mercy sees Mary trying to climb over the fence of the school and grabs her by the hair and brings her back.

Mercy forces Mary to wash with hard gray soap. The soapy liquid runs down her face and stings her eyes.

"*Wallawa*, stop! I want get away! *Bimung gurai*, stupid! Soap stink," says Mary.

"You learn not run and you talk English quick and foller me or you get flogged by Cook. And she flog me for letting you go. I get blame! You live here now; you got five pounds bread in week, two pound meat. A pound rice, half pound sugar. You eatem all up yerself."

"*Naiya*, run, *nalla yan*."

"You not *nalla yan*. If you run away, you gonna get lost. All the time mens shoot native; they all gonna die. Mrs. Shelley tell us that. Captain Wallis kill chiefs near Appin. Kill all family. You forget about alla native business; you and me *waibala* now. You gotta stay and help me," Mercy pleads.

Mary struggles to force Mercy's hand away. There is strength in Mary's body—she is more powerful than a boy. The soap is dropped and Mary turns to face her torturer. There is recognition and newfound respect. Mercy has power over the children, but the two girls are now friends—sisters perhaps. Mercy mutters that she is sorry. She reaches out and strokes Mary's hair.

———

Some months pass and one morning a school inspector rides into the yard on an old brown horse. He walks in without knocking.

He is as thin as string and has a long mustache of gray fur, like kangaroo skin. His dusty coat has ragged sleeves, and a fob watch hangs glinting from his dark breeches. He walks with a shuffle and sneezes constantly while peering closely at the children and wiping his pointy pink nose with a white handkerchief. He walks up and down the classroom rows and examines the children for spelling and Bible study. Mary can now speak English and has learned to write, and Mrs. Shelley shows her pride by singing their praises, in song.

"The children are our pride and joy, pride and joy; Hallelujah praise the Lord!" she sings.

The inspector frowns and combs his hair with a yellow bone comb and pulls strands out to let them fly around the room. Mary sneaks behind him and puts some hair in her pocket, just in case she needs to use it for magic.

He tells Mrs. Shelley that the pupils must poo on some paper so he can check it for worms. The children go under the tank, squatting and pooing and leaning down to look between their legs to see if there are any crawly yellow threads.

"I got some here. I got five," says Mary.

"Oh, you can count. Castor oil for you. Here you go, drink it up. Make you better," says Mrs. Shelley. She makes her drink the medicine and Mary vomits.

The inspector checks the dormitory, where the neatly folded government-issued blankets are laid on the beds. He checks the wooden shutters for dust and says, "Tut-tut." Mrs. Shelley moves behind him and looks worried because this man can close the school. His head is shaking, and he writes something in a ledger. Mr. Shelley nods and pats the children's backs.

"We put a Darug magic spell on that fella with words and stealing his hair. He might go mad," says Mary.

Mrs. Shelley smiles at the inspector and puts a sign in copperplate writing on the wall. She reads it aloud: "Rule one: Thou shalt be clean. Two: Thou shalt be chaste. Three: Thou shalt not pick nits from each other's hair. Four: Thou shalt honor your teachers. Five: Thou shalt not run away. Six: Thou shalt not pick your nose and eat it. Seven: Thou shalt not sleep in a huddle with dogs. Eight: Thou shalt not speak in yabber and shall endeavor to use English at all times. Nine: Thou shalt eat at the table and not on the floor. Ten: Thou shalt be grateful for the government's benevolence."

The inspector nods and smirks at the rules. He is full of praise for the school and has none for the children. When he rides away on his poor horse, they whoop and dance. Mary writes on the list of rules, when no one is looking: "Rule eleven: Thou shalt not fart."

"Who has endeavored to disgrace this list?" demands Mr. Shelley as he glowers at the class.

"I practice my writing," says Mary.

"Stand and take punishment," says Mr. Shelley. He grabs Mary by the arm and flogs her with the cane as she stands stiff and unbroken. The other children stare and hope they will not be next.

Mrs. Shelley rushes into the classroom and takes hold of her husband's hand to stop the beating. There is a struggle, and the children are astounded at her courage.

"Will you indulge me," says Mrs. Shelley to her husband. "The children are trying but so much needs to be learned. We must give them time to be playful. This will not help them read."

He searches the room for an answer but coughs to retain his dignity and places the cane on his desk and pats it.

Mr. Shelley whispers fiercely to his wife, "It was pure insolence! Please do not speak back to me in front of these innocents. I have my mission. I seek out the wandering tribes and preach earnestly to them. I will save souls from the void of eternity. I wish to be able to record '*veni, vidi, vici.*' But darkness rests upon these native peoples and gross darkness envelops hearts."

Mrs. Shelley smiles, nods pleasantly, and replies, "Not the innocent children, surely." She pats his arm and the children look up at her for guidance. They long to be let out to play—the sun is shining outside, the gum trees are beckoning, kookaburras are laughing. The bush is calling.

"We go play now. Mary and me want to run. We will get some lilly pilly for you," says Mercy.

"Let them out. It will do no harm, my dearest," says Mrs. Shelley.

"Rubbish. Work is what they need. Oh, that the Son of Righteousness would arise and dissipate your every dark feeling," says Mr. Shelley.

"No, I love and respect all your doings," says Mrs. Shelley.

Mary sees Mr. Shelley staring gloomily at his wife with his pointy nose all red from sniffing. He seems to be sick.

"I feel you resent me bringing you here to the end of the earth," he says.

"My dear, I won't dissuade you from your great work and conversions in this Garden of Eden or from performing acts of charity for unenlightened heathens. Why, this morning I baked a raisin cake to give the poor destitute creatures camped out on the hill." Mrs. Shelley is beaming at Mary as she speaks and is stroking her hair, which is a strange feeling, but pleasant. The mention of raisin cake has made the other children sit up and cheer up, their eyes glowing.

"Of course, the girls will just run away like they all do in the end. Why, the well-respected chief, Bungaree, was asked to bring his son Bowen to be schooled and he refused!" says Mrs. Shelley.

"Bowen my cousin. He live in Georges Heights. Grow lot of fruit and fish all the time," says Mary, but no one is listening.

"The very hide of him to refuse education! The young man will be ignorant. I don't know why we bother," says Mr. Shelley.

"Outside to play!" calls Mrs. Shelley, and the children rush into the garden.

Mary feels alive at hearing about her tribal cousin, *babana* Bowen. She longs to see him. But he never comes. No family comes—or if they do, they are turned away. She suspects that this is what has happened to her father, for surely he misses her and regrets making her come here.

This summer, the noise of cicadas is a thick rackety noise. The hot air smells of burning gum leaves as men clear the bush of the beloved trees. *Crack, crack, crack*, as tree spirits fall and are hacked and split with wedges. It rips apart the spirit pathways to the sky. An endless cracking of death to the Darug.

Pale dingoes, *mirri*, walk around a destroyed world and are lost in an empty landscape. Mary is also lost in this new scalped place. Every day she makes a circle in dust and places a stone in it to represent her father. She asks him to come to her, but he does not.

The picture of the spirit of the Lord is above her bed, his long white beard shimmering among angels. She gazes at the shadows crossing the sky and blotting out the rainbow serpent in clusters of tiny stars, *kimberwalli killi*. She can hear *murrungal*, thunder that tells her the *Gullaga* Giant Hairy Man is coming for smelly girls. Shuffling through leaves. Mary rubs her armpits and sniffs; no smell, just eucalypt soap. She shudders in her bed at the bone-crunching sound. She knows that a fire can keep these spirits away, and she reaches out for the sputtering candle and pulls Mercy into her bed. Whispering, Mary tells her how her grandfather and grandmother used to sit with her in the firelight, telling the old stories that are sung and danced. She wants to hear Mercy's stories.

"We got Gundungurra people story," says Mercy. "That old *Ga-rangatch*, he giant eel, like *burra* eel, winding under *bulga*, hill, and make that river by dig, dig. I see him real deep in caves; he got white shining finger. He makes all. *Bunggawurra, bulga*. He make mountain then rush underground. He make sky with real big rain. He chase by big tribe, call them quoll cat mob *Merrigan*."

"My true name like that, *Muraging*," says Mary.

"True, eh? *Yuranyi*, he that black duck, diver duck, they want him real bad. They track him, *pittuma* looking for him and alla time, dig dig and looking help from all tribe," says Mercy.

"What? They want to catch him real bad?" says Mary.

"Yep, that spirit, *Merrigan*, real brave one. He dive deep, deep with that *mootin* spear in cave full of water and he spear him. You know cut him, little bit, then he brings flesh and they eat it up." Mary squeals.

"Real tasty. He must be mad, that *Garangatch*?" says Mary.

"Everyone chasin' that spirit but not catching him. No way, he too fast. He like lightning. All those fellas go into sky and rivers and deep waterholes, and that serpent, he still lives in one cold dark waterhole in that mountain. You see his eye glinting in moonlight," says Mercy.

"Them fellas go to sky, *kimperwalli*. True, eh? Now *nangi*, we sleep," says Mary.

The story leaves the other children with huge eyes, and Mercy cuddles up to Mary and sighs.

"My *biana* tells me lot of story," says Mary.

"Forget him; he's not coming. Not never," Mercy whispers.

CHAPTER THREE

Late 1818: Mr. Shelley's Illness

Poor Mr. Shelley is ranting about his days as a member of the London Missionary Society in Tonga when his friends were murdered by islanders. Back then he became a distiller of rum to ease his grief. He tells the children stories about being in the Tuamotu Islands on the ship the *Queen Charlotte*, and about murders by pearlers. His stories leave the children terrified.

He is not well.

The school now has many pupils and there is a morning roll call: Betty Cox, Milbah, Betty Fulton, Tommy, Peter, Pendergrass, Amy, Mercy, Nancy, Buddy, Sally, Maria, Winston, and Charlotte. Some children arrive and later are taken back by their parents, but most are orphans.

In the darkness of his study, Mary sees Mr. Shelley counting from a bag of silver pearls. *Clink, clink, clink.* He pounds the floors at night like a *goong* ghost and is convinced they are going to be killed by marauders. He rages with a tropical fever and then goes all quiet and soft and loving as he strokes the children's heads. Mercy tries to work out his moods in the morning so she knows what's to come and can tell the children what to expect.

"When he blows a whistle, you must run to him and line up, like soldiers," says Mercy.

The children are afraid and pray to escape being hit. Cook is a large, angry, orange-haired woman with whiskers on her chin. She hides the glass decanters because Mr. Shelley has started to drink rum that he has begun to distill.

One night, Mary sees Mr. Shelley standing at the top of the stairs holding a candle, gazing through the window.

"They are out there! I can smell the stench! They are planning an attack! Is it of no consequence that I cannot save you all? No, it's a bushranger!" yells Mr. Shelley. "He will disgrace my wife and steal the children. He'll shoot me and take all my earthly chattels. Mary, we must erect the shutters at once! Hello! Everyone awake! Attack is coming!"

Mrs. Shelley runs down the stairs and calls to him, "You have woken the whole house. My dear, come back to bed. We see no attack. Come quietly; there is no need to get your gun." She closes the door and leans against it. He sighs as she leads him to his bed. Later, the children can hear him crying.

Thunder sounds and they are terrified; they know that devil-devils are around; angry spirit-lightning smashes the earth from where they live—in volcanoes and deep pools. Mary also fears the walking dead, who are wrapped in paperbark on forked stick platforms.

Later, the children hear screaming and cursing. Mrs. Shelley yells at him and they hear glass smashing. The children huddle together. Mary has heard these cursing words from convicts, but now they are in the house and dear Mrs. Shelley is upset. Mary wants to run to her and hold her and tell her that she loves her. Mr. Shelley runs up and down the stairs and takes a gun from the rack. Now the children are truly terrified. They know what a gun can do. Mary hears a gunshot upstairs. Then there is silence.

"He get taken to that Parramatta Lunatic Asylum," says Mercy.

"He might shoot us. We got to look out," says Mary.

Mr. Shelley pushes his weight against the heavy wooden bars across the shutters. They have holes in them for poking guns through to shoot countrymen. No one can get in, but if there is a fire no one can get out.

Mrs. Shelley takes the children out of their beds and they huddle in the lounge room while the rain pours down outside. Mr. Shelley has a white, white face as he walks to the cupboard to take out some gunpowder.

"No lassitude. No useless ambulation. Keep away from windows! Tonight we will board up the windows. No one can access this humble establishment," says Mr. Shelley. "As in Tahiti, we must pray to be saved." Some of the little children begin to cry.

Mary hugs Mrs. Shelley. She is calm as she takes the gun from her husband's hands and hums. Mary closes her eyes and the music of a corroboree echoes through the dark. Mary thinks it is a welcome ceremony.

"I can see the *myall* fires and hear their heathen war songs. They are eating worms and vermin. Like Zulus of Africa. Cannot you all hear the witchdoctors? *Karadja?*" says Mr. Shelley.

"Not that word, Master; we only whisper that word 'cause one might come find us," says Mary.

"They are chanting that accursed song? It does not stop, the *clackety-clack* of boomerang. Like Samoan drumming," Mr. Shelley says.

Mary thinks he is crazy because all she can hear are native songs about rain. She senses that her uncles are out there singing.

Through the cracks in the wall, the children look out and see a row of warriors with spears high on the hill near the town. They are silhouetted against the light. Mr. Shelley is terrified. He sweats and paces, mumbling.

"Why you lock us in, Mr. Shelley?" asks Mary.

"Sweet innocent girl! Can't you see that the heathen perpetrators of murder want to break down the doors and kill us and eat our hearts?" says Mr. Shelley.

"They dancing, Mr. Shelley. They not hurt us; don't be frighten," says Mary.

"The savages will not care that you are dark. They will only see you as a human sacrifice to cook over fires. Oh, God! Save these little ones!" He grabs Mary to his bosom, but she is not frightened. She wriggles in his sweaty embrace; he smells of pipe smoke and beef gravy.

Mr. Shelley paces the room and piles wood on the fire. The older girls read stories to the little ones. The children are as quiet as bush mice. The air is tense and the clattering boomerangs fill the night.

"My *biana* tell story 'bout him fly on top back of beast, like devil-devil. He fly then dive deep in mountain and red-eyed spirit live there. He wake up, he know he been chosen *Karadji* man," Mary whispers. "Clever one, fix up sickness or kill someone with magic. He got secret things in dillybag. I never see that."

"Don't talk about all that thing!" says Mercy.

"*Quai bidja, jumna paialla jannawi,*" Mary's father whispers in her head: Come here, we talk together.

Mary stands and peers through the cracks in the shutters where she can get a better view of the tribe's fires. The tribe is sending smoke messages, calling for a meeting. Mary cannot understand why Mr. Shelley is so afraid. The families are gathering for corro- boree business.

After a few days, Mr. Shelley is exhausted and falls into a deep sleep. The next morning he wakes with a fever that never ends. He burns up hour after hour, night after night, until one night, he is dead. Dead at forty-one years. His spirit flies out the window like a hot wind. His wife weeps for one week and Mercy secretly burns some leaves in his room.

He is buried at Saint John's cemetery in Parramatta and the chil- dren attend the funeral. They watch the coffin as it is lowered into the grave. Some of the little ones are frightened that if he wakes he will not be able to get out again.

———

Mrs. Shelley takes over the running of the school and tells the children she has employed a Mr. Barnes, an ex-convict, as the teaching assistant. He is sweaty and pale with a long, thin, pink face and whiskers sprouting from his ears. He wears a grand gray wool coat and a purple necktie that is supposed to give him a dashing air. He carries rolled-up maps and a box of books and sits in the dining room to sharpen his quills. He writes long letters to anyone of importance who might listen to his opinions on the doings of the colony.

But Mr. Barnes is not just an ex-convict assistant; he fancies himself as an explorer into unknown interior country. He has rendered his services to this humble school, knowing that he had not a delicate knowledge of the human heart, which must be important to such endeavors. He takes the position on condition that he could engage in the exploration of the dark land to the west and north.

CHAPTER FOUR

1818: White People Things

From the *Sydney Gazette*, December 1818:

Settlers in Turmoil on Hawkesbury River

After the military campaign of previous years, such as those of Magistrate William Cox, there are rumors of dark and dismal events and dreadful excesses. There were places on the Hawkesbury River where the hand-picked mobile troopers have hunted down natives and shot them with impunity. Massacres in Appin, Grose River, and Emu Plains occurred around 1816 to 1817, and it is claimed that no fewer than four hundred Blacks were killed in Cox's expedition alone. Many encounters with hostile Blacks have led to reprisals and punishments.

There are terrible stories of warriors from a ferocious tribe killing three soldiers, taking their coats, and cutting off the men's hands.

East of the Blue Mountains, there has been little trouble with natives, as they are now suppressed and have resigned themselves to living as workers on farms. The inducements of tobacco and flour have helped them to make up their minds in this regard. The flourish of a musket has a desired effect also. However, some hostile groups congregate in the Kurrajong area who are believed to be planning attacks on outlying farms and shepherds. This information is most distressing to new settlers.

═══

Time passes and Mary James learns about white people things. She is making a knitted doll for the little ones and is adept at baking scones in an oven. She can read, write, and speak English better than Mercy.

She pushes her love for her father into a tight ball so it won't poison her. She knows longing can make you sick.

═══

One day as Mary holds a baby on her lap, Mercy brings an old lady into the dormitory. Mercy found the old woman hiding in the flour shed, where she had broken in to try to find something to eat. Shards of sunlight flicker over the old woman's face and Mary wishes this woman was her true granny—but this woman is from a mob she does not recognize. Yes, she is from her clan, the Burruberongal, she says, but from far away.

Her cheeks hang in folds and her eyes are piercing black lights. This granny is a tiny woman with a stooped bearing and a black pipe permanently stuck in her mouth. She has a red scarf tied around her head and wispy gray curls on her forehead. She wears a long dark skirt and apron with a dillybag on her back full of useful things, including a billy can, a pannikin, stringy bark for making string, a small kunni yam stick, and a coolamon of bark full of dried wild figs. She looks frail but has a warmth and a strong, soulful gaze. The girls can see that she is not afraid of anything.

"This old lady is called Granny Wiring and she is real hungry, so we give her our tucker tonight? That alright?" asks Mercy.

"*Wattunga*? Where you from, Granny Wiring?" Mary slips in, close to the old lady, wanting her love.

"*Naibala*, finish up," says Granny Wiring.

"All fella belong you, he gone? He *baletti*?" asks Mercy.

Granny Wiring nods and tears flow as she slides down to sit on the floor. The children all think the same thing: she could be their granny and the *waibala* have taken her food and her place. Mercy hugs her.

"Our Burruberongal Darug mob up near Cattai. They your people, Mary girl. All people come quiet, after all fella been shot," says Granny Wiring. "All been burnem up. *Waibala* shootem. No more run away in that place. Might as well give up," says Granny Wiring. "War been finish. We safe now. No more body in wombat hole. Bits of broken boomerang everywhere. We run, real frighten. They saddle up, load musket, shootem all mob. We tell everybody about that killing. No good. Blackfella been settle down now."

Mercy wraps Granny Wiring in a shawl and the children are still.

"We look after Granny, hide her here, and feed her up. Make her real fat. She's only got one blanket. No country," says Mercy.

All the girls fear that Mr. Barnes might find her during inspections and throw her out. Mary thinks of the shining table in the schoolhouse, how it gleams with beeswax polish and her elbow grease. The old granny can be hidden under that table during the day and at night she could stay with the girls and she could teach them about their country.

After a week, Mr. Barnes finds Granny Wiring and he drags her out from under the table to face Mrs. Shelley.

"Whose grandmother is she? And why is she sleeping in our house?" demands Mrs. Shelley. Mercy pushes Mary forward.

"All our granny. Belong to all us girls. But she from Burruberongal mob like me and she might find my daddy for me. We feed her up. She's starving," says Mary.

"Yes, I can see your Christian care and I am glad of it. I too care, but it won't do," says Mrs. Shelley. "I feel the utmost kindness and good intentions toward all you natives, but she will have to be taken back to her correct family."

"They all dead, all rotten on trees with corn cobs stuck in mouth," says Mary.

"Come now, Mary, that's simply not true. No lies here. We will find her home," says Mrs. Shelley.

"Granny Wiring says that *dyin* women got nothing, but she not want government handout; she says she butter her own bread," says Mercy.

"Please don't use that word *dyin*. It's not nice. We are all trying to use proper English, aren't we? Now, girls, please oblige me by hastily returning to the schoolroom. I will deal with Granny and we will provision her with appropriate attire and arrange for her care. She reminds me of an old dear I used to know in Cornwall."

"I go on long foot walk now; you come find me one day soon, eh, Mary and Mercy?" says Granny Wiring. The children watch Granny Wiring hobble away with Mrs. Shelley and they cry for her, and for themselves. They see their families walking into the distance. She is the only link with the old people they have had, and that is all that they long for.

———

One day, a dusty lieutenant rides his mount down the road and arrives at the school. He has ammunition strung about his chest, knee-high leather boots, and a blond mustache. Over his saddle dangles a new child for the school. His red jacket is stained with blood.

The lieutenant enters the house, but Mr. Barnes does not want any more pupils and Mrs. Shelley looks suspiciously at this man. The children watch as the boy is laid down on the couch in an exhausted sleep. The boys stand nearby ready to help find clothes to dress the lad.

"I have brought you another student, one of those saved by Captain Woodrow near the penal settlement of coal town. It is a wonder
that I made it back from the northern frontier. It is wild country,"
says the lieutenant. "I regret that the child is not well-disposed. Perhaps the traveling on horseback did not suit him. Or perhaps it's just
a high degree of shyness; he seemed mightily afraid of the horse."

"A drop of medicinal laudanum will fix him quick," says Mr.
Barnes. "We are honored to accept this innocent, so please thank
Captain Woodrow and remind him of my intention to join him on
an expedition. He is said to have been a veritable demon in battle
when he was on the subcontinent, and so fashionably dressed when
not in uniform, the ladies are all aflutter."

"I have heard that he has shot many of our sable brethren," says
Mrs. Shelley with a worried glance at Mary and Mercy.

"I couldn't be sure, madam," says the lieutenant.

"We will nurse this child back to health, won't we, madam?
Teach him to have manners and dress him like a proper Englishman," says Mr. Barnes. Mary looks at the trembling little body, and
as he wakes, she takes him in her arms.

"*Biana, biana,*" says the child.

The little one huddles against Mary and she thinks how silly he
would be to believe that he will see his family again. She knows
there is not much happiness here and she feels like yelling it to the
boy, to his beautiful upturned Black face.

"Please, if I might be so bold as to make a suggestion: don't
overteach him. We want compliant servants, not upstarts. They are
stupid, and humility is best," says the lieutenant.

"You *bimung garai*, stupid!" says Mary and the children laugh.

"Enough cheek, young lady," Mr. Barnes warns.

"Subservience paves the way for exploitation of wealth in a colony, where the landed gentry get wealthier. The poor get poorer,
and the Aboriginal people will get nothing but degradation," says
Mrs. Shelley with fervor.

"You sound like Mary Wollstonecraft. You have a touch of revolutionary zeal," says the lieutenant.

"We are the civilizing mission overseas. I am a model of propriety," snaps Mrs. Shelley.

"What will become of society if women feel they have the right to speak as such?" the lieutenant mutters.

"We shall endeavor to whitewash his soul of heathen ways and we will protect and love him. He can be baptized Harry," says Mrs. Shelley.

"His name's not Harry. He tells me his name *Yuranyi*, like duck," says Mary.

"He needs a good English name, to be sure," says Mr. Barnes.

Mrs. Shelley stands upright suddenly, her gaze on the lieutenant's hand as it strokes his saber in its leather casing.

"While I am grateful that you bring us a child, I fear what may have happened to his parents," says Mrs. Shelley.

"He is from the Hunter River," says the lieutenant.

"Awakabal and Wonnaruah mob there," says Mary.

Mr. Barnes casts a warning glance at Mrs. Shelley, but she ignores it, clears her throat, and continues:

"I have heard all manner of atrocities committed in the name of bringing progress to the natives and I cannot approve of your methods or accept that you have no choice. Why, you have gore all over you! I would, if I could, seek justice for those miserable people who are God's children also. We have heard enough of your military violence. You are not wanted here, sir. Get out of my house now!"

Mary is thrilled with this daring speech. She opens the door and waits to escort the soldier out. He takes his hat and bows curtly to Mrs. Shelley. Mr. Barnes is silent with indignation on behalf of the military man and his endeavors. Mary gives the visitor a shove and slams the heavy door behind him. She leans against it and Mrs. Shelley smiles at her.

"You cannot treat our military like this. There will be gossip. He was most respectful. Did you see his garb? A nice pair of breeches and those boots with silver clasps; how does he afford such things?" Mr. Barnes asks, but no one is listening.

Mary helps with little Harry as he lies still and hot in a crib. They need medicine from the town, but Mr. Barnes has refused to allow the older girls out of the premises. He wishes to control every aspect of their lives. He paces the floor and cleans his musket in the dining room.

Mary hears the stories of her Burruberongal Darug people making raids on settlements and wonders if her father is among them. She imagines him with spears standing against the sky.

But Mrs. Shelley is adamant. "Mary will go for the medicine, and you let her out, Mr. Barnes. She is our fastest runner and has the best English. We cannot be patient with your fearful fantasies and wait any longer or the child will perish," says Mrs. Shelley. Mr. Barnes opens the door and Mrs. Shelley gives her instructions. Mary flies out.

She runs through the streets and marvels at the busy markets and storefronts. Even the church seems busy with settlers gathered outside for a wedding. At the apothecary Mary asks for the medicine and receives the precious mixture. She runs back to the schoolhouse and is met with gratitude; the medicine will save the child.

That night Mrs. Shelley is feeling melancholy and writes to her sister to cheer herself up.

Dear Sister,

How I long to see you in a few years' time. How are the lovely children?

I am now a sad widow, as you know. I have adjusted to life, although I tire of wearing black.

The town of Parramatta is growing and my students are a joy. As you know from my past letters, my husband was always looking for ways to improve the Aborigines, and the children can now all read and write. A miracle.

I have recently been honored with a visit from Lady Macquarie, who informed us that the governor has set up a small farm for Chief Bungaree at Georges Head overlooking Sydney Harbor. The governor holds this Aboriginal chief in high regard as an ambassador for his people. This is also a home for the chief's family, including his dashing son, young Bowen. He is only a youth but is held in high esteem because of his father.

This native has proved himself worthy of our trust and in 1803 he returned from circumnavigating Australia with Matthew Flinders. There have also been other voyages of exploration.

The family of Bungaree have a timber hut, but you will be amused to hear that all his sable brethren prefer to sleep outside. They also have been given a boat for fishing.

The governor granted some convict servants to help them in learning agriculture and they have grown trees of peaches and apricots.

There are visits from governors and French explorers dripping with soft talk. They talk to the people, but no gift is given to the clan. They lack the English sense of generosity.

The Russian Arctic expedition with Captain Bellingshausen and Mikhailov has arrived in their sloop, the Vostok. *They have drawn some splendid pencil portraits of Bungaree's family, and I enclose one for your interest.*

I do trust that all your family is well, and my sweet nieces and nephews are in good health. Please write soon as I am desirous of news from home.

Your loving sister, Eliza Shelley.

CHAPTER FIVE

1819: Elopement

Governor Macquarie is planning his departure from the colony after a leading role in the social and economic development of New South Wales. Convicts are still nearly half of the population, but it is no longer a simple place of penal servitude; free settlers arrive by ship every week from Great Britain. An inland settlement of Bathurst, west of the Blue Mountains, has replaced the illusion of a mythical Arcadia beyond the mountains. Now is the golden age for squatters, and it heralds the continued destruction of Aboriginal society.

The Parramatta Native Institution has been improved, and there is now a pretty thatched cottage with a white picket fence surrounded by tall eucalypt trees. The cottage, of thick pisé walls, built by convicts, has glass windows, while the garden thrives with vegetables, young fruit trees, and chickens. The children climb the lemon tree and nibble the green fruit. A muddy road leads into the center of the busy town, where chain gangs of convicts sweep the paths outside the school and load wheat from outlying farms into carts to take to Sydney.

Mary is three years older, and her English is nearly fluent. She writes a letter to the governor asking about her father and fears she will never see him again. The image of his face floats in front of her and she tries to keep him there all day. One day she thinks she can hear his voice arguing with Mr. Barnes. The voice demands his child, Muraging, but he is told to go away. Mary runs to the door but there is no one there. She rushes outside, convinced she will see him, but the path is empty.

The days continue and the seasons change. Cold winds blow from the mountains and Mary can hear the whistling of birds telling her to be strong. She sees other children's families camping near the schoolhouse, but still no sign of her own.

One day, Mary watches as Mercy hands a baby boy to his mother under the fence. Mrs. Shelley holds out her arms to take him back, but Mary is standing with her and shakes her head as she points to the mother and says, "Baby wants his mummy, please, Mrs."

Can't she see this baby needs his mother's milk? Mrs. Shelley relents and smiles. She walks away with Mary's hand firmly in her own.

Lady Macquarie visits the school in her horse and carriage. She shimmers in silk and a pale blue colored hat as she pats the girls' heads with her white-gloved hand, which makes Mary feel strange and light-headed. The lady's presence makes Mr. Barnes and Mrs. Shelley bow and mumble. She moves like a swan, gliding across the floor of the schoolroom, where she takes off her glove and places a hand on Mary's.

Mary gazes at the pale pink nails and gold rings as the hand directs hers to the inkwell, dipping the nib. The lady places a piece of parchment on the desk and directs the writing of Mary's name. With a flourish and a firm grip, she pushes the nib to write curls and no blots. Mary inhales her perfume, like some strange hypnotic flower, and the lady whispers:

"My dear child. I guess that you can smell my perfume from India, *Harum bin Ali*. Let me anoint you—dab some on your hand. Such a pretty thing, and so clever," says Lady Macquarie.

Mary allows the perfume to touch her wrists and ears and she swims in fields of flowers. She wonders if a smell can take you away into the sky and take away sadness.

Lady Macquarie reads aloud from the *Sydney Gazette*:

"Every human heart must have fondly dilated with the glorious and humanizing conception of beholding so many children, snatched from the wilds of barbarism, ignorance, and misery . . . the Native Institution must then have shone forth with all the resplendency so vast and glorious that an object is capable of emitting: The civilization and salvation of fellow creatures, at present involved in gross darkness."

"Lovely, we are so very proud," says Mrs. Shelley.

"I will undertake to make certain that, after the arrival of the next ship, you all have some Canton cloth, Scotch cloth, and lovely Pondicherry cotton to make new attire for all," says Lady Macquarie.

Mary swoons with love and watches the lady sit near the new female students who are struggling with their writing. These girls have a wildness about them, and they whisper about escaping in a language she cannot quite understand.

———

One day, two of the newer girls, Betty Fulton and Nancy, elope into the wild. The girls are seen throwing away their clothes and running naked through the bush. Before long, however, they are both returned to the school and native police constables are swiftly rounded up to marry them at Saint John's Church in Parramatta.

Mrs. Shelley informs the children that the young couples are to be given a hut, a farm, and a cow. They will live near Nurrugingy, beside Richmond Road, in the bush. They will also be given tea and loaves, three petticoats—that Mary has sewn—and a quarter pound of soap, two yards of print cloth, and the same of calico. Mary is jealous of these girls and their newfound freedom and wonders at the justice of it.

Death comes to the school—the babies die in the night of pestilence. Harry, too, is sick and his feverish head lies in Mary's lap. His hands clutch the blanket and he thrashes back and forth. Mary prays to God, but Jesus does not come to heal him. She makes a medicine of sarsaparilla vine and drips little bits into his mouth with honey. They boil up willow bark for pain and fever and rub the eucalyptus oil from steamed leaves onto the child's chest. Other little ones are sick, and Mrs. Shelley paces the room with her lantern.

Mary and Mercy wash the little ones' heads with cool water. Harry does not survive. The baby's ghost is now among them. Mercy takes some sticks and makes a fire in a bowl in the babies' room so they can cleanse the area. But as the blue smoke winds up to the roof, Mrs. Shelley runs in with a bucket of water and puts it out.

Mary thinks she cannot stay in this terrible place a moment longer. The *waibala* force them to stay in rooms full of death and spirits. Mr. Barnes takes Harry's crib and washes it with turpentine, but the girls will not go near it. They can feel the baby's face looking at them, and the light from his crib fills the house.

It is cold and Mary escapes the dormitory—she would rather curl up by the kitchen fire and sleep with the dogs.

———

Time moves slowly and the long year has made Mary stronger. She keeps the memory of her father safe and will not talk about her aunts. Perhaps they are gone forever. The mob's camp at Freeman's Reach is a secret thing and only Mercy is allowed to know about the people who live in this fading place.

"You'd better not eat with your fingers, you dirty guttersnipe. My da would fix you, *gach maidin*," says Cook. For many years she was a convict and her suffering has made her angry and bitter. A Presbyterian from Ireland, she waddles when she moves and always eats more than her share. When Mary reaches for more bread, Cook hits her hand with a metal spoon.

"You go and empty the chamber pots quick fast or feel my stick. You *Sambo san Afraic,*" Cook bleats and Mary runs to do her work.

Mr. Barnes sits in the kitchen when Mary runs through and grabs a piece of bread to eat. He is furious and chases her with a wooden spoon—she laughs and escapes to the yard. He calls to Mrs. Shelley, but she is preoccupied with the storeroom and has lists to make.

"That heathen Black girl will be the death of me!" he yells as he enters the storeroom.

"Leave her; she shows unending spirit,"

"Which is to be . . . condemned," says Mr. Barnes.

Mrs. Shelley reads from the list she is making: "Ten yards of cotton cloth, caps and bonnets, smocks, aprons, candles, beds, and blankets." He surveys the yard to search for Mary for punishment.

Meanwhile, Mary runs her fingers down the shiny, smooth glass windows in the backyard. She admires her reflection with her hair in braids and her prickly starched smock. She has come to admire the English sewing and her own ability with making a neat French seam.

One day, Aboriginal Chief Nurrugingy comes to the school door. He stands outside with his spears, woomera, and cloak. Mary recognizes him as a Burruberongal Elder. She silently begs that this man has been sent by her father. All the children gather at the door.

"Hello, old man, what do you want?" Mr. Barnes says in a surprised voice.

"Give daughter. Come," says the chief.

He points at a yellow-haired child hiding behind Mary's back, but Mrs. Shelley is businesslike and holds the little one's hand with a proprietor-like firmness and says, "I will not attempt to dissuade you from taking back your daughter but, if you insist on taking her, there shall be consequences. In my humble opinion, she will not acquire the advantage of an education to help her to adapt to a new life."

The man snatches up the little girl and runs out with her over his shoulder. Mary leans against the wall and watches as he dashes away, throwing the girl's pinafore and apron into the paddock. She imagines herself running behind them with the sun on her face and the smell of eucalyptus. She is diving into a clear pool and floating among pink waterlilies with white herons standing nearby in orange and purple light.

Mary can now write compositions and recite the Lord's Prayer. Her annual examination results will be adequate, with a second prize. They will print this in the *Town Gazette*.

"Mary, come to me, my dear child," says Mrs. Shelley. Mary is not sure what she wants but stands before her with hands behind her back.

"Would you like to indulge me and learn to play the violin?"

But before she can answer, Mr. Barnes interrupts: "No, Mrs. Shelley, this is unconscionable. You will spoil the wretched child. We cannot afford more of our time on such wasteful occupation. They need to be singing God's words." Mr. Barnes knows about the proper education of natives. But Mrs. Shelley does not listen to him; she places the delicate instrument in Mary's hands and shows her how to hold it. The bow screeches on the strings. Mary is learning to play the violin. She grins glaringly at Mr. Barnes.

"Idleness will not be tolerated. I have often thought about sending out the older girls into occasional service to teach them for their future employment," says Mr. Barnes. "Heaven forbid that you have to feed them forever. I see enough idle laziness in the sable brethren around the town. I have offered them as servants to that superb man, Reverend Masters. He requires them only when he entertains, as does the governor, for heaven's sake."

Mary is alarmed at this news and whispers to Mrs. Shelley, "We don't want to be servants, Mrs. That magistrate, he's a bad man; he whips people," says Mary.

Mrs. Shelley nods at Mary and puts her finger to her lips to shush Mary. She eats her scone and dips pieces into a teacup, as she inclines her head to Barnes.

"Well, you should have spoken to me first. But since you have made up your mind and you think that you are my admirable superior in all matters, I shall allow the older girls to go to work," says Mrs. Shelley.

Later, Mrs. Shelley sits on a milking stool by Mary's bed. The candle glimmers with yellow light and she looks pretty. Wind blows a shutter somewhere and it clatters. Mary can hear the wind sing of the great gum forest, the rivers, and tumbling stones.

"The Lord's my shepherd; I'll not want . . ." Mrs. Shelley sings gently like a whisper.

"I don't want to be a servant," says Mary.

"You will be, tomorrow. But don't be afraid; no one will hurt you there. I will see that you and Mercy are treated in a compassionate way. Nothing to fear. I will remonstrate with any employer who does otherwise. Sleep, child."

———

Mr. Barnes is smoking a pipe on the veranda while humming a tune from his hymnbook. The acrid smell spreads across the field. He searches the hills for gathering tribes, men in topknots with bones in their noses and men with painted shields. He searches for men with flying sharp spears and clattering boomerangs, men bringing terror and bloodied bodies. The air is buffeted by a coming storm.

CHAPTER SIX

1820: An Expedition

Some years earlier, Governor Macquarie had raised the flag in the new town of Bathurst, west of the Blue Mountains. It was intended to be the administrative center of the western plains, where orderly colonial settlement was planned. However, the Wiradjuri warrior Windradyne led his people in open warfare against the newcomers.

Governor Macquarie writes in his diary: "I inspected ten new settlers for Bathurst. I have agreed to grant each fifty acres, a servant, a cow, and four bushels of wheat, and to receive into King's Store all the wheat they can grow for the first twelve months."

Recently Mr. Barnes has been on a long and tiring expedition with Captain Woodrow, who has been observed about the town riding his horse, and who is said to be tall, handsome, and commanding in his uniform, with golden epaulets and brass buttons.

Mary and Mercy are now the senior girls of the school, because they are about fourteen years old, so Mrs. Shelley gathers them in the drawing room to hear about the adventures of Mr. Barnes and the captain:

"I feel obliged to elaborate on the story in the newspaper about my excursions with Captain Woodrow. Everyone is talking about my noble exertions," says Mr. Barnes.

"I have heard rumors of atrocities committed against the sable brethren," says Mrs. Shelley, but Barnes ignores her remarks. "Perhaps your exertions were less than Christian?"

"I had the opportunity of speaking to a tribe of native Darug Blacks in the interior as they were getting ready to go to war with their neighbors. We put our horses up at a settler's house and walked into the camp. The children ran away, but King Yarramundi came to speak to me. And lo and behold, despite my poor skill in linguistic matters, I have learned some of this dialect. *Quai bidja* means 'come here,' so you girls *werowi* will need to hear this and obey."

Mary is alert now. She sees the old chief standing in their camp. A feeling of elation and expectation rises in her. She wishes she was standing with that old grandfather now.

She asks her question: "You see the old chief? You ask him about my daddy? Where he's gone?"

She receives no answer, but her eyes link with Mercy's and they lean forward to hear every thread of evidence that the Darug and Gundungurra people are still living in the Kurrajong camp. The girls grip each other's hands; they are desperate to hear about Yarramundi's people.

"I spoke to William Cox, a landholder, and a very well-dressed man in a black velvet smoking jacket. Quite handsome, I thought. And I much admire good English black velvet; silver clasps would be nice with a French cut," says Mr. Barnes. "He said that we are wasting our time trying to educate the Blacks. He said it would be better to shoot them all and manure the ground with their carcasses. I was sorry to hear flawed judgment and kept silent. He was a disgusting man, albeit with a nice sense of fashion."

"Perhaps it would have been beneficial to speak out. Some might say it was cowardly not to. I am shocked that you do not support my views. Perhaps I should find another teacher," says Mrs. Shelley.

Mary and Mercy watch with growing alarm. Will they ever find out about their families?

"I regret that you hold me in such low esteem. Others have said I am much admired about the town. Some have said I should be in uniform; I should look splendid, I think," says Mr. Barnes.

Mary nudges Mercy, and her eyes betray her fear as she blurts out, "I want to know about my daddy. Does this chief say where my daddy's gone?" Mary's voice is louder than it has ever been.

"Tell her! Mr. Barnes, we often use good manners instead of utilizing our higher calling and speaking out against such wrongdoings. The child needs to know about her family! We will all be judged!" yells Mrs. Shelley as Mary rushes forward and slips her hand into the mistress's. Both hands tremble.

Mary watches Mr. Barnes's nose. The clumps of hair look like possum tails, and she wonders why he has them growing in his ears as well. She is beginning to hate him and his little hymnbooks even more.

She imagines her father standing up to the soldiers. She must find him. Perhaps Mercy will come, too. But her friend is now putting her finger in a dish of butter on the mahogany table. She rubs the buttery finger onto her scaly legs. Mercy admires her shiny skin, all golden brown, and has lost interest in adult words. She sucks butter from her knuckles.

Mr. Barnes hangs his head and moans. He sneers at them as he fills his pipe, then reties his necktie while gazing in a mirror on the sideboard.

"Where is your family now? Who knows? No such heathen family exists anymore. Are you an imbecile, child?" He is about to walk out of the room.

"My daddy's not finished up. You might be finished up!" Mary yells as she leaps at Mr. Barnes. Her fists strike him on the chin and she flails at his chest. She cannot bear the stupidity and cruelty of this man. Mr. Barnes pushes her away and she falls on the floor.

Mercy jumps up and the butter dish clatters to the floor. She stands between Mary and Barnes and screams, "Don't touch her! Or I'll kill you!"

Mr. Barnes pinches Mercy hard on the cheek and shoves her to the floor. He leaves and slams the door. Mrs. Shelley strokes Mercy and soothes her.

"You are like my daughters. Nothing will harm you. Shush."

Mary can see her father walking into sunlight with crows above his head.

"They might be dead. We're all going to perish in that great judgment. That is what we must all the time think about. We must think about Armageddon like we are taught in the Bible. Everyone must face God and be judged, or get burned," says Mercy with authority.

━━━━

Mary and Mercy are walking about town on errands for Mrs. Shelley when they come across some Darug farm laborers sitting in the square. The men laugh at the latest story about the reckless exploits of the military. They hear that soldiers who followed Nurrugingy, the Aboriginal guide, returned to Windsor empty-handed, exhausted, and sun-sick—no prisoners, no killing. They didn't even see a Blackfella. The children laugh because they know that Nurrugingy tricked the expedition and led them nowhere. Mercy declares that all the Blackfellas will attack the soldiers next time for sure.

━━━━

That evening Mr. Barnes walks in from the local inn and reports to Mrs. Shelley, "Captain Woodrow—too good for the likes of me! He has been seen in the company of some lieutenants striding around town in ridiculous red gaiters. The foolish peacock! Next he will disport in a braided jacket. They make up the uniforms as they go. All fancy puff and no substance," says Mr. Barnes.

Mrs. Shelley calls the children to talk about the latest military exploits of the captain.

"The captain has been forced to arrest some native people. I'm sure he is sorry about what had to be done to protect us all," says Mrs. Shelley.

The girls whisper and fidget.

"That captain won't arrest warriors in the Blue Mountains. He is going to be afraid of Blackfellas *whu karndi*. He will be scared big-time," says Mary.

"He is not always a noble man," says Mrs. Shelley. "He says he protects the farmers but sometimes we are aware his soldiers murder with impunity. A terrible shame."

"He's going to shiver in the wind like a baby, because Blackfella will hunt him down," says Mercy.

"Quiet, girls. He is under orders and cannot disobey military commands. You must not say terrible things about him," says Mrs. Shelley. She holds up a musket.

"Mr. Barnes has tutored me in the loading and firing of a weapon, although for what purpose I am not privy to. I shall instruct the older children in case of future need. Mary will be first, so she must step outside with us to the garden, while the other children remain inside. Safety first!" says Mrs. Shelley.

Mary skips forward with glee to learn about the placing of flint in the flint screw and how to cock the trigger and fill the shot and other useful tasks. She wishes she owned such an implement because it could be useful through life. She hugs the oak stock of the musket to her shoulder.

Mr. Barnes taps his pipe and leans close to Mrs. Shelley. He whispers loudly: "That captain will have to be successful, because I have heard he has certain financial requirements. He is beholden to Magistrate Masters, at least fifty pounds."

Next day the sun shines and the flowers bloom by the window. Pink roses are covered in bees and the children are happy in their occupations. Mrs. Shelley embroiders on a frame, having shown the young girls how to sew blanket-stitch on sample cloth. They learn quickly and produce small blankets made of rags.

Mr. Barnes has recently taken an interest in native things, and he arranges his collection of native curios on a desk. He questions Mary and the others endlessly for information. He shows them a crystal from a kangaroo pouch, but they are afraid of the object from a *Karadja* man. Mr. Barnes does not realize how dangerous this thing is and does not know that touching it can cause sickness or death.

Mary whispers, "*Karadji kibber*, doctor stones are not for girls." She turns her head away, but he insists on her looking. Her face grimaces in pain. This thing can cure a spear wound, but only the *Karadja* doctor can use this special stone. Her hair stands on end; the powerful stone is making the room shudder. She tries to get away, but Mr. Barnes holds the stone above his head to catch the light. Mary expects thunder and fire to erupt. This man will bring terrible things to the house: the spirits that protect this stone will take revenge.

Mr. Barnes is a fool. He even tells them that he has been a witness to digging up graves to get the skulls of buried people. Mary is horrified and prays he does not make them look at these.

One day Mrs. Shelley has an unexpected visitor: Captain Woodrow knocks on the door. Mary watches him and sees that he is good-looking for a *waibala*, but his nose holes are too small. His brass buttons are coming loose and his blond hair grows long over his collar. He has a sunburned face and a crinkled smile with startling pink lips under a carefully trimmed mustache. Mrs. Shelley seems flustered by his visit and she trembles as she pours the tea.

He says he is dedicated to soldiering but looks at Mary and the other young ones as though he longs for a family. He is almost playful toward them. He gives Mary a tiny brooch with an eagle on it, but Mercy is jealous and there is a tussle in the hallway as she tries to grab it.

"Give it to me! I am here the longest; it should be my brooch," says Mercy. But Mary grips it tightly and growls with newfound strength. Mercy backs away.

The captain does not drink or swear but he does smoke. His pipe is always clenched in his teeth and he has a tobacco pouch in his pocket. Mary thinks her father would like that pouch. The captain keeps tapping the ash from his pipe.

———

Some months pass and Mrs. Shelley is often surprised to find Captain Woodrow at her door. He seems to visit when he knows Mr. Barnes is away. The two gentlemen have fallen out over arguments to do with expeditions that do not eventuate. One day a leg of pork is delivered to Mrs. Shelley as a gift from Captain Woodrow and she dares to host a dinner party.

There have been days of fussing over the food and decorations. She rushes about giving orders and arranging platters of roasted vegetables and modest foods to be served on the lawn. Mary wears the brooch and waits on the table, which sags under the weight of the pork. Cook wipes dribbles of blood from the plate and pushes the platter into Mary's hands to deliver to the table.

Captain Woodrow carves the meat and offers Mary a piece while winking at her. She shakes her head, but Mercy bounces up and grabs the morsel and hides it in her pocket, all sticky with fat. They seldom eat such meats, and it is unbearable to see the food and not try to taste it. The girls stand straight and wait to take the plates away. As they clear the table, the smell of the leftover meat is too much, and Mary's mouth waters until Mercy takes another morsel from a used plate and secretly hands it to her.

Mrs. Shelley sits next to their honored guest, Captain Woodrow, but she is shy and blushes when he looks at her; he flirts with her. He tells the assembled dinner party about his latest escapade and holds court as he draws a map on the tablecloth.

"We formed line ranks, entered, and pushed on through a thick brush toward the precipitous banks of a deep rocky creek. The dogs gave the alarm and the natives fled," says Captain Woodrow.

"Thank the Lord for that! Please don't tell us any more; I cannot bear it!" says Mrs. Shelley.

Mary drops a jug of gravy. Her shock at hearing of native deaths is terrible and she doesn't see the sudden hard slap that hits her face. Cook has her by the hair, out of sight of the table, behind a screen.

"Slattern Black!" hollers Cook. Mary holds her cheek from the blow and slaps the cook back in the face. The shocked woman cannot close her mouth as she lashes out again.

"You clean it up quick smart or I give you a beating later," whispers Cook, and Mary takes a cloth and mops up the spilled gravy.

"A smart firing ensued in the gray dawn of morn. We saw their figures bounding from rock to rock."

Mrs. Shelley interrupts: "No more of these stories. Have you no heart?"

"I had ordered my men to take as many prisoners as possible. I regret to say, my dear madam, many were shot and others met their fate by rushing in despair over the precipice. 'Twas a melancholy but necessary duty," says Woodrow.

Mrs. Shelley stares at the captain with outrage.

"I note that your civilizing of native peoples seems to require that you massacre them, women and children," she says.

"'Tis a shame. But I'll admit that our towns like Parramatta are abounding in sin and wickedness where the Blacks are victims of crime, prostitution and slavery, and countless cruelties," says Woodrow.

"We protect our children from these outrages," says Mrs. Shelley.

"I hope you will allow me to visit more often and protect you all," says Captain Woodrow.

Despite his horrible stories, the captain becomes a regular guest at Mrs. Shelley's house and Mary washes his clothes and starches his shirts. His recent campaign is written on his clothes. She burns his shirts with pleasure. At bedtime, Mary creeps out to the shed and sees him washing his saber. She wants to grab that sword and run it through him. She watches in horror as he opens his small saddlebag and pulls out black ears—*benna*—strung along native string. There are at least ten of them in different sizes. Full of fear and loathing, Mary takes the brooch he had given her, spits on it, and hurls it out the window.

———

Cook and Mrs. Shelley help the girls hang flapping clothes on the line with wooden pegs. The season of kangaroos, *Jenneli*, when the young 'roos are easy to hunt, has begun. Mary is told to remember only the names spring, summer, autumn, and winter. Soon it will be the season of quolls, *Tugra Gori*, when the south wind blows. Mary hears their squealing outside the kitchen door; they are looking for scraps of meat and are not afraid of dogs or men. She imagines that she is growing to be fearless like a quoll because her name *Muraging* means quoll.

Out in the yard, Mrs. Shelley presses the clean sheets to her face. She tells them that she is dreaming of sailing boats that will take her home to England. Mary asks her when she will go, but she shakes her head.

Mrs. Shelley shows Mary a tiny painting of her dead child. He has blue eyes and yellow curls. Mary remembers her own little *bobbina*, cousin, and his laughing and playing and sweet little white teeth and how he died of sickness for no reason. She thinks that the spirits of these little children are walking about this house.

Mary hears little boys calling to her and she listens for them late in the night. They are night wraiths who swim in the air and hover above Mrs. Shelley. Mary wonders if she can blame herself for her brother's death. Her burden is to have so much to eat, and she can drink tea from a crockery cup, and he is probably dead. She had loved him well when he was a baby on her hip. He brushes his face against hers and laughs. She must go on living with the most precious loves gone.

With strict instructions not to bathe, Mrs. Shelley allows the oldest children the privilege of walks along the river. They walk along a track by the swirling water and smell fires coming from across the plains. They know the eels are spawning upriver and imagine them eating sucker fish spawn. When the rain comes, Mercy sings an old song to lure the creatures to the bank and Mary waits with her *mootin*, a spear fashioned from willow. They catch the little eels as they slither from river to pond and roast them in a fire of wood coals.

Christmastime is here, and Mary and Mercy are excited to be going to Government House in Parramatta with Mrs. Shelley and Mr. Barnes. They will wait on the governor's table for the first time, clothed in black dresses with white aprons. They are scrubbed and preened with their hair pulled into tight pigtails. They are told that the governor likes to share a table at Christmas with a wide selection of people to show his gregarious nature. The governor has shown his appreciation of the progress of the Parramatta Native Institution by inviting the teachers to Christmas lunch. The girls know that being a temporary servant is not so bad, because they can sneak snippets of delicious food. The school lends them out to other houses on occasion in order to gain some remuneration.

Mr. Barnes drives the cart to Government House and hurries the girls into the back of the building to begin work in the kitchen. The kitchen has two large woodstoves, and black pots hang from hooks over the cooking plates. Some carcasses of swans and ducks hang above the worktables. Another hook has rabbits and the haunch of a kangaroo that is being skinned by a convict servant. The cook has a red face and her hair tied up in a bun; she pounds dough for bread. Flour flies into the air, and the smell of boiling fish makes the girls hungry. There is a great Christmas pudding to be shared with servants and guests. It has fruit and glacé cherries; Mary and Mercy pick the red fruit out of the pudding when the cook has her back turned.

They are to work hard serving a roasted black swan at the table, its head still intact, along with Indian pickle, chicken, eggs, salt beef stew, kangaroo tail, potatoes, and fish. When the governor arrives, the girls stand at attention at the side of the formal dining room and murmur as he enters and removes his cockaded hat with white feathers. Mary notes that he has gold braid all over his coat of red wool. So many buttons! She is a fancier of buttons since coming to the town.

"O Lord, bless this Christmas and this colony. Take us to your bosom. Oh, let us hear heavenly voices of thunderous angels, and let all the brethren, both white and Black, gather at this governor's table to partake of your benevolence. Amen," prays Mrs. Shelley.

"Mrs. Shelley, you seem to have achieved a remarkable feat after your husband was taken from you," says the governor. "The children can speak English and, lo and behold, some can read and write. I also hear of murder on the roads, the rush of prostitution in the new towns. The settlers wish to give a love of liquor to the natives so they can be rendered helpless and become the victims of tyranny and plunder. You, Mrs. Shelley, have achieved a miracle in civilizing these dear children." He smiles at Mary and Mercy, and they curtsy.

"We have achieved this with the continued hindrance of insufficient funds and the ongoing visits from unwanted Black fellows who claim to be parents," says Mrs. Shelley. "One such man, Nurrugingy, took his little child back and will not be coerced into giving it up."

"The way of a noble savage, is it not?" The governor looks at Mary and touches her shoulder. "Who is this pretty servant? She is familiar."

"Mary James, sir. A promising—and sometimes outspoken—student brought into the Parramatta Native Institution at a tender age. She is now a young woman who can recite her catechism and has a remarkable vocabulary, and she loves her dictionary and music," says Mrs. Shelley.

"Excellent. I remember her. She will make a fine maid."

Lady Macquarie's hand flutters toward Mary. She looks into Mary's eyes and smiles as she asks, "And what will become of her after she has completed her education at your school?"

"That is a problem, madam. Many of the girls elope into the wilds," says Mr. Barnes.

"Soon we are to depart for England, but I believe we should celebrate our early days of relative harmony with the Aborigines," says the governor. "They are British subjects, plain and honest. The Aboriginal females exhibit virtues of modesty and bashfulness. In time you will find them suitable tame native husbands."

"I shall endeavor to carry out that task. I also hope, sir, that you can send me some books from London for my instruction. I wish to explore relationships between privilege and education, natural birth rights, and its connection to property. It has deep moral implications," says Mrs. Shelley.

"Madam, Rousseau says males are active and strong, while females are passive and weak. Your role is the teaching of your charges, not encouraging simmering revolution," says the governor.

"Thank you, sir. At school, we are endeavoring to teach our charges about the human soul," says Mrs. Shelley. "They are under the misapprehension that the souls of their deceased relatives pass into the bodies of living humans, such as our own race. They believe in transmigration of souls, like the Brahmins. I asked Mary to kill a snake for me. Mary, tell them what you said."

Mary bows and speaks, "I cannot kill it because he's my brother, my *bobbina*," says Mary.

"Quite so," says the governor. "When other natives visit the school, be ever vigilant—no free flour is to be given without labor. Anyway, they are suspicious of our flour, which is the inevitable consequence of the poisonings at the river branch near Colo. They call it green seed flour."

"Hear, hear. We agree. Deplorable action, but effective. They don't realize what we can do to our enemies; after all, the wild tribes wish to eat our hearts," Mr. Barnes mutters.

Mary and Mercy are stunned to hear this information. Who would want to eat their greasy cheese-smelling hearts? They nudge each other and mime eating a heart.

Mary and all the schoolchildren climb into carts to travel the long journey to Sydney Town. They travel in an open cart that has carried grain, and the chaff bags are placed on planks to give the children seats. It is a rough but joyful ride. The children sing and choose which horses are best of those they see along the road. The sun shines, it is warm, and the road has countless people on horseback or in carriages. The road is all mud and holes, but the rough jerking of their cart fills the children with laughter, especially when the horses fart!

Mary has never seen teeming Sydney Town before; the small dwellings crowd together near the Rocks and the stench of sewage is everywhere. She sees Koori natives fishing by the harbor and some sing to the settlers and receive payment. The children are herded into two longboats with a sailor on the oars. It is thrilling to see colored pennants from tall-masted ships flutter in the air along the dock of Port Jackson Harbor. Mary and Mercy cuddle up to each other in delight. But there are pitiful sights as well. A line of shackled convicts staggers past them, and the girls are shocked to see women and children in irons with their ragged clothes unable to conceal their nakedness.

On their arrival, they travel in boats behind the government barge around Garden Island and then to Elizabeth Bay. Governor and Lady Macquarie are their hosts. Today is a celebration for the governor's son, who is turning six. His name is Lachlan, after his father, and he is dressed as a highlander in tartan dress.

The students of the Parramatta Native Institution are special favorites of Governor Macquarie and he is keen to show them off to his great friend Chief Bungaree, who is living in a village at Georges Head, overlooking the harbor. This village has been built to house sixteen Guringai families. These families traveled from across Broken Bay to take up the governor's offer to replace the Aboriginal clans that perished from the terrible scourge of smallpox. Few of the Borogegal, Gaimariagal, or Gadigal people who had lived on both sides of the harbor are to be found.

The village was built by convict servants for Bungaree; one of these servants is a Prussian ex-soldier called Ferdinand, who is famous for having been at the Battle of Waterloo.

A big mob of local Guringai people are feasting on damper and beef when the children are rowed to Georges Head to meet the great explorer Chief Bungaree; his two wives, Aunty Queen Matora and Queen Gooseberry; and Mary's cousin Bowen. This young man has gleaming black eyes and throws a spear with great skill before the giggling girls.

Chief Bungaree strides toward them wearing a cockaded hat that was a gift from the governor. He, however, is not wearing trousers and the girls squeal with shock. The governor chats amiably with his friend and they seem to exchange jokes. Mary is astounded to see such friendship between men of high degree.

The chief proudly shows the children a pathway down a steep incline to his longboat anchored below. They reach up to the young apricot trees to grab green fruit, but are scolded by one of Bungaree's wives, Queen Cora Gooseberry; the apricots are not ripe.

Mary cannot put the chief's son, Bowen, from her mind; he is eighteen years or so, a little older than the children, and has strong muscled arms. He seems so confident, and his English is as clear as an Englishman's. Mary looks at him with admiration and, while clutching Mercy's hand, she dares to speak to him: "You go walk-about a lot; you seen my daddy? You hear about him from your mob?"

"No, he might be finished up now. We have not seen him long time," he tells her.

"Sorry for that news," says Bowen as he walks off to the men's camp.

Mary sobs a little but looks away so no one can see this.

They eat peaches in Bungaree's orchard and drink some *bool*, which makes their heads ache. Lady Macquarie gives Queen Matora a breeding sow, seven pigs, and a pair of Muscovy ducks. Mary knows that she will eat those ducks quick smart. She remembers swimming underneath wild ducks and pulling them under the water, then later roasting them on a fire.

On their return from the excursion, Mary sleeps deeply and

dreams that her father has something in his hand. She reaches out from her bed. He gives her a present of a downy bird's nest with a tiny blue wren's egg. He tells her that he only ever takes one because the Jenny wrens wouldn't like to lose all their eggs.

━━━

Mary and Mercy are growing into courageous and reckless young women. They are often scolded by Cook for climbing out the school-house window in the night to find trouble in the town. They walk among the young Darug people who congregate beneath bridges and by fires along the riverbank.

Every Koori they meet claims to be a cousin of some distant kind. Intermarriage of Darug clans is causing a mix that will not allow them to follow kinship rules for marriage; it's all very mixed up. But they are mostly from old Grandfather Gomboree's mob. Polly and Betty are new daring school students and they meet their boyfriends, Yarringguy and young Nurrugingy, under the trees. Meanwhile Mary and Mercy are becoming wild in their expeditions.

A few weeks after their visit to Bungaree's village, Mary and Mercy meet up with another one of Mary's cousins in Parramatta, for there are countless—every native is somehow related to Mary or Mercy. Everyone is a cousin or uncle or aunt, for the numbers are dwindling and each person in a clan is precious. They walk to the end of the town, where the vineyards grow with the smell of sticky grapes in the air. Wasps, bees, and flies rush past them looking for the dung around the vines.

Before Mary has a chance to say no, they are all climbing over the fence and into a white woman's yard. Mercy has a look of pure glee as they get under the wire chook house and into the nesting boxes, where the hens are nesting on fresh-laid eggs. Mary is hungry, so she stops to crack an egg and swallow it down. She knows that the whole escapade is a bad idea. As she eats another egg, Reverend Masters arrives in his buggy and—to her horror—stares at Mary with outraged comprehension. She pretends to be feeding the chickens, but she knows she has been seen. Mary feels like punching her cousin for his wildness—he will certainly end up in the asylum and she will probably go to Parramatta Jail, but it is too late now to change her mind. She quickly stuffs five fowl in her shift while the mother hen pecks at her. She hurls herself over the fence to find her cousin waiting with an open linen bag, and they all run back to town where they sell the fowls to a farmer. Mary and Mercy race home while the cousin saunters back to join his fellow crooks.

Mary knows Masters saw her and that it will come back to haunt her.

———

The Parramatta Native Institution girls have been invited to dance at the Parramatta Government House. They crowd into an outhouse to dress in Tahitian grass skirts and are given feathers to hold. The music comes from boomerangs clattered by old Nurrugingy and a possum skin drum played by his son Bobby. This Koori man has been granted thirty acres of land with Colebee along the Richmond Road and has a small farm, but he makes some money playing music for the governor. The girls are sent in to dance. At first they are shy and awkward but, as they warm up, boldness takes over and the girls twitch their bottoms, wiggle, and prance. Mary enjoys running and stopping, sweeping her feathers in the air, while Mercy flirts outrageously with the audience and sticks her cheeky tongue out at them. Mrs. Shelley bends her head in mortification; her instructions in physical culture are all but forgotten—the girls show no "decorum," and they are creating a scene, a shameful spectacle. But when they meet His Lordship, the governor, he bows to them and claps his hands.

They shuffle into the kitchen to be given jam tarts and tea, only to be given a lecture by an Irish ex-convict manservant: "You are much used by these so-called Lords of the Land, the landed gentry. They take your land and you Aboriginal natives become lackeys of the upper classes," says the Irishman. Mary knows he is right, but for now she stuffs her mouth with another jam tart.

CHAPTER SEVEN

1821: Boothuri

Parramatta has grown and has many solid whitewashed houses with thatched roofs. The stumps of once-great trees are scattered about the surrounding fields. Sir Thomas Brisbane arrives in the colony to replace Governor Macquarie, who has sailed back home to his beloved England. The new governor takes up residence.

A young, shy Aboriginal man, Boothuri, begins a week's employment in the Parramatta Native Institution garden. He has come from the mountain people and speaks little English. The girls peer at him through windows and the school overflows with giggling.

Mary, now nearly sixteen years old, is collecting eggs in the chicken pen when suddenly Boothuri appears beside her. He is a tall, muscled young man, handsome in his gray opossum skin cloak, and when he laughs he shows his shining white teeth. Mary cannot stop looking at him and feels the energy that pours out of him. She is fascinated. They laugh at each other and she gives him all the eggs. He carefully covers them with his cloak and bounds away over the fence. He appears again, just as suddenly, in the orchard where he eats an apple, standing close, right in front of her.

As the days go by, Mary is enchanted by his ability to turn up anywhere. He has feather feet, so Mary never hears him approach: he is the perfect thief.

One day she is in the paddock milking the cow when he appears. He puts his head under the cow and sucks on a teat. It is warm and he is near naked, and close. Mary is bursting with excitement.

Mary grows to expect him, and one day he stands beside her near the garden full of blooming jasmine. He leans down and rubs her face while she smells the flowers; they speak for the first time. "*Naiya* Boothuri. You?"

"Mary, daughter of a chief," she says and hides her face.

Mercy watches the two of them, and she is jealous.

"You don't talk to him; he might steal you," says Mercy later on.

"I like him, but you know I love you, too," says Mary.

Boothuri waves to Mary and sweeps across the field like smoke while Mercy pulls at her, trying to take her inside.

"You can't run away. Lot of bolters in that bush waiting to *nguttatha* you or eat you or both might be," says Mercy.

Mary can see no signs of his tracks in the dust. She thinks about the possibility of loving this young man but pushes away the idea as too dangerous. She would have to leave the protection of the school. But perhaps she could search for her father?

Mary pictures herself running into Boothuri's arms as she lies awake at night. But what if his Gundungurra and Darug mob reject her or see her as a *waibala* spy?

After the week is up Boothuri leaves. She grieves his departure and daydreams during the day and at night as she waits to find him in her dreams.

One night the sound of crickets is broken by the call of a boobook owl and Mary wakes. There is someone pulling at her shoulder. The soft tugging on flesh is like a cat nuzzling—Boothuri is in her room! She can barely breathe. Maybe she should scream, but his smile is so enticing.

"What do you want?" she says.

"*Ki barley. Me burribi* husband. Come," he says, and his gentle voice makes her brave as it drips and cajoles. Like a calling from the mountain or river, it sings in her bones.

"You *jinmang*, wife for me," he whispers, then mimes her packing blankets and running away. What is this talk of "wife" when she is barely a woman? What does it mean? Will she have to cook for him? Will she survive with Boothuri in a camp after years of a soft bed? Her school family will miss her, and Mrs. Shelley might even send out a search party with police—and then what terrible catastrophe could occur?

She is afraid—afraid of the journey into a forest where so much has been transformed. Will she recognize any place that her family lived? Will she be wanted? Is she an outcast now that the English school has changed her? But at the same time she is more alive than she has ever been, and she is brave. Mary will do this thing that is almost unbearable to contemplate. Yes, this will be her moment of escape and redemption.

"You come now, tonight, *jinmang. Naiya* Boothuri," he says.

Still, she hesitates. She imagines herself walking behind a white husband, weighed down with children and work. She turns to her bedhead and a picture of Jesus looks down as she tries to remember another life, her Aboriginal life.

Boothuri laughs silently at her, but his manner is soft and tender as he takes her hands and presses them against his bare chest. She sees the cicatrices carved in his skin and sighs as a lump rises in her throat at the prospect of leaving dear Mrs. Shelley and the children who need her.

"You *jinmang*, wife, come. You wife, you come, me Gundungurra and Darug man. You Muraging," he says as he pulls her to him, and the soft, gray opossum fur rubs against her neck as he nuzzles her hair.

She fills a basket with flour, tea, and clothing, leaving the best calico dress with a lace collar in the cupboard. She will have no need for lace.

Mary is shaking as she dresses. She sees that he has sharp spears and an axe in his belt like he is going off to war. His face stays on hers and she trusts him. It is madness. No more warm bed or meals at Mrs. Shelley's table. She fights off her many doubts and she wonders if he is frightened also. Boothuri leaves and waits outside.

The night is cold and Mary steals two blankets and some bread. As she wraps the food in cloth, she hears Mercy behind her.

"Don't go away. I'll die without you here. Please stay. You get killed!"

Mary shakes her head and reaches out to hold her friend, but Mercy stands cold and stiff, alone and angry.

"Come with me; come find your tribe, too. I am looking for my father. You can look, too," says Mary.

"Everyone's dead. Your mob dead, your father dead. Look at the true story. You'll soon be dead like all Blackfellas."

Mercy is wondering what it would be like to have a warrior husband. He would do things to her at night and it might be lovely. She is a woman and has a *mulamundra* bleed; she is ready. He would have big shoulders and strong hands and he would be kind to her and give her a kangaroo tail to eat. But she does not want to eat a tail crouched over a fire. She wants a table and a plate. She will stay with Mrs. Shelley and wait.

Boothuri whistles from outside and climbs up to the window. He frowns at Mercy and she shoves Mary away from her. There is a long, sad silence between them.

Mary begins to climb out the window and Mercy cannot bring herself to say farewell. Instead, she whispers, "I hate you!"

Mary and Boothuri climb under the fence and Mary looks back and sees Mercy's shadow in the window as tears roll down her face.

―――――

The stars are out and gleam as Boothuri opens the school gate. She hurries through, picturing Mr. Barnes coming after them with his gun. Mary imagines him packing the barrel with shot like he did to shoot birds! He could pepper their fleeing backsides, but they hear nothing except night birds.

After walking quickly away from the town, Mary crawls up rocks and half falls. Boothuri puts out his hand and pulls her up; they smile at each other. They have nothing and everything, with no home except that everywhere is their home. This night Boothuri knows where they are going. It is west to the mountains and he does not falter. Mary is tired and slow, but he smiles and waits for her to catch up.

Boothuri sniffs the air and looks at marks on the ground, then takes a gum tree branch and brushes their tracks away. No one can track them now.

He trails the leaves behind them as they walk into the shadows of the forest, and they stop under the cover of trees to look back one last time. Now they can see a glimmering candlelight in the window. No doubt Mrs. Shelley is making tea, but Mary knows that they will not notice she has gone until breakfast, and for now the cockerel has not crowed. "*Wattunga* Darug?" Mary asks him; he inclines his head to the west.

Mrs. Shelley will know that she has left of her own free will and will not search for her. She is not the first. She will walk into her drawing room and see that the violin has vanished, along with Mary.

CHAPTER EIGHT

1821: The Mountains

Early in the morning, they hear lyrebirds singing in many voices across the escarpment. Then a whipbird whoops. Two yellow-tailed black cockatoos chew casuarina seeds in a tree overhead. The white mist lifts from the fern forest and there is an eerie beauty and tranquility that is broken by a striped sparrowhawk diving for insects.

Mary and Boothuri are tired and stop to drink from a creek. The dogs in the settler shacks bark at them and Boothuri hisses a peculiar sound, like a dingo, and the dogs fall silent. The land is newly logged and broken trees litter the ground. It is a kind of sorrow for them to witness this new *waibala* destruction. Through the trees they hear the banging of stone against stone and the sharp crack of sledgehammers as convicts build a new road. The couple skirt the edges of the clearing up the mountain, where Aboriginal tracks have long been, but they avoid all contact out of fear of attack.

Boothuri is strong and certain, and he will lead her to a promised land, like Moses did. He bends down beside a creek and scoops fresh water into his mouth. He cups his hands for Mary to drink and his fingertips brush her mouth. He grins. Now her life is with

Boothuri. She is brave with him, and his voice seems to come directly from the mountains and rivers. Now she will be *jinmang*, wife.

When they stop under a huge fig tree to eat some bread, he lifts her blouse to gaze at her breasts. His eyes glow but he does not touch. She is shaky. This is where her life begins, on this road, running away with a man who wears the opossum cloak and has spears and an axe in his belt.

"*Wattunga*, where we go?"

"Kurrajong," he says.

"*Biana*, he's there?"

"No, but maybe not far," he says.

He walks on and looks back at her—at his wonderful prize. His eyes flicker over her body as he laughs. Mary struggles with her dillybag piled with linen clothes and a heavy bag of flour. He puts out his hand and she gives him the flour to carry.

She wonders if she should have said no. Should she have said, "Go away; go back to your Gundungurra mob"? There is a lump in her throat as she thinks of dear Mrs. Shelley and all the children who have become brothers and sisters to her. She is miserable at the thought of Mrs. Shelley's face when she sees her empty bed. Mary will be seen as yet another reason for the governor to shut down the school. Another failure in civilizing the natives.

As the miles pass, the moon shines over the quiet water and fear gives way to excitement. They gaze at each other and touch hands. They walk an ancient pathway through sturdy white gum trees lit with moonlight and through open grass plains beneath the Blue Mountains.

"*Ngulluwa, nangi*, sleep," says Boothuri, as they arrive in a deep rock shelter. Boothuri sweeps the floor with casuarina branches and lays the soft needles underfoot. He makes a bed of bracken ferns piled high, then flattened by his feet. He lays the possum cloak over the bed and the blankets on top. He murmurs and pats the creation. They lie down and look at the blackened roof of the shelter. How many thousands have camped in here? Red ocher handprints show the passage of many children.

Boothuri brings flames to life with a twirling stick. Watching him brings back the longing for Berringingy. She sees her father's hands cupping a small flame and thinks that this longing will kill her. Can you die of sadness and dimming memories? Mary asks for information from every kind Koori they meet along the track, but the shoulders shrug and pitying faces tell her there is no trace of her family. No one knows where they have gone.

They pile charcoal around the fire and among the black ash are shards of silcrete stone, scrapers like thumbnails, fine and sharp. This is a place to make native stone tools. She holds tiny blades that have been used for scraping the flesh from opossum skins. These tools are like the ones from her father's tool kit, and she takes one and hides it in her dress, hoping to bring her father back—a stone to wish upon. Mary examines the triangular points in the yellow firelight. "*Garmai*, spearheads," Boothuri says, and he takes her finger to test the needle-sharp point. She pulls her hand away, but he uncurls her fist and lays translucent spearheads in her palm.

"*Buru*, kangaroo, your totem." He nods and points at her. His hand is warm, sending pulses of life through her body.

"*Naiya burru*."

"*Naiya waiali*, possum," he says, and he knows he will not be permitted to marry her because she is the wrong skin group to marry him. But he doesn't care and Mary doesn't know.

She feels Boothuri's breath on her neck as he leans his head against hers and sighs. She quivers. His body is tender and close. His face strokes hers and his eyes shine. She dares to kiss his forehead and he gently brushes his lips on hers as they tumble into their first joyful sex.

The morning dawns and they are in each other's arms on the bracken bed. Currawongs sing out across the mountains. Boothuri fetches water in a coolamon that lies for this purpose beneath a ledge. She runs her fingers across the spear-sharpening grooves at the back of the shelter. Forty people might have slept in this spacious cave at one time. She is beginning to be frightened of the unknown. Mary unpacks her basket and holds up a billy can and some tea. Boothuri grins. They blow on the fire, and it comes alive. His eyes are lowered but then they hover on hers. He is shy even though they have embraced in a night of love. King parrots flash red and green as they eat damper.

"*Pittuma Darug.*" He runs his fingers across the rock grooves. Many warriors have passed here. She freezes because she had been taught to fear wild people from other tribes.

"*Karmai?*" Mary asks if they might be killed.

"*Beal*," he says, they are safe.

Mary has heard talk of murderous mountain Blacks, savages who chop off the heads of lonely settlers.

"*Dullai*, not killem you. Darug kill soldier, not you," he says.

They walk into the rough bush below Kurrajong Mountain and he climbs a tree with speed. When he comes down he whispers that he can smell native smoke.

"*Dullai*, Darug."

Boothuri teaches Mary skills in tracking. She remembers being shown the tracks of goannas and other animals as a child. Boothuri stops to feel the ashes in a fireplace and tells her he can find the people by the fading warmth of the coals. The movement of a twig or pebble is another sign. If you practice these skills, then you will always be able to track people. He finds the hiding place of an echidna and kills it swiftly. They roast it on coals and it is delicious, like the flesh of young fowl.

They push along a narrow track and come across a clearing with soft yellow grass. It is a paradise valley before they reach the mountains. Bush turkeys bound away, and one scrapes at a mound where eggs incubate. Mary helps Boothuri uncover the eggs and they eat them raw. Above them, white waterfalls pour down orange stone cliffs. Many Darug people camp nearby and Boothuri tells her that other tribes are here, all mixed up. They walk into the clearing and he looks for his mob. People sit among paperbark *gunyahs* next to fires, with dillybags hanging in trees next to dozens of spears. They look up and stare at Mary.

Mary and Boothuri are viewed with some suspicion, but as his family stand to greet him there is joyful singing and clapping of boomerangs that builds to a crescendo. The camp dingoes prowl around them to sniff out danger but are soon licking their hands.

The people are Gundungurra and Darug. They are scarred by *gal gal*, smallpox, and have an air of desperation. They speak in both languages and Boothuri understands and helps Mary to find her Darug words. His mother is Gundungurra and she looks warily at the newcomer and will not allow her to sit nearby. The government blanket is shifted away, and Mary stands awkwardly. At last, some ancient women brush a place for her next to their fire. One old woman takes her hand and warms it in her lap in the possum fur. Mary feels relief and her chest begins to relax.

She looks at the tiny circles of scarring on the old woman's hand. She is told that this camp of people are all that is left of a great mountain clan, and many are dead or so poor that they now must rely on government blankets to keep warm. She begins to notice more wounds and scars from illness all around her. "Let Baiame, the sky god, and Jesus punish the *waibala* for all that has happened here," she silently prays.

Mary worries that she will not be accepted. She is informed with frowning faces that her skin group is not right for Boothuri. But Mary is a Burruberongal Darug woman and the daughter of a famous warrior; surely the elders will respect her. And Boothuri is a Darug man. And the tribes are now mixed in because of so much destruction. Everybody knows her and her family for a hundred miles in any direction because every Aboriginal knows everyone else, or of them, and certainly how they are related.

She learns that some clans have traveled long distances for initiation ceremonies and the Awaba, Wonnaruah, and Darkinjung from the north come to join the Gundungurra and Darug to fight the *waibala*. Mary sees that some girls have had the little finger of their left hand removed to show they are the fisherwomen. She hopes she is too old for this.

The camp shimmers with little flickering fires and elders warm themselves and shelter in *gunyahs* of bark and stones. Mary sees they wear long, gray possum-skin cloaks wrapped around their bodies, which makes them look like huddles of gray fur. Every man has a pile of spears and a woomera beside him. Some fashion spearheads from silcrete stones chipped from a core at their feet. Fire-heated resin from ferns is used to adhere the deadly points. Other men lie under small trees and *gunyahs* smoking pipes and cooking delicious-smelling meat. Children play string games between two trees, jumping and skipping. Mary can see her brother's spirit drifting above the playing children.

"*Barrio nguyangun*, give me!" A tall naked woman has a head of tousled black curls decorated with kangaroo teeth woven through them. She thrusts her hand in front of Mary's face. Mary looks at the stretched palm with dark lines crisscrossed; the hand demands a gift. She tries to look away, but the woman persists until an older woman pushes her hand down. What does she want? The clothes? The dillybag? Everything?

"She want present," says an old granny with a smile. Mary nods and the old woman points to herself. This old woman looks with a certain familiarity; she is an old relation.

"*Naiya Baayjin.*"

"*Baayjin.*" Mary nods. She then hands over a precious apron and the naked *dyin* ties it around her waist and saunters away.

Boothuri beckons Mary away from Granny and points with his lips to a new spot where she will be more welcome. These women will teach her how to behave, while Boothuri sits with the men. The women move a pile of sleeping dogs to make room and they pat the ground beside them and brush away leaves. They look her over and one aunty loans her a possum-skin cloak. It is cozy and warm.

Mary smiles as one old woman squeezes her chin and stares into her face. She pats Mary's back, then offers a shell full of water, grinning at her. This woman knows everything about them in one look. Mary stops trembling and more women come close and reach for her white garments. She sees they do not trust her and lowers her eyes.

Beside the fire is a *gunyah* full of furs and baskets of wild fruit, like lilly pillies, geebung, and sandpaper figs. There is a rich damper made from burrawang nuts that have been soaked and ground up. Yams of different colors are piled ready for baking, and string dilly-bags hang around in the trees. These dillybags are brightly colored and woven with dyed wild grass.

Two women argue over clothes from her dillybag. A beautiful young woman with blazing black eyes parades in the best petticoat. Mary doesn't mind and watches with interest.

They eat dampers and roast turtle, goanna, possum meat, baked emu eggs, freshwater fish, and, best of all, a stew of emu rich with yellow fat. They celebrate the sky goddess, Birrahgnooloo, who is the emu spirit and the goddess of fertility. They will make a ceremonial dance for her, a corroboree.

At last she asks about her father, "*Biana*, Berringingy?"

The people tell her he is well and that he has gone farther north with his clan. Here it is almost as if Mary's thoughts can be read—her fear and discomfort, and her world of *waibala* somehow polluting her. Some women ignore her and talk behind her back. She notices that the Gundungurra headman, old King Louis, is watching her, puckering and licking his lips below the bone in his nose.

Mary sleeps a way off from the others with Boothuri, but the ground is hard on her back. She tosses and turns and wonders what will happen to her. She wonders whether she has forgotten her people's ways. Dark figures move against the black night sky and weapons are placed outside *gunyahs*.

In the morning, some women take Mary by her hands and lead her to a possum cloak, where they pat the place for her to sit.

"*Ngulluwa*, sit down," they say.

The women paint her face with yellow ocher, her hair is plaited with white cockatoo feathers, and a necklace of tiny gray and silvery shells threaded onto a human hair string is hung around her neck. Small animal teeth are scattered among echidna quills that are on threaded necklaces around the women's necks. The women are happy to see her painted up for the renewal of earth ceremony. The waratahs are blooming, and the women teach her some steps with the accompanying beating of possum skins stretched over their knees. Mary is told that the waratah is a sacred flower for these women. The Dreaming story tells of two mobs fighting by the river with much blood spilled, filling waterholes; the sky spirit wept and the waratah appeared from the earth to heal the land.

The women dance in a small group echoing each other's light steps. They stretch stringybark thread between their hands and they sing the old songs. They sing tales of the Dreaming and how *Garangatch* the giant eel chases the quoll cat across the mountains and lives in deep pools. The dancing by a fire goes on late into the night.

In the camp, piles of kangaroo bones lie near the fire and some camp dogs chew on them and snap at each other. Mary's flour is used to cook dampers in the ashes, and she eats one with cooked goanna, its skin curling in green and white patterns; then she tastes turtle and possum.

That night, Mary takes her bundle to the fire and magically produces her precious violin. She plays to the tribe and they laugh and tap their hands on their thighs in time to the music. It is miraculous to hear such sound from a wooden object. The women gather around Mary to touch the instrument.

Two men appear in the clearing. One is a majestic Wonnaruah warrior from the north and has a commanding presence. The other man, thin and staggering, carries many spears and has a wound on his shoulder. The old women surround the wounded man and help him by applying red gum sap to his wounds and binding them with spider web and paperbark.

Mary watches with eyes lowered. These men are curious about her. She cannot look at them as some are in taboo relationships, but she is yet to work out who is who. Only some skin brothers and sons can be spoken to. She will make many mistakes and be laughed at. Her kinship teaching was so long ago. They seem to want to dissect her and explore all her belongings and body. She is shy and covers herself in a cloak. Some men seem to regard her as a potential wife. She is frightened.

The night crickets chirp as she holds tightly onto her violin and her remaining *waibala* clothes. Mary tells herself that she will be safe, but a louder voice screams that these men will change everything. These warriors will decide what happens to Boothuri and he has no say; by law he must show his allegiance to them first for they are warriors and messengers from the frontier wars.

Her senses are alert and she cannot sleep because she can feel her husband slipping away, abandoning her. Boothuri will be forced to leave her to go out on raiding parties with the men, even though he means to return to her. She holds tight onto his shoulder, and he murmurs in his sleep.

Before dawn, Boothuri takes his spears and joins a party of men hunting kangaroos with their dogs. Mary follows behind with some of the old women. The group arrives at sunrise in a clearing where a large group of animals feed on grass. They make camp and wait for the hunters' return.

Wombats lumber past and hide in burrows. Baby joeys poke noses from their mothers' pouches and an old man kangaroo scratches his chest as he leans back grandly on his huge thick tail, his ears erect and twitching. A smaller group of rock wallabies are close to Mary, grazing.

Birds call in the soft golden light and Mary is enthralled by the cooing of topknot pigeon and the shrill whistle of a whipbird.

Meanwhile, the men slink through undergrowth and motion to each other. They are covered in kangaroo shit and earth to disguise their human smell. The old man kangaroo sniffs and stands tall and alert. He scratches his chest again, his head on one side listening for danger. Mary follows some distance behind the hunters and watches from behind a tree as some of the tribe's dogs run off, sniffing their prey. Yelping and growling, the dogs catch one young male kangaroo and bring it down. Mary looks away. Kangaroo is her totem; she cannot eat it or kill it.

Quietly, the hunters creep along the ridge. Men close in on some fighting kangaroos and woomeras whir as they let fly a flurry of spears. Mary watches as a kangaroo is dragged back to the camp for cooking. The women open the animal with a silcrete knife and they rip out the entrails to feed the dogs. They have built a deep pit of fire and filled it with hot stones to place inside the gutted animal. The animal is placed on coals. The men strip sinews from the legs to use for twine and hafting spearheads. Boothuri singes fur off the tail and offers some bloody flesh to the oldest men, who blow to cool it and chew the delicious meat, spitting out pieces of fur. When the feast is cooked, the old ones are given the best pieces of meat, then the hunters, and last of all the young women and children. Mary is given a half-eaten kangaroo bone but shakes her head.

Later that day, the hunters speak of fighting the *waibala*. They plan to join Gundungurra in attacks on *waibala* near Picton or to head west to join their onetime enemy, the Wiradjuri. These people have made raids on their camps to steal women for countless years, but now they must join forces.

The headman, Wargun, has a deep hatchet-scarred brow and he looks at Mary. She shrinks from his intense gaze, her heart pounding. The thought of running back home to the school is intense. This terrible talk of battle is hard to follow, and her lack of language makes it a struggle to understand.

"*Werowi*, girl, *nguyangun*, give me," says Wargun. Boothuri shakes his head and will not answer. He hangs his head so the old man will see his respect, while Mary stands next to him. She lowers her head and hunches her shoulders and grimaces as though she is deformed. She is still and silently begs her lover to choose her over his tribal obligations, but she knows he will always leave her if asked.

"*Nyindi, molliming beal, nyindi mittigar, naiya, gumirri*," says the old man. Boothuri hears him say that he cannot marry Mary because his skin is wrong. Wargun wants Boothuri to give Mary to him. He wants her *gumirri*, her vagina. Boothuri refuses to give her up and a heavy atmosphere descends around the young lovers. Boothuri leads her away, his head low. Perhaps he cannot win.

Mary can taste the misery of being forced to sleep with the old man and she can smell his sweat and power. She knows he can use *Karadji*, cleverman, magic to call her if he wishes. She would be one of his five wives, the youngest and the most desired, but distrusted by her sister wives. The old man smiles at her, and a lightning bolt travels from her head and into her guts and vagina. He is powerful. Mary knows enough to understand that she could be beaten if she doesn't obey. That night, she can't sleep and presses her shivering body against Boothuri.

That night Mary dreams of Boothuri speared in the neck with his skin torn off and a dozen spears in his chest—they are hook spears that cannot be removed. Blood weeps from his wounds. The color seeps from his face, leaving only his skull. She dreams of dead humans walking with animals' spirits as they rise in the air. And she dreams of her vagina stolen and taken by the old magician; she wakes with a jolt, hot and sweaty. They both hear old men discussing the marriage on into the night. To their relief they hear that the men will accept this marriage. So many tribal rules are being

disregarded in these killing times. Mary can continue to sleep with
Boothuri for now.

At daybreak, the old leaders, Wargun and Old King Louis, agree
to let Boothuri keep Mary as a wife, providing she can offer information about *waibala* doings. Boothuri hands over his precious
woomera and best spears as payment to satisfy the old man.

———

In the morning, Mary hears the men speak about the frontier war
and the warrior bands who attack outlying farms. She hears of
Aboriginal families hung from trees to rot in the wind and bodies
strung up alongside the stretched corpses of wedge-tailed eagles and
dingoes all in a row, like so much vermin. She still shudders as they
describe the deaths of troopers, and Boothuri sounds as cruel as the
senior men. She has known soldiers who are not devils.

The men discuss the thousands of newcomers arriving in ships
in Sydney Town and how they crash through the bush smashing
the fragile undergrowth, cutting down the oldest, tallest, and most
sacred trees—even carved burial trees. Log-splitting men follow the
axe men, and the sound is deafening, night and day. Fiery pits burn
all night with wasted bark. Her peoples' footpaths have become
bullock tracks with deep greasy mud churned by huge wagons full
of logs. The tiny fruits and flowers are being crushed. Nothing is left
of the forest's ceremonial sites. Their stories cannot be told if the
places and sites of the ancestors are gone. The waterholes are ruined
by cattle and the *goona*-filled water cannot be drunk.

But then a man with hard eyes speaks. He is Old Jack and is
much feared by all women because he has taken many of them by
force. It is a shameful secret. He is known to rape and kill *waibala*
and Aboriginal women from distant clans, but he has gone unpun-
ished in these confusing killing times. He tells them that the tribesmen are preparing to destroy corn crops and drive the *waibala* from

the country and that a man had been speared in a nearby farm and that he was half-eaten by wild pigs.

They hold a discussion of war strategy and plan to raid isolated farms for goods. It is a matter of survival to take the *waibala*'s corn where once daisy yams had flourished. Mary sits quietly with the old women, close enough to hear their talk.

She has a terrible foreboding.

Boothuri offers information about the town, and Mary grows nervous as plans are made. She pictures Mrs. Shelley with the children and knows she will be asked to reveal details of the white men and the troopers. Someone with her knowledge of English is valuable property, and she sees Old Jack watching her. He has a stone hatchet and a coiled rope for scaling trees in his waistband. The rope is like her father's and this makes her sad.

Mary is given a stone by a granny and told to care for it. It is held in a tiny woven bag. The old woman smiles and seems to see everything that Mary has been or ever will be. It is unnerving—she feels like her insides are on the outside.

The old woman takes out the stone and twirls it in her hands. Her eyes close, and she conjures a vision for Mary. Flashes of power, out of a mist is a cliff, a site, a special place alive with a spirit and someone swimming underwater. An eye stares at her from the clear fresh stream. Unblinking. It is giant eel, *burra*, and it pierces her forehead with its power, as if it will rush straight through her.

Old Jack comes toward Mary as she crouches next to the granny. Her breath quickens and her mouth is as dry as dry wind. He is old but still tall and muscular and is covered in battle scars. He is terrifying. He carries a shield with a tribal design and holds a hard wooden club. His cheek has a fresh sword slash across it. How many men has he killed? How has he been able to lead all the Darug and Gundungurra warriors and not be shot? The tribes have become mixed up, what with the destruction of their tribal boundaries. He is laughing at her, and she pushes away her fear as she stands up. She clenches her fist with her head bowed and thinks, *If you touch me I will kill you with my bare hands.* She hopes to be protected by the old women as she stares at the man's gnarled toenails. He demands that she tell them about troopers and guns. She shakes her head.

Mary tells him she is a schoolgirl with no knowledge of these things. Her eyes do not look up. She prays they will not ask Boothuri about Mrs. Shelley's school. She would rather die than let these men know about the school. Boothuri is quiet and looks away when he is questioned. Mary watches his hand as it quivers by his side, with the slightest signal to her to be careful and very quiet.

In the early hours of the morning a band of warriors, laden with spears, leaves the camp. They are painted with ocher and their fierce faces are lit by fire. Boothuri does not go with them. He watches, stiff with anxiety. If he had left, Mary knows he would not come back.

After a few days, Mary wants to move on to a place away from her fears. The sound of bellbirds and kookaburras echoes across the mountain but she is restless and unhappy gathering geebung fruit, grinding seeds, or making *bool*. Mary wants to walk back to the town of Parramatta or to a camp near the school. The thought of returning to live near *waibala* town tests her confused loyalties. She thinks she can be in two worlds and not have to choose.

"*Naiya yan*, I want to go back to town," says Mary. She pleads with Boothuri to go back to Parramatta and, in doing so, feels that she has failed a test.

Each day comes and goes, and they sleep on Boothuri's cloak by a fire. At any moment she fears he will be forced to give her up. However, there is comfort in sleeping under the stars.

One morning, Old Jack arrives back from a raid accompanied by Dutburra, a red ocher-painted warrior who is feared by the clans. He has a *waibala* musket with him. She wonders how he found this weapon. Did he kill the owner? Did he steal from a store or farm, or did he steal it from the school? Was Mrs. Shelley lying dead in her own blood? He smells of murder and is full of mysterious power. Women weep when they see Dutburra, for he is an executioner for white and Black.

"*Nyindi*, come!" says the warrior.

The warrior is caked in red earth and his elegant hair is coiled like a turban, smelling of sweet goanna oil and eucalyptus. He shakes the gun at Mary. The gun is black and heavy as he holds it against her throat. Boothuri shouts to protect her, but an older man stops him. He needs to obey or be speared. Mary is not important to them. Two old women intervene. They argue with the man and shake their waddy clubs at him. He shouts back and pulls Mary aside. He wants her to teach him how to use the musket.

He wants to fire this weapon, but she claims to have no knowledge. What she does know is that without flint and shot he will not be able to fire it. The warrior throws her to the ground and walks away, but then he is back, in a rage. He shouts that all the tribes are in terrible danger, for a *waibala* posse is sure to come after them. They must not stay in this place—the Bells Falls Gorge massacre, near Sofala, is still fresh in their minds. People were shot down over the falls and women raped. Dutburra stares at Mary and she is terrified.

Old Jack has cuts all over his body, raised welts from battle. He is a dark storm of anger and Mary will be partly to blame if he cannot fire the musket. Boothuri tells her that the old men will punish her, so she crawls into a *gunyah* to escape their eyes. No one helps her. She knows nothing about finding the flint and powder to make it shoot. She can work in a kitchen, read a book, or play a violin, but not this. Boothuri seems ashamed and she sees him collapsed, his head in his hands. Then he stands in front of the old men with his head bowed. He is trying to save Mary's life and she suddenly understands what she must do.

Mary knows her father would want her to stand proud and be resilient, so in an instant, she changes. She's not afraid to face them. She takes the musket and shows them what to do and explains as best she can about the missing powder. The men nod. Mary carefully hands back the musket. They will need to carry out another raid.

The following day, Mary wakes up and finds that Boothuri has gone with Old Jack, the Darug, Gundungurra, and Wonnaruah men, and Dutburra, the executioner. Every man who can travel has left on the war party. They have gone to collect other men deep in the mountains near Katoomba. She realizes that she may never see Boothuri again.

=====

As the weeks pass, the men do not return. The women grow anxious. Mary plays her violin in the dusk to find serenity and remember her life at the school. Her drive for freedom has vanished. She now has only a need to survive.

The women in the tribe cannot gather enough food to eat. There is little game nearby, and the women gather yams and wattle seed. But it is not enough and they must move on. The white hunters have massacred all the local kangaroos and there is no hunter to search farther away.

The women take up coolamons and hoist the small children on their shoulders and walk the tracks to other camps. Some *waibala* along the way give them food, setting out flour in bags outside huts for the women. The women are careful; they have heard rumors about poisonous green-seed flour. Even clean water is hard to find because the *waibala* cattle have dirtied it. Their horses have dropped *goona*, but the women know that if they float charcoal from the fire in the water, the water will be clean to drink when the coals sink.

The rain comes for days on end and the women cry out to Birrah-gnooloo, the sky spirit, to stop the deluge. They are traveling in Blue Mountains country and cross many icy-cold creeks, where they stop to refill woven palm dillybags with water. One creek floods in the rain and kangaroos swim across the swollen torrent. Mary squats to refill her water dillybag and sees a *waibala*'s struggling dog trying to swim against the flood; she reaches out and helps it up the bank. It shivers with a begging look and runs off.

━━━

The weeks turn to months and the women and children walk toward Katoomba. They gather lomandra seeds and yams, but the rain has long gone and now they are hungry in the hot, dry summer. They are constantly alert for *waibala* men on horseback, as they are known to kidnap Koori women and rape them. The land has less food, and cattle graze over yam fields and destroy what little food there was. Mary is growing thin and worn and has lost hope of seeing Boothuri again. She guesses that he is dead but still hopes that if she stays with his tribe, then one day they may be reunited.

One day, as the women pass a remote hut, a farmer's wife calls from a window. She has a beautiful smile. Mary is in rags, but she smooths her wild hair and knocks on the door and the woman appears, kindness shining through her as she beckons to them. Mary wonders how she could live like this, all alone in this wild country. The woman puts fresh damper on china plates outside the hut. She spreads each piece with plum jam and it smells wonderful. Mary is afraid that it could be poisoned, but they are starving. They are out of control as they rush toward the food, screaming and scratching. A girl with wallaby teeth plaited in her hair is first to the pile, and Mary uses all her strength to push her away. They might have ripped each other apart for a piece of scone. Hunger tears you up.

CHAPTER NINE

1822: A Soldier in the Bush

Governor Macquarie departs for England on the *Surry*. He is sent off with affection by *waibala*. He is sent off with relief by the families of Aboriginal people whom he has massacred.

━━━━

A striking, gangly young woman with a beautiful broad face and deep brown eyes, Mary walks along a dirt track. Her tangled, curly black hair is tinged with gold highlights from the sun. Filthy rags now replace her clean smock. She has become accustomed to sleeping on the earth with a dog or two to keep her warm. Now she has new sisters, mothers, aunties, and grannies. Mary polishes her violin as if it were a precious child.

The women walk all day and eventually come to a tranquil valley where they make their camp. They unload coolamons and digging sticks and make a fire. Mary pulls sheets of paperbark from a tree and builds a shelter *gunyah*. Others make low roofs of bark and lay down their cloaks for the children to sleep. This place is full of cycad palms and towering tree ferns. Small cascades of fresh water trickle nearby, and blue wrens and silvereyes skip in the low tea tree bushes. Bandicoots and echidnas covered with prickles are scarce, but one of the women catches a small goanna to roast.

Mary walks for miles through bush looking for *wirriga*, goannas, *burriga*, bandicoot, and *buduru*, potoroo, by checking for small scratchy tracks. She eats some wild *bambal* orange and sucks the water from axe holes she cuts in the roots of a gum tree. She finds a fertile place near a rock overhang and is digging for *midin*, yams, when she hears the terrible sounds of marching, tramping boots, and soldiers' breath. Then gunshots and screams. She hides behind a tree. She is so starved she feels she can disappear. She holds her breath as the men pass by, and when she comes out of hiding she is disoriented and cannot find the women or their tracks. She is lost.

In the afternoon, Mary stumbles upon a bush shack in a clearing and finds that it has a fireplace and a tea kettle. The coals are still hot, and she makes herself at home and boils some water to pour on the tea she has discovered in a tin. Around the room are papers and even a telescope. So, this shack must have someone living there who studies nature. She is reaching for a tin cup just as the door opens. A young soldier stares at her in surprise. She is terrified because he is blocking the doorway, the only exit. He looks at her and momentarily seems not sure what to do. She charges at him, but he puts out his hands in the way that a man would calm a wild horse. He makes a shushing noise and holds up a leather bag of coins. They clink as he smiles at Mary. She is terrified as he moves closer.

"No! Get away! Don't touch me!" she says.

"You speakee English. What wonders next, you pretty thing. Come on."

She makes no sound as he edges forward and puts his hand over her mouth. She struggles and he pushes her to the floor. This red-coated soldier is young with dark fluff for a beard and sweat on his skin. His bright green eyes flutter at her and she can't breathe. He takes his hand away and mumbles something, but she cannot understand. Then he opens his coat and presses her against the dirty white shirt front. He strokes her cheek and eyelashes and smiles. She is still and stiff as he unbuttons his pants' placket and his pizzle, his *windji*, sticks out like a pink beacon. He growls and Mary bites him on the cheek—a deep teeth-gnashing bite that shocks him and gives her time to slither out of his grasp. She swallows the blood and is out the door, sprinting. She doesn't stop until the shack is long gone.

She is exhausted but must continue to look for the women's camp. All the rest of the day she searches and it is nightfall when she comes across it. The fires are still burning but there are no women or children. Just smoke, like a silent song, weaving into the sky. The coolamons have been tossed into a pile, the broken fishing *mootin* spears and digging sticks tossed into the bush. They have flown, have been captured, or are dead. She calls out but not with full voice, because she is scared that any cry will bring the soldiers with their muskets. Perhaps they will come back one last time to make sure everyone is dead, or maybe the old granny will return to find her; yes, she will wait. Among the broken coolamons she finds the miraculous parcel of fur that hides her violin and bow. She takes it in her arms—it is warm and alive and a message to live.

Mary lies down and pulls paperbark over herself. She hopes to be taken into the heavens with the sky people. She falls asleep but soon wakes and peeps out of her cocoon. Some meat had been cooked on a fire near the edge of the clearing—it looks like a goanna tail, but she is too afraid to move. In the growing dusk, she hears the cries of swooping swallows, the insect catchers, and falls asleep again.

In the morning Mary crawls into the sunlight and darts to where she had seen the cold black meat, but it's gone. Only a smudge of grease remains on the stones. It must have been taken by quoll cats. She sucks the grease off the stones, retrieves a waddy to use for hunting, and gets clear of the camp. Mary drinks water from a spring surrounded by maidenhair ferns and, with her thirst slaked, begins to muddle together a sort of plan. A plan to live, even though it seems everyone she knows is either dead or gone to the *waibala*.

It comes to Mary that she must return to Parramatta and not wait for Boothuri. So she sets off on her long walk toward the east. At night she sleeps in terror. Between the rocks there are spirit beasts with red skins and helmets of horns. She sees devil-devils everywhere where *goong* spirits teem across the earth and she has no fire to ward them off, but she is determined to survive.

Finally, Mary arrives in Parramatta. She speaks aloud to herself and promises not to be abused again. She remembers the weight of Mrs. Shelley's musket and its shiny barrel. She longs to buy or steal such a weapon. She can feel the fierce ancestors' blood in her veins. This is what regaining her soul is about. She will murder or maim any man who tries to rape her or harm those she loves. She knows how to prime a musket and how to hold it steady against her shoulder. Her fingers twitch at the possibility.

As she walks through the streets she is surprised to see men of all types steal glances as she glides past. She is admired, despite the filthy rags and her worn-out appearance. She has a *waddy* and possum skins to trade tucked in her skirt, and her wild hair flows around her face.

In the town, Mary sees food in abundance. She has been sipping from creeks and eating any *midin*, yam, or *damun*, wild fig, she can forage and sipping nectar from waratahs and nibbling bracken tips. Here there are piles of potatoes on carts and overflowing sacks of green and yellow corn. She observes the ladies carrying lace parasols made in England, who laugh as they tiptoe through the mud and rubbish and order their convict servants to purchase goods. It is market day and men carry sacks of flour and are paid for their labor by a fat man in a waistcoat. She looks at them receiving money and wonders how she can earn some coins to buy a meal. She plays the violin, and one man tosses her a ha'penny.

After a long morning, Mary stares at the cake stall but no one else is paying for her music. Some children throw rocks at her. She throws them back. She does not beg and her defiance radiates from her eyes.

The new governor of New South Wales, Major General Thomas Brisbane, comes to a gathering of natives on the edge of the town to satisfy his curiosity about the "Indians." His aide-de-camp follows him with a ledger. A phrenologist doctor is there too, measuring the heads of any Blackfella he can find. He pays them with a coin, so they line up. He places his cold iron caliper on their foreheads and records measurements to deliver to Joseph Banks from the Royal Academy in London. The doctor is a celebrated grave robber who will receive native skulls from any contributor. It is said that Banks also owns Chief Pemulwuy's skull and has preserved heads of countless others. This doctor is a flesh boiler. A bone weigher. He stinks of English sweat as he feels Mary's head. He wants to take it with him as a fine specimen, but it is, inconveniently, still connected to her body. Mary's head would be studied as an example of pure native blood who has learned to read; she is an interesting specimen.

Mary listens to him talk about the rebel natives who were run into a dead end and shot. There were sixteen men, and they were hung on a hill. Some freed convicts cut off the heads and took them to Sydney, where the government paid them thirty shillings and a gallon of rum each.

"Why do you want our heads?" she asks.

"Young lady, I am a scientist. And my craniological specimen studies indicate that the intellectual abilities of natives are by no means despicable," he says.

"That might be; the people who take our heads are wrong. And, if you take them, you might be despicable," Mary replies.

When the phrenologist has finished pawing her skull, he hands her a coin.

Then she sees a ragged Aboriginal man crawling in the mud and she thinks that he must be starving, as he waits for something to happen. His eyes dart to every food stall. He is searching for his life, his lost country, his dignity. White people press handkerchiefs to their noses and avert their gaze. To them, he is like a worm or a snake that has to be skipped over on the way to buy bread or perfume or rum.

Mary watches as he sits holding up a cup. His face is turned toward the mud. He has no strength to look up. She has a lump of damper that she shares with him. She takes her violin and reaches down to touch his shoulder. He shudders and she leans down and whispers:

"Music."

She plays a jig and is rewarded with a smile. After a few tunes she waves at him and walks away. The square is crowded with settlers and Mary hopes she will not meet Mrs. Shelley, who would be shocked at her disreputable appearance. In the distance, she sees some Parramatta Native Institution children walking in a line. In her hurry to escape being seen, she nearly knocks over a fragile old woman—it is Granny Wiring. They greet each other with joy.

"Where you been?" asks Granny Wiring.

"*Molliming ngalbunga*," says Mary.

"You got *molliming*, husband, good girl?" asks Granny Wiring.

"No, gone, he's gone," says Mary.

"I don't want you marry *waibala*! You wantem your tribe."

"I'll not marry, no more," says Mary.

Granny Wiring sighs and shakes her head.

It is a hot and dusty morning when a famous Wonnaruah warrior, Chief Myall, from inland of the Hunter River, walks down the cobbled street with his wives beside him. His eyes burn from behind the white ocher on his face. He strides with his possum cape flowing behind him, and the red marks on his chest glisten in the sun. Strong muscular arms scarred with cicatrices hold ten fighting spears and a woomera. The talk flies around the town that he is going to attend the Annual Native Feast Day. The native grapevine is frantic: Does he intend to kill the governor? Will he set fire to the houses?

Servant girls gather at the gate to watch the great man pass. All manner of people fall in behind the warrior and it becomes a procession. This chief is not afraid of white men or their guns. He cracks his knuckles as his black eyes travel along the line of young women's faces in vague recognition. He smiles at Mary and she blushes.

After entering the main square, the chief sits under a tree with his wives near him. All around, the native feast is being prepared with bowls of *bool* and meat cooking on fire pits. Flags fly and the music of a military band fills the air. Piles of government blankets are on the grass, where a soldier waits to hand them out to deserving and tamed Aborigines whose names are on his list.

The chief summons the crowd to listen to him; he holds up his hand and waits for quiet.

"Soldiers kill lotta men. *Wolbunga koori*. Huntem down, finish up. In mountain, Gundungurra join up all mob: Darkinjung, Wonnaruah, Worimi, Awakabal, Biripai—all fighting. Lotta *waibala* people. Too many. I not take breastplate!" says Chief Myall.

The chief takes his large collection of spears and walks toward the military buildings and the courthouse, where some motley settlers have gathered. There is a festive air with a fire-eater and traveling players performing music.

The settler families stare at the chief while ten troopers from the Forty-Seventh Regiment, led by Captain Woodrow, march toward him with muzzles loaded and muskets raised.

Mary sees the chief's two wives coming out of the shadows. They are worn out and wear torn possum cloaks and bend over with sorrow. One of them carries a large bundle of paperbark, tied with bush twine. Is it a gift?

Captain Woodrow approaches on his piebald stallion in front of his platoon. Morning sunlight glints off his raised saber. Mary hides her face in her cloak.

It seems all the town is assembled to witness this meeting with Governor Brisbane, who has been summoned from his house; he hastily adjusts his wig. They meet on a road lined with bending gum trees. Hot winds blow hats from heads.

Mary walks behind the chief now and trots to keep up. He stops in front of Woodrow and glares at the soldier, waiting for him to dismount. Woodrow climbs down and stands, shorter than the warrior; his English boots are no help. There is silence except for the occasional child's voice or a cacophony of cockatoos and crows. The governor strolls toward the scene with his aide-de-camp and begins to sneeze into a white handkerchief. A Scottish piper begins the mournful wail of a bagpipe; it grates on Mary's ears. But, at last, it has come, this long-awaited confrontation.

"You wish to meet with me, Chief Myall? Well, I stand here at your request. As you see, I am quite naked of weapons," says the governor.

The chief strikes his woomera against his leg and a terrible apprehension grips the crowd. Some white men crave the Black man's humiliation and long for a show of soldiers' strength.

"Shoot him, the blaggard!" shouts a man in the crowd.

Chief Myall does not blink. He holds his head high.

"*Nyai kummai,* spears for Governor." The chief places a pile of spears on the earth in front of him.

"Are you surrendering?" No one speaks; only birds cry out. The governor coughs and wipes his face with lace.

"Do you promise to stop your depredations against our settlers?" the governor asks as he nudges the spears with his boot. The chief just stares.

One of the wives steps forward and solemnly places the paperbark package before the governor's feet. She unwraps a portion of the blanket and the governor leans over to peer inside. He sees the dead child. He reels back in shock.

"*Budjil budjil* measles killem *gurng kurung*," says the wife.

Mary squeezes through the crowd. She touches the child's mother on the arm.

"Don't surrender, Chief. They'll hang you; they are *kulara* angry," yells Mary.

"Draw and quarter him," shouts a man.

The governor raises his hand.

"All assembled here, let me assure you, there will not be any punishment today. It is our Native Feast Day! He will not hang. You, Chief, must carry this message to your renegade brothers and sisters: We will hunt you down!"

The chief pushes the paperbark bundle toward the governor, then wraps his possum cloak around himself tightly, and walks slowly away through the crowd with his wives behind him. Many Koories follow him.

The governor shakes his head and gestures for a soldier to remove the dead child. He quickly reaches his hand to the brass gorget that hangs on a chain around Captain Woodrow's neck.

"Give me your gorget! Quickly, man!" says the governor. The captain pulls the brass breastplate from his neck and hands it over.

"Chief, wait! My solemn duty is to represent the English Crown and to prevent treason," says the governor. "Will you not accept a reward?" The chief, however, does not stop or turn his head. He keeps walking away as the crowd parts to allow him through. The governor is left with the gorget hanging limply from his hand.

"He will beg for your recognition and your generous help when we hunt down the branch renegades from the Colo River," says Captain Woodrow. The troopers move the crowd to allow the governor to get into his carriage and, at that moment, Woodrow sees Mary. His eyes pierce hers and he nods with a grim smirk.

Mary hears stories about soldiers under the captain's command. Two native girls, just past puberty, who were captured near Hunter River by troopers and paraded in neck tethers through the village to an audience of people leering and laughing. They were auctioned off to a settler who wanted them as maids for his wife. The soldiers who brought the girls demanded that they keep them overnight. Next morning the captives were released near their new owner's abode. They collapsed by the gate all covered in gore. They had been tied to a tree and continuously ravaged throughout the night. Mary thought the captain was a bad man.

Some stories are not so terrible. Mary hears how the Parramatta Native Institution has been relocated to Richmond Road to the new Black Town, near the Aboriginal farming family's land grant of Nurrugingy and Colebee with his sister Maria Locke, who Mary knew from school.

Mary and Granny Wiring walk along the Great Western Road to Prospect and on to the new Black Town, arriving at the Parramatta Native Institution mission house. Mary walks up to one of the six cottages on the Aboriginal family's land grant, on the high bushy ground above Bell's Creek. She sits alongside Granny Wiring with Maria Locke, who boils them an egg each on her little fire. Mary strolls among the cabbages and cabbage moths and watches the chickens and a few cows in the fenced paddock. She envies her old school friend's fortune. The corn is ripe, and she leans over the railing and breaks off a few cobs to chew. Wheat struggles in the next row and even tobacco grows near where Mr. Locke, the ex-convict husband of Maria, hoes the earth.

"Do your children go to Native School?" asks Mary.

"Some days they go, but mostly they go when they get rations from the government store," says Mr. Locke. "But they can read already. Not like me; I cannot even write my name."

Mary hears Maria Locke's stories about the ships in Port Jackson and how the English vessels disgorge countless white settlers into their country.

"I might see those ships. They a real wonder. I might sail away myself," says Maria.

It is time to move elsewhere, and Maria Locke's stories of cousin *babana* Bowen and his adventures as a policeman enthrall Mary. He is employed as a Black tracker near Palm Beach and he has made a name in the colony as a protector of farms and by working for the customs officers. He has captured many bushrangers who run illegal stills, making grog. She wonders how he can work for the *waibala* police who have murdered so many of her people.

She will walk with Granny Wiring to Sydney Town to seek him and her future. The next day, the two women start walking toward Port Jackson. The roads are often dangerous places for women, but this one has become a highway, with carts and bullock wagons carrying goods to the government settlements; they hitch a ride on a bullock cart.

CHAPTER TEN

1823: Woolloomooloo

John Oxley has published his Journals, *Two Expeditions into the Interior of New South Wales, Undertaken by Order of the British Government*, which give detailed descriptions of inland Australia. He hoped to find an inland sea and his explorations opened the way for squatters to invade the rich lands of the Liverpool Plains. He also carried out naval surveys on the coast and recommended a new penal colony at Port Macquarie. He plans a further exploration on his ship, the *Mermaid*, as far north as Moreton Bay. He will take on board the well-respected Aboriginal guide Bowen, son of Chief Bungaree.

＝＝

On Parramatta Road, Granny Wiring and Mary travel toward Sydney Town. They hope to see cousin Bowen before he sails away. They rest after a day's walking and Granny boils water in a billy pot. She carefully pinches tea leaves into it from her pocket. Mary sips the tea and smiles with her hands pressed between her thighs. Her thoughts are of Boothuri and where he has gone. If the troopers didn't kill him, maybe he fell in with the fierce Darkinjung warriors from over the Deerubbin, the Hawkesbury River. Or was he punished for his transgression with her? Perhaps the headman had him killed. She shakes her head to dislodge such thoughts and looks forward to nights dreaming of him.

Granny Wiring finds a stray dog. It is part dingo, ragged and yellow. It follows them on the long road and keeps Mary warm at night, despite Granny cajoling him into her blanket with scraps. The dog's furry warmth next to Mary's chest sends a wave of safety through her.

She is fearful at night and tries to conquer this by murmuring the names of her missing loved ones. She can't accept their loss. She folds her arms around her body and prays for strength and an end to running. She hears crickets and mosquitoes buzzing and a rustle in the dry leaves near her makeshift bed. A snake perhaps. She shudders, reaches out for the dog and his reassuring snore, and winds the blanket tight. The insects do not worry Granny Wiring. Mary watches her. Her head is tilted back and her mouth is open— breathing the restful sleep of a baby.

The morning light comes with a chorus of kookaburras. Mary calls back at them to keep laughing. She needs a good laugh. The women stand on the edge of the Parramatta Road and try to jump into the back of another bullock wagon, but it is overladen with bags of flour and the bullock driver bellows at them to get off!

The plains stretch out before them as they walk—Mary's feet have thick soles. They stop to drink from a swift-flowing creek in a clearing near the road and soak their bodies in the cool fresh water. Mary floats and stares at the wide, blue sky. The purplish mountains behind them are shrouded in mist. Ducks are on the water and Granny tries to pelt them with stones so they can have a duck dinner, but she misses.

As they walk into the haze of burning fields after harvest, a group of Aboriginal people pass the other way, traveling from

Sydney Town. The man has a bunch of spears on his shoulders and the women have children in slings across their backs. The group wave and they exchange greetings. They are Burruberongal clan, like Mary, and she once again calls out to find if they know her father's whereabouts; once again there is no answer to the question.

Granny tells Mary many stories and even whispers about the secrets that old women have. Mary listens with hushed silence about the clevermen, who must be avoided because they can take some of your hair or spit and attach it to the arm bone of a skeleton and chant to a spirit to carry out a curse on you. It could kill you or make someone sick. Magic can kill for sure.

Finally, they arrive and walk into Sydney Town, longing to see the great sights. They stare at the tall, pale stone buildings and grand carriages that make their way down the teeming main streets. The carriages nearly knock them over with their iron wheels. They walk into Circular Quay, which is bustling with sailing ships moving to and fro. The wharves are piled with boxes and pallets of goods, and sailors of all colors lounge around smoking cheroots. Crowds of people are eating, laughing, shouting, and doing business of all kinds. Her countrymen are also there, selling peaches and fish from baskets, while their children dance for coins.

Granny Wiring has told Mary that Bowen has a reputation as a fine tracker and has many contacts that might lead to her finding a position with a large household. Mary is full of hope that he will welcome her. She remembers him from her childhood visit to Bungaree's farm on the harbor at Georges Heights and from encounters in the streets of Parramatta.

It rains heavily and the water runs down Mary's body in rivulets. When the sky clears, a brilliant rainbow bursts through the mist over the harbor. Mary looks and is excited—something wonderful might happen. Mary and Granny wash their faces in the rain and hurry to join an excited crowd that has gathered to follow the explorer John Oxley and his horse team as they move toward the wharf.

Before they can find Bowen, Granny pulls Mary away from the crowds because a riot has broken out beside a grog shop. Men hit each other and shout obscenities.

Mary and Granny try to sleep at the Aboriginal camp in a wooden hut near Circular Quay, but the drinking and fighting keep them awake. Tired and hungry, they leave in the morning with the dog following along behind.

The streets teem with hundreds of *waibala* arriving from endless ships, and there are countless supplies being unloaded on the docks and carried by horse cart up George Street.

Mary and Granny hear that Bowen is fishing by the harbor and has not yet boarded the *Mermaid*. They walk toward the tall wooden ships with their furled white sails and watch as small native canoes pass by with people fishing. They spot Bowen leaning over rocks unrolling a fishing line with a shell hook. He looks at Mary.

"*Nyangu nindi bija*? Why you here, little cuz? Welcome to War-rane, this Sydney place got lotta *waibala*, lotta tucker," says Bowen.

"*Pittuma nindi*, we're looking for you," says Mary.

"*Narr*, true? I hear you got *molliming*, eh?" asks Bowen.

"No more husband," she says.

"Too bad, you pretty one," laughs Bowen.

He offers Granny a pipe of tobacco and welcomes them with a salute. They admire his handsome face and his white linen turban bound up with cockatoo feathers and dingo teeth. Mary offers him some damper from her bundle and he smiles at his tribal cousin.

"You want to work for *waibala*? Can't help you with that because I go on big ship across sea, same like my father, Bungaree," he says.

"You can take me too. I want to go across that sea," says Mary.

"You gotta wait here. No woman's on ship," says Bowen. "You can go to Barrenjoey, near Palm Beach, see my mother Gooseberry. You can go live there. Good place, plenty tucker," says Bowen.

The wharf atmosphere grows chaotic. *Waibala* rush by with wheelbarrows and piles of English goods. Mary stands back from the turmoil while Granny and Bowen smoke together. Mary sees he has a wound.

"What happened to you, *babana*?" she asks.

"Got beat up by Gadigal with waddy at Woolloomooloo. My fella countrymen, they chuck spear when we fight. I got it right in my *kobbera*. Big payback punishment for my Guringai tribe, after some fella dead. Too right, look out they might come back now, looking for trouble," says Bowen.

Mary watches as a crowd of tall, imposing Gadigal men from the south-harbor side stroll toward them. They call out that they want more fighting, blood, and revenge with other Aboriginal men, but Bowen declines. The men arrange themselves in a row on the side of the wharf road as people gather to watch. These men have faces and arms painted in white ocher and they stand with spears of the lightning serpent. They take their wooden clubs and line up like white clouds in eastern rain. Mary watches this performance as they play fight in front of an audience of *waibala*. She is alarmed at the casual use of battle but knows that they must make a living of some kind like this.

Bowen walks away with Mary and Granny Wiring in case the Gadigal call him to fight. He knows these men by name and knows what they desire. He will bide his time and then one day return to take part in the display-fighting to make money. But today Bowen tells Mary that he has other matters to arrange for his sailing trip.

"Take me with you," says Mary. But he laughs and shakes his head. Granny Wiring takes her arm, and they all walk together among the heat and dirt of the harbor. They see an old lady roasting rabbits and native pigeons on a fire from a barrow, and women in bonnets huddle around squeezing the pigeons to find the fattest. Mary nudges Bowen and the smell pierces their nostrils. They are hungry, always hungry. Bowen produces some pennies from a kangaroo leather purse and buys a cooked rabbit for them to share.

Now it is time for Bowen to look for his ship among the British maritime flags and the stench of rotting fish and seaweed. Bowen must match the name written on the ragged paper, but he cannot read, so Mary reads it for him, and they search the wooden hulls for the painted writing.

She calls out that she has found the *Mermaid*. It is a tall vessel with a big-breasted gold statue with a fishtail twisting around the wooden flagpole. Granny admires the statue and nudges Bowen and laughs.

"*Nabung*, big titty eh?" says Granny.

"But she got no legs!" says Bowen.

"No good," says Granny.

They all laugh and walk along the wharf looking up at the ship while searching for Oxley, the surveyor general, among the throng of seamen.

"Hey, I got a letter for Master Oxley!" yells Bowen.

A seaman holds out his hand and helps Bowen aboard, but Mary is left on the wharf. She feels discarded. She bursts with longing and aches to follow. He soon stands by Mr. John Oxley and handles the map with certainty, proving that the surveyor is right to trust him. He is the son of Chief Bungaree, who sailed the seas and fed Flinders's cat, Trim, pieces of black swan meat.

Oxley shakes his hand and introduces him to the first mate. It is agreed, Bowen will join the expedition to the northern coast. They will sail with the tide.

"We will travel to the proximity of Point Danger, where Captain Phillip Parker King has gone before us with your father. We will endeavor to explore and map Port Curtis and Moreton Bay, and we shall hope to inquire as to the well-being of two Englishmen who are reported to be shipwrecked but alive due to the kindness of the natives. You, Bowen, will no doubt avail yourself of communication with the said native personages," says Oxley.

Mary watches and waves to her cousin. He is radiant with happiness, and she wishes that she were a man and could go on great adventures across the sea. She weeps inside while Bowen, wearing a cockaded captain's hat, waves goodbye.

"Take me too!" she calls.

Oxley smiles at her and whispers something to the mate as they admire the beautiful Aboriginal woman standing on the wharf.

The smell of the ship is pungent, and Mary holds her nose and watches with envy as an audience of *waibala* stare at Bowen talking with Oxley.

Their attention quickly turns, however, to a nearby ruckus and a young white man who is making a loud disturbance. Tall in black clothes and a white clerical collar, the man calls out that he is the newly arrived Reverend Smythe. He sets up on a wooden box, holding pamphlets, and begins a speech, telling the audience about a plague upon the people of Egypt and about the battle where Joshua chased the Israelites at Ai and utterly destroyed them and burned their homes. Mary looks at this performance and laughs. He is enthusiastic and somehow compelling.

Bowen helps load guns and gunpowder as sailors coil ropes and load tubs of limes aboard. A young sailor climbs the rope ladder to the crow's nest and looks down at the reverend.

The young Reverend Smythe has pale skin and a hooked nose, high cheekbones, and blue eyes. His dark hair curls out from his black clerical hat, and he radiates a kind of pleasant energy. He wears a black cassock and stands on his box while calling out to the crowd. Mary is captivated; no one but she listens:

"Come, my brothers and sisters. By the rivers of Babylon, there we sat down, when we remembered Zion. We hung our harps upon the willows in the midst thereof. O daughter of Babylon, who art to be destroyed; happy shall he be, that taketh and dasheth thy little ones against the stones," he declares with fervor. He looks down and sees Mary for the first time. She smiles and he blushes.

When he has finished his speech, Reverend Smythe moves among the gathered crowd and hands out pamphlets about Jesus. He sees the lovely face of Mary watching him and hands her a pamphlet. She is polite as she folds it carefully before she rips it to pieces and drops it into the sea. He watches and shakes his head. Granny's dog growls at him.

Mary taps her cheek and smiles at the reverend. He gulps and she can feel his eyes on her as she sashays down the wharf. Looking back, yes, he is still watching her. She laughs and winks at him.

Mary dares to blow him a kiss before hiding her face. Granny Wiring laughs and snorts as Mary takes her arm and they saunter along the wharf.

"Look out, his *windji* after you," says Granny.

The young minister follows Mary and taps her on the shoulder; he has a note in his hand.

"I already have your paper. I threw it in the water," says Mary.

"No, this is different," he says and nods with embarrassment before walking awkwardly away with the dog barking at his retreat. Mary reads his note and is surprised to see an address for the Parramatta Native Institution.

Bowen is now happily on board, and the *Mermaid* sails with the tide. Mary and Granny stand along the shore and wave, and Mary runs along the dock to see the ship sail out toward the Heads. The crew call to each other while the first mate bellows orders, but the flapping sails, winding ropes, and winches swallow the sound. She holds her hand up to shade her eyes and stands for a long time after the ship has disappeared beyond the blue horizon.

Mary and Granny continue their visit with their relations, fishing for their dinner and cooking on coals with cousins at the Woolloomooloo camp. The *gunyah* huts sit among sand dunes and rocks, and women hang washing on bushes and brush the earth with brooms of cabbage tree fronds.

They have failed to gain useful employment in Sydney Town. Mary declines the offer of a place at Palm Beach; it seems too far from her tribal country. But the note the young Reverend Smythe has given Mary is an offer to visit him and find employment. The next day they begin the long walk home to the west.

CHAPTER ELEVEN

1824: The Parramatta Native Institution

The *Sydney Gazette* has much news about government and massacres. Bowing to the demands of an increasingly free society—if you are a white fellow—the first Legislative Council forms in New South Wales to aid the governor in the legislative process. It is heralded as the start of responsible government for the expansion of many parts of Australia. The council meets in the Chief Surgeon's wing of the Rum Hospital—so called because it had been built by the government through the selling of sixty thousand gallons of rum. At the same time, martial law is proclaimed in the Bathurst area, where seven settlers were killed by Aboriginal people led by Windradyne. In retaliation, soldiers, mounted police, and stockmen kill at least one hundred Aboriginal people.

———

Mary and Granny Wiring arrive on Deerubbin near Parramatta, where Aboriginal families camp near an estate and have employment cutting timber or harvesting. The corn crops are bountiful and the new English gardens flourish in the bush soil. Mary and Granny marvel at the brightness of the roses and daisies and stop to gather bunches to sell along the road.

Once again, Mary asks about the whereabouts of her father's mob. There are many stories of where they may have gone but no real directions are offered. She is afraid they are all dead.

Mary and Granny camp along the river. They dig yams and gather oysters, but hunger stalks their every move and they must find a better way to survive. It is time to seek work at the Parramatta Native Institution. This will require some new attire for Mary. Granny barters the dog for a clean smock from a farm, and Mary dresses herself in the rough hand-spun garment and wraps the violin in a cloth to carry across her back.

Granny puffs on her black English pipe. She has tied a piece of torn blanket around her head, and she looks neat and grand in her government blanket. Mary stands beside her on the banks of the shimmering Deerubbin. The river is deep and dark green with a mist rising from it as it weaves through the country. Gray herons lightly pace and feed in the shallows among tall yellow reeds, and black and white pelicans sail gracefully along the surface.

Mary stares at the huge, gray stone building, with its many windows and black shutters that look like eyes. The Parramatta Native Institution is three stories high and, as such, is the tallest building in the area. There is a sign pinned to the fence that advertises, in looping cursive script, a situation for a maid. But Mary turns and begins to walk quickly away. She does not like the look of this terrible building; it is terrifying. Granny Wiring catches her arm and firmly marches her toward the school.

They climb the stone steps to the great wooden doors and it seems like an evil-looking place, full of *goong*. Mary feels these ghosts and tries to walk away again, but Granny pulls her up the steps, insisting that Mary will take a position and no longer starve.

"*Whu karndi nindi mingangun*, why you go?" asks Granny.

"*Naiya yanna naiya yunga.* I want to run away," wails Mary.

"What you gunna do? You not *waibala*, you not Blackfella. You in between. Gotta live! Not alla time looking for husband, he gone. Not alla time look for father, he gone. Look after self now, not starve. You speak English. Work for this place, not hungry alla time, you live," says Granny Wiring.

She pushes Mary in front of her just as it begins to pour. The drenching rain and blowing wind forces them under the shelter of the arch at the front door. This stone is now covered in mist and Mary stares at the foreboding doors, like doors to a prison. She tries again to turn away, but Granny holds her wrist fast and batters at the door. There are hinges of hard gray metal and a knocker embossed with bronze lions. The huge bolts are pulled back from the inside and Mary looks up into the small iron-barred windows. The air seems rank and poisonous; it smells like death. She is very afraid, but Granny's fist still grasps her hard.

Mary heard about this orphan school from Mrs. Shelley, who used hushed tones of righteousness to describe the good they did. Here, small children could be saved from the evil of drink or lecherous parents. "Most," she said, "are orphans with no one to care for them, so the benevolence of the colonial authorities allows unwanted infants to thrive under its roof."

But Mary senses it is a place of many deaths. She can feel the little spirits pounding at the windows and she can see tiny gaunt faces pleading for life. She turns to run but Granny puts out her stick and trips her, then yells for someone to greet them. Mary lies miserably on the cold stone step, cursing Granny and looking up at her with pleading eyes. She wants to disappear in the rain, but a young man opens the door. He is the assistant curate and, Mary recognizes, Reverend Smythe, the preacher from the wharf.

He is formidable with his black bushy beard and black silk clothes and a wide, pink-lipped smile. He is handsome and strong all at once. Reverend Henry Smythe, the master of the Parramatta Native Institution, has warmth pouring from his eyes, and Mary thinks he is as attractive as the day she first saw him. He takes Mary's hand and pulls her up, continuing to hold her hand. He looks at her sodden dress as Mary brushes herself down and wrings water from her clothes, before arranging her wild hair. She still carries her violin, and he gazes with curiosity at the bundle.

She looks at her dark hand in his pink one and can see that his nails are clean and trimmed while hers are dark and filled with ash. He smells of camphor, Russian leather Bibles, and cedar trees. She smells of eucalypt and smoke. He can see her beauty; again it disarms him.

"Come in. Don't stand outside freezing. Terrible weather, is it not?" says the reverend. He grins and holds an embroidered cloth to his mouth. He can sense the fatigue, the hunger—and the anger. Mary wrenches her hand away from his touch.

"Girl here," Granny says, pushing her forward, and Mary's eyes are wild in apprehension.

"I am not of your acquaintance, dear old lady, but I see you have brought this lovely young lass with you," says Smythe. "Let me guess. You have responded to my note and wish to offer her as a native servant? Oh, she has lovely light brown skin, like warm drinking chocolate."

Mary stands very still. She will turn and run fast into the bush at the first opportunity, and she will punch this smiling man on the nose if he dares to touch her again.

Granny accepts some tobacco from him, and he replaces the silver tin in his pocket.

Mary sees something else in him. He is lonely and young, wanting something he cannot have. She watches him, his shapely body and lovely eyes.

"This Mary James, servant. She work," says Granny.

"Ah, I have heard," he says. "You must be about sixteen years old, yes? Of course, you have no idea, do you? What is your true native name?" asks Reverend Smythe.

"Muraging, but they gave me a new name," says Mary.

Mary stares at his chest. He is wearing a white shirt with lace, and a black hair pokes above the neckline. This man will surely imprison her as a servant. She looks about for possible escape routes. Yes, down the steps and over the fence, or she can swim across the river. This man keeps nodding and smiling.

"Oh, dear. I know who you are, dear girl. Your old teacher, Mrs. Shelley, will have to be informed, but don't worry. I do not care about it," says Reverend Smythe.

"No! I don't want work here; I don't like you or this place!" says Mary.

Mary stares straight into his eyes in the way of English insolence.

"We shall see. Don't be too hasty, please," says Reverend Smythe.

"Girl speak English. Can read write. Girl workem hard," says Granny. Mary grimaces.

"Mary, please don't be frightened. Let's look at you. My, my, jolly good. Has your mistress allowed you the privilege of an English education? Do you cook and sew? Laundry, I'm certain. Would you be disposed to living here, not as an inmate of course but as my indentured servant? I can make arrangements. I can sign the papers. You will be most welcome and will have a generous allocation of board and food and a small stipend. Come along," he coaxes.

He holds out his hand and takes Mary's gently. He leads her inside the door and she is hypnotized. A lamb to slaughter.

"Off you go, Granny. You may go to the kitchen to receive as much tucker as you like. I believe Cook has cold mutton with Indian pickle," he says.

Granny nods and lights her pipe. She hobbles off around the back of the building without a backward glance.

Smythe leads Mary along polished wooden floors with rich carpet runners. On the way, she glimpses inside a room with a piano, red Persian carpets, and blue glass bottles that gleam like bright sparkling stars. Along the walls are hundreds of books.

"We shall see what training you have had at the hands of Mrs. Shelley. And we have also a succulent apple tart, with whipped cream. Would you like some?" he asks.

"Irish beef stew but made with kangaroo. One can only assume that you would like that as well. That is, if your wild tribesmen have not succumbed to temptation and killed all the beasts," he says.

"Terrible times, Mary, the suffering of the tribespeople. I am so sorry, you see. Taking you on is my redemption for Jesus. Do you know Jesus? Of course, Mrs. Shelley has seen to your Christian education. I am quite certain you can read and write. Oh, we will have such a nice time, you and I. And you will play your violin, such a curiosity!" Smythe continues.

Mary fears this place that has few windows, like a prison. Mary is taken to be bathed by the plump middle-aged matron, who is Welsh. She is ferocious. She glares and shoves Mary's head in a basin of soapy water.

"Keep still, you dirty thing! I don't know why he brings you to me for looking after. Covered in lice, I bet. I have too many to look out for," says Matron.

Mary sleeps in a cold dormitory alongside the white servant girls, who snore all night. The children sleep nearby, in another cold dormitory.

Mary's curiosity about the reverend and the school stops her from running back to the bush. He has books with drawings and wondrous paintings hang on the wall. They reveal strange countries and beasts, like lions and elephants; she is mesmerized. He shows much kindness toward her.

Each day she rises before the sun to fill boxes with firewood and light stoves in the kitchen. She carries heavy trays of food and washes dishes by the hundreds. The food is good and her bed is warm and clean. Mary stays.

Mary becomes acquainted with polishing the shiny, waxed floors in the Parramatta Native Institution corridor, where the children buff them on their knees. The five-year-old girls in gray smocks push cloths along in front of their knees until the boards shine brightly. It is a game to the little children. The rooms have high ceilings and cracked beige walls; on the windows—shipped from London—are black iron bars. Once the windows were used in the hulks for African slaves. Not far away there are African children in Dixieland, also called Baulkham Hills, born to the ticket-of-leavers from Jamaica. Mary has seen them in Parramatta, dancing to drums.

Late one night, Mary hears shouting from the hallway and the sound of Matron's voice as heavy objects are thrown and girls squeal. Someone is in trouble for breaking a glass decanter. There are smashing sounds, more broken crockery, and the Matron is cursing.

Mary recognizes the bad words because she has heard them from drunk men. She has seen men bashing each other and screaming; she saw a man break another man's arm, heard it snap like a twig. Mary knows when to be quiet, when to run away and cover herself in blankets and not utter a sound, when to hold her breath and keep still, away from the shouting and madness.

Crawling down to the bottom of the bed, Mary waits, for she fears that Matron will one day choose to scream at her and beat her with a broom handle until she bleeds. Matron paces the corridor and holds a lantern to check that the servants are all in bed. The pale shapes of quiet girls huddle in iron beds.

The laundry smells of fear and drudgery and is under Matron's constant surveillance. Mary washes hundreds of small sets of clothes, and her hands soften and bleed. She works in the nursery, where she sees tiny white orphan babies crying as they lie in lines on straw mattresses—the children of fallen women. She walks among them and as she touches each one, they give a little shudder because they are so unused to human warmth. They will surely die miserable deaths.

Mary wants to cuddle all the babies, make them warm and loved. She holds three at a time and thinks about how she might one day be a mother with her own sweet little one at her breast.

Reverend Smythe strolls with the Matron along the rows of babies, sprinkling holy water and reading from the Bible. The servant girls balance as many babies as they can on their laps, feeding them pap and milk as they offer kisses and wipe their bottoms. The smell of poo and vomit is always on them.

Alice May is an English servant, and she smiles when Mary picks up babies, balancing them in her arms and singing a native children's song. Alice May laughs and imitates Mary's sounds—Mary is sure it is with affection. The girl sits on a milking stool with a little boy on her lap and plays clapping hands with him, then she holds him up to see outside the window.

"Can you see the trees? Can you see the horses? Can you see my home in London town?" sings Alice May. The little child giggles and she nuzzles his head. A glimmer of loving hope.

They take babies into their beds to keep them warm in the freezing winter. They tiptoe into the nursery with candle stub lights and steal them. They are the night *minnek wirawai*, walking to find babies before they are taken to their deaths.

Alice May is now her friend, and they seek each other's eyes when they feed the babies. She sees Mary but seldom speaks directly as there are too many critics about. They whisper to each other and begin a friendship of mime. Mary teaches her Aboriginal sign language.

"Where you going?" Mary's hand flicks toward her. "What are you doing?" is a thumb up and head inclined. "Where did you get that food?" is fingers to lips and head inclined. "Give me some" is a palm pulled toward head. Alice May is her secret and her salvation.

"At one moment, these young babies have health and spirits and next moment we behold souls in the arms of death," says Henry Smythe. "We must pray because he who is faithful has promised when thou passest through the waters of death, he will be with them, and the rivers shall not overflow them. God is a refuge and a strength and very present in our hours of need. We may meet these babes in that place, where sin and sorrow and sighing are forever done away." Mary listens but has little idea what he is talking about. These babies need their mothers' milk.

"If I have baby, I will not be parted from her. I will die before the *waibala* can take her to a place like this," says Mary.

"I already had a baby and he died here in this place," says her friend.

"I'm sorry. You would be a good mother," Mary whispers.

When Mary finishes the washing, she picks up a few babies and they turn their pale mouths to her empty breast. The porridge and cow milk spoon-fed to them by the servants is pale and thin, and their hungry mouths howl. She lies awake at night listening to the wailing and feels always cold. She watches the stars tumbling through the crack in the shutters and sometimes thinks about all that she has seen.

"The other girls say you are a strumpet and you work that night shift near the town hall. They say you got piles of shillings in yer bed," Alice May tells her one day.

"I've got nothing, do nothing, I just wait for my granny or father to come for me," says Mary.

Mary wishes the shillings were true, but she hates the cruel gossip. Servant girls shun her. She is mostly alone in her toils and, except for Alice May, no one seems to trust her. Most of the time she is vacant, living in a dream. Perhaps she is invisible.

She tells herself that she can try to fit in with these convict girls. They sew patchwork and Mary sits nearby hoping one will ask her to join, but she is shunned. They wash her cup twice. Perhaps she can find a blade and cut their throats.

Some days, ghost women walk back and forth in front of the building. They look up to the high windows. Some squat under trees and hide their faces in shawls. Some search for their children. Others want to give their children to the Matron. She sends them away. The school cannot take a child without a letter from the governor.

Mary walks to the barn in the courtyard where a cow is milked; the cows are also prisoners. Morning frost cracks on the milk pails when Mary dips her billy kettle in. She takes a bucket of milk to warm for the babies. She squats back on the floor in front of the woodstove and hums to take away her feeling of desperation. She must wash these floors every day—Matron will beat her if she neglects this duty. Then Mary takes the dirty water down two flights of stairs to the laundry. It is cold in the stone room. And it is full of spirits: girls who have had their hands caught in mangles or scalded by tubs of boiling soapy water, those who are boiled with the sheets. A bat flies past the windows and then an omen, *budawa*, the owl, calls out. She blocks her ears.

———

Reverend Smythe changes Mary's role. Now she has the title Native Servant. It's a position of respect and she has special jobs. Alice May will not talk to her anymore. The reverend has written to Mrs. Shelley to explain this new position, and Mary is given a new set of cotton shifts and aprons, but also one fine respectable dress bought by the reverend for her to wear to church. She can barely breathe when he hands it to her. She fingers the pale blue cloth. She now sits in front of Saint John's Church in Parramatta, admiring the black wooden pulpit and glass windows. The soldiers sit in one gallery and the settler families in another. At the back sit the poverty-stricken, ex-convict, ticket-of-leave families. The minister is the Reverend Marsden and his bellowing voice is much feared.

Mary is the only Native Servant at the orphanage. The others are convict English girls borrowed from the Female Factory. They are fierce and hardened and tear her hair if they find her alone in the cellar. These girls are from Glasgow or London and other places of mystery across the seas. They sing about their suffering. They have stolen shoes or tricked men into giving them their watches. They have sold their bodies and drunk gin by the gallon.

Alice May is now her enemy; she hates Mary's rising and hisses at her: "You turn your back now and I will flog you. You'll be fucking the master. Trollop! Strumpet!"

CHAPTER TWELVE

1825: Dinner with Reverend Masters

There is consternation when the ship *Almorah*—chartered to deliver supplies such as rice and flour from Batavia—is seized in Sydney Cove for carrying tea contrary to the East India Company charter. The ship carries news of the *Lady Nelson* to inform everyone that it has been captured by Malay pirates and all her crew murdered. Despite these setbacks the colony thrives, and Reverend Masters presides over the trials of convicts who have escaped and have been returned. He has obtained considerable riches and property.

———

Mary and other servants journey to wait at table at the wealthy estate of Reverend Masters. As they approach in their bumpy horse and cart, Mary stares at the unfolding scene and Masters's grand colonnaded home. Rows of English oaks lead up to the entrance while Black and white farmworkers, clad in white shirts and trousers, dig and hoe in the fields. It is like a scene from American slave plantations. Beside the barn is a mob of gray wallabies that scamper off as the cart stops.

The house is by the clear South Creek—once the source of fresh water for her people. The doors are as thick as a man's muscled arm and were transported up the river by ship. The locks are huge and were brought from London. Masters wears black silk and is fat and arrogant with muttonchop whiskers. He brags about this grand house of sandstone with its mahogany staircases and thick carpets.

"No thief, murderer, or marauding Blackfella can gain entrance," says Masters. "You know I pride myself on discipline, morality, and industry here and I beat my convict laborers with my own hand."

Reverend Smythe escorts Mary through the back door and into the kitchen. He pinches her chin then leaves to join the party on the front terrace. She waits for instructions from the butler and, as she waits, she admires the surroundings and leans down to inspect the Indian carpet with its marvelous patterns of lilies in crimson and blue.

She tiptoes into the library and runs her fingers down the huge books. She sees *The Odyssey* and wants to tuck it in her dress. Not stealing exactly, but borrowing, but it is too heavy. Then she sees *A Thousand and One Nights*, with pictures of princes in purple headbands and queens in sheer dresses and capes, with jewels cascading down their breasts. There is gold on the pages. The women, kneeling on lounges, are pictured with their brown nipples peeking from open blouses. Mary sniffs the pages.

Reverend Masters assembles the servants. He stands with his hands on his hips; his gold rings gleam on plump fingers. He looks at Mary and remembers her as a child at the Native School.

"So, little Mary has grown into a fine young woman. How interesting, is it not?" he says.

She finds him repulsive and imagines herself atop a horse, stamping Masters to pieces. He has thinning black hair and a large red nose that protrudes over a long, black cassock with a starched white collar—kept neat by the slave work of the girls at the Female Factory for wayward convicts. A small, tight leather cudgel hangs from his belt and his black eyes wither her. His reputation for flogging precedes him.

Masters's servants are a source of information. They say he marches up and down in the library reciting Shakespeare. They say he sleeps naked with a large porcelain doll dressed in a silk nightshirt, but surely this is a silly rumor. Why, he has a wife! They say he abuses his dark-skinned butler, Rodney, the Jamaican, who calls him a beef-eating shitty Protestant behind his back. All the female servants love Rodney.

Masters raises his twitching white fingers above his head. It is said he likes to whip the face, leaving a red welt across a Black or white cheek. Sometimes he uses a switch of willow tree to reveal pink flesh. Afterward, he is known to cry with remorse, dabbing his eyes with a handkerchief and sighing.

The older girls are instructed to wait on the long oak table, where Reverend Masters sits in a great oak chair. He commands the table with the company of Reverend Smythe, Captain Woodrow, and Mrs. Masters, who is fat and freshly arrived from London. The captain sits beside Mrs. Masters, who wears the latest English fashion, with chrysanthemums in her curled hair and a green Empire gown with short, puffed sleeves. Mary looks at her with admiration, but the lady glances back in annoyance, fingering her necklace of silver and pearls and holding her glass just so to show her golden wedding ring. Mary is conscious of her gray smock and linen apron, but she tosses her proud head upward. She will not bow down.

Captain Woodrow smiles at Mary and nods to his fellow diners.

"Mary, come here, let us examine you. This girl was at the Native School. She reads and writes very well," he says. Mary stands with her hands pressed stiffly to her sides.

"Her role is to wait on tables, not read Shakespeare or play her confounded violin. Why, it's an abomination, like a cat playing whist," laughs Masters.

"I would like to hear her play," laughs Woodrow.

Mary carries a platter of baked potatoes and waits by the table amid laughter and clinking crystal glasses. In the center of the table is a big roast bush turkey surrounded by onions. Reverend Masters gobbles a leg with gluttonous pleasure.

"A wager, Captain—you like a bet? I bet that Mary can play a passable jig on her violin," says Masters, as he waves the turkey leg.

"Are we to expect a cat to dance as well? A shilling says she can't," says Woodrow.

"No, Smythe here says she can," he says as he beckons Mary to the table.

"You, little Black lass, play for us. You can show off your white-fellow music skills. Bring an instrument, Rodney," Masters commands as he wipes his mustache.

A violin and bow are placed beside Mary.

"I cannot play well, sir. I will not play for you," says Mary.

"Hush, girl. Play for him," says Reverend Smythe.

"You will obey. An Irish jig on the violin. Come. We will clap. Play!" orders Masters.

"I won't play," says Mary.

Masters pushes the violin into her hands and drags the bow screeching across the strings. Smythe grimaces at her. At last she nods and gently places the instrument against her chin. She plays a jig and the music is competent and delightful. The party claps.

"Pay up, Woodrow, or add it to your debts," says Masters.

Red wine dribbles down Masters's immense chin as Captain Woodrow tosses him a shilling. Mary can smell the delicious meat and imagines that she is sucking the bones. She waits for the guests to finish eating and then helps to clear the table.

In the kitchen, Mary sips the wine dregs and sniffs the dessert plates. She runs her fingers in the cream.

A crashing of plates in the outhouse draws Mary's attention. To Mary's surprise, Mercy comes through the door carrying a great plate of golden wild birds and pigeons. She is all grown up, her face glowing with health and her hair dressed in a white lace cap. Mary is astounded by Mercy's stature, the majesty in her buxom frame. She makes signs trying to find out when she came here and how she is treated, but Mercy lowers her head. She hands Mary a dish and they both wait in the dining room, with Mercy pretending not to understand her friend's silent inquiries. The pair see Reverend Masters scowling at them and Mercy sticks her tongue out. Mary laughs, then mimics her friend.

Rodney grabs and admonishes Mercy, but she wriggles out of his grasp and flirts with the young, handsome butler; he flirts back.

"*Wirawi, yellun yanna weh*? *Nalla yun*? Want to come and get away?" Mary whispers to Mercy.

Rodney smacks Mercy across her backside and she laughs, then she is gone. Mary moves to the side of the polished dresser, out of the butler's way.

"Come, Mary, are you stupid as well as savage? No yabba-yabba, ooga-booga here," says Masters.

Captain Woodrow shakes his head at the insolence and motions with a finger against his lips for her to be quiet.

"I feel it is an excessive burden for us white men to have to tolerate such behavior. You are insolent and loud, Mary James," says Masters. "Do you believe in the Lord our Savior? Has your precious reverend taught you your catechism yet? Do you honor the Sabbath? Perhaps you have sold your soul to the devil? Oh, don't fret. Learn your prayers. Rodney, give her some lemonade. In a tin cup, not a glass. No, in fact, she shall have wine. Now, where is that saucy girl, Mercy?"

Mercy steps up to the side of the table.

"Yes, sir. What do you want?"

"A drink of wine for the cheeky fiddle-playing girl," he says.

"I don't drink wine," says Mary.

"You do today," says Masters as he offers a cup of wine. Mary shakes her head, but he pushes it at her.

"She must learn compliance. Mercy, do you remember her?" asks Masters.

"She was at the Parramatta School with Mary. They can read!" says Smythe.

"Tell us if this Mary is to be trusted," Masters says, staring at Mercy, who looks defiantly into his face.

"I don't know nothing, but she been to our Native School," says Mercy.

"Know *anything*, for God's sake. Grammar is everything. Without it, and manners, we are all savages," says Masters.

"She might be a thief. But just fowls," Mercy mumbles, and Mary looks at her as if she might punch her.

"Oh no. One cannot tolerate dishonesty in servants," says Mrs. Masters.

"I did not steal anything," says Mary.

"Yes, but she is not a common garden thief. She did steal food from her generous Mistress Shelley," says Masters. "Thou shalt not steal?"

"Not a thief," says Mary.

"No, I suspect she is a liar. Someone who denies the good education given to her, then takes off to be a Black concubine," Masters continues. "A woman who sells her quim for money. The Irish lasses are the worst, or best, trollop quims, depending on your point of view. What say, eh, Woodrow? You would know—a lusty young man such as you?"

"Never," says Woodrow.

"Scared of pox, I'll wager."

Masters licks his lips and leans under the table and puts his hand up his wife's skirt. She screeches and hits him with her fan.

"Really, Mr. Masters! Decorum," she says.

"This is polite society, please, Reverend," says Smythe.

"Polite be damned. I began my work here preaching in an Irish convict hut when it was full of rats. Stinking of gas and worms. Fornication, buggery, quim and twat for sale all about," says Masters.

"The Irish have a lot to answer for," says Woodrow. "The English commanders in Ireland flogged Liam Duggan for three hours and still he did not give up his O'Connell comrades who had burned a Protestant manor house. He rotted for six months in solitary. They called him the Pride of the Land."

Reverend Henry Smythe finds his voice despite being among his superiors.

"Please, I can't abide these stories. They will distress the ladies. I implore you, Captain, to desist," says Smythe.

"The ladies don't mind. This is the colony! We draw and quarter anyone who stands against the lawful English government, including Blacks," says Woodrow.

"Jolly good. Plenty of 'em here. Observe the Irish in the prisons, all rebellious scum. If there is ever a mixing of Irish and the natives, what an insolent lot they would be," says Masters.

"I want some cake," says Mercy as she sticks her finger in a gleaming sponge cake on the gold-rimmed plate.

Mary cannot take her eyes off Mercy. She cannot believe that her school friend has become so obedient. How has the young woman's face bloomed into radiant beauty in the face of such servitude? The pursed full lips, the hair piled and pinned like a lady, with her shapely figure revealed by her maid's dress and tiny lace apron. In comparison, Mary's wide linen bonnet hangs around her ears.

"Really, we have not trained her at all," says Masters. "No speakee unless spoken to. I suppose you can have cake. But first you must dance for the captain, to show that you are a good lass. I will tap a tune on my glass. Come now, entertain us. *Tu vas au bal ce soir?*"

He clinks his stemmed glass with a silver fork and Mercy wiggles and prances like a ballet dancer. Mary is astonished. Then Mercy turns her back and lifts her skirt to show her round bare bottom, and the whole room laughs, except Mrs. Masters, who shudders.

"Oh ho, ho! That's how we like 'em. Make 'em laugh, make 'em cry. You could do well at old Drury Lane Theatre," says Masters. "We will need entertainment at the governor's costume ball next month. What do you all think? Mercy, you had better have some cake. And some for Mary because she has earned her repatriation to the orphan school where she is learning to respectfully hold her tongue, eh, Smythe? Don't hold back on whipping her. Or whatever you fancy, what-ho?"

He takes a slice of cake and licks the icing before giving it to Mercy. He holds up a finger that has been dipped in cream; she licks it like a cat, then gobbles the cake like a starving child. Mary shakes her head. Doesn't Mercy see that this yellow cake could choke her? Like rat poison. Mary hides her piece of cake in a potted palm.

Reverend Masters keeps drinking while speaking loudly and banging drunkenly on the table. At every slam of his fist, the glasses shake. Mary stands frozen to the spot.

Reverend Smythe turns to Mrs. Masters. "Your journey was not too distressing, madam?"

"It was such a relief to arrive in this colony and travel down the river to this fine village. Well, at least it was until I had to be carried through the mud and mangroves on a sailor's back," says Mrs. Masters.

"Thank heavens for your laudanum, madam," says Captain Woodrow.

"But then I stepped onto dry ground and beheld a new and delightful country. I was delighted to see wildflowers in great abundance. The yellow wattle trees are like the English mimosa with the same almondy smell," says Mrs. Masters.

"There are evildoers all around us in your Garden of Eden, murderers at every turn. Evil walks this land, believe me," says Masters. "We have a blind benevolence that drives us to save and indeed my kindness has saved many a tribal person from starvation. I would not deny your countrymen bread, eh, Mary?"

"I don't know. Only they are hungry," says Mary.

"Bread, of course. But we need to save souls and instill morality. God will save you all," says Smythe. "But really, Mrs. Masters, this place is not as bad as people say. Many people are very civilized. Some natives come to my church wearing garments such as pantaloons. Look at our lovely Mary here. She will eventually become a willing servant of God and master."

"I want to improve my situation, sir," says Mary, but she is ignored.

"On one occasion I was made conscious of some natives along the riverbank," says Mrs. Masters, "but they were not numerous. They seemed to have short curly hair, no doubt crawling with vermin. But what is peculiar is that they had white teeth." She looks at Mary's teeth and Mary rubs them with her apron.

Mary wants to tip gravy over their heads.

"We fixed 'em, didn't we?" Masters jokes.

"They are by no means as ugly as one had expected from my husband's letters. I also hear that if you give the native one thing, they will always expect to be given things," says Mrs. Masters.

"Rubbish. They are given weekly rations or, like your native girl here, suitable employment," says Masters. "And I see to it that the native servants learn an appropriate demeanor."

"Quite. One's race, color, or birth has little consequence in the eyes of God. Shepherds are butchered by Blacks and then they, in turn, are butchered," says Smythe.

"But no gratitude. The settlers and the military all together go in search of the felons who shout about choking darkies, shooting black crows," says Masters. "All spitting speeches about hangings to find retribution for the outrages against innocent white women, which gives them the reason to commit outrage and torture the natives. As if our evil has not already been passed on in pestilence, syphilis, and smallpox."

"I saw it when I arrived in 1789. Natives call it *gal gal*, all covered in yellow oozing pustules brought by La Perouse's ship in a cordial. Sadly, they died like flies," says Captain Woodrow.

"Oh my, how terrible!" Mrs. Masters cries, reaching for her napkin.

"As Pater would exclaim, 'Truth is admirable.' More Madeira wine, anyone? I will myself. Good for my health. No cases of small-pox on the First Fleet, clean as a whistle. The natives abandoned those that demonstrated disease and fled into the bush. But wherever we British traveled, the natives rolled over and died," says Masters.

"It was like the Indian slums pestilence," says Captain Woodrow.

"After a while, we saw no bark canoes fishing in the harbor. It had been alive with natives, then silent," says Masters.

"Piles of bones in caves," Masters continues. "Oh dear, look at little Mary's face. Sorry, dear. She has a great heart, I am informed, great compassion toward others, especially Smythe's pet orphans. All those dying whore babies. That right, Mary dear?"

Mary does not lift her head. She wants to feed him to the dogs. He enjoys watching her face when he speaks his venom. There is much she could say to these pieces of evil coming from his mouth, but the chasm of ignorance is too deep. She imagines him chewed up, in mud.

"David Collins has written about it: the dead left to bury the dead. No need for military action; nature took care of it all," says Woodrow. "That old Chief Berringingy also died with a small boy at his side; not sure why. He was found with his weapons all laid out as though he expected it."

"Influenza, I suspect. A shame," says Masters.

"Who, sir?" asks Mary.

"Berringingy and a boy."

Mary is stiff. She shudders and tries to recall the last time she saw her father. She tries to conjure him up from the mist. Her head pounds. She falls to the floor in a faint.

The party guests stop and stare.

"Whatever is the matter with the girl? So impulsive and headstrong. Mary! Stand up straight! Say a prayer for our Lord," says Masters as she struggles. Mary's eyes flutter open and she lifts her head.

"He's not dead. You liar! You tell lies! He's alive! He will come for me. He loves me. Not dead!" Mary hisses and sobs.

"Calm yourself! All will be well. We will find out the truth about this Berringingy. No crying," says Smythe. He waves his hand like a flag of truce.

Masters watches Henry Smythe, who is clearly resisting his desire to hold Mary. Smythe wants to say that he suspects the dead man is her father and is sorry for it. Old Granny Wiring had given him this story of Mary's family. But he stays at the table and holds his head in his hands and prays. Finally he pushes back his chair and takes a handkerchief to Mary. He mops her face as the room watches with curiosity. She has become their entertainment.

She silently begs to leave the room. Her father's face smiles at her. She closes her eyes and breathes him in, for he will never leave her waking and dreaming thoughts.

"Does she conjure devils? I hear they speak to spirits and dance naked for abominable purpose," says Mrs. Masters.

"Perhaps she flies at night," says Masters.

"They burn them at the stake back home," says Mrs. Masters.

Mary's rage and sorrow become intolerable and she reaches for the tablecloth. She wants to make glasses break and plates shatter. But she cannot move. She holds her arms tight, her anger imploding.

Smythe returns to his seat, and they ignore Mary now and carry on their conversation.

"I hope that he who fed Elijah in the wilderness will not let us feel that calamity of famine," says Masters. "Then the natives might get the upper hand with murder and rape. I have been partial to a little rape of the Sabine women myself . . . Pass the salt."

Mrs. Masters faints and Smythe picks her up and passes smelling salts under her nose.

"Get Cook. She can loosen her corset. Oh dear, I have gone too far," says Masters. "I should not drink so much Madeira. I am sorry, dear wife!" he says as he fans his wife.

Mary reaches forward and rips the cloth from the table. Roast turkey, wine, cutlery, and glasses crash onto the carpet in a terrible scene. She throws plates and cruets at the people, who scatter, terrified. They rush all over the room crashing into each other in confusion.

Cook runs in and belts Mary across the ear, then the butler tries to grab her. She escapes and races out to the kitchen yard to be alone. She wipes her nose with her hand and hides, curled up into a ball on sacks of onions in the corner. But Masters is upon her with a whip. "You dare to destroy my dinner party! You Black slave!" he shouts.

The beating is severe. She feels his whip on her legs, back, and across her face. Mary holds her hands up trying to protect herself. She turns her head into the sack. The whip slashes her body again and again. She screams. Masters stops and regards her upturned bloodied face with some satisfaction. He prods her ripped smock, and she cringes as he turns his back and walks away with a snort. She grits her teeth and watches him.

"Pig!" she shouts.

Masters stops and slowly turns to face her before coming at her again, lifting the weapon high and lashing her yet again with fury. When he is exhausted, he lays aside the whip and wipes his hands. As he leaves, he sees that Smythe has been standing at the door, alarmed. Mary does not look. She is silently pressing her hands by her sides to make herself disappear, too consumed by emotion to feel her pain.

The servants pile into the cart to return to Parramatta, and Mary can barely crawl into the cart. The road is long and dusty, and she hides her face in her apron. She has lost all hope of finding

her family. She fears that they have all perished. Her wounds bleed
and the pain is unbearable.

Weeks pass and Mary's physical wounds slowly heal thanks to
the soothing balm Reverend Smythe prepares for them. She walks
in the garden and stares into the grevillea bushes full of chirping
wrens. She feels as tiny as a honeyeater, as if she could fade away
and dissolve.

CHAPTER THIRTEEN

1825: Seduction

Lieutenant General Ralph Darling is received in the colony with his separate commissions for New South Wales and Van Diemen's Land. The conquest of lands by violence and bribery extends through a western boundary to include Fort Dundas on Melville Island in the tropics. The southern boundary extends to Wilson's Promontory.

Back at Reverend Henry Smythe's Parramatta Native Institution rooms, he has installed modest amber glass windows. Tall oak trees shade the yard, a garden of roses adorns the porch, and a field of yellow maize grows abundantly at the back of the buildings. He also experiments with wheat, barley, and root vegetables. These are green pastures with earth as warm as blood. His days are long and peaceful.

Mary no longer works with the orphans. Now her duties are entirely with the reverend. During the day Smythe writes his sermons and Mary washes and starches his clothes. At night he writes his journal by a flickering candle while Mary brings him cocoa and picks up his clothes from the floor. She sees that he cannot keep his eyes from her body; he is going mad with love and lust.

She often feels his attention upon her. She knows that he observes her as she bends to gather the white shirts. Lately she admits to her own desire for him. This night is no different from others, except that he has been watching with an open hunger. His eyes are glazed over. She crouches on the floor before him as if looking at a stain, so that he might see her shapely backside.

One morning, Mary sees Henry's shadow against the window of his office as he arranges some botanical specimens. The house is empty. The moment has come. She enters the room and is excited at the sight of his elegant thin hands. She wants him. She hears her own breath as it pounds and catches.

She moves swiftly to stand behind him. He faces the cross with Jesus pinned to it and murmurs a prayer, but she whispers in his ear and kisses his neck. Surprised, he turns around to face her. Silence, except for their breathing. His shirt is lifting, and as he pushes it back into place, his hand brushes her bare arm. She takes his hand and places it under her shift and moves her nipple against his fingers. She presses her body against the wall and hooks her leg around his thigh. He pushes her dress up and over her arms and her golden skin greets the sunlight. She thinks he has never seen a naked woman before.

She strokes his curls, helps him take off the clerical clothes, and unties his undergarments. He steps out of them, and she pushes him to the floor. She momentarily wonders if he has ever done this before and straddles him and takes him inside her with urgency. She forgets her grief and sadness, and her body arches with pleasure. He has tears on his cheeks. He quickly dresses Mary, then himself, and dabs his brow with his handkerchief.

The next day, Mary dusts the room with an emu-feather duster. It is full of the aroma of potpourri, ink, and musty Bibles. Smythe's long gown hangs behind the door smelling of camphor; she inhales. Mary smooths the cloth as though nothing has happened.

She remembers Boothuri and that love is a thing that must be cherished, like living in the sunlight and playing along the river with joy. She is now Henry's lover at the Parramatta Native Institution, beneath the blackbutt desk, on the Persian rug, beneath the oil painting brought from England of the crucified Jesus. A thorny coronet. It cost twenty pounds. The other servant girls seem to know, and they do not blame him. Mary hears their laughter but ignores them.

Henry Smythe is aware of the consequences—of being sent back to London in disgrace or of being reprimanded by Masters. He knows of God's wrath and the rotting corpse of guilt. But Mary is his long night in the desert, his temptation. He holds her hand, light as a sparrow, and brushes his lips against it.

"When I look at you, the air is laden with heaviness, and I fear an apoplectic convulsion coming upon me. If I'm agitated, O Lord," says Smythe. "This thunder in my heart is deafening; my eyes are the lightning, and they glitter with intense longing for your body!"

"Don't be afraid; you're not bad," says Mary.

"They will judge me. I must tiptoe in this school. Sometimes, I cannot speak because lies might fly from my mouth, like flies," says Smythe.

———

Mary has taken refuge in this lover's embrace; she hopes to find protection and security with this weak man. After suffering so much, she needs this love and intimacy. Smythe visits her bed every night. He is not restrained in their turbulent lovemaking, but in public he is silent and brooding—torn by guilt and fearful of discovery. She will wait to see the outcome.

But she becomes like him. She learns to stay inside the house like him, as this is what the English prefer. Her humor is now restrained and she laughs aloud only when she is with other servants. Occasionally it feels like she is dying in a trap.

Henry gives her a big English dictionary and an encyclopedia full of facts. He tells her to learn new words. "I walked in the beautiful Norfolk Cathedral, much bigger than our Saint Jude's in Windsor," says Smythe. "There are Gothic high arches of stone. It is a holy place with soft singing and a glow from stained glass windows. I walked in the iridescent blue and red light. Come and imagine this joy. Let's close our eyes and I will take your hand and lead you there."

One night, Mary and Henry venture outside to sit in the garden under stars. He holds her hand and places an object in it. "I have a new telescope so I can see Mars. Do you know of this planet? A red light is actually reflected from the sun; can you believe that?" he asks as he laughs and hugs her.

"I have brought you something that tastes better than honey— lilly pilly jelly," says Mary. "It's bright pink and sticky; taste it." She holds a finger dripping with the sweet syrup, and he sucks it.

"Delicious."

"I cooked it on a stove," says Mary. "You can try geebung fruit when it's in season. We call it 'snotty gobble.' That planet you talk about is not Mars but a boy who steals food from his mother and he goes to stars. The great serpent sweeps cross night sky; you can see him in a thousand stars."

"I love you, my dearest, but you must accept the Christian worldview, as Satan is a beast who lurks within our hearts. I fear he is awake and following you," says Henry.

"No, only little hairy men, who might eat children. Why should I believe your story? You are scared of ghosts, like me, eh?" she asks.

"I have infinite patience with you, because you are like a child," says Henry. "I wish to cleanse your heathen ways and expose your native intelligence to European knowledge. The music, you have already embraced," he says.

"Blackfellas come from the earth, out of a waterhole when a great mother put her digging stick in this earth," says Mary. "All creatures come from that place. She is born from the sea. Like that story about Noah's Ark."

"Sing for me. In your language?" he asks.

He looks at her with kindness and a willingness to understand. So, she stretches her dress over her knees like a stretched drum, just as her aunts had done with possum-skin cloaks, and beats time with her hands and sings.

Werowi tuabilli bulga, dungarra bayley,
Girls from mountain tribe, dancing swinging their hips,
Karabi yan kaundi, dun gittan,
Black cockatoos fly above, yellow tail feathers.
Gundungurra werowi, muruku mulamundra.
Mountain girls, dance in rain, droplets run down legs.
Mula muruku
Kuthaling kaianyung.
Darkinjung, Darug kaianyung.
Nguttatha werowi.

She looks up and his face is transformed. She doesn't know what she has done.

———

Mary accompanies Henry into bushland as he looks for exotic insects and flannel flowers. He has jars full of plants and insects in his study and a board with hundreds of butterflies all pinned and dead. They sit beside a chart of drawings of seahorses and fish.

They walk along the creek bed, and he stops to catch a big green beetle in a small wooden box. Over their heads wattle birds eat nectar from bottlebrush bushes and tiny honeyeaters run up the trees. He catches a cicada and is about to pin it.

"No, don't kill this little one. This is *Yarramundi*, like our chief, his totem," says Mary, as she takes his hand.

"It will be swift. Death for an insect has no meaning. It cannot feel like us."

"You're wrong; we all the same: insect, people, all like you. There are lots of cicadas called *jirrabidirrin*, Floury Monday, Greengrocer, Black Prince, and the Pisswhacker. You must only kill when you want to eat animals." Mary shakes her head and holds tight on his hand. The cicada flies away thrumming.

"In God's world, we human beings rule over all the animal domain," says Smythe. "I have heard that the Hindus believe in many gods, and some are indeed animals, but we are Christians. You will come to the Lord in good time, although, being out here with you in this wild, terrifying new world, I sometimes experience a doubt. I wonder why on earth we are here at all. You see, I have been blinded by forbidden fruit, my Eve. I have committed a ghastly sin." Henry sits down and clutches his head.

"Loving is not bad. It makes us happy. It's not bad to feel happy," says Mary.

"I don't think I can ever feel truly happy, not after my journey out here on a convict ship. I was minister on board and the men were chained in the hold with seawater around their legs," says Smythe. "It was a filthy stench, and they were in starving misery. And I, absurd as it was, was forced to lead the wretches in prayers and hymns. I held my Bible aloft, singing aloud like a lunatic in front of the damned." Mary pats his hand.

In the afternoon, Henry Smythe looks across the table in the dining room, where afternoon tea is being served. All butter cake and jam, the English women titter and sip tea, their poverty hidden in ten-year-old dresses and homemade bonnets of cabbage palm leaf. Mary is rendered invisible. She is asked to fetch cups and plates from the kitchen. She catches his eyes and senses the look of love. She inclines her head and purses her lips upward.

Smythe hurries from the room and kisses Mary in the kitchen; then, with a dreamy expression, he returns to the table. He spoons cream onto a fairy cake, flushed and sweating slightly as he discusses Genesis with an Englishwoman.

Mary thinks she might be carrying the reverend's child and the congregation might run him out of the town.

CHAPTER FOURTEEN

1826: Pregnant, Bindimari

King George IV is the English monarch who reigns over them, and the governor of New South Wales is Lieutenant General Ralph Darling. He has the power of life and death over all the people of New South Wales. He has overseen the installation of the colony's first streetlamp in Macquarie Place, Sydney, burning pure whale oil.

━━━━━

Mary walks with Henry in a forest near the huge old spirit gum trees of Windsor. Three men could join hands around one trunk and still not meet. They walk in deep-ferned gullies, among weeping staghorn ferns, mist, snakes, strangler fig trees, and a cacophony of birds. A giant emu with huge yellow claws is eating purple fruit and ignores them. Henry takes a sample from a shrub.

"Look, some lemon tea tree, leptospermum."

"That's called *budjor;* it's good for wounds," says Mary.

"Let me write that down."

"Henry, you know I'm *bindimari*," says Mary.

"Is that a type of berry? Can you make a jelly with it?" asks Henry.

"*Bindimari*, I'm pregnant. Baby," she whispers and strokes her belly.

"Oh my, no!"

"That Birrahgnooloo, she is an emu spirit in the sky who brings babies," says Mary.

"I don't think so," says Smythe.

He freezes and cannot move but he turns and there she is, with the bump in her body clear as the alarm in his face. She knows he will not come to her again.

He packs up his specimens and they travel home in silence. Mary caresses the growing baby, but her mouth is dry and her lips cling to her teeth. She falters on the path, but he does not try to help or comfort her. She is now his enemy. Poisonous thoughts rise up like bile, and Mary vomits into the bushes.

Henry avoids her now. He shuffles off into corridors and locks his bedroom against her. This baby will be born with no father named on its baptism certificate.

Mary's shift grows tight and the baby quivers incessantly. It will be a gold-skinned child and she will name her Eleanor.

=====

The reverend is not home the night his daughter is born. He has fled at the sound of the labor pains, and the cook helps Mary by making a clean place for her to lie down. She births the baby on the kitchen table and it is bathed in a basin. Cook moves Mary to a cupboard bedroom and the baby is wrapped in a flour bag and placed in a washing basket. Later, Cook feeds Mary pudding and syrup. When Mary is alone with her baby, she is struck by the feeling that this is the first human who will not desert her.

In the early morning, Henry knocks on the door of Mary's room. He enters and gazes at his daughter.

"Please, may I hold her?" he asks.

Mary places the baby in his arms and Henry Smythe cries and hums at the child, rocking her back and forth. Mary touches his arm, and he looks lovingly at her while the baby struggles, little legs kicking at him. The swaddling cloth falls to the ground and the golden limbs stretch up with tiny fists that push at his chest.

"I had no idea they could be so strong. Look at her taking my finger. This child will be a fighter. She is in a hurry to grow up. Look at her chin, dimpled like mine," he says.

"She is healthy and always hungry. Her name is Eleanor. You will love her?" asks Mary.

"I will protect you both, I promise," he says.

Henry spins the child around in his arms and laughs with joy and Mary has a moment of pleasure. The warmth swims up her body and she is humming in hope of a life of being loved. He smiles into her eyes and tilts her chin toward him. All hurt is gone.

Mary recovers quickly from the birth and goes back to work in the laundry with her baby tied to her back. Eleanor does not cry. She is a smiling, beautiful baby.

As the months pass, Henry becomes more and more uncomfortable when others are nearby. He does not want them to notice Mary and turns his back as he pretends that she has nothing to do with him. He watches Eleanor playing beside Mary while she scrubs the floors. He watches the child growing from a painful distance.

Mary visits Mercy at the Masters estate. Mercy declares the baby is a gift, saying she will bring Mary good fortune. Mercy is her aunty.

Not long after her visit, there is surprising news from visiting servants: Mercy has disappeared from Masters's estate. She was seen packing things into a bag and, the next day, she was gone and only a crumpled pile of clothes was left on her pallet—Mercy had stolen a white lace gown. She vanished in the night like a spirit.

———

Henry calls Mary into his room. He sits her against the fire so she can warm herself and he takes Eleanor and hugs her tight. He sighs and smiles and Mary thinks that their former intimacy may begin again.

"It is time; would you like to join your people in one of the camps? You must miss your tribesmen. I can pay you some money to assist with your relocation," says Henry.

"No, we like it here. We're happy," says Mary.

"Please, I will raise the child," says Smythe. "As you must see, your presence is an embarrassment for me, even if no one knows I am Eleanor's father. You see, I care for you both and love you deeply, but I can't be seen to condone immorality."

"She's a happy baby and no trouble. She's not going to embarrass you. And, anyway, everyone here knows you're her father," she says.

"Well, quite, that is the point. Please think about my position. I can give you silver coat buttons to help you pay for your travels."

"You're going to throw me out?" Panic rises in her throat. She can hardly breathe. Memories of being given away hit hard.

"So, you will not go, then? Well, just stay away from the church," he mutters.

"I will not."

"You will be damned," he says.

Henry strokes the baby's head and walks around the room. He sings nursery rhymes and smiles into her face, but something has changed in him. He will not look at Mary.

Another year passes and Mary keeps her distance from Henry and cares for her baby while working in the laundry. There are few friends, but she hopes she will see Mrs. Shelley in the street in Parramatta. Mary doesn't attend church anymore, because she is shunned. She hopes that if she runs into Mrs. Shelley, the lady will admire her daughter, but never ask about the father, because she is far too kind.

But there are changes happening in Reverend Smythe's household. There is a rustle of constant letter writing. Henry has plans to marry a woman from England whom he has not met. He orders a new suit of clothes and some modest jewelry for the wife-to-be.

CHAPTER FIFTEEN

1830: Mistress of the House

One third of migrants who come to Australia after 1830 pay their own passage. Conditions for settlers and ex-convicts are much better than back in Europe. The Emigration Commission is established to assist females to move to Australia. There is a need for women as domestic servants and agricultural workers. Some come as engaged future wives to men they have never met; one is engaged to Henry Smythe.

Governor Darling makes a decision to invite all the tribes to a meeting and corroboree at Parramatta. It is time for the twelfth annual Conference of Tribes and the Annual Native Feast.

The chiefs Blang, Dual, Cogie, Boodeny, and Nurrugingy arrive in the town. They will receive blankets and clothes for their tribes. There are rumors whispered among the native servant girls that the famous warrior Windradyne, the Wiradjuri chief from over the mountains, will not attend this meeting. He will not pay court to the white-man king despite the promise of gifts of tobacco and rum.

Mary talks with the other servants. "Last time Chief Windradyne rode a big horse to that feast. He came with three *waibala* and walked all over Sydney like he was the king himself," says Mary. "That other chief, old Bungaree, he is finished up now. Too bad."

Mary hears about the abundance of food at the party that she cannot attend. There are forty loaves, twenty-two monstrous dishes of roast beef, thirteen plum cakes, a huge hogshead of soup, several tubs of potatoes, and a hogshead of three-watered grog. But the servants are not permitted to attend the annual feast, for they have jobs to do and, what is more, have been lectured by Smythe about being civilized Aborigines with no need of interaction with their sable brethren. She groans at the unfairness of being kept indoors away from such a meeting and feast.

The *Sydney Gazette* reports gleefully about a future war between the Cowpastures tribes and the Liverpool mob, who are clans of the Gundungurra people. Much bloodshed is expected, and the serving girls talk about the possibility of interclan fighting.

There are, however, more important things to talk about: the new bride, who will be Mrs. Henry Smythe, is about to arrive and take up her position as mistress of the home. Reverend Smythe beams with pride. He has married Susan in a swift service performed by Reverend Masters, which was all hymns and candles. Mary was not invited. She is working in the laundry among blue bags and Borax starch.

Mary leans against the piano and squeezes the red velvet piano cover in her fists. She sniffs at the sight of the buggy pulling up in the courtyard. She is tired from pacing and not sleeping. Her starched apron scratches and lace frills strangle her. She pleads for the strength to remain controlled, with no outbursts. She will bite her lip and maintain the picture of a docile servant even when it is repellent—all this ridiculous curtsying and bobbing!

Mary holds her hands in fake prayer and watches out the window at Henry's nervousness. He looks uncomfortably up at the window as he takes the gloved white fingers to steady his new wife as she climbs down from her carriage. Mary titters to herself as she sees that Smythe has left a Bible page marked: "Thou will crawl on your belly and thou shalt eat dust all the days of thy life."

She watches his face glow red as he looks up again to the window. Mary's eyes latch onto his and, in this glance, the whole betrayal is before her. He blushes and sweats and stinks up his suit with nerves. She hears him call out, "The serpent beguiled me and I ate . . . Thou art cursed above all livestock and all wild animals."

Reverend Masters accompanies Mrs. Smythe and Henry as they enter the drawing room. Mary stands by the door waiting for orders. A cool wind blows with Susan Smythe, for she has the haughty air of the English gentry and sniffs the room like a fox. She is tall and thin and elegant in a fashionable gown.

"I find it quite shocking. This country is so dry with so many dead trees and crackling leaves. It seems a barren landscape from hell. I already miss the verdant pasture of southern England," says Mrs. Smythe.

Even in this first moment of meeting there is an unspoken friction as the bride looks disdainfully at the furnishings and at the servant. Mrs. Smythe's eyes rest on Mary's pretty face and a snarl comes from the white woman, for instinct tells her more than words. Henry shows Susan his home and his nature display.

"My dearest. I have a superb specimen collection of eucalyptus, the family Myrtaceae. You must see them later. I have over a hundred specimens," says Henry.

"How peculiar you can be, and dull. I prefer my pale pink tea roses. I brought the cuttings from England," says Susan.

The room has new furnishings, including curtains made of dark red damask, and there are glass bowls of waratah on the oak table. Mary brushes the chair with a duster and shows the bride where to sit. For a moment, she thinks she might place an upturned pincushion on the seat. She decides against it but comforts herself by imagining the bride holding her arse and howling.

Mrs. Smythe leans over the wildflowers and inhales, then smiles at the simpering Smythe as he sighs a nervous breath. A perfume of lily of the valley wafts after her and Mary secretly holds her breath, for this smell is overpowering, sweet, and sinister. It reminds her of vomit. Mrs. Smythe wears a dress of purple shot silk. Its huge, lace petticoat rustles beneath voluminous layers. Mary wonders if the husband will be able to find his bride's *moondra*, her quim, among the frills.

The house is gleaming thanks to Mary's elbow grease, and she watches the new bride's every move. She is unsure of how this new person will fit into this house of secret sighs and longings.

She is now summoned to bring in a tea tray and serve her new mistress. Mary places a plate of pink ice candies on the tray before Reverend Masters and the newly married couple. She fantasizes about pouring hot tea on the bride. Instead, she retires to her room and sulks.

Mary thinks about Henry's skin and how it glistens with sweat when he rides above her with clenched teeth. She thinks about his long artistic hands and penetrating, white, titillating fingers. She thinks about Boothuri and lying beneath ghost gum trees on a soft gray bed of possum fur. She thinks about Granny Wiring and her supposed wisdom in bringing her here. She might never see that old woman again.

She wonders why she is so easily led and has no steel to leave this ridiculous prison. She wonders what will become of her daughter. His daughter. She wishes she were somewhere else.

She knows she must snap out of this way of thinking—or she will be doomed to misery.

That night, Reverend and Mrs. Smythe host a welcome dinner party, with Masters, Woodrow, and some other ladies and gentlemen. Mary polishes the silverware and helps prepare the meal. Candles are lit in the candelabra. The party will eat golden roast fowls with potatoes gleaming with butter, accompanied by decanted Spanish wine. Mrs. Smythe has supervised the cooking of colonial dishes, such as yams and boiled wild spinach with roast mutton, followed by creamed lilly pilly fruit with goat's milk custard.

Mary wonders if she should leave before she is thrown out. It would be good not being cooped up in a dark house. She imagines herself walking back to Kurrajong or working on an estate with a good young husband. She collects plates from the table and stands at the side, listening.

"Mrs. Smythe, are you enjoying your new life in the colony? You will no doubt enjoy the availability of meat and grain. In the early days we had little," says Masters. "You have heard that Old Mr. MacArthur is suffering from insanity? Daft as a dill brain. Not meeting his government wheat quota. Half the settlement is dependent on government handouts. Eh, Henry? And that Captain King is regaining his spirits, which have been much depressed owing to the losses of sheep to natives and the wild dogs and dingoes. He also collects botanical specimens."

"I would like very much to share my knowledge of native species," says Smythe.

"No one wants to talk about botany," says Masters. "But life here is quite entertaining. The mixed company of the colony is sometimes alarming, but some native tribes are *tres intéressant n'est ce pas?*"

"Very interesting. And married life, does it suit our previously lonely curate?" Woodrow leans toward Henry and grins.

"I was never occasioned to complain of being lonely," says Smythe. "I have my native plants and I am interested in the tribal languages and, of course, we have our crops of barley, wheat, and maize. I have committed to new crops in spring." He is quick in his own defense.

"Plants. Rather dull. My humble congregation is bursting with merry company, what with the odd praiseworthy mulatto from the Americas and even, for heaven's sake, a contingent of Maoris from New Zealand," says Masters, "full of fulsome praise for their church back home. I thought they would have cannibalized all the English by now. Boiled in a pot! But no, here they are all sitting up in our church, tattooed and respectably dressed. *C'est la vie.* What next? Asiatic wives in our beds? At it like wet rabbits. That would be a bit exciting, eh? We have all sorts here—an exotic persuasion, eh, Henry?" Masters laughs and slaps Mary's bottom. She drops a blue-and-white plate and it smashes into shards.

"Silly girl! Get a brush and sweep it up," says Masters.

Susan and Mary exchange a look—a moment of shared vulnerability. In some ways, they are both servants to these men.

"I concede that I, on a few occasions, felt loneliness," says Smythe.

"Oh, here we go!" says Masters.

Mary feels tension between the married couple. She feels a terrible burden of knowledge.

"Very lonely but not too hardworking, eh? Naturally, Henry had plenty of time for the . . . um . . . natives. The pretty lasses are amendable or bendable, what-ho?" says Masters. "All those misplaced starving wretches. Pass the bung-head liquor; it is so much more satisfying than weak wine." He drinks a glass of the fiery white liquor.

Masters looks at Henry, who is staring with a pale face at his new wife.

Mary can't keep quiet in the face of Henry's ridicule. She steps up to the table and with uncontrollable emotion speaks out. "Reverend Smythe cares for us and the orphans and is very kind. He gave the children some sugared ginger from China yesterday. Without him, we might be all starved," says Mary.

"Mary, ginger indeed. Are you not aware that you are just a servant? Don't speak of Reverend Smythe. He is not your concern," says Susan.

Mary looks at Susan, and she realizes that the wife knows every-thing by sheer feminine intuition. It will be an uneasy atmosphere in the house, a place where whispers will be heard.

Masters laughs loudly and pushes his napkin against his mouth. He is quite taken by the drink.

"Golly gosh! The Reverend Masters has drunk too much, haven't you, sir?" Henry Smythe helps him to his feet while Mary moves to the corridor.

The new wife is from green England, where the witches and fair-ies come from. She has brought along a Scottish piper from the old country. He plays a horrid noise on a bagpipe after the dinner party, and the singing goes on until after ten.

Mary is with an Irish maid in the kitchen and as they wash dishes she whispers, "I listen to him making love to his wife and I need to escape from this place. He says he will care for us, but he lies. If I go, they will send police to get me. I'm indentured. I might get put in jail; he tells me this," says Mary.

"Leave it alone. You must forget about him. He is a rascal, like they all are," says the maid.

———

Susan Smythe begins her life in the Parramatta Native Institution and starts to take an interest in the experimental corn crop and the new Indian maize and vegetables. She is not a bad mistress, giving orders with a nervous flutter to her Black servants. Mary watches Henry behind her back and the tension is palpable. He is terrified that Mary will reveal his sins.

An icy jealousy courses through Mary and she cannot stand the sight of Henry embracing his wife. She imagines the new wife caught in the laundry mangle or eaten by dingoes or falling down the stairs. The desire to kill her mistress is a shocking surprise and it makes her sick.

One morning Henry Smythe summons Mary to the library as he has some information to share with her. She sees her beloved books now placed on a high shelf, out of her reach. She gazes at the volumes and wishes she could steal some.

"I have made inquiries and it seems that the tribe from which you were taken has dispersed. They were close to Windsor, on the creek near Riverstone, which is of course the old reverend's land. I have asked about your release from your indenture and the suitability for you to join the Windsor Burruberongal mob, however I hear that they have walked off too, and no one knows where they are. So, what to do now? It must be the Liverpool tribe, after all," says Smythe.

"Don't worry. We'll go in the summer. You won't need to worry about us," says Mary.

Mary folds the linen clothes, stroking the cleanliness, inhaling the smell of lemon and lavender. She places dresses in her basket and thinks of a time in the future when she will carry them on her head with Eleanor walking beside her. Mary dreams of the path to Liverpool and has heard that Chief Gilbert and King Geoffrey might welcome her. She is their distant kin from her mother's side.

Her beloved aunts might be there. They would love her and not despise her for being enslaved by *waibala*. But she finds it hard to leave, despite her thoughts. She is forced to watch the new loving couple and aches with wanting her lover. The anger inside her grows. She scratches at insect bites and is distracted and fierce with anyone she speaks to. She hides in corners listening to the married couple's banter so she can find some torment to inflict on him. She puts a poisonous funnel-web spider in their bed, but the Irish maid finds it, takes it in a pot, and empties the spider outside. She squashes it and gently leads Mary back to her work in the laundry.

One night, Mary slips up to Henry's bedroom to listen at the door. The lovely marriage room is no longer a single curate's room and is still hung with the wedding garlands of wildflowers.

She can hear his familiar sighing as a hot pulse of love runs through her body. She feels sure the embracing couple will hear her heavy breathing.

Mary looks through the keyhole and sees the wife lying as still as death, with her body rigid, her hands pressed against the sheet, and her teeth clenched. This must be a shocking event for an English lady. Mary presses her hands between her legs and a sigh escapes, then a sudden quiet.

"Is someone there, Henry? Outside our door?" asks Susan.

"Nothing, my love. A mouse."

A mouse? Mary will give him "mouse"! She slams the stairs with a broom. She wants to shout but nothing comes out.

The days grow colder and Mary is usually in the kitchen cutting up salt beef or making porridge with her daughter by her side, learning as little children do. Eleanor grows into a headstrong and excitable girl, and Cook often takes her by the wrist to punish her for stealing or spitting in the flour bowl. Eleanor runs about the house and jumps from couch to couch, and the maids chase her with brooms.

———

A year later, Mary has still not left the house and a change is in the air. Henry has become less vigilant, and he now admires Mary openly when his wife is absent. Mary has accepted the role of wife number two—for the moment. Mary's violin playing is beautiful and Henry lies on the settee in the sunlight, listening to the music and conducting with his finger. He holds Eleanor in his lap and plays horsey with her. It is a scene of domestic bliss.

Mary indulges Henry's irresistible longings as he touches her when she brushes past. One day in darkness, he finds Mary in the pantry.

"I am so sorry, Mary. I love you and know I have committed crimes. I am a bastard son," says Henry Smythe. "Have compassion for a poor sinner. I will protect the little one and you. I can love two women equally."

"You might have married me. Other white men marry native women," says Mary.

"As a respected minister of the Church of England, I must lead the way in respectability and moral order."

Suddenly, they realize that Susan is at the door, looking hard at the two of them.

"Henry, may I have a word with you?" Susan's voice is crisp.

"Of course, my dearest. What is it?" asks Henry.

"What is it? You must know what I am about to say! It pains me, I can barely speak," she says.

"I have no idea! Are you ill? I am not a mind reader. Speak!" he demands.

She stands stock-still and stares at Mary. Henry reaches out and touches her arm, but Susan brushes him away and snaps at him.

"I will not tolerate your harlot in my home," says Susan.

"You are going quite mad; it's the heat, my dearest. Why don't you lie down and we will get some tea?" says Henry.

Mary walks quietly from the room and Henry gently holds his wife's hand.

Days later, hushed speaking trickles down the corridors. Henry engages in hot and desperate coupling with Mary against the piano after her violin practice. But it is quick, almost as though it did not happen. She smooths down her smock and straightens her hair.

Early the next morning, a loud howling seeps from the corridor and Susan Smythe stands in front of little Eleanor, who is crying. The mistress has her hands behind her back holding a large spoon. She looks at the child as though she would like to eat her. Mary runs to the child and kneels down.

"What happened?" asks Mary.

"Mrs. Susan hit me with spoon," Eleanor cries.

Mary turns, shaking with anger, but she dares not speak. Susan Smythe throws the spoon across the kitchen and tosses back her hair, which is falling free on her shoulders. She is still in her night-clothes and there is blood on her nightdress. Mary looks at the stain, which Mrs. Smythe tries to cover with her hands.

"I did no such thing. The child is a liar, and we should teach her better manners. I will begin her education with others in the orphan school," says Susan. "We can't afford to keep every half-breed creature who comes to our door."

"Sorry, Mrs. Smythe. I'll take her along to the kitchen. She won't bother you," Mary whispers with a quiet, tense voice. She hides away in the pantry and squeezes Eleanor in next to her.

"You must be good, *nyindi, kurung jannunggai*, and daughter."

Mary fears she will die if Eleanor is taken. She must do everything she can to prevent this. Perhaps she can find a position elsewhere or find her long-lost aunties?

All night, she is awake with fear, listening to the beating of her heart and the sounds of the house. Somewhere, someone sighs. Mary fights with her impulses, with the need to be with Henry.

Mary takes some embossed writing paper and writes a letter.

Dear Mrs. Shelley,

I am Mary James who you brought up by hand. I run away but now I am back living in the home of the master of the Orphan School, as you must know.

I hope the Sunday School examinations have gone well.

Would you think of taking me back to live with you? I can be of

*service to you because I can read and write and play music. I would
like to be a teacher. You might hear I have a girl, and she is mostly a
good child. I wish to bring her and live with you.*

    Yours sincerely,

    Miss Mary James

A week passes and Mary receives a return letter delivered by
Cook, who is amazed that there might be a letter for a native servant. She is shocked that she could have written a letter, let alone
received one in reply. She looks at her as if she is a dog who can now
walk upright.

Dear Miss James,
*My dear young friend, I am sorry to hear about your situation, but I
cannot help. I have so many charges to care for already.*

    *Please do not presume to write ever again about this problem. I
can send some linen for your child, but not much else.*

    *I am so sorry to write that you are known as a woman of
corrupted virtue—a person of scandal and low native morals. I am
afraid that we English have taught you nothing. You have flaunted
your illegitimate child in the streets of Windsor. I am crying as
I write these words to someone I love. Have you no shame? I
thought you to be a good girl. I also know that you are kind. Ask
for forgiveness and it shall be given. Much gossip attends your
continued presence as a so-called servant. That the minister can
tolerate you is indeed evidence of God's supreme mercy.*

    *My dear girl, the other students you were with at our school grew
(mostly) into respectable members of society and have married in
the church to suitable ticket-of-leave husbands. You, I hear, have no
visible husband. Perhaps you are, indeed, a fallen person. I pray for
you every night.*

    Yours sincerely,

    Mrs. Shelley

Mary keeps the letter folded tight in her shift and is filled with regret every time she reads it.

———

One morning, Henry Smythe is tending his corn patch with a hoe. When he scratches the mud from his boots and returns to the house, Susan calls him to the drawing room. "Henry, where is my new blue gown that arrived on the *Perseverance* from England in the package with the peacock screen? I am most distressed at its disappearance."

A look of alarm spreads over Henry's face like a stain.

"It was here in this tea chest. I want to wear it to meet the governor's wife at the ball. She is fashionably attired. I thought it would match my bonnet with white ribbons."

"Oh, I was under the impression that it was a box of rags," says Henry Smythe, "and I gave it away to the poor . . . well, to Mary, actually."

Susan Smythe is horrified and storms in a rage around the drawing room.

"No, it can't be! Have I married an idiot? Tell me that I misunderstand your words? It was blue shot Chinese silk, worth many pounds! And you gave it away . . . to her?"

Mary pours the tea, but her secret is written on her face and the air is thick with moist, mysterious suspicion. The truth is aching to come out.

Sex with Henry after music practice has become routine.

That night, Susan tiptoes down the stairs and sees Mary wearing the blue dress, which now is lifted, bunched up under Mary's arms, the azure ruffles caught in brown fists, the embroidery crushed beneath Henry's thrusting knees. Susan's shocked face stares out of the candlelight; Henry gasps. Mary pulls down the dress and runs to hide in the cupboard under the stairs.

"You monster! You deceitful fornicator! You adulterer! I will kill your strumpet!" shouts Susan.

"Reverend Masters shall hear of your doings, your pathetic life," she screams.

She runs past Mary's hiding place, up the stairs, and into her husband's dressing room. There she attacks Henry's clothes with scissors, cutting them and ripping them with her hands. The servants hear the ripping and screeching. Mary stays hidden, quivering, wondering how it will end. Will Henry beg for forgiveness?

"There you are, you evildoer!" yells Susan as the cupboard door opens. Susan is unhinged. She grabs Mary by the hair and pulls her across the floor. She attacks her with ferocity, and her strength is huge as Mary struggles to keep this betrayed wife from scratching her face.

Cook, who has been wrestling a leg of kangaroo into a pot, runs into the room with the leg still in her hands. She rushes in and uses it to hit Mary across her back. The women part, and Cook drags Mary into the drawing room and throws her at Henry's trembling feet.

"What will be done with the slut, Reverend?" asks Cook.

"My, my! Too much noise on the Sabbath. Leave her there," he says as he takes up his quill and dips it in ink. Mary cowers on the carpet.

Mary does not feel afraid for herself but fears for Eleanor; defiance is perhaps uncalled for. She bends her head in a suitably ashamed manner. Henry cannot look at her. He is hiding his face as he bends to his writing with trembling, coward's hands.

"You are desirous of my attention, dearest?" he poses to Susan, who has entered the room.

He steps away from his writing desk and over the prostrate Mary to pour himself a glass of claret.

It is now clear to Mary that Susan can do anything—nothing is off-limits. Once unleashed, her anger knows no end.

The furious cook drags Mary to the laundry.

Days pass and the house is silent, as they all pretend to go about their work. Susan weeps in corners and Mary knows she must stand her ground while appearing docile. She sings ditties and plays mournful Irish tunes on her violin.

One night Mary hears a crackling noise and smells smoke. She presses her face to the kapok pillow, coughing. She crawls up on her knees to peek through the window, where she sees a small, creeping fire that looks like a snake. She covers her child with a blanket.

Mary hurries out to the field despite being afraid of being attacked and murdered by corn thieves. There, against the light of the yellow flames in the cornfield, she sees Susan in her nightdress, carrying a lantern. Her other hand holds a sheaf of burning straw. Mary thinks of the reverend that morning tending his field of beloved maize, as he walked through, testing the corn for ripeness.

Mary runs to fill a bucket of water and races toward the dancing flames, shouting, "Help! Fire! Fire!"

Then she sees him. She has heard of the attacks on outlying houses by the renegade warrior Chief Jerungi and his band. Jerungi is silhouetted against the hill, holding a woomera, a dozen long spears, and a *boondi* stick with a lumpy hammer end. His head is a mess of plaited hair tied with white kangaroo teeth. Around his shoulders a kangaroo-skin pelt hangs by a rope, and he sports a waistband of plaited reeds. He is nearly naked. He turns toward the building and the light shines on his ocher face and red-painted chest. Mary is terrified. His eyes fall upon Susan in her white slip as she trips across the field, setting fires, unaware of his presence and hers. Mary runs as fast as she can toward Susan, at the same time screaming out to the house, "Henry, your wife is burning the corn!"

She sees Jerungi lift his woomera and swiftly place his spear. His arm stretches back, taking aim. His spear will split Susan in two. Mary stumbles on the corn shafts as Susan delicately places the fire on each stalk; quickly Mary recovers and seizes Susan, taking her to the ground and saving her from the whirring spear. Susan struggles under her.

"You would harm me? Harlot!" she hisses.

A hook spear lands with a thud next to their heads. Mary turns her face toward the hill. Susan is at last aware of the danger.

"Don't move. That Blackfella might kill you," whispers Mary. "Lie still!"

Susan's eyes are wild with fear, and she pushes her face into Mary's shoulder. Amid the confusion, the lantern has tipped oil onto the earth, and it catches fire and burns along the ground. They can hear the clamor of people from the house and school buildings arriving to fight the blaze.

"Susan, where are you?" yells Henry, as he lumbers from the building.

Mary looks up and Jerungi has gone, but she knows they can't hide from him—it is a game he always wins. He has feather feet.

Susan stands up, wiping black ash from her face, her hair disheveled. Mary wipes the mistress's eyes and smooths her hair in a moment of quiet. Susan coughs and straightens her nightdress as they walk toward the house. Mary has her arm about Susan's waist.

"You will not speak of it to him. Please!" pleads Susan.

"I will not."

"Good. I take no responsibility for the work of the devil in this godforsaken hellhole," says Susan.

Susan removes Mary's arm from her waist and walks ahead.

All around, the servants and neighbors run with buckets; they form a chain from the well to douse the flames. Henry is among them in a desperate effort to save the crop. They bucket water onto the flames until the fire is under control. Henry stops to rest and his face is black with ashes. He sees his wife and Mary silhouetted against the smoke in the field.

"What happened?" Henry shouts with a puzzled and wild face.

"Mary set the fire, the native you protect! I tried to stop her," says Susan.

"Lord save us! We required this harvest to survive the winter. The church does not provide enough for all of us. Mary, did you do this?" Henry holds Mary's arms and shakes her.

Mary does not answer; she faces him with a steady gaze.

"They are right! You people cannot be tamed," says Henry Smythe, then turns to his wife.

"Thank you, my dearest Susan, for your valor. We might have lost the school as well," he says tenderly.

Susan stares and smiles at Mary; then Henry carries his wife in his arms across the burned field. At that moment, one of Jerungi's warriors, who had been hidden, rushes down beside the barn and, in an act of revenge for past doings, belts Henry across his back with a waddy. The man flees across the field, like a shadow. Henry collapses and Susan screams and falls to the ground beside him. She leans over to nurse her husband in her arms.

The servants carry Smythe to the house and lay him on the sofa to be cared for by Cook and Susan. He will not die, but he has broken ribs.

The cook tells Mary that she is not needed and Mary walks back to her room and throws herself on her bed. She has run out of options but will find strength and take her daughter away. Her hatred for Henry overtakes all other emotions. She will now happily leave his loathsome house.

Over the next week, Mary makes ready for her departure, and the inevitable long foot walk, with Eleanor, into God knows what. She prepares her belongings carefully and remembers the day she arrived years before at the Parramatta Native Institution, when the dreadful cook gave her a savage scrubbing with a bristle brush, as though to wash off her dark skin. Mary remembers Mrs. Shelley and running away with Boothuri.

She will not ask for anything from Smythe except what she has earned and paid for herself. He must release her from the indenture. But she will have no hesitation in taking whatever provisions she needs. To take from white people is not a bad thing. She ponders the word "thief" and how it refers to her somewhat pathetic pilfering. A few silly chickens and some flour. Now, if she stole a horse or cow, that would warrant the name.

====

The next day, the sun shines and the sky is a radiant blue. The river sparkles and small boats make their way along it; diving ducks plunge into the water and emerge with wiggling fish. The grand sandstone edifice of the Parramatta Native Institution seems untouched by last night's fire.

All the servants and orphans are busy in the field trying to save what is left of the corn. Little children dig and replant seedlings, carrying precious water to each one. Mary wipes her hands on her apron and looks at the place where she saw the warrior standing. She thinks that Jerungi, and perhaps Old Jack, planned the attack, but there is no sign of them. The tracks have been brushed away.

The afternoon is full of work and Mary is polishing silver in the dining room when she hears Henry and his wife walking toward the room. She hides behind the peacock screen.

"Get rid of her!" Susan says with a clear high voice. Henry twitches and ruffles his black hair with nervous fingers. He sits on a couch by his writing desk and taps his quill. He laughs like men do when confronted by a wronged woman.

"Must we discuss this now? I am penning a sonnet and working on my native language book," says Henry. He dips the quill in ink and examines the tip.

"Sonnet? Are you insane? I shall call the doctor to bleed and purge these dark humors," rages Susan.

"We must buy more quills—make a list. . . . She is just a Black servant. Don't be foolish, Susan dearest," says Henry.

"You must choose between rich cream cake and soda bread," says Susan.

Mary leans forward to hear his answer. She holds her breath.

"Don't be ridiculous, dearest. It was a mistake such as many better men than me have also on occasion made. You must forgive me. I command you to find forgiveness. I am only human," says Henry.

"I have heard about such servants! The other colonial wives have spoken of these creatures!" says Susan. "You are shaming me and have no respect for the sacred promise of our marriage. You are a colonial joke. Everyone laughs at you—behind your back—at your lack of Christian fidelity or conscience as you preach your pious sermons on the Sabbath. Look at you now, damaged by a violent savage and yet you dare to defy me and let her stay."

Mary can tell that it can't be going the way he hoped. It must end, of course, it must. She looks at the painted silk screen. There are iridescent Indian peacocks, lilies entwined with bluebells, and pink roses up the edges. She picks a hole in the silk with her fingernail, intending to put her eyes to the hole, but her hand rips the silk and the tear trickles down through the flowers.

"Stupid, stupid girl!" Susan sweeps the screen aside to expose Mary. "You have broken the screen! Am I to pay for everything? Chinese silk is very expensive. Am I never to be free of you?" says Susan.

"I can pay," says Mary.

"With what? Your concubine wages?" asks Susan. Henry squirms.

Mary rises and stands with her head bowed, submissive. She watches the two of them together with teeth clenched. Every scrap of her body rebels. Heat rises up through her neck and bursts through her head; her scalp tingles and a powerful surge of emotion explodes. She sees Susan shaking. Then Henry and Susan lean toward each other like an old married couple. Mary takes off her apron and lays it carefully on the floor. Her face is strong and rebellious. She can no longer play at being a docile maid. Her dark eyes and lustrous lashes gleam as she clears her throat, and the two of them stare at her.

"Are you cold, madam? You look like ice," says Mary. A groan of horror escapes from Henry as he stares at each of them. Susan stands shocked, with her mouth open. Her hands are clasped as in prayer.

"Please, Mary, have some decorum. If you could allow us some privacy," Henry wails from the couch.

"She set fire to that cornfield, not me! It is her fault you were injured. She is an arsonist!" Mary says to him.

"Liar! That thing is your prostitute!" says Susan. She turns to Henry as if she might scratch his face. Susan is young and perhaps has never used this word before. He coughs, then takes a glass of sherry and downs it.

"I have taken vows and pledged my love to you alone, Susan. I carried your miniature in my pocket for three long years while awaiting your arrival," says Henry. "Did you instigate this destruction?"

"Your servant burned the corn with her accomplice renegades. Not me!"

Susan holds her head high and floats from the room like a ghost.

He sighs a deep, sad sigh and they are alone together, but Mary knows the once-gentle love is gone.

"Mary, you will do as I say, or I will be forced to summon the constabulary. If I do, you will be arrested and locked away in the lunatic asylum," he says. "Do you have any conception of the gravity of what you have done?" He is miserable and looks into Mary's face. "Go and get your belongings. Put them in a basket. You must, of course, leave the child and depart this dwelling tonight."

"You cannot have her!" Mary screams.

Henry hangs his head. Mary walks to the door and, through the crack, sees Susan with her ear pressed to the door.

"We will find my mob," says Mary.

"Some of your people are living by the Liverpool clock tower. The word is *ngurra*, is that correct? You can go there." Henry points to the door and looks away.

Mary goes to her room. She is strong and determined. She puts on the blue silk gown and combs her curls. Henry had been unable to resist her in that dress; it still has his smell.

Suddenly an enraged Susan bursts into the room and stands before her. Her face is scarlet. She runs at Mary and tries to rip the dress from her body. Her pale fingers scratch and tear at the dress. In Susan's other hand is a riding crop and she brings it down on Mary's back. She beats her in a frenzy and then attacks Mary's face. Blood drips onto the floor.

Henry bursts into the room and takes Susan's wrist and bends it backward and twists it. She cries out, "I hate you; I hate you!"

"Drop the whip, Susan, dear. I am so sorry. Let God forgive me for this," he whispers as he holds out his hand. Susan drops the whip into his hand and faces him, weeping.

"Really, you surprise me, Henry. And her child, little Eleanor, she is your own true bastard child, isn't she?" asks Susan. "She's yours, isn't she—and hers? Her standing here in my English dress!"

Mary speaks slowly, as if to an old person.

"He gave me the dress. And Eleanor belongs to him. Henry has ridden me many times," says Mary.

"No, Mary. Oh God, please! Don't speak! *Wari wari*," implores Henry Smythe.

He takes Mary's arm and tries to force her to the door, but she grips him by his thin arms and shakes vigorously. His wobbling eyes, her spitting anger, a burst boil, at last out, out. A teacup breaks. She is free inside, something has lifted.

Susan is a pile of desolation as Henry helps her to stand and takes her handkerchief to blot her red face. She whimpers and falls against his chest. Holding the bottom of the torn dress in her hands, Mary backs out of the room, heads to her bed, checks on Eleanor, and collapses, exhausted.

Mary is jolted awake by intense visions. She is fighting off the giant eel spirit and his fierce eye looks directly into hers. He calls her to wake up! He has sharp snapping teeth. Its eel head is tipped on the side and talks to her, calling out for her to play music. Coins fall from the serpent's mouth. It is an awakening! She sees clearly now how she will escape servitude and oppression: She will make a living as a traveling musician.

Mary imagines her warrior family standing before her, painted in white ocher. She will make a new life and become someone who stands apart from the *waibala*. Her bending in subservience will disappear and she will be the valiant one, free from their trickery and seduction. She will find a way to move against the people from the ghost ships who would take the land and imprison her.

Early the next morning, Mary washes her face, dresses in her oldest clothes, and fills a basket from the kitchen with food. Eleanor is asleep, wrapped in a blanket. A cold, stern Henry is at the door.

"That particular English cane basket belongs in this house," says Henry.

"Don't touch it," says Mary with steely determination.

"You never fold properly, let me—" he says as he touches the clothing in the basket and begins to flatten the material. Mary snatches it away, but he sees that she has taken a silver box, carved with phoenix birds and petals. His finger strokes the incised pattern. He covers the box with the cloth and their eyes meet and he says nothing further. He strokes Eleanor's face and sighs.

"Mama, what are we doing?" Eleanor asks.

"We're going away. Come on, little one. We'll go for a big walk," says Mary.

Mary is trembling but feels strong. She cannot spend another night under his roof. She no longer desires him. He could never be a husband—she should have listened to Granny Wiring.

"Of course, as you wish. I could perhaps walk with you to the outskirts of the town. No, my stupidity," says Henry as he mops his forehead. He stretches out his beckoning hand to Eleanor; it hovers and Eleanor clings to her mother.

"You must do as God wills," says Henry. "I leave it to you to decide upon the correct actions. The Lord knows that I have tried to show you good behavior and—"

"You are a devil, *weri waibala*. You preach goodness up in the pulpit but do something else," Mary says, and Henry pulls at his hair.

"I have confessed and been delivered by God's grace," he says with pious tones.

A carriage pulls up outside and they hear the servants welcoming a visitor. Footsteps approach, and in a moment Reverend Masters pokes his head around the door. He holds his black hat under his arm and suddenly he is standing stiffly beside Henry Smythe.

"Ah, there you are, Reverend. I have been summoned by your fearful wife. What ails you, sir?" he asks Henry.

He looks at Mary and her child as though they are rubbish. Eleanor is scared.

"What mischief have you created, girl? She must be turned out immediately," he says to Henry.

"Now, Smythe, I have suggested to Captain Woodrow that he take his troopers and shoot all the Blacks who dare to come into the town and attack your corn—the ones who are armed to the teeth. Renegades. Make manure of them. It is outrageous! Woodrow will collect their heads in a basket like the Frenchies did. Boil them down for Joseph Banks and the Royal Academy. The rest, the tame ones, can be loved like Jesus would." Masters coughs into his hand and Mary is consumed with hatred.

She takes up the basket and heaves the frightened child onto her hip. Henry puts his hand on Eleanor, but Mary's look moves him back.

"I beg you, Mary, leave the *kurung*, your child, with me. No more crying, *yunga*. You can't feed her on vermin out in the bush," says Henry.

"Let the slut go, for God's sake!" implores Masters.

"It is not clear. The world seems full of clamor. Alright, but I will help you on your way. Let me carry the child," says Smythe. "Quickly, before the house is awakened, we can find our way through the kitchen." He tries to take Eleanor, but Mary pulls her away. Meanwhile, Reverend Masters has helped himself to a glass of claret and wipes his face with a lace napkin.

"I will not slink away like a thief. I will go out the front door!" says Mary.

"Leave like a savage, you mean! Slamming doors like a wild creature. You have no manners, despite our best teachings. No grace," says Masters. "I'm certain Henry will miss your fiery presence. Everyone else is so dull."

"I am sorry, Reverend, for you to see this unseemly mess," says Henry, his eyes protruding.

"Your wife, she is stitched up, stiff back. She has got a hard eye. She is like a witch; she's got skinny *nabungs*," says Mary.

"Oh, yes, this is priceless. I must write this down in my language journal. Skinny *nabungs*. Oh, how funny! Write down that word, Henry!" says Masters, and he chuckles with merriment.

"Come, we are going. We can butter our own bread," says Mary as she hugs Eleanor and laughs. The little one holds her tightly.

"There will be little butter where you are headed—to become a harlot in a bawdy house for a penny a go," laughs Masters.

Mary walks down the hallway and straight out the front door, slamming it behind her. Henry Smythe collapses onto the couch.

———

Mary has taken cotton shifts and aprons in the hope that she will find work as a house servant. She has also taken a loaf of bread and a bottle of claret wine from the kitchen, despite Cook's glare. Her violin and bow are wrapped in a blanket.

The dogs follow her even though she tells them to stay. Dogs are smart and know she is leaving. Their tongues loll out and they trot down the path away from the stone building.

Mary walks down the dark road with Eleanor skipping alongside her, singing and clutching her rabbit toy, knitted from brown wool, to her chest. She is blithe and too young to realize how terrible the scene has been.

"Come on, good girl. We will go to find aunty, cousin, grand-father," says Mary.

They walk under a sharp blue eucalypt mist. After a few hours of walking, they are tired and squat against a tree. Mary holds her arms tight around her knees, waiting for some animal or something to give her a sign about where to go.

That night they sleep by the road, Eleanor wrapped in Mary's arms. In the morning they wake and keep walking until they pass a farm. Dogs bark. Mary carries Eleanor on her hip and balances the basket on the other side, and, after a long walk, they arrive in Liverpool town. She sees the tribe happily camped around the big clock tower and wonders what kind of greeting she will receive from the headmen of the Darug Cabrogal mob—King Geoffrey and the other chiefs, Cooman and Gilbert.

CHAPTER SIXTEEN

1832: Liverpool Blacks' Camp

K ings School at Parramatta opens with fanfare, and three small boys of the gentrified squattocracy are delivered to the sandstone gates. A royal heraldic shield reminds all who walk beneath it that the crown of England rules.

Meanwhile, another Englishman, the settler John Macarthur, is formally declared insane and sent to the asylum. A life in the colony can do that.

Not far from Parramatta, the fine sandstone buildings grace the square at Liverpool and the houses around are neat, with thatched roofs and pisé walls. There is a stone bridge and archway, and some young elm trees grow alongside the dirt road. English flowers grow among corn and vegetables. Settlers walk along the street, carrying loads of wheat and fruit to the market. The clock tower is high and impressive, and there, underneath, is the Liverpool Gundungurra tribe. They lounge happily in the shade of trees and cook some ducks on a fire.

As Mary gets closer, she strips a green bough from a wattle tree to show her friendship. She holds it up high in front of her. Red Rose, Blue Poppy, Prince Harris, Nancy, Horace the Duke of York,

Charles the Third, King Geoffrey, and Janet the Cripple. Then there are the cricketers: Willy and Billy Creek. Everyone is happy to see Mary and her child.

Aunty Nancy is at the camp, and she sings with joy to see her long-lost relative. Mary is welcomed by her skin uncles and aunties and cousins. They are responsible for her.

King Geoffrey has many wives and looks at her as if she might be the next one. Mary is not the right skin for him, not the right group for marriage, and he knows this. He is not *molliming*, not a suitable moiety for a husband. If her father were here, he would tell the old man that Mary was not for him, or he might spear him.

No one asks about Mary's life. The here and now is more important. The old women are from both Darug and Gundungurra mobs and have authority to teach her about her relationship to everyone—her kinship—because they are her mother's people. The women pinch Eleanor's face and squeeze her cheeks. They hold her hand up and examine the cuticles for their color. She has golden curls, and they admire her pink ribbons.

The old women take Mary and her child to the nearby bush to paint ocher mud on their bodies for a welcome corroboree—they will be safe from the great eel spirit that lives in the nearby lagoon. The middle of the lagoon has a whirlpool that can suck you down. The eye of Garangatch lives there, and old women call out to the spirits to introduce them to the newcomers.

After the corroboree, old Nancy stands by a termite mound and listens to the white ants making buildings and preening their queens. She takes Eleanor's hand and rests it on the red mound so she, too, can learn to hear this.

They settle in the camp, making a *gunyah* of paperbark, but Mary sees some of the other tribal woman laughing at her. The women snicker and hide their mouths, whispering. They see she is an outcast, not grown up under the protection of King Geoffrey, not a true member of the tribe but a runaway from *waibala*. Her clothes mark her as a servant, and so the women begin to take away her things. Poppy wears the apron over her naked body. Mary holds on to her shift and growls as they laugh and grab little Eleanor. She is stripped like a corn cob with her pretty dress gone and then her bloomers removed to much laughter. Eleanor stands naked and shaking, her eyes large and pleading. Mary grabs her daughter and hides her in her arms. She manages to wrestle back a shift for Eleanor to put on.

But she must learn to share others' things, even her child. She must be like the old people and not like a *waibala*. They huddle by a small fire as the other human bodies and dogs make a wall of comfort around them. Mary and Eleanor are protected and wanted. It might be the easiest thing in the world to become part of this tribe.

Mary remembers her childhood and her joyful aunts—swimming for lily pods and chewing the roasted seeds from the pods; smiling with them while listening to stories of dreams and spirits; and calling out to the little spirit hairy fellas, "Shhh, hairy fellas," so they wouldn't steal the lizards and bush tucker like yam, *midin*. Those little fellas were everywhere wanting that food.

The old women smoke clay pipes. They smile and, with upward signs, ask Mary for baccy, but she has none. She presents the bottle of wine to King Geoffrey, and he laughs as he uncorks it. The bottle passes from mouth to mouth and soon it's empty. Then it disappears into a dillybag. The glass will be used to make spear points.

Mary's basket is empty, the clothes are worn by anyone who can get hold of them, but she has managed to hide the silver box and her violin in her blanket. In her basket, she has brought a booklet for writing. Mary writes her name on the page, and everyone gathers around to see this magic. Poppy takes the pencil and tastes it. Then she breaks it on the ground. Mary retrieves it and carefully keeps the broken bits. This ability to write is a gift; her teachers and the tumbling years of school are a safe memory.

After a few days, there is no food left in the camp, and everyone forages for something to eat—geebungs or small goannas. Mary sits by the fire but is still unsure of her rightful place and can't work out what to do—she feels useless. She is not used to a rough life on hard ground. Mary sings an English song, then plays the violin for Eleanor; the women clap and laugh.

Mary knows she has been called back to her country. The beautiful land has called her, and she is with her own people, so she makes some tea in a billy to share among the ten of them. One chipped cup is passed around and everyone mutters about finding some more food. The senior women are strong and knowledgeable about what bush food they can gather, and they discuss the ripening lily bulbs they can harvest from a billabong and roast.

Eleanor takes up some bright orange seed pods from a cycad and an old aunt rushes to stop her. She explains how this food is poison and must be handled with paperbark, then ground on stones, and soaked for a long time. Then it can be baked in ashes and eaten. Mary listens intently because such a mistake can make you die— *baletti.*

King Geoffrey is tall and dressed in a blanket tied at the shoulder with kangaroo sinews and he uses Mary's skirt as a cloak. He has a belt of human hair string with a wooden fighting club hanging down, and a topknot with wallaby teeth. The women wear English bonnets and voluminous skirts or nothing at all. Some of his wives wear white pipe clay in a cap covered by bark string on their hair to remember the dead. They all burn red termite bed to keep away the mosquitoes.

In the late afternoon, the women help Mary make reed-and-shell necklaces, while one plaits kangaroo teeth on leather to decorate her hair. Another wraps her in a warm possum-skin cloak, and she feels alive with their love and kindness. Her memory of the time with Smythe and Masters is fading; her servitude seems horrible and she wonders how she could have lived in such a way. Her reliance on *waibala* is now shameful.

A few days later and it is another Native Feast Day in Windsor town, and the clan walk all morning to attend. They will receive blankets from the government and have their names recorded in the big ledger. Mary carries Eleanor on her shoulders and tramps along in a line of native women. She is one of their tribe. But there is constant hunger and illness.

Flags and flowers decorate the town of Windsor for the feast day, and fifty natives gather in the main square near the Macquarie Hotel. Sitting among some women is Mercy, who has also run away from English service after being insolent to her employer, Reverend Masters; she now lives a hand-to-mouth existence with the South Creek mob. Mercy has displayed her resilience in moving away from being a servant: it is rumored that she left a pile of *goona* shit on Masters's bedroom floor. Mercy is round and beautiful as she stands up and swings her hips in the white dress she stole from Masters's house. She smiles with recognition of Mary.

"That old fella too stinky for me, all the time he grab me and I run away again," says Mercy.

Mary hugs Mercy but detects something new about her. She has named herself White Rose and seems to be making money by selling herself to selected *waibala* males.

The clan build a fire in the town square and sit down to wait for the gifted English food and *bool*, a drink of rum and water.

In the distance Mary sees Chief Jerungi walking with some other men. He is unaware that he is wanted by colonial police. Mercy waves and smiles at him. She flirts and he looks at her body with a grin—she is tempting even though she is the wrong skin for him. He strolls toward them and squats by the fire in front of Mary and Mercy.

"*Wiang* sister, *naiya* Native School, remember me: Teddy. You can talk to whitefella, *paialla waibala*. You write letter for governor, take letter," says Jerungi. Mary shakes her head as he tries to find the words to convince her.

"*Jumna ngandu*, Mercy *naiya nallawalli* she stays here," says Mary.

"You write letter, save people from big trouble," says Jerungi.

"*Bobbina*, brother, no letter. *Pittuma karndo*. We're nothing," says Mary.

Mary is quiet and will not be forced to do the will of this chief. But Jerungi is not happy as he strides away with his companions, and she is ashamed that she won't help him, that she has no power. She fights the rising confusion again. Her feelings of insignificance stop her from writing any letter to a governor.

The women are now hungry and Eleanor grows thin and sickly.

"We might get job again with Masters, he pay me good money and food. We gunna starve here, you come too?" says Mercy.

Mercy takes Mary by the hand and asks her to return to Windsor and try to work again with Reverend Masters. It is a thought that repulses Mary, but she is desperate and senses the need for survival from her friend.

The women sit for hours in the shade waiting for food, and Eleanor is tired and thirsty. At last they get the feast of beef and damper. A soldier brings a basin full of drink; the men drink a lot of *bool* and get drunk, but not Jerungi. He sits warily alone under a tree watching them.

Mary searches the crowd of English people but can find no acquaintances and marvels at how quickly she has become invisible to them. She is now one of the tribe and of no consequence to the colonial authorities. She feels as if she has stripped off her paler skin and now wears the skin of native women.

By sunset the clan has walked back to Liverpool and is back at King Geoffrey's camp. Men fight and club each other, and the women hide in the bushes. Mary prays that it's not her head that will be broken tonight. Mercy asks her again to run away to Windsor soon.

Next morning, Mary gathers wood and starts the fire from ashes. She boils water for tea.

"Mary, *karndo*, damper!" This is a command from the king, as if Mary can perform magic. She knows that she is not a slave to the king, who has ten wives to wait on him and countless children, but he is frightening because he is a *Karadja* man who can use his doctor stone, his *Karadja Kibba*, which cures spear wounds or illness. He keeps it hidden and wrapped in skins.

One night, Mary accidentally sees him unwrap the crystal quartz stone, which means if she had been seen, she could be "sung to death by magic." As a child she was taught the importance of staying away from the old men's objects. The king senses Mary near. He turns around suddenly and, in a moment, Mary knows he could kill her. She sweats with fear and pretends to brush the ground with a twig as if she has not witnessed anything, but, still, she is terrified of him.

Mary sits far off from King George and his wives. The chief approaches them with a stern expression and Mary's fear grows. He indicates the dillybag she carries. Mercy nods to her friend. He knows what is in it. Mary takes out the silver box and offers it to him. He points to the ground in front of him and she places it down on the earth. This is the payment for her transgression of seeing the stone; she watches as the box is placed in the chief's own dillybag. Gone forever. He motions to her violin, but she shakes her head.

She finds Mercy and says she is now willing to run away with her and find employment, as it is dangerous to make a chief angry. Mary waits until dawn and then grabs Mercy and takes Eleanor's hand and walks onto the road, carrying her violin.

The child is dressed in rags and a scarf, so she is not naked. A few hours later, they see other native families begging for food, standing with their heads bowed. She feels the shame and Mary knows she can't do that—but she can play her music for coins. But Mercy has no problem begging. An Englishwoman holds lace to her nose when Mary passes. She burns with anger and bitterness.

Mary and Mercy give every morsel of food to Eleanor, but she is still hungry and cries pitiful tears. Mary hugs her tight.

"I'm sorry for this life," says Mary.

Mary curtsies to a passing Englishman.

"Pardon, sir," Mary speaks in her finest English voice. "May I work for you, so I can earn money to buy food for my child?"

The man is well dressed. His eyes sweep down the poor clothes while his wife grips his coat.

"Husband!"

"Sorry, lass, I have no employment for you, but have a penny," he says and flicks it to Mary, who sees it roll in the dirt. She watches it but doesn't move. Eleanor picks up the coin and grips it tightly in her fist. Eleanor and Mary continue down the street and repeat the performance. Seldom has Liverpool town seen a native woman dressed in a dirty white petticoat who could speak perfect English. She is a perfect mimic. She buys loaves of fresh bread and flour and treacle.

The road to Windsor is long and a few days later, Mary lies against a stone wall in a miserable cold wind and presses Eleanor to her chest to warm her.

All day, Mary and Mercy walk toward Windsor town and are closer to Masters's estate, but they are afraid of being caught up in the fighting of the town drunks, white men and Black men tussling outside the hotel. They are exhausted and camp near the South Creek, by a small fire. They have had nothing to eat except wattle gum, and Eleanor cries. Her arms and legs are stick thin.

The next day, as they walk along the track to Masters's estate, a carriage approaches. The ornate vehicle comes to a halt, the black door opens, and the steps are lowered. A black shoe with a silver eagle buckle appears, then a white stocking, followed by a plump girth. It is Reverend Masters.

"Hold the horses, driver. Come here, my girl," says Masters to Mercy as he crooks a finger and holds his frock coat out of the mud.

"Yes sir, we want work," says Mercy.

"You are on your way to ask me for employment again? After your disgraceful departure? I see you are destitute. You always come crawling back. I can forgive your insolent actions. But really, my dear, you left shit in my slipper! I do love a bit of fight in a woman. Come along and bring the others. I am not a cruel man and I have ample work for all Blacks who wish to earn a decent living. No thieving or cheeking me, mind you! Follow along the road to my estate and go around to the kitchen. Hop to it!"

Mercy is delighted and she takes up Eleanor in her arms and trots off behind the carriage. Mary shakes her head and follows.

CHAPTER SEVENTEEN

1833: Masters's Estate

The lunatic asylum operates at Saint Luke's parsonage in Liverpool. The inmates receive moral treatment involving purging of the body to eradicate black bile, a treatment known as "blisters to the head," and bloodletting with leeches. These are used to treat mental patients. Milk of poppy is introduced by juicing unripe opium plants, and this is considered effective.

Reverend Masters visits the more gentrified of the inmates to ensure he is not forgotten in their wills.

———

It is many years since Mary entered employment with *waibala* like Smythe. Now Mary and Mercy work for Reverend Masters on his large sheep and wheat estate on South Creek. The house has tall pillars of white stucco out front and a steep thatched roof. English oak trees grow down the road that leads to the house. A kitchen garden at the back is full of pumpkins and fruit trees. Outhouses cluster around stables and the kitchen, which has a huge woodstove. Mary has a position as a servant in the kitchen and the laundry. Her job is to chop wood and keep the stoves and boilers alight. Mercy is a house servant in a starched black-and-white uniform. They are as close as two mice.

At the estate, they are sure of shelter and food, and will not take to the road again. They have heard about the *gal gal* (smallpox) in the Kings Town up north. The disease is killing hundreds of their people, and they die miserable deaths; the stories are terrible.

Mercy hopes to escape the rough life of a refugee and enjoy a life of leftover cake and nice dresses as a maid. If she can secure a person to look after her, forever. Yes, that would be a plan. She sees no need to be self-sufficient like Mary wants to be. As she works, she thinks of her parents, and Mercy regrets having lost her family when they tried to escape from troopers. To remember the scene is cruel. Her parents fled over a fern-covered cliff. Well, she was only five years old, and it seems as though they had flown like birds. Her father was hit by a firestick, causing a spout of red blood, and her mother took one last look at Mercy and dropped into the misty air and crashed on the black rocks under the mountain waterfall; the noise was terrible. It was part scream, part thundering torrent. Mercy was picked up by a trooper and delivered to the Parramatta Native Institution.

And buried deep down in her memory are her little ones, floating in the watery sky, choking on a gray membrane that covers their throats. A sob now escapes from Mercy's mouth, and she stifles it as she waits at table.

"Buck up, girl. Stand up straight, for God's sake. The cause of smallpox, pestilence, and death is natives searching for the devil. It must be a punishment from God to bring light to all heathens," says Masters.

Mary hears that the governor is coming over the rough roads to South Creek and she climbs up on the barn roof in time to see soldiers galloping past the house to check for his safety. Some wear red woolen coats and helmets of gold; some hold the reins of horses without saddles, their dark flanks glinting in the morning light. The men have ammunition strapped to their chests as if they are going to a foreign war. She hears a mournful sound overhead and, looking up, sees a flock of black swans flying toward her, flashing and beautiful in the pale pink sky. She thinks of herself flying away like these swans.

In the kitchen, she has been given responsibility for peeling garlands of garlic, tubs of onions, beetroot, carrots, and turnips that are stacked on benches ready for a feast. In the garden, she picks a pile of beans and cabbages and gives them to the cook. She checks the outhouse meat room, where the hooks are hung with upside-down native quail and pheasants, wild swans and ducks, and kangaroo legs. There is abundance here.

Working in the kitchen allows Mary to watch these men and listen to their gossip. She hears about Chief Jerungi and how he will come to speak to the governor at Masters's house.

Next day, Mary serves the tea at the great dark wooden table and keeps her head low. Her thumb is in the sugar bowl, and she licks her fingers. She takes a pinch for her daughter. Eleanor is in the kitchen near the stove, where she plays all day, until she is taken to bed in the servants' quarters near the barn.

Mary is invisible in the great house, but she listens. She gathers any snippets of information she can. The talk is serious and dark: all about killing, as though it is sport. Bushwhack, take a crack at a Black. She has a vision of herself on horseback, riding to tell the renegades that they must not trust any governor and that the troopers are coming. Their guns will bring death and misery. But she has never ridden a horse.

Mary has matured and become more astute; she finds determination brewing in her heart. She digs in the garden and talks to visiting birds: the rainbow lorikeets, white cockatoos, and warbling currawongs, all waiting for her to treat them with a handful of oats or grain. She pours a pitcher of water out onto a tray for the birds to drink and finds their friendship heartening.

Captain Woodrow is a guest at Masters's house and Governor Ralph Darling is about to arrive, so there is a flurry of preparation. The estate must show all its glory, with all the Black servants dressed in white as they line up near the colonnade of English trees. Masters has arranged a display of great wealth with ivory tusks and a canteen of silver cutlery. Mary rushes back and forth with platters for afternoon tea. She has become a valued servant and this position ensures her child's safety.

Governor Darling steps down from his carriage. He is an imposing man with a balding head. Woodrow holds out his hand to guide him. The rumor among the servants is that this governor is a tyrant who tortures prisoners and bans theatrical entertainments in the colony. He was once a dictator over the people in Mauritius. He looks about at the opulence and nods.

"I have seen estates as rich as this in Mauritius when I was stationed there. The Frenchies grew sugar cane with Negro slaves as labor, which we endeavored to outlaw," says Governor Darling. "I trust this estate is not profiting from government spending?"

"Oh, heaven forbid," Masters replies.

Rodney, the Jamaican, ushers in the governor and welcomes his aide-de-camp. After much bowing and scraping by Masters, they settle into the drawing room. Mary serves tea and waits at the table; it is an opportunity to listen to the events of the colony being recounted.

"Sir, if you receive this renegade chief, perhaps he can bring some peace among his people," says Captain Woodrow. "They are not all untrustworthy. I actually trust the natives more than the convicts. I had an encounter on the road to Hunter River with a Black Jamaican. He was seven feet tall and had a gang of thieves. We had to ride for days with our pistols in our hands. They would hunt us down and kill us just to get our guns and horses. After a week, we smelled like a Calcutta sewer. What do you think, Mary James, of such a story? Speak up!" The governor and captain are looking at her.

"One day she may be able to lead us to capture her rebellious countrymen in the mountains," says the governor.

"She is just a servant, sir," says Masters.

"I know nothing, sir. I just work here," Mary says as she gives a curtsy and places the teapot on the table. Rodney motions to her to be quiet.

"Oh yes, you can read, as we know. But you are also known for stealing, but not able to follow a track? You resided with your tribe for months, I hear. This might be your best skill; we shall test you," says Woodrow.

"Leave her. She is reformed, aren't you, Mary, my pet? A bit of stick is a great reformer, do you not agree, Governor? She knows her place now," says Masters. "Keeps me well fed, too. She is motivated by a need to feed her illegitimate daughter. I think she hopes I will explode like ripe fruit. But she has become docile; no insolence, nothing like what I have to put up with from naughty Mercy. Oh, the natives can fight alright, especially the women, like cats. The men are quite valiant in battle. However, between them and us there is little compassion, no real deals, or peace. What do you say, Mary, about this chief? What have you heard?"

"He can turn into a crow and fly above men's heads. He has wings as wide as a tree. But he cannot be killed," says Mary. Woodrow laughs.

"Crows are known to eat the traitors after they've been drawn and quartered in the Tower of London," says Masters.

"I have reports that Jerungi has the ability to organize rebellion. It will be an eternal war until they die out, or until we have strict adherence to regulations. They will come to learn obedience," says the governor.

"We hear how Governor Phillip dealt with them," says Woodrow.

"Pemulwuy killed seventeen Englishmen and he was decapitated, along with six of his warriors—Bennelong gave him away. Captain Watkin Tench of the Royal Marines and his men of the New South Wales Corps—they thought they could take 'em. But now, now we are outnumbered fifteen to one by convicts. Those were the days, days of action, not pontification."

"Ask the Aborigine lass here. What does she think?" says the governor.

"I'm just a servant, sir. But I think this chief wants to talk peace. We are people too, not animals," says Mary.

Rodney quietly pulls her away from the table.

"A little insolent, aren't you, Mary?" says the governor. "We all want peace. You are of no consequence in the great world. Discipline is what all the colony needs. Sometimes I think that the fear of native insurgency is nothing compared to the home-grown monsters whom we have around us."

"In Newcastle, we have transferred the majority of felons to Port Macquarie. No more penal law," says Woodrow.

"We have built the beautiful Christ Church Cathedral," says Governor Darling. He sips at his tea, eats his scone, and continues, "And I established the Church and School Corporation to complete the division of settled parts of the colony into counties and parishes."

"Indeed, I agree that we need more order. I fear that some escaped convicts have turned to cannibals. Our men ride in fear of every sound, every crack of a stick," says Woodrow.

"I have issued statements regarding native felons," says the governor. "On any occasion of seeing or falling in with the natives, either in bodies or singly, they are to be called upon, through our friendly native guides, to surrender themselves as prisoners of war. If they refuse to do so, or make the least show of resistance, or attempt to run away from us, the soldiers will fire and compel them to surrender. I have summoned Chief Jerungi here today to examine him. We will see what he thinks about our orders for the soldiers to break and destroy the spears, clubs, and waddies of all those we take as prisoners. Such natives that happen to be killed on such occasions, if they are grown men, are to be hanged up on trees in conspicuous situations, to strike the survivors with the greater terror. However, just for today, mind, we have promised Mr. Jerungi a safe passage."

Mary hears the governor's words about Jerungi's band and understands the meaning. He will be hunted down and end up on a gibbet. The governor is looking at a cream cake and she pours yet another cup of tea. She pushes the dish of red jam toward his hand and her eyes meet his. He holds the gaze for a moment. There is a hint of suspicion that she might be an enemy. He is correct.

"Sir, we must carry out the best methods by which to make our colony safe. Jerungi may offer a truce, or we will have to eradicate them all. You know we search for coal, but I observe many indications of tin and copper. I carry a divining rod and, no, it is not witchcraft," Woodrow says and reaches for his divining rod.

"Sounds like it to me. Would God approve?" Masters frowns.

"This is simply made from willow twigs picked at the right time of year. You wish to try it, sir?" asks Woodrow. He hands it to Rodney, who passes it to the governor to hold. He measures it in his hand.

"Is it science? Here, Mary, try the magic stick. It will tell us where water flows."

The governor hands the stick to Mary; it wavers in her hands, and they all laugh.

"It points to water under this house," says Mary.

"You might have the power for divination," says the governor.

The aide-de-camp enters the room and speaks to the governor. "Governor, he is here, Mr. Jerungi. He is waiting but I warn you, sir, to be very cautious. He is volatile and unpredictable."

Masters and Woodrow stand and gesture to the door.

"We could have done with the skills of Bungaree, to interpret. However, I hear he is dead," says Masters.

"Poor Bungaree. He circumnavigated the continent but all he could do in the end was make a living selling peaches at Kirribilli," says Masters. "Oh, and apricots. However, his son, Bowen, is held in high esteem. He is said to be an excellent tracker and boatswain. He speaks countless native tongues and, as such, went on the Oxley expedition. Extraordinary."

"Before he enters, tell me about this highly regarded native you are about to bring into my presence," says the governor. "You see, we have a pressing need to build the roads and get access to the Hunter River to Newcastle in the north, and I do hope he can assist us to achieve this zealous endeavor."

"I suspect that Chief Jerungi is guilty of committing depredations against settlers, but he begs a pardon from you in return for our military's safe passage around the new townships," says Woodrow.

"You, girl." The governor crooks his finger at Mary. "Does he speak on behalf of all Blacks?" he asks.

"He speaks on behalf of humanity, sir. He seeks justice, a pardon," says Mary.

Masters coughs. "What nonsense, a pardon indeed. Off with his head! I know for a fact that Mrs. Masters almost had an abomination committed against her." He looks pointedly at Mary as if she is to blame. "She was assaulted by one of Mary's heroes. In Mrs. Masters's own bed, in her own house on a Sunday afternoon, when I was detained with my church obligations. Not nice, is it? Terrible. I am beside myself with guilt for not being able to protect her. Why, she has gone home to England, just like that, and I am all alone."

"I am sorry to hear that, Reverend. Now, however, we must cordially receive this servant's countryman," says Woodrow.

"I desire revenge for my wife, but I am forbidden by the church. Henry Smythe took some of my muskets and he has been practicing his shooting," says Masters.

"This assault on her is indeed an outrage," says the governor.

"Do you wish to still see Jerungi?" asks Woodrow.

"I will allow Chief Jerungi to approach my person as I am eager to make friends with the peaceful natives. We can't take offense at every native in the whole country. Some must be tamed so that they can be used as ambassadors for their people," the governor says and grins benignly.

Captain Woodrow beckons the aide to fetch the visitor. Mary strains to see the warrior.

Rodney ushers in Chief Jerungi. He is tall and imposing and wears military trousers and has a topknot of white feathers. The warrior has cicatrices carved in his chest and shoulders and large, muscled arms. He has a strong brow and no shirt or shoes. He lays down ten sharp spears with flint tips and a carved hardwood woomera by the hat stand. He strides forward as though he is entertained by a governor every day. He stands by a plush green chair as the governor takes a monocle and examines him like a specimen.

"Welcome, King Jerungi. I take it that you wish to bring peace. Take a seat. I believe that you speak some English. You were educated at our Native School, is that correct?" says the governor.

"They call me Teddy. But I run away." He does not sit down but walks about the room nonchalantly and lifts glass paperweights to look through them.

"Of course, you did," the governor says. He grins and indicates for Mary to pour some tea in a cup for him. Jerungi pushes the cup away and pours himself wine in a glass. Mary nods at Jerungi and he smiles at her and winks.

"Talk now about my mob. No more killing," Jerungi says and stares directly at the governor, as an equal. No one seems to be sure of how to proceed. Everyone is tinged with nervousness, except for Jerungi, who is at ease.

"You are safe here. I see you as an esteemed envoy for your people. Be assured, you will not be harmed," says the governor. "I am a man of my word, and I believe you can be the man to lead your people through these challenging times."

The governor holds his chin and continues to stare with fascination. There is a tension in the room, as though something were about to break. And it does. Jerungi snaps the stem of a crystal wine glass and Masters jumps up and shouts.

"Take care, you barbarian!"

Captain Woodrow also rises and stands to attention by the governor while Rodney reaches for the broken glass.

"Don't worry, Mr. Jerungi, there will be an excess of such glasses, all shipped at great expense from London," says the governor.

Jerungi pushes up his kangaroo-skin garment and sits down at the table opposite the governor; the aide-de-camp moves to his side.

"Governor, you trust captain?" asks Jerungi as he looks at Captain Woodrow.

"He will be made a major, because of his coal discoveries near Hunter River," he says.

"You want peace, for our mob not attack English?" asks Jerungi.

"That would be absolutely correct. How can we achieve this?" the governor asks as he nods his head.

"This captain kill lotta mob," says Jerungi, glaring at Woodrow.

"Of course, I understand. Out you go, Woodrow. We can manage quite well in these delicate matters without you. They must have good memories of you," says the governor, not concealing his sarcasm.

"Tiddle off, Woodrow, there's a good fellow," adds Masters.

The captain walks out of the room. He is furious.

Mary looks through the window and feels the strangeness of Jerungi sitting on a red velvet chair at the table with the governor.

Masters looks uncomfortably hot and pulls at his collar and rubs his face. The air is as thick as jam. Suspicion dribbles from the walls.

"If I may speak, Governor. This savage is not to be trusted," says Masters, while Mary waits by the table with intense interest.

"Well, Mr. Jerungi, you have all managed to bring insurrection despite our trust in your chiefs," says the governor. "The old governor promised you a generous feast day and I expected on my arrival in the colony to also have a harmonious coexistence with your fellow natives. Is it not so?"

"That old governor sometimes good. Sometimes not," says Jerungi.

"He remembers the punitive expedition of 1817. He won't look upon colonial authority with any acceptance," says Masters.

"If I am ignorant of the apparent motivations for the attacks against us, how can I understand?" asks the governor.

"He is a natural killer. White women and children have been butchered by his band of savages. What on earth can we hope to gain by simply talking to him, a heathen? I pray to God you know what you are doing, sir," says Masters.

Mary feels a rush of fear and clutches the windowsill and can sense a terrible thing may happen.

"Peace. It is my personal wish to have a peaceful settlement under my guidance in this new world," says the governor. "English men and families are coming here in thousands—not just felons, but respectable immigrants with considerable assets. We must offer security. Trade, Christianity, all will flow if we can come to some peaceful arrangement with the hostile natives." The governor is passionate and loud. He faces Jerungi with an imploring look, and Mary watches with growing anxiety.

Suddenly, Jerungi moves in his seat. He reaches forward and strokes Reverend Masters's collar. Mary holds her breath. Jerungi takes hold of this collar and pulls Masters's plump face up against his own. He seems to breathe in the *waibala*'s air. The governor is alarmed and the aide-de-camp rushes forward to seize Jerungi's arm, squeezing it to make him release the now-choking Reverend Masters. There is loud coughing and Captain Woodrow bursts into the room, cutlass drawn, and Mary ducks to the floor.

"Unhand him!" the captain demands, and Jerungi laughs like a storm.

The captain, Rodney, and the aide-de-camp grab Jerungi and drag him from the room. As they do, he reaches out for his cup of tea and sips it as he is pulled away. The tiny china teacup is covered in pink roses, and he hands it to Mary, who is dumbfounded. Mary looks at the cup. She is awfully fond of pretty china.

"Death for *waibala*!" Jerungi yells as he is hauled to the stockade outside. Masters is still coughing and trying to regain his voice.

"Damn scoundrel!"

The governor wipes his face with a handkerchief and everyone is quiet. Mary slips out of the open door to watch where Jerungi is taken. No one sees her go.

Later that evening, Mary visits the wooden stable where Jerungi sits, imprisoned. It has been boarded up on all sides except at a small door. Mary has no fear, only a need to help this man. The coming darkness covers her; she is a creature of the dusk, a gray kangaroo leaning softly against the wood. She scrapes at the door and digs a hole at the bottom.

There is no guard, and she whispers to Jerungi, "*Bobbina, karndo.*" She pushes an orange under the door and some damper. A Black hand takes the food.

"*Wiang*, help me?" he asks, then says, "*Yuin, womra*, dig."

Mary runs to the shed, finds a garden trowel, and puts it under the door. She quietly walks back to her bed and sleeps soundly knowing that the great warrior will be gone by daybreak. He will fly through the night on dark wings—no white man can hold him long.

In the morning, Mary wakes and Captain Woodrow is there. He stands by the bed with the trowel in his hands. His thumb caresses the rusty metal; it rubs along the edge and his eyes do not leave her face. She hangs her head and suppresses a laugh of victory.

"You did this? You helped him escape," says Woodrow, "like an Indian fakir with magic at your fingertips. You are a naughty girl. Do you want to end up in the stocks?"

Mary pulls the blanket up to her chin and sings, "The grand old Duke of York, he had ten thousand men; he marched them up to the top of the hill and he marched them down again." The captain pulls down her blanket and glares at her.

"I swear that if I can prove you had a hand in this escape, I will have you tried and locked up for eternity. You know the Female Factory? Well, I will make sure you go to the prison and rot. And we will remove your little girl. I hoped for loyalty from you!"

"What loyalty? Me, all alone with no tribe. You will not take my girl," she shouts.

He turns and walks out of the room, and she hides her face under the blanket. She can hear him swear as he steps with his clean boots into horse shit.

Later that evening, the captain's plans are being discussed. The gathered white men sit by the fire and Mary listens but is invisible to them.

"I have a splendid notion that is as simple as the Blacks themselves are. I will offer this renegade Jerungi power—everyone likes that, even the primitives," says Woodrow. "We as colonial authorities will appear to be conciliatory, to want to keep the peace between our Black brethren and ourselves, the superior race. I will offer conditions for their surrender. Modest ones, mind; the man is not stupid. Then, there will come a time when this treacherous leader will want to barter with us. They do like to trade. We will quarrel and there will be an accidental skirmish and a shot and that's the end of it. The land is quite ours already, anyway." The captain puffs on his pipe and leans forward to stare at Masters.

"A bit ruthless, isn't it? Smythe would say: 'Where is God's word in this?' How can we bring the natives to the faith if we keep killing them?" Masters says while thoughtfully picking his teeth. "Surely, a gentle coercion is what is needed, the taking of children to train for service. Some kindness and the love of God. They are useful for farmworkers and we require them if we are to grow the colony."

"You have a righteous belief in our conquering a lesser race of mankind," says Woodrow. "Of course, Jerungi can lead his people to your church, you will offer tobacco and blankets, and that always works. Of course, you have noticed the decrease in their numbers? Disease such as measles and whatnot."

"And bung-head or *bool*—it makes them daft as a dill brain," says Masters as he crooks a finger to Mary and she pours another sherry into the captain's glass.

"I often wonder what we are doing here. We deserve some medals for this service for king and country," says Woodrow, "but I tire of medals; I have a pile from the European wars. What madness made you leave your comfortable living in Cornwall to come to this shithole, anyway? And don't say God told you to come. Because that is bunkum." The captain is standing now, poking his finger into Masters's chest. He is drunk, or they both are.

"*C'est la vie*, eh? No, I will not make a trite answer, although the Lord did appear once with a demand that I give up my life for Him," says Masters. "Don't you laugh at my deep and abiding commitment to religion. Mary, more wine!" Masters yells and she obliges.

"I am waiting," says Woodrow.

"I was drawn to my great work ordained by God because of some unfortunate occurrence back home."

"I ascertained as much. We are nearly all on an adventure to escape from something, we New South Welshmen."

"You must promise not to divulge any information, no gossip please, I beg you. I was caught doing something," says Masters.

"Ah, an indiscretion of a moral kind?" asks Woodrow.

"I was cruel. I beat them. Badly. Oh, we are not nasty folk. In fact, my family treated our slaves well in Jamaica, and I now regret slavery," says Masters. "My Black butler is here of his free will."

"I see. Disgrace," says Woodrow.

"I had no choice but to take up the bishop's offer of this position in a far-off colony. It was either here or Patagonia and fever," says Masters, as he coughs into his handkerchief. "But now, I have damned gout! Is that right, Mary? Gout? More wine, girl!"

Masters has his face in his hands and Mary stands nearby pouring wine. She pushes his handkerchief toward him on the table. She wishes she could jump on his head and push her fingers into his eyeballs until they pop out.

"Yes, I see. Have another drink," says Woodrow. "That impenetrable forest is our insurmountable enemy. But we have ongoing coal extraction and perhaps even gold. We have a lust for it, do we not? But that northern forest exhausts my attempts to find safe passage to Hunter River. A place of murder and rapine. Too many *myall* natives."

"The good and the bad," says Masters.

"I go with my armed men but even the trees are homicidal. They fall in the wind and are hundreds of feet tall. The timber cutters go at it day and night. I have taken shots at fleeing Blacks and seen them drop after one shot. A crack shot. Once we were surrounded by forty of them, armed to the teeth. A fearsome sight, bones in their septum, hideous war paint, and a fearful drumming of spearthrower on shield. But we can strike terror in their hearts," says Woodrow.

"And you have no conceit," says Mary.

"Mary is always here with an uncalled-for opinion. It is extraordinary to hear her apparent intelligence. Lots of English words. And damned musical. And I agree that some of the warriors have valor. Pemulwuy was an extraordinary fighter; it seemed he could not die. He had but one eye but could see for miles. Head in a bottle in London now," says Woodrow.

"Oh yes, pickled Pemulwuy."

"There was a battle, reported but briefly in the *Sydney Gazette*," says Woodrow.

Mary leans against the table to listen.

"Move off, girl," says Masters.

"No, let her report this back to her countrymen," says Woodrow.

"We were camped in a small valley and the tribe that came were called Darkinjung. It was before dawn, toward Hunter River, and, other than one killing of a native the day before, we hadn't seen any. We had left that body with arms asunder; then the lieutenant had the idea to leave his corpse as a deterrent, as we had done this often before. We hung him on a tree, like Christ. One soldier made a wreath of thorns."

Mary's face turns pale; her hands clench her smock.

"Blasphemy, I know. Don't be shocked, Mary. It is, after all, war."

"No governor proclamation will protect settlers and shepherds out there," says Masters.

"I didn't want them to follow and ambush us. I was of the mind to frighten them," says Woodrow. "To show them who is boss. You see, you don't know they are there. It's a superhuman ability to be one with the forest. There were bird calls, loud and piercing in the mist, and we woke to see the hill above us had a row of silhouettes. Natives by the hundreds, all loaded with countless spears. They kept coming like Zulus. The rattling began, a terrifying noise of spears and waddies against shields. My men were caught unawares, and we were in a panic as we grabbed our muskets and shot." He refills his glass.

"Tales of derring-do! You'd like to be one of those warriors, eh, Mary? And cut off our heads," says Masters.

"I held my spyglass up and focused on the leader as he stood tall among the other men," says Woodrow. "Totally fearless, they tore down the hill as the men fired again and again, and faced our guns as if they were nothing. We scrambled for powder. The hook spears tore through our men and they died in agony, if not that day, later by infection and miasma. We ran away from the carnage, Black and white bodies piled up in that lovely valley. We ran all morning and into the night. Certain that we were followed, we were tortured by the smoke signals and echoing bird cries. It was them, of course, mimicking the wild creatures. We arrived at our destination at the penal settlement of Newcastle. We were all wrecks—only six of us alive. Jolly good thing I was rewarded with promotion, a major now, you know."

"Mary, you must play your violin for us now! Go on, fetch it at once," yells Masters.

They both nod and Mary is sickened. Reluctantly, she takes the instrument and plays a sorrowful tune. When she finishes, she takes the wine carafe away to refill and spits in it. She lets her dribble trickle in a long tendril toward the lip of the glass. The spit forms bubbles on the wine surface. She puts her finger in to mix it up. Then Masters's shadow crosses the kitchen table; he has followed her.

"Mary, you dirty, dirty girl! I will not stand by and see you show such lack of respect for our guest." He takes her by the arm, wrenching it as he grabs his whip from his belt. He holds the weapon above her, and she looks at him boldly as the whip crashes down. She does not cry out.

"No, no hitting, I wasn't spitting. I was cleaning the bottle." Mary looks down at the reverend's boots. Full of hate. She will piss in the milk churn next.

Masters has a rage upon him. He wants to punish her for being part of the surviving race. For having ears and eyes. He wants to punish his Cornish wife for leaving him, and the clergy who sent him far from the green shores of home.

He grabs her arm again, but the captain takes his hand and stretches it backward until Masters calls out in pain. Mary falls from his grasp. Next time she will shit in his lamb stew.

"I am sorry, so sorry. I don't know what comes over me. I lack control. A consequence of dark humors that should be bled. A sickness. Mary, I'm sorry, girl," says Masters.

"Enough, Reverend, just leave her to clean up after us. Then she can play her violin for you another time. Go on, Mary, run away. That is what you are good at." The captain pulls Masters's hand from the whip and throws the lash into a corner.

He can beat her all he wants, but she will not bow down for him. He is not a man of God, for he has no compassion.

Captain Woodrow tousles her hair and grabs her chin.

"Oh, I think we can make you do anything we wish. Can't we, Reverend? You will be useful one day. Go on, out you go." He slaps her backside and pushes her toward the door.

She feels anger coming but beats it down. Not now, not at this moment; she will wait for a better one. As she walks out of the room, she knocks another wine bottle over. The precious English claret flows like blood and the cook flogs her again with a wooden spoon for being careless.

The next day, Mary hears that Jerungi and his band have stolen from an outlying farm and have taken muzzle loaders and lead shot, and wheat. She wonders how the governor will make his peace with them now. And the kitchen is alive with rumors of her helping the prisoner escape. Mary is now also the enemy. She must run away or face imprisonment.

Before she leaves, Mary sneaks into Masters's bedchamber. There she sees Mercy sound asleep with Masters's leg pushing her against the sheets. Empty wine bottles lie about the room. Mary quietly finds the reverend's medicine cabinet and takes his Epsom salts and stool softener and adds them to his wine glass by his bed. That should fix him. She imagines him hurtling to the thunderbox with his buttocks squeezed together.

In the early light of morning, Mary confides to Mercy that she must leave her, and there are tears. Mercy clings to Mary and sobs. They fetch Eleanor from the servants' quarters and the child is delirious with joy to have her mother take her on a journey. Mary dresses her daughter and tiptoes into the night carrying a bundle of clothes and her violin. Eleanor skips beside her with the pleasure of being out in the night, to watch the stars and wonder at their new adventure. She is like her mother—she is full of amazement for new places. They look back and see Mercy waving from the gate.

Mary stands by the road with her child and bundles and looks both ways. Which direction? She thinks about heading to Freeman's Reach, where her true country calls, but there are stories about bountiful employment in the wineries at Lower Portland on Deerubbin, the Hawkesbury River. What taunts her is the worry of not knowing where she will sleep along the road or when the next meal will come. Eleanor chatters and sings. She is not afraid.

CHAPTER EIGHTEEN

1834: Portland Head

The quiet, green Deerubbin near Portland Head is now a wide creek and Mary and Eleanor are escorted by a ferryman. A hand steadies them as they cross the mudflat to the tin shacks where fifty Aborigines work picking grapes. The workers camp by the river and play music at night. The sounds of a violin, concertina, and gum-leaf musicians fill the air. Despite the wine that is pressed, this is a place where Christianity rules and hymns are played. The workers are sober people.

Mary takes a job as a grape picker, and a big Italian foreman shows her how to pick them and load them into baskets for crushing, and how to tread them into wine. The man loves her violin playing and requests a nightly recital down by the river at sunset.

The men play cricket on the flat in the afternoon, and the best players are wanted by the town teams. Mary plays violin with the wife of the owner, Signor Florentino, and life is at its best. She meets some of her long-lost Darug family and feels a kind of peace at last.

The land nearby is rough and stone-ridden, but it belongs to two Darug men. They hold deeds to prove ownership. Little huts dot the steep incline, and there she makes their home, where no one can run them off—at least for a few months. They grow corn and have a government boat for fishing, and they receive rations for picking grapes. As usual they get flour, sugar, fat, and tea from the shed at the back of the estate house. Some families collect rations from the local farms in return for working the cornfields, and Mary learns to trade her fresh-caught fish for vegetables and meat.

Months pass and when the grape harvest ends, so does the time of plenty. There is no more work and the vineyard foreman tells Mary to move on. She pleads for herself and her child, but nothing can be done. She feels they will be a burden to the good Darug families who can now barely feed their own children. The women watch her walk down the road. She sings out to the currawongs to guide her.

———

Mary and Eleanor sleep alongside the dusty road as they head toward the town of Prospect. She has been told that here the estates are prosperous. As they arrive, she sees the native workers in fields of wheat and corn, dressed in white cloth trousers and shirts, while a foreman stands guard with a cat-o'-nine-tails. She passes with her head low and keeps Eleanor close. He mustn't see them.

The magpies sing and she follows the insects as they fly in the air; she is like one of those flying crickets. A native man sees her and secretly wades through the field with a hessian bag of fresh corn. He is sad and beaten. He hands the corn to her without a word, and Aboriginal women sing to her that she must keep moving because this work breaks hearts. They are slaves—indentured without freedom or wages.

Her eyes reach out to the women; she uses signs to say "run away," but they reply that they are too frightened of the lash. The overseer spots them in the long grass. Mary crawls and the aching pain in her heart causes her to hide with Eleanor behind sheafs of wheat. The overseer walks toward them. He is gaining ground and the Aboriginal men give piercing warning whistles and she heaves her daughter onto her shoulders and rushes to the road, stumbling, breathing hard, with sweat pouring from her body.

Days later, she is still walking. She does not know what she is looking for, but she needs to find shelter for herself and her child. Eleanor cries with hunger. Too much raw corn has given both of them stomachaches. The child clings to Mary's back and the heat presses on their bare heads.

A small but tidy pisé house is before them. Mary looks in the window, holding Eleanor, and sees a white woman carving roast beef brisket with yellow, dripping fat. They both drool. The settler woman's eyes flash at hers and she screams as Mary ducks down into the garden bed and trips on a rake.

"Look, husband, there is a wild native at the window! We will be murdered in our beds! Get the gun!" shouts the woman.

Mary is too exhausted to be afraid. She falls to the ground.

The farmer's boots are at her head, nudging her. With all her strength she manages to cover her child with her body. He shouts at them. He is afraid. His memories of Black incursions on his farm are fresh.

"Get up, you Black mongrel. You come around here stealing! I'll take a stock whip to you," he screams at them.

"No, sir, we're hungry. We want work," pleads Mary.

"Get! And take your piccaninny with you," he says.

"Let us stay. I read and write; I can play the violin," she says.

He stares at Mary and before he can react, she picks up her violin and starts to play "Londonderry Air." Little Eleanor dances in front of them like a spirit, her body bouncing. They are the minstrels, wandering outcasts in their own land.

The farmer stops in his tracks as the full meaning of this accomplishment penetrates. His wife drops her saucepan, clutches her bosom, and stares in wonder at this freakish person before her. Her visions of screaming Blacks and axes and heads cut off disappear, and scenes of the old country take over.

Averting her eyes to concentrate on the music, Mary plays with passion and the music of an Irish jig pours out into the landscape. His eyes fill with tears when she plays "The Star of Munster"—he is Irish. The man drops his gun to his side. Mary is "taming the wild beast," as Mrs. Shelley used to say: Androcles and the lion as she takes out the thorns from their paws.

Mary finishes and puts down her violin. The woman hugs her thin body. She has fallen in love.

"*Neamh thuas!* Heavens above!" The man bows to them.

He takes off his coat and places it over Mary's trembling shoulders—now he can see her hunger and her desperation.

"*Ay cailin,* ay girl, you play like a professional musician," says the farmer.

"I can work for you, too," says Mary quickly.

"We will give you food. There's many a Blackfella we have fed," says the farmer.

Inside the house, they are given warm milk in a pannikin. Mary looks over their strange slab structure. It is full of *goong* ghosts.

"We need a place to stay," says Mary.

"I can't offer a place for you to stay. My wife, Mrs. Byrne, would not want that," says the farmer.

His wife looks hard at them and says, "They can stay. I need a servant. She can work for her keep."

Mary smiles her brightest, willing smile.

But now Mary becomes more aware of the overwhelming problem of the *goong*. Ghosts creep around this place. Maybe it was a place of deaths or a burial ground. Mary can hear a howl from some unseen forces. Granny Wiring taught her to recognize these. She argues with herself, thinking that this house is not a good place for her child. Little Eleanor pulls on her arm with her hair prickled around her face; she also looks at something in a dark window. Mary and

Eleanor get up to leave but the farmer's wife beseeches her to stay. They are hungry and dirty and need shelter, but this place is infested with bad things and her intuition tells her to run like the wind from devil-devils. Before they can flee, Mrs. Byrne takes Eleanor's hand and leads her into the kitchen and offers stew and they both fall on it with relish.

"Eleanor, we can live here. We might be happy," says Mary, trying to convince herself.

When darkness comes, Eleanor stirs near her mother. They are on blankets by the stove. They are warm and have been fed, but Mary can hear something strange—the beginning of the *goong* haunting, like a soft creeping animal; this is a ghost with a deep sadness lurking upstairs.

"Don't be frightened; we need shelter," says Mary as they huddle together and sleep as best they can.

The next morning, Mrs. Byrne serves them a breakfast of porridge with cream and Mary smiles. She is in a mood of great optimism, and they move to the sleep-out at the rear of the place.

"Now, what shall we call you? We will call you Mary and she will be Girly," says Mrs. Byrne.

"Yes, Mum, but my girl is Eleanor," says Mary and curtsies.

"First you will scrub the kitchen floor, then the dining room; then you will dig in the garden," she orders.

"Yes, Mum. Then I will look at your ghost place," says Mary.

The woman comes in close to Mary and whispers, "Do you feel the banshee, too? I'm so scared here but my husband will not leave this house. He built it and he will not take us back to England," she says. "It won't be long before that ghost scares me to death. Every night, I feel it as it paces in our bedroom and points at me."

That night, Mary wakes to find Mrs. Byrne standing in front of the light in a pale nightgown. She is crying. Mary takes her by the hand and walks into the house and up the stairs.

"Give me your words of wisdom. Can you save me from this

thing? God has forsaken me," Mrs. Byrne cries. Mary takes her in her arms and leads her to her small bed, for she does not sleep with Mr. Byrne.

"You have some stones? Like crystals?" asks Mary.

"I have such things," she replies.

Mary looks through them and finds a purple stone.

Mary sits on the bed and discovers she is right: the room bristles with the power of *goong*. He shimmers and has no legs; his dark eyes glow. He is hideous. He points at them and Mrs. Byrne retreats under the covers, shaking and cold. Mary holds up the crystal.

"Go away ghost, go away *goong*, go away ghost!" she cries.

He has hair down to his feet. *He has to be a dead countryman*, she thinks, *and he wears shredded clothes as if from a fire.* He seems to know Mary. She is terrified also. The ghost shimmers and speeds through her body with a finger outstretched.

"*Yan*, go away, *goyong*, white thing, *jebuggali*," says Mary.

The next day, the women gather peppermint gum leaves and smoke the house to rid it of spirits. Mary carries a saucepan full of smoldering leaves, as Granny Wiring taught her, and Mrs. Byrne follows her in a kind of trance as they flick the smoke all through the house while Mr. Byrne laughs.

"Are you trying to get rid of the *taibhse*, ghost?" he asks.

Mary nods at him. This is the truth, but he does not see it.

A wind blows through the rooms. It is a silver light that whispers along the rafters. Mrs. Byrne holds Mary's hand and grins for the first time in her presence. The house is free of spirits. She picks up little Eleanor and dances her into the living room. The child holds out her hands to the mistress and is pulled into her arms. Mary watches and feels jealous—maybe this woman wants her child as her own. Maybe this would be best, and Mary could continue the life on the road instead of having to be a servant. Mrs. Byrne could give the child her heart. She would be fed and protected—safe.

Mary considers how love for her child might make it possible to leave her behind.

Weeks pass and Mr. Byrne watches the growing friendship between Mary and his wife. He is angry for something he cannot express. His wife must be all his. He sees them laugh as they sit up late, sewing clothes for Eleanor, and he hates them. He longs for his own child that has not come.

Mary is trying on a beautiful evening dress in Mrs. Byrne's bedroom while the couple are out. The room has some silver engraved boxes open on the table, but the lovely dress is her downfall. She has seen it in a cupboard—long, soft, yellow taffeta silks—and lifted it out in front of the mirror. She puts it on over her dirty shift and it fits like a song. She twirls and lifts the hem to examine the fine stitches and her eyes shine in the mirror. How she longs to wear pretty things.

Then she sees the farmer behind her, snarling like a dog.

"Take it off, you filthy whore! I will thrash you for this," he says. "How dare you touch my wife's *culaith*! Her dress!"

He takes hold of her arm and wrenches the dress from her body; it rips down a seam, and they both stare in horror. This is the end for Mary here; there will be no more protection. The constables will be called and she will be sent to the Female Factory to starve and work to death. She stumbles out of the room and leaps from the high windowsill into the rose bush, and there, standing, holding Eleanor by the hand, is Mrs. Byrne.

"Mary, why are you crying? Why are you crying?" she pleads for an answer.

"I will go away!" says Mary.

"You can't leave me; why are you leaving?"

"I have to go. I am not safe here. Your husband will call the constables. I want you to take her," says Mary.

"Why? She is yours."

"I can't look after her. Please care for my daughter until I return," says Mary with tears streaming down her face.

"I will; she can be like my own. I will love her," says Mrs. Byrne.

Mary walks out the door, gets her bundle from her room, and walks off down the path.

"Mamma," little Eleanor calls after her. She runs after Mary, and Mary shouts at her, "No, go back. I can't take you anymore. The policeman will come and take me, and that Benevolent Society will take you! They'll send you to that children's home and I will not see you again. Stay here, safe with Mrs. Byrne. She can love you. I will come back, soon, I promise. I promise!"

"Ay, let her go, child. She needs to go. You will be safe here," says Mrs. Byrne, but Eleanor screams and tries to fight her off until Mrs. Byrne holds her down with force.

Mary looks one last time, then she runs through the trees, runs and does not look back. Eleanor's shrieks echo through the forest.

Mary gulps and sees her little ghost brother, also holding out his arms to her in the mist. She keeps going, running in terrible misery, as far as she can. She runs until she can't turn back. She will find the child when it is safe, when she has a way to make a living and a shelter.

But she sees her daughter's face ahead of her in the clouds. She stops still and all she can hear is her beating heart. Should she go back and get her child? Surely, she can't leave her; she is still a child. But Mary walks on. It is the saddest day of her life, and she feels a granny spirit standing there, twirling her long gray plait.

Mary talks aloud to her shadow. She tells it to be still and look after her and guide her and give her a strong mind. She calls out to the little spirit fellas and keeps walking. Walking. She will be back and the child will never leave her side, but first she must find a way to live and feed her. This pain brings back to her memory the day she walked out of the Parramatta Square, held tight by Mrs. Shelley. She never saw her father again. Mary looks ahead and forces herself to not turn, because if she does she will break her resolve.

She hears the distant sound of a military drum and bagpipes, like the roar of angry beasts. Then she hears a whistle—the cry of a great white bird across a sea bringing more hell to her life.

A few hours pass and she sits by an immense Port Jackson fig tree. The red-and-black flying foxes hang over her head and chatter, and she thinks, *What will I say to a daughter I have abandoned? Sorry for this and that, sorry for my abandonment and cowardice. What will I say to her when at last I see her again? What will I say when she blames me for this betrayal?*

Many miles later, Mary sees an inn ahead with a yard full of wine barrels. She sees a worker from the vineyard unloading empty bottles into a crate and nods in recognition. Perhaps there will be work? But Mary hears people laughing inside the inn and a heckling sound like crows. The door opens and startled white faces gape at her. The air smells of tobacco and dirty old, sucked pipes. A man yells at her to get out.

The road ahead stretches out in front of her. All she can see is cold, hunger, and fear.

CHAPTER NINETEEN

1835: South Creek and Prison

A year passes and when Mary sleeps, she remembers there was a time when she had been a child of moonlight and rivers, when she glimpsed the power of the great serpent eel in the mountains. She had sat at Freeman's Reach in her mother's lap by a fire and played with lighted sticks. All around were linked ponds, *bardo*, and fresh clear water flowing into South Creek. *Yuranyi*, the black duck, swam nearby. She remembers diving under a brown duck, drowning it and plucking it, then eating it. That water was so clean they could drink it while swimming. Its sparkling water was fringed with ferns and there was a platypus on the bottom. They caught the scattered red yabby crayfish in pools and cooked them in hot ashes. They roasted the long-necked turtle, and the people drank soup from their shells.

In her pockets now she has crumbs of old damper, smears of jam glued in the cotton thread. Each day when she begs, she hides a tiny bit to eat later. Her skin is dry. She is starving and cold. She remembers a wool coat from the mountains and longs for that coat, for her family to appear.

BENEVOLENCE

205

Mary is willing to eat anything. She will scratch out eyes and tear at faces. Somehow, she survives in the bush with its *butaeen*, brown snakes, under the dry leaves. She has dreams of making incantations. Yes, she will get some nail clippings of Smythe's. She will find some of his hair and make magic. Half-remembered chants come from her mouth. She is battle-hardened and knows that her aunts could conjure his death from mist and create sadness with the help of rain. She dances in the morning light and is covered in dirt and visions of revenge.

She steals fowls again; this time she has five big fat leghorns in her arms. They will be delicious.

But Mary is arrested as she sits in Windsor Park. Her foot is on her violin, and she quickly hides it in a bag. She is called a vagrant, a thief, an outcast Black, and a beggar.

Incarceration is her punishment and the sound of her violin soars over the watch-house walls as she sits in the cell. The guard asks how she can know such celestial music.

Mary looks out the window at the new grand building of the Magistrate's Court in Windsor and marvels at the white columns in the front.

Mary is a felon and all the felons are kept in fetid cells out the back, while the magistrate has his tea. They are led into the court in a row with clanging chains, strung together like convicts. Women, even children, hobbled in ankle manacles, trudge with their heads down, along the corridor to wait to be summoned.

"All rise! Court is in session," yells the court official to the rowdy courtroom.

"The matter of thieving by Mary James of five fowls. Witnesses saw her at it some months ago, and again a few days ago," says the gentleman in a black suit and white collar. He is standing by the dock, and Mary's cheeks flush with embarrassment. The men around her have committed crimes such as murder and arson.

"How do you plead, Mary James?" asks the magistrate, who is none other than Reverend Masters.

"Not guilty, Your Honor," says Mary.

"You were seen running from a backyard with chickens sticking out of your shift and two hanging from your shoulder. They were white leghorns. Is that correct, madam?" asks the policeman.

"And a prize rooster, a red one," says the owner of the fowls, who sits fat and cross at the front of the court.

"I took no rooster," says Mary.

"You would be sentenced to ten years of hard labor if I had anything to do with it. I know this felon very well, yes, very well indeed. But the law is the law, and we have no witnesses to testify about the crime," says Masters as he raps his pencil and sips sherry.

"I was not there. I didn't do it. I don't even like eating fowls. I am a good girl and I was a student at the Parramatta Native Institution set up by Governor Macquarie." She is certain that this will sway opinion. The gavel swings down.

"You absconded from the Native School. You absconded from employment as an indentured servant at the orphan school. Perhaps you do not like work or schools? You absconded from my estate! You are found guilty and sentenced to three months. There will be no lenience next time, Miss James."

"I work for you, sir, when I'm released. I'm a good servant, you know, and I read and write. If you might find my daughter—she is missing—it would be appreciated, sir," says Mary, as mild as can be. But Masters ignores her and with a flourish she is led away.

"I left her with Mr. Byrne but I heard he's gone somewhere!" cries Mary. But nobody is listening.

"What about my poultry?" the fowl owner asks. She has turned bright red. Perhaps she will find her chooks running down at the native camp. Or at least find their white feathers in the Darug headman's hair.

In Windsor Prison, Mary wears a gray blanket with a red stripe and the printed words New South Wales Aborigine. Just in case she forgets. Mary has many hours to ponder the injustice of being locked up for taking a few birds while the English take everything from her and her people. She wonders at how complete this destruction is in such a short time. Her people have nothing but blankets and are constantly told to move on by constables in Windsor town. No sooner do they find a place to sit than they are again moved on. They are acceptable only if they are willing to be imprisoned in uncomfortable clothes and dark sheds to work as slaves.

Perhaps she will go to hell and burn all through, just broken fragments of bones and bits of bird feather all in a sooty mess, tipped onto the ground or floating in the air, for Mary cannot stay underground and she will be missed by some spirits. She carries her mother's blood, her connections to the past, her flesh, her life. She knows that to have been given away as a child is a curse. Mary has become a liar and a thief.

She nibbles some gray damper and tries to suck out any goodness, but it is tasteless. Her eyes grow used to the darkness, but she is afraid of the ghosts that live in this cell. She begs the guard to take her out, but she sees there is no *ngubaty*, no love.

One day is the same as the next. She hears the guard's breathing, farting, and snoring, and stares at him through the bars. She longs to squat under a tree to piss, but in here she must use a bucket. It stinks.

"Let me out. I only stole five fowls!" she cries, knowing how futile it is. And it only makes him laugh. She is of no consequence. She will cease to exist in here.

It is morning and Mary feels the sunlight slip under the main door. Tiny flies swirl in the beams. The guard stirs. His eyes find hers and she looks away very quickly. He takes a bowl from the meat safe, picks out a piece of cold mutton, and chews at it while gawping at Mary. She is still and doesn't say a word. He throws the chewed bone just outside her cell and she stretches out her hand to pick it up. Mary wishes him to hell.

He comes back and Mary hides the bone in her shift.

"Stealin' food, is it?"

"No."

"Stealin' chickens, stealin' silver boxes. I heard about you, a dirty Blackie thief," says the guard.

"No."

Her porridge arrives with a dribble of treacle in it, and she is overjoyed. As Mary eats she imagines herself in Smythe's house, eating from silver platters. She looks at the last scrap on the enamel plate for a long time.

———

At last, her imprisonment is over and she is released.

"I don't expect to see you in my courthouse again, you understand?" says the magistrate.

"Thank you. I can go now?" she says impatiently.

"Let her free and give her back her musical instrument. How strange that she can play a violin. Many have never heard of such a thing," says the magistrate.

Outside the jail, the steps of white stone beckon her down. Her feet touch the wet grass, and she goes around the courthouse corner. She is out of sight and she breathes in fresh morning air.

Windsor is quiet and only the owls and cows are awake, with their eyes watching her slow walk across the fields. An old fig tree stands nearby, older than the arrival of the British. The old man spirit in the tree whispers to her to be quiet and brave. He sings to her, beating time on a possum-skin drum. He holds her in his arms, and she rests before moving on.

A stranger walks toward her and strolls past. She watches this tall, thin man who has feathers tied in a plaited topknot and carries an animal-skin bundle. He could be shot on sight just for being a Blackfella. He stands near her, smiling with white teeth and flaring nostrils pierced with a bone.

"*Worri* native? Where our people?" he asks.

"*Wiannamatta*, South Creek," Mary answers.

He speaks a little English. He is a mountain man, a handsome Gundungurra man. Mary tucks the violin under her chin and plays and he sings in a high-pitched croon. They smile at each other. Mary slowly turns around and when she looks back, he is gone.

She finds wombat meat on a fire at a camp. It looks black but she eats it and walks into the bush. She is embraced by the trees and feels warm and safe. She is home. She quickly finds a track from her people and follows it.

The ridgeline is on her right and she climbs toward mountain safety. She gets a feeling of foreboding and when she comes upon a clearing, the feeling of alarm grows. This is a *bora* ground. She cannot be here in this secret men's place, where boys are made into men. No place for a woman. The ground is raised in a ceremonial animal figure, and the mounds on each end are joined by a path. Mary moves as fast as she can but is caught in thorn bushes, which tear away at her shift, and she can hear the shouting of the spirit men.

She leaves the *bora* ground; red scratches sting her legs and she spits to wash them. Her hair catches in a tree branch, causing her to stumble and fall among cool, soft ferns. There are grubs in that tree trunk eating the wood. If she was in the mangroves near South Creek, the grubs might be tasty *cobrah* worms that can be cooked on a fire to heat the body and stop the cold.

After days of traveling on tracks, looking for her Burruberongal people, she sees smoke down by a creek. It is Aboriginal smoke—

not a *waibala* with a gun. She creeps into the line of trees above and looks down to where a kangaroo is gutted for the fire. Although she cannot eat her totem, it would taste good to someone who is very hungry. A man puts the meat on the fire to singe the fur, and the dogs bark because they can smell her. She stands up.

"*Nindi, bado*, you got some water?" Mary calls out.

"*Nyangu?*" a woman answers.

"Thirsty," says Mary.

"*Djin.* Who you belong? *Nyannungai?*"

"I'm Mary. South Creek Burruberongal mob."

"*Quai, quai, bado* here for you. Drink," says the woman.

The woman welcomes her and holds up a pannikin of water. Mary walks slowly toward them, nothing to lose. One old man has a bone in his nose and is dressed in possum skins. The women have golden skin and are dressed in *waibala* clothes. It is not until she sits down by the blessed fire that she realizes how very cold she is. The women give her a blanket.

"*Wattunga djin?*" they ask.

"From Windsor courthouse jail," says Mary.

"You murderer?"

"No, thief," says Mary.

"That alright, we all that. *Waibala* big one," the woman says and they both laugh.

Mary feels free and she once again travels by foot to the house where she last saw Eleanor, but it is a desolate place with empty, fire-blackened rooms. No person has knowledge of the Irish farmers and her daughter; they have vanished into dust and *goong*. The road back to Windsor beckons and she makes a living by playing music and singing. She hears a story about a troupe of traveling players, on their way to the town. Her curiosity burns; perhaps she can join them?

CHAPTER TWENTY

1835: Deerubbin, the Hawkesbury River

In 1835, His Excellency Major General Richard Bourke passes the Proclamation of *terra nullius,* upon which British settlement is based. This states that the land belonged to no one prior to the British Crown taking possession. Aboriginal people therefore could not sell or assign the land, nor could any individual person acquire it, except through distribution by the Crown.

Another proclamation regulates the rates of tolls to be levied at markets. There are thirteen public houses in Windsor and a market that is licensed to sell butcher's meat, pork, beef, mutton, ham, butter, cheese, milk, eggs, poultry, game, fruits, and vegetables. It is here, near South Creek toll bridge, that Mary has made her camp, quite close to the jail.

———

Mary wishes she could evaporate into the clouds in Windsor town. She is heartily tired of trying to make a living playing a violin. She dreams of a new husband. She no longer thinks about returning to traditional life in wild Burruberongal country, because the people are dispersed. She sits on a blanket by the South Creek toll house and waits for sustenance.

The renowned wandering troupe of *waibala* actors and Aboriginal musicians sets up in the town square. Some men play gum-leaf music, their white teeth piercing the leaves trembling with song, and, to Mary's ears, it sounds like a band of violins. A handsome young blond man wearing a red velvet cape stands beside Mary. He glances at her hands. To outstretch them, to beg, is difficult. She wishes her fist would open and ask for a coin, but it will not uncurl.

The other musicians put up a tent in the square by the Macquarie Hotel and the river. Nearby, a cart festooned with pretty colored pennants carries a piano and a troupe of white and Black misfits. Some are drunks and some are madmen. And Mary can't help but notice the bags of flour and fresh loaves piled on the cart.

The blond musician plays a mandolin and begins singing in a strange language. She wonders if it might be French. She is drawn to his beautiful voice, and his eyes beckon to her.

Apart from hunger, there is another desire within her—the desire for another child. The sight of every mother with a child is a kind of punishment. Envy shoots through her like snake venom. She aches with the memory of lost Eleanor.

Her eyes meet the blond man's eyes; she gives a nod, and he follows her in a playful dance—and they suddenly kiss. He is also a puppeteer who plays Mr. Punch—he will probably have a Judy. He invites her into his cart.

Mary offers her body to him for some of his fresh loaves of bread. He takes hold of a loaf and feeds her a piece with pale creamy butter. She holds it in her mouth, savoring the goodness.

They lie down in his cart on top of costumes of velvet and torn lace. His hair curls down to his shoulders and he wears turquoise beads and wooden seeds around his neck. Gems on a chain glisten on his golden, hairy chest. His chamois shirt is open with a leather cord against his skin. He is perfumed and newly bathed and this makes her want to bathe also. She jumps out of the cart and tips a bucket of water over herself and snatches another piece of bread. Now she is ready.

In a moment, Mary climbs dripping wet and naked back into the cart, shaking her long shimmering hair. He arches back and rests his hands beneath his head to look at her, and she is embarrassed to be so exposed. But she likes this fella with glowing cheeks and pink lips over perfect teeth. His tongue pokes out a little and he laughs with his blue eyes in hers.

"You are *très* beautiful, so pretty. I am Timothy and today I am *heureux*, lucky man," he whispers.

A family from the circus climbs onto his cart rummaging for clothes because they have been swimming in the river. Mary sits up and covers her body and cannot look at them. She is shy. But they are happy and bickering and take no notice of her; she is just a cushion among the theater props.

"You have wife?" Mary asks.

"*Non*, these are my fellow *jongleurs*," he says as he pulls her back to him. The others laugh and leave them alone.

"*Une belle brune. Creole n'est ce pas?* You are beautiful."

They make long, slow love and later they lie back as he smokes an Indian cheroot. He climbs down from their bed and takes a large bag of flour from his cart and hands it to her. He also offers a worn blue gown with a lace collar; she nods her head. He kisses her hand and she feels somehow shy again. She clambers over the side of the cart with the flour and hurries away, smiling into her scarf.

———

Nobody seems to belong to the native women who walk along the tracks, refugees in their own land. At first, they were covered by hot and hungry family members—brothers, sisters, mothers, fathers— all over them. Whining, hugging, and moaning for more and more love. Uncles and aunts in a field with their arms full of corn, then shot like crows, the smiles wiped from their faces in a blast of gunpowder.

Mary moves from camp to camp along the river and meets her Burruberongal people and pleads for information about her daughter, but to no avail. She forages for food and her hands are purple with blackberries. The blue dress is bartered for food.

Months go by and one morning, after sleeping in a pile of dirty blankets, she feels her breasts ache and she realizes that she is pregnant. A *wibbung*, magpie, sings in front of her; he is a message spirit to guide her.

She walks back to where she met her Frenchman lover, but the players are long gone; only some forlorn pennants flap from a post.

———

Mary travels back to Freeman's Reach, the *waibala* name for her true country, where she was born near Deerubbin. The soft lagoon was a place of plenty, and she had hoped to give birth there. But Mary stands by Bushells Lagoon, now choked with willow trees. Carp slash the surface, the native fish are gone, and the yabbies are already eaten. It has so quickly turned from paradise to a muddy hole. She clutches a willow branch to keep from falling in. Even now, in the distance, she can hear trees being felled. Piles of timber are near the track, waiting for a bullock team to haul them to Windsor. Fires burn in the bark piles. The smoke seeps into her skin.

Anxiety fills her. If she could find help to get down the river, where no *waibala* could find her, perhaps she could give birth in peace and the child would not be taken away. Fear tugs at her chest and she aches for some quiet place for her new baby. She remembers giving birth in the Smythe kitchen and the burst of love for baby Eleanor, then her abandonment. How could she have left her child?

She slams the side of her skull as if she can punch away the dark memory.

She keeps walking along a riverbank alive with Aborigines building boats and splitting logs. Mary continues until she is on the edge of a small settlement by the Hawkesbury River. She longs for a boat to take her far away. She needs a canoe like the one her father made long ago to travel the length of the river.

Over on the riverbank she sees an Aboriginal man watching her. She has a flash of recognition. He is an old cousin of her grandfather, a Darkinjung man. He works as a timber man on the estates near Windsor and he beckons to her. He remembers her family well and asks after them, but the shaking of Mary's head tells him all he needs to know. All gone.

He is a kind old man, and she leans against a tree as he takes his axe and calls her to follow him. He will build her a canoe. Mary walks along a path toward the last remaining gum trees. She is wary and looks around for some unnamed danger. But she must trust him.

Sunlight and bellbirds fill the air in a beautiful clearing. The man whittles a canoe paddle from wild hibiscus while the yellow flowers lie in piles around him. He chews the bark to strip it from the length of the branch and rolls the fiber in a ball to use later as string. The canoe bark comes from a stringybark tree. He places a log against the tree. Despite his age, he is agile as he shimmies up with bare legs that grip each side of the trunk. It is almost unbearable for Mary to watch because he is so much like her father.

The man has a rope slung around his hips and the tree, and he edges it up to support his weight. In his belt is a *waibala* axe; it is sharper than his stone *mugu*. He notches the tree trunk, climbing until he is as high as three men, then carefully hacks at the tree, digging a knife into the space between bark and wood. The sap oozes as he pries away the thick covering. He shimmies down and makes another axe cut around the base. Further hacking and he has split the bark sheath down the middle. He grins at her, then leaps down to take hold of a suitable stick to pry the bark from the tree. There is much grunting and then the tree is naked.

Mary runs her hand over the pale-yellow wood—it is as smooth as skin. She mourns the death of this tree, but this thick sheath of bark will become her canoe. She helps the man lay it on a big smoky fire, and they drag logs and stones to place on the stretching bark. The heat and weight will make the shape right for a vessel. It flattens in the steam, and after a long time, she can see the boat emerge from the curved bark.

The sun has risen high in the sky and around them the sound of axes rings through the remaining forest. The old man shapes the ends of the canoe by cutting them into wedges and bending each one. He uses thick woven twine to tighten the ends; then he examines the boat for holes and uses fern tree resin heated in the fire to fill any cracks. He smooths the bark with his knife.

They wait several days for the bark to harden and the canoe is nearly finished; he motions to Mary. They carry it to the river, where he tests the craft, and she can feel a rising happiness. This canoe means freedom. He sits lightly in the middle, balanced and comfortable on a pile of paperbark. He demonstrates the new paddle of sticks tied together and laughs out loud as the boat flies across the inlet. He waves at her, and for a terrible moment she thinks he will keep rowing and it has all been an awful prank. But no, here he comes. A bursting smile and he leaps out and helps Mary to sit her pregnant form onto the finely balanced seat.

The first canoe journey takes her along a narrow creek, where she sees trees scarred from the marks of *cobrah* worm hunting. She collects the young mangrove fruit to steam on a fire and eat. She collects geebung from the nearby bush, and the berry fruit fills her mouth with sweetness. A pile of sarsaparilla leaves lies on a possum skin in the canoe; she will make a tea from these to soothe her belly. The tranquil water is soothing and she sings in the sunlight to her unborn child.

When the baby is ready to be born, Mary takes refuge in a Burru-berongal camp along the river at Eastern Creek. The women know Mary as a cousin, and they huddle around her and build a fire to warm the birthing possum rugs. After a quick labor, her baby is born. Mary is alive with joy. The boy baby is pale, a yellafella baby, *gurng*. The women cluck and touch his little face and wash him with eucalypt leaves and whisper his totem, *wibbung*, the magpie. He brings his love to all the women, so they take turns to hold him above the warm ashes and rub him with goanna oil. They massage the tiny human and hand him to Mary to nurse. She feels such joy in this new life as his eyes meet hers. Mary swears to herself that no one will ever take him from her.

CHAPTER TWENTY-ONE

1838: From Wiseman's Ferry to Gentleman's Halt

The office of the Protector of Aborigines is established after a recommendation in the report of the Parliamentary Select Committee on Aboriginal Tribes. The Protector would be required to learn Aboriginal languages, and their duties would require them to watch over the rights of Aborigines, guard against encroachment on their property, and protect them from acts of cruelty, oppression, and injustice.

———

Mary finds a job with a kind employer—Colin, a quiet farmer who treats her well. In return she cooks and cleans for him. The farm grows corn and wheat, and Mary cooks loaves from fresh-ground flour milled by a horse-turned grinder. The kitchen becomes her domain, and she turns out plum puddings—but with no currants—and gingerbread. She learns to sew dresses from satinette and cassimere and decorates them with jet buttons. The farmer sells all these items in the market in Portland.

The farmer tells her about Gentleman's Halt, an abandoned house up the river toward the town of Spencer. When her son Wibbung—or Timothy, named after his French father—is three years old, Mary decides to move on to find this house along the Deerubbin. Colin built the house himself and has no further need of it. He draws a mud map for her and when she asks if she will be safe, he nods his head.

Early one morning, she and Timothy wave goodbye to the farming families who have sheltered them, and she pushes her canoe onto the river. The water is not so deep or dark, and reeds grow along the bank. Cormorants dry their wings on branches and the sun dapples on the water. Mary has a bundle of blankets, her violin, some coins that she has saved, a bag of flour, tea, and sugar.

The fresh water has turned to salt water and the river becomes fast flowing and she has trouble paddling. Her son sits in the middle on the pile of paperbark, as she fears sharks. The bark twists and lurches to one side, and water spills into the bottom.

The river becomes deep and treacherous in places, but there is still a singing beauty as a mist rises in the early morning. Diving gray cranes swish before her, ducking under the green waves and rising with wriggling fish in their beaks.

Mary paddles down a narrow stretch of river and sees the place where it splits in two. The Colo River on her left has a thin strip of settler shacks, with corn growing and sheep grazing. She will not go there as it has a reputation for wildness and the stealing of Black and white women. She chooses Deerubbin, her mother river.

Soon a distant sound of rocks splitting and explosions of dynamite tell her she is close to a settlement. The steep red and yellow sandstone cliffs tower over her with huge ghost gum trees and thick bush. She continues toward Wiseman's Ferry, where the convict road, the Great North Road, has been recently built. Perhaps she will find work in the nearby inn.

Wiseman's Ferry is a large raft, where loads of flour are winched across the river by a metal wheel pulled by a horse. The old ferryman and innkeeper is Solomon Wiseman. His inn is called The Sign of the Packet; he is an ex-convict and a boatman from the Thames in London.

Along the riverbank, the convict road workers stand about in torn, dirty shirts, their skin tanned from the sun and hunger etched on their faces.

Mary ties her canoe to a tree and walks up to the thin, well-dressed Wiseman, who is operating the metal wheel of the ferry. Mary puts Timmy on her hip and tightly binds him in her possum cloak as she gathers courage to speak to the ferryman.

"Sir, do you have work at your inn for a woman who can read and write? I do laundry and sew as well," she says.

He looks her up and down and notes that she is golden-skinned and very handsome.

"I have no work for such as you, sorry, lass. You would not wish to work for me anyway; it is punishing hard work. It killed my first wife, who died of natural causes, or unnatural, depending on your point of view," says Wiseman and he chuckles. He collects a toll from the driver of a cart, then turns back to Mary. He winks as he pockets the coin with a look of deep satisfaction and then leans down to a wooden crate. He holds up a bag of salted meat and waves it at her.

"Salt beef. Want to buy some? A penn'orth?" he asks.

Mary watches his movements closely. She has heard the stories about this powerful, shrewd man from people downriver. He has been known in years past to threaten ticket-of-leavers if they did not accept more of his meat, with which he serves the convict gangs who work on the Great North Road to Wollombi. Wiseman rubs his hands together. He views Mary, an unprotected woman, as a possible source of profit. Mary nods and takes the bag of salt beef and pays him with a handful of British farthings; he counts the copper coins. He notices she has a silver shilling in her bag.

"You got a shilling there; what else you need?"

"I will keep that," she says and tucks the money into her skirt.

He hands her a bag of wild lemons and a sugar stick of boiled lolly.

"Take a lolly for your child, and we have a surplus of wild lemons. No cost. I suggest that you go on quickly as this place is no good for pretty women like you. The desperate men hereabout might fuck you." Wiseman grins.

The convicts who are unloading the bags of flour whoop and call out to her. They are not accustomed to seeing lone females on the river. Mary sees no malice in them and feels only compassion. They are in leg irons and chains, covered in sores, and she watches the overseer walk toward the cringing, starving men with his cat-o'-nine-tails flicking in his hand.

Up the bank, a few staggering drunks are returning from the inn. They call out to her. They yahoo and offer crude gestures. They would like to grab her.

Mangroves grow thick around the riverbank and Mary drags her canoe quickly into the water. She must escape this place.

But even in the water she is not safe. Two drunken men in a fishing boat wave at her. The yellow-haired one grins at her like a devil. He puts up a sail and heaves to. He means to chase her. She paddles furiously to get out of the channel, but the tide is stronger than her paddling. She crisscrosses to a tiny rivulet in the mangroves. The fishermen laugh at this good sport. Wiseman calls out for them to leave her alone but they ignore him.

"Hey, girly, you better paddle fast," one of the drunks shouts, "because we are going to catch you and rape you!"

The drunks lean over the side of their boat, but Mary keeps paddling with an occasional glance of her head to make sure her little boy has not fallen out. She pants and her chest heaves with sweat and fear. Timmy giggles at the speed of the canoe. The men are closer now, sideways and grinning, like fools.

Suddenly the wind changes and the men are blown off course

and struggle to keep up with her. They end up tangled in mangroves while Mary skims across the river and gets way ahead of them.

"Alright, *koochoo*, good boy, hold on," she says.

The oysters are thick on the small rocks. Mary rows by a section of the river too narrow for the chasing sailboat. She can hear the men howling with regret as she paddles faster into the shadow of the mangroves—her shelter.

She pulls up on the muddy bank and tugs the canoe up the black slime. Soldier crabs scuttle around. She ties up the canoe with the stringybark rope. The ground is black, stinking slush, but it feels safe, and she hopes they won't find her among this stench. For many hours she can hear them searching the rivulets. She huddles with Timmy in her arms in quiet terror.

"Hush; you must be very quiet, Timmy, or Mummy will be hurt by bad mens," whispers Mary.

Hours pass and Mary gathers fat oysters by chipping them off the rocks with a piece of silcrete stone. She pops them into Timmy's little mouth. He laughs, little hands clapping. Then, with an axe, she digs *cobrah* worms for him from the mangrove branches. He knows nothing but what his mother feels, his eyes upon her searching for clues about her mood. He asks endless questions. She loves him so very much.

"We going for corn? We going for swim?" asks Timmy.

"Yes, we'll get corn to cook," says Mary. "Now, *nyannungai*? Who owns this?" she asks him and holds up his small fishing line.

"Timmy's," he laughs and grabs it. "Me *kurung*."

"Yes, a little boy."

The shadows grow in the cool afternoon. From their mangrove sanctuary, they can see gray herons on the bank and spoonbills scooping up water. They climb onto a firm bank and the crabs scuttle in armies of gray helmets; Timmy runs after them laughing. Mary can let him laugh now; surely the men have given up hope of catching her. There is no sound of men on the river.

She shows Timmy the curved grass nest of a satin bower bird with its collection of blue shells and some small bones. Mary picks one bone up then quickly drops it. This death bird has collected a human finger bone—a bad omen.

They sleep in the canoe under the possum skin on the darkest of nights. Mary stirs under a thick fog of gray dreams. She is floating in deep water, swirling with pulsing eddies, then her eyelids flutter and she is awake. The canoe is drifting and she leans back on the flimsy bark to gaze at the night sky. Her breath slows. In among the mangroves she can hear creatures all around her scuffling for food. Crabs and eels most probably, not men, so she can breathe again and not be torn by fears.

The dawn breaks. Pink glowing light and birdsong trickle across the creek. Her back aches. She washes her face in the water—time to give Timmy her breast and the last of the damper. She holds him close, murmuring, "Coo-coo, my baby, not far now."

A day later, they come to a tumbled-down, grand, two-story sandstone house on the edge of the Deerubbin. This is the secret house of the farmer friend. Its name is written on a board, "Gentleman's Halt," and there is an abandoned convict-built road at the back of the dwelling. She camps in the house and finds beds, pots, and the remnants of a garden. In the darkness she hears a python in the roof, but it slithers away. She finds a supply of dried beans and weevilly flour in wooden tubs. She marvels at the wide verandas, wooden-shuttered windows, and high ceilings. There are orange trees heavy with fruit, a jetty, and countless oysters, birds, and kangaroos. The view from upstairs is of a wide arc of the green river and mangroves. She sucks an orange and peels another for Timmy. Pelicans and cormorants entertain the child.

Weeks pass into months and Mary collects plump blackberries to make syrup and uses the meager supplies of flour to make a kind of sod pudding cooked in the camp oven on the fire in the main room. Her arms are crisscrossed with scratches from the briars. The spring near the house has fresh water and Timmy laughs when he is bathed in a tub by the fire.

Mary tends the cornfield in its ruin from kangaroos. She builds a fence from twigs and erects clattering tins on string to warn her when they try to steal corn.

As each day cools, she drags a bucket of water to drip on the new corn shoots and cabbages. Each tiny plant is a joy. On her walk back to the house, she is alarmed to see the door ajar and hear the sound of someone breaking sticks inside. Panic rises in her chest. Can it be a runaway convict who will harm her?

Mary motions for Timmy to get down and be quiet, and they crawl to the door. To her astonishment, her old friend Mercy is standing in the kitchen, grinning. It is pure joy to behold her because it has been nearly six years since they were together at Masters's house. Mercy had heard rumors of this abandoned house and followed the gossip upriver to find her friend. Mary had spent many hours thinking about Mercy; now her laughter fills the room and the bright face glows. She is mature and beautiful with curls piled on her head, with a white scarf and a necklace of silver abalone shells and knitted grass around her neck. Timmy is shy and peeks out at her from behind his mother. Mercy tickles him and chases him around the kitchen in a game of hide-and-seek.

"Where you get that little *naoi* rowboat?" asks Mary, as Mercy settles into an armchair, patting the seat while looking at the uncomfortable surroundings. Mercy picks up a filthy cushion, sniffs it, and throws it to the floor.

"You got a cover for that?"

She unties a bundle of food.

"I barter for a watch chain. Don't ask about that. I here with you and *koochoo* baby. No worry," says Mercy. "I got presents for you and the little fella. I got new clothes and flour, tea, sugar, dry beef, and a fruit cake!"

"You want stay with us? Be an aunty for my boy?

"Lovely *wungar* boy. Call me aunty. It look like you got a good place here. Plenty fish. Nice chair, nice roof, nice fire, no *waibala* boss to shout at you. Nice. It's pretty good. Reckon I stay for a bit?" says Mercy. They hug and are happy to have each other. No one wants to be alone because loneliness can kill.

"Where you been?" asks Mercy

"I'm here a little while, but mostly hungry. The last year has been no good."

Mary tells Mercy how she survives on the river by growing corn and by bartering fish, oysters, and prawns downriver in the township of Spencer. Mercy nods and holds her hand. The friendship between them is of sisters and they must care for each other and not separate.

"Masters is not bad, he's like old man now. Not much *nguttatha* anymore. Doesn't want my pretty *gumirri*. Just ask me to help him dress and look after him. He got no wife. She go to England and never come back. He keep me for a long time, lot to eat, good warm place for sleep. I like it quiet now, not run here, run there," says Mercy.

"But he bosses you all the time; maybe now you want a soft life?" asks Mary.

"A soft life not bad. Better than hard life. I got nice things now. But I had little ones."

"What, *gurng* babies?" asks Mary.

"Gone now," says Mercy sadly. "When you go away after you help that chief, I have to leave Masters's place, too. I live in Parramatta and I find nice husband. One of my mob. We happy—so happy— but then it's a real cold winter. Not much food so we live in a bark shed. Not warm. Have babies. My babies gone now. That strangling disease, diphtheria. Two girls. Twins, Mary and Mercy. They got real sick. Can't breathe, the throat swelling and swelling. They turn blue and cold and gone. Just close their eyes and sleep forever. I scream and howl and try to hang myself. My husband make smoking song for me. After that he's gone. Not coming back."

Mary hugs her and they hold tight to each other.

One morning the women take Timmy for a swim in a billabong nearby. It is murky and full of turtles and eels. They catch a turtle and cook it on a fire.

"That Reverend Smythe told me once about a pretty place in England for a swim. He called it 'the blue hole,'" says Mary.

"Well, I reckon this is a brown hole," laughs Mercy.

Gentleman's Halt is a huge sandstone building. It is only half-built, as though the grand design were too much for her farmer friend. But the kitchen is dark and warm with a wood fuel stove. Mud and newspaper line the walls that are then painted with a whitewash. In a shed, they find a bag of seed corn, and they find other vegetable seeds in tins stacked on a shelf in the earth cellar; the women plan a bigger garden.

Mary and Mercy dig the earth to extend the garden of corn but it's a battle with the large gray kangaroos who try to get to the sweet young corn. The women build a higher fence of branches to stop the huge male animals, and every morning they check it for damage.

Mercy washes clothes in a tin tub by the fire after she has bathed Timmy. He seems to grow in love with her and, as days pass, Mary sees the closeness growing between them. She cannot help but be suspicious. She cannot relax. What if Mercy takes him away when Mary is sleeping? She sees Mercy's eyes on him like a greedy spirit. Mercy enjoys his love and ignores Mary. What if she let him drown or burn? Mary stays awake half the night with Timmy warm against her.

Months pass and the three of them eat well as the corn and cabbages ripen, and they drink from the small, fresh, spring-fed well with straight stone walls near the back of the house. Timmy scoops tadpoles into a tin cup and his little hands grab at the tiny animals. He holds one with legs and laughs as it tickles his palm. Despite the frog spawn that floats in the ferns, the water tastes sweet and fresh. They use a leather bucket to carry it to the house.

It is soon winter. Timmy has developed a swollen belly and there is no flour left and nothing to eat but lomandra seed damper and wild fruit, like lilly pilly, wombat berries, wild grape that is hard as stones, and sweet yellow geebung. The oyster stews are beginning to make Timmy sick and Mercy makes a medicine of sarsaparilla leaves to feed him with a spoon. One day, they walk to the billabong and swim in its fresh water. They dive for the waterlily stems, which they peel and eat while floating. Mary notes that the flowers of these waterlilies will soon turn into edible seed pods, rich in nutty oil. They will return in the right season.

It is a cold drought and small game like possum or goanna are hard to find. Each evening Timmy cries with hunger and Mary is frightened that he will sicken and die. Mercy catches an echidna with a snare made of devil's guts twine and roasts it on the fire. The women give their portions to the child; they lick the drips of juice—it tastes wonderful. They are hungry too and suck the bones greedily. The echidna quills go to making a necklace for Mercy.

One morning, they row their boats to the township of Spencer, near Mangrove Creek, to barter for food. Mercy has a stolen silver watch, which she holds high to catch the light. She asks for flour and milk, but the shopkeeper is silent and sneering as he reaches for the old bags of flour, full of weevils. The women stand their ground until he passes them a large bag of clean flour, salt meat, fat, tea, and some sugar.

They take off down the swift river toward their house and the feeling of going home is luscious for Mary. She imagines herself tucked up with a cup of tea in front of her fire. An arrogant shopkeeper cannot hurt them.

Mary ties up her canoe, but the tide is out, and she struggles to get to the shore through deep mud while carrying Timmy. She climbs up on the tree trunk jetty near their house. She usually balances along the tree trunk with nimble skill, but not tonight. Mary has Timmy in her arms as she slips and falls into the deep, gray, stinking mud and sharp oyster shells. The child screams.

Mary howls out for her friend, who comes and lifts the child from the mud. Mary tells Mercy to take him up to the house and to not worry about her. She feels her nose and it seems to be broken. Blood fills the oyster cuts as she crawls up the bank and along the track to the house.

Inside the house, Mercy has lit a fire in the stove, and Mary staggers into the kitchen to wipe the mud from her face and body. She is dripping brown ooze.

"You look like you covered in *goona*, shit all over you," laughs Mercy.

"No worry about me. I was thinking I was in the circus and I can balance; then, bang, into the stink," says Mary.

"You just pick up Timmy and run on that pole like a possum—but you're not a possum, you're head over tit," laughs Mercy.

Mercy winks at Mary with good humor and produces a parcel of tea. Mary moans in pleasure because they have been stewing the same old tea leaves for weeks and the native sarsaparilla is not as good to taste. Mercy boils water in the billy and they undress Timmy and wipe him down. He snuggles against them. Timmy begs for a spoonful of sugar to suck, then dips his fingers into the white crystals. *Without this child*, Mary thinks, *there would be no point in living*.

"He's like my child, too. My little ones all gone. I would die for him," says Mercy.

"He loves you, Aunty," says Mary.

Timmy traces his fingers around Mercy's face and kisses her, but then leaps into his mother's arms and falls asleep. Mercy washes the deep cuts on Mary's knees and hands and carefully picks out bits of oyster shell. She steeps *Eucalyptus paniculate*, gray iron bark, *muggargru*, in water for disinfectant. Mercy takes red sap from their collection of bush medicine and presses the cuts closed.

"You're a good nurse. I'm glad you've come," says Mary as she sits with Mercy in the firelight.

"*Ngaia yunga* for *wungar*, you still know that talk?" Mercy looks at her and strokes her hair.

"*Yuin*, yes a little bit," says Mary.

"One bossman hit me when I spoke lingo. I just speak English all the time now," says Mercy.

"True, aye? You know, I think I am a big coward. I leave all the people who need me, before this. But now I will never leave my son," says Mary.

Mary has an idea to barter with the families downriver at Marra Marra Creek, off the Deerubbin. She tells Mercy she has heard about her cousins living there on a small farm. They have orchards of oranges and peaches and a white German father, Ferdinand, who protects his native wife and children by going alone to town for dry goods. His family is safely hidden back behind the mangroves. It is a secret valley of plenty. She will row along the river again to safety and the quiet haven of Marra Marra Creek. She will find her cousin Biddy's farm.

But Mercy has had enough; she longs for the comfort of Masters's estate. She looks at the thin stew of cabbage in the billy pot and stirs it with her fork. Mary watches her. It is greasy and watery.

"I can't eat this *goona*. We're starving here. See my ribs here! We need *karndo*. You can go downriver, chase a stupid dream place. But watch out your boy doesn't die! I'll paddle back up to the town to see what I can get from that old Masters man," says Mercy. She has a strange look on her face.

"Come with us to Marra Marra Creek. We can be safe together," pleads Mary.

"No, you all the time run, run, like a rabbit. You ever want what *waibala* have got? Lots of food, lots of warm places. I want to go Windsor town. I need tobacco and maybe work a bit for him," says Mercy. "I can ask that Masters again. He likes me. He's got a lot of money. You come or maybe Timmy might die."

"What? My boy will get strong. That Masters, he likes you? You *bimung garai*, he's not *mittigar* friend. He beat me, he beat you! He spits on us. You can't work for him," says Mary.

"I'm going. I'm getting skinny. Straight away like that. You coming? You going to stay watch that baby get really sick?" asks Mercy as she packs a small basket and walks toward the door.

"No. You've got to stay here with us where it's safe. I can protect you always. You make lots of mistakes. All the time you chase the wrong fellas," says Mary.

Mercy howls with laughter and says, "Look at you! Talk about choosing wrong fella, ha! And now you're starving, your boy is starving!"

She walks to the water's edge, steps into her small boat, and is off.

"Don't go!" Mary screams.

"You got to follow me; you're my sister!" Mercy screams back.

She paddles in the direction opposite to where Mary wants to go—she is going a day's paddling back upriver toward Masters's estate. Her bowed head in a pink scarf becomes a blur in the river's mist. Mary stands by the canoe with Timmy, torn between staying or following. Eventually, Mary packs her canoe with Timmy and some food and reluctantly follows Mercy toward Windsor town, and Reverend Masters. She seems to have no will against Mercy's insistent power.

CHAPTER TWENTY-TWO

1838: Masters's House Again

Dear Sir,

Thank you for your kind hospitality on our recent visit to your splendid estate at South Creek. We much appreciated the religious interviews with yourself and your servants.

On our departure, we ventured to the other side of the creek, to see Black natives, who resort thither. In comparison to other tribes, the South Creek natives may be considered to be remarkably half-domesticated and they often are employed in the agricultural operations of the estate. The wife of our guide can read, she is a half-caste, educated in the Native School at Parramatta. It is to be regretted that this school was abandoned, for though many who were educated in it returned to the woods, yet an impression was made upon them, favorable to their future progress in civilization.

Yours sincerely,

James Brownly, Missionary

Masters's house leans against a stony hill, and in the few years since Mary worked there, it has undergone major improvements: an extra floor has been added and extra pillars enhance the white colonnade. The thatch roof has been replaced by sturdy orange tiles from the convict brickworks. The building sits majestically against the gray sky while currawongs sing all around. It has many sandstone chimneys, and smoke drifts in white clouds over the oak trees. A sumptuous garden rambles over the land around the house. English flowers are in bloom—marigolds, purple fuchsias, and white daisies are all in rows. Orange, lemon, and peach trees grow in straight lines and a greenhouse abounds with plants bearing ripe tomatoes.

Mary, Timmy, and Mercy stroll down the grand pathway and stroke the carved stone statues of several lions that guard the way on either side.

An Aboriginal gardener is planting seedlings in the kitchen garden and Reverend Masters clips his red roses while balancing his wine glass on a nearby stool. His old friend, Captain Woodrow, reclines on a chaise longue on the veranda, sipping Andalusian sherry. Bees perch on the flowers and the perfume of countless daisies and lavender bushes wafts over the lazy scene. Mary, Mercy, and Timmy stand as yet unseen.

Captain Woodrow reads a newspaper, the *Sydney Gazette*.

"Oh look, here are some dark-skinned trespassers!" He waves his wine glass at Mary and Mercy.

"I don't read the newspaper. I prefer to be indolent imbibing Andalusian wines or the sweet wine of Malaga," Masters replies.

He drinks another glass of wine.

"I rather like the idea of some kind of Utopian vision. All brotherhood together in peace, et cetera, and a nice drop of yellow this," says Masters as he holds his glass to the light.

"When I was with the garrison on the subcontinent, I was in-

structed in Buddhism by a brown-skinned monk, but I had a per-
sistent ague. He recommended that I cure myself by drinking his
fresh urine. Cheers!" says Woodrow while finishing his glass.

Woodrow puts down his empty glass, waves, and jumps on his
horse. He trots down the path away from the house and toward the
town. He has errands.

As she approaches the door, Mary hides Timmy under her dress.
Suddenly she notices that Mercy has gone, run off without a word.
This is so much like her—pushing Mary into trouble, then doing a
flit. Timmy's thin little hands grip her legs.

Rodney holds the door ajar and whispers for Mary to go around
to the kitchen. She takes Timmy out and walks along the outside
path and looks through a window to see a fireplace and glasses of
yellow wine. The room shimmers with a foreign allure. It is a dark
interior of bloodred walls and velvet curtains. She is shocked to see
Mercy already in a servant dress preening herself before a looking
glass. Rodney walks toward her smiling and smoothing his crinkled hair. They whisper and cuddle and Mercy has her legs crooked
over his open breeches in a scandalous embrace, followed quickly by
sounds of sighing and humping.

Mary is furious. Mercy has led her to a place she doesn't want to
be. She has been duped. She inhales deep breaths to quiet her heart.

Mary is ushered into the room and there, in front of her, is Masters's huge back as he shrugs on a green satin smoking jacket and
lights his long Dutch pipe. His head tilts toward a vase of flowers
and he inhales the scent. Mary has an overwhelming desire to steal
something. She sees a small carved ivory skull with emerald eyes.
Her fingers touch it and straightaway Masters's voice booms, "Don't
touch the antiquarian objects!"

Timmy bursts out crying, and already she wants to escape the
reverend's presence. Masters swivels in his big wooden chair and his
gray eyes, like beacons, alight upon Timmy. The child shivers and
tightly holds his mother's hand.

"A child! You have brought me a magnificent blond child! Wonderful!" says Masters.

Mary looks at him closely. He is a weaker man now, with a florid face, and he seems to have trouble breathing. Masters reaches out a plump hand for Timmy and the child recoils. Mary pushes Timmy behind her.

"No, sir. I want work, like Mercy. We are hungry," she says.

"I remember you. You helped a felon escape! You want to return to my house?" he asks as she nods and her hands tremble. She is fuming inside—it is like eating poison—but her son's survival may depend on this odious man.

Masters twists a gold signet ring around his pinkie finger as he licks his lips and leans forward. His breath is fetid.

"I do have compassion for you all. Especially lovely Mercy, that naughty wench. But otherwise one needs to 'Smooth the dying pillow,' et cetera. Firstly, you must give a creditable demonstration of your skills. Go to the kitchen and make some tea. Use the fine Indian tea leaf. Mercy will help you. Off you go. And leave the boy so he can be warmed by my fire."

He leans forward and wiggles his fingers at Timmy.

"Don't be afraid, little boy. Would you like a boiled lolly? Or an apple?" he asks as he bites into an apple.

"He must come with me," she replies.

"If you must. But, if this is a true capitulation, you will crawl on your hands and knees and beg for this opportunity. Show me," says Masters.

"I cannot, sir." Her head sinks down, but she will not crawl.

"Lower . . . like the potentates of India; they learned to submit. Hmm, it will do for now," he says. "I am sorry for your recent hardship. You do look a little famished. Need a bit of fattening, eh? Chin up, little boy—all will be well. Did I give you an apple? Oops, I ate it. Jesus teaches forgiveness. I might even find your mother a suitable 'ticket-of-leaver' to marry. How's that?"

"Kind of you," she says.

"Here, have a sweet red grape. I grow them on the estate," Masters says, handing Mary some grapes. Timmy grabs the fruit and stuffs them in his mouth.

She watches Masters and fears him, knowing that starvation is not the worst thing. Worse would be if she had not known the love and protection of her father or teachers. If she had been raped or tortured. But she endured one beating by this man's hand, and she managed to keep this boy. He matters more than life itself. She would do anything to protect him, to see him eat well and thrive.

Mary follows Rodney into the kitchen. He has strong muscled arms, a Jamaican African build of handsomeness and an ability to be quiet in the face of any eventuality. He smiles and whispers that she will be safe in the house. She returns with a pot of tea on a tray. She pours tea into a porcelain cup; Masters tastes the tea but grimaces in disgust. He spits the tea on the floor.

"Are you trying to poison me? It tastes of something foreign; is it a native herb?" says Masters. "A spell? A witch's brew? I cannot trust you. Do you dance naked in the forest summoning up devils as well?"

He takes a tendril of her hair. He twists it in his fingers as if testing the quality, then lets her go. She twists out of his reach.

"You very much wish me dead, do you not?" asks Masters.

"Yes, Reverend," says Mary.

"Ha, you are amusing. How would the death of one white man make a difference? There will always be more to come."

He can read her thoughts. Her chest is heaving, and Mary shakes her head.

"No poison," she says.

"We shall see. Mind you, I shall be on constant alert. You want Madeira cake? You always liked cake," he says and reaches to eat a piece. Her mouth waters. What is he thinking? Will he harm her child?

"Don't want it," she says.

"You haven't learned the manners or the good grammar we hoped for. We had such high hopes for the native servants. We thought you could be better than the Jamaicans. Oh, and I am repentant of your past treatment—shouldn't have occurred," he sighs.

He chews and brushes the crumbs from his lap. Mary watches the cake and Timmy implores her with his eyes. They are so hungry.

"I need employment. My child will be with me. He can help me," says Mary.

"Need, is it? Your baking is bad. I hear that your bread is lumpen like a lead ball. We could shoot it out of the cannon that we used on Napoleon," says Masters.

"Yes," she whispers.

"Nothing begets nothing. *N'est-ce pas?* Let us raise your child in our orphan school," says Masters.

The blood drains from her face.

"Never, he stays with me," says Mary.

"You learned to read and write—a magnificent accomplishment. Why seek to deprive your infant? Let me touch his hair. My, goldish, isn't it? The father must have been very white."

Mary snatches Timmy out of the reverend's reach. This man wants to steal him from her. She has lost one child and now she must be courageous in holding on to her son. His little hands point to a bowl of fruit: bananas, oranges, apples, all delicious looking. He is whimpering and Mary takes an orange and hands it to him. She looks at Masters and he laughs.

"Go on, steal a banana, too. Don't be frightened," he says. She peels the fruit for her son while her eyes do not leave Masters's face.

"I want to ask about my daughter, Eleanor. Is she in that Female Factory? Where is she now? I wrote a letter," she says.

"You have given up this child, this Eleanor? Had a lot of inconsequential men, have you? As for a letter, I don't think one letter from your type of personage will mean much to the colonial authorities. Or have your circumstances changed that much? Do you by any chance happen to have a husband? A place of constant abode? Have you purchased land, like Maria Lock?" he asks. His sarcasm drips from the walls.

"No," says Mary.

"Tut-tut. You look like something a cat vomited up. Like a beaten dog. Are you a doggie? Can you woof? No. Hmmm," says Masters. "Just a harlot mother and destitute runaway prisoner who dares to come begging to me. Not a good look, is it? Give me the boy and you can visit your Eleanor. We will find her somehow, I suppose. Not take her, mind, but see her for a few hours. If I can locate her. I am not an unjust man. I will make inquiries. That would be pleasant, would it not? Turn about; let me look at you."

Mary is struck dumb; she cannot even howl. She stands with gaping mouth and for a moment it seems that Masters will pop a sweet into it. He fingers a chocolate wrapped in silver paper lying in a glass bowl. He tosses it in the air and swallows. He pours red wine into a crystal glass and sips it slowly while staring at Timmy. He leans toward the child and whispers.

"Have you ever heard of King Nebuchadnezzar? From Egypt? In the Old Testament? No, why would you?" says Masters. "He took all the boy children and burned them alive. Or cut off their heads with a very sharp sword. Can you picture that, little boy? I have an illustrated Bible; I can show you pictures. That is also what happens to people in hell, who disobey God's word. Burned alive."

Timmy has buried his face in his mother's skirt and is crying loudly. Mary summons up all her courage and hunches her shoulders as she speaks. She thinks Masters is mad, but she can also see that Timmy is hungry. She could snatch all the chocolate and fruit, right here, in front of the reverend.

"I need employment in the kitchen, like before. I'm a good worker. You already have given work to Mercy," says Mary.

"Not for long. Mercy is a slattern. But we have other service for her; she is willing and beautiful at least," says Masters. "We have countless Black girls in the kitchen and whatnot. I am not an unfeeling man. I have a duty to help. I used to fuck them when I needed. But now my pizzle will not do my bidding. Tragic. They received a coin. A farthing or such. As for you, you are quite dispensable, I am sorry. But the boy could be saved, given English manners. There are many men who could use a boy like him. Tidied up, hair cut, nice little black suit with ribbons. Blue, I think, to show off his blond curls. Oh, I could eat him up for supper. Nice little bottom. In the Orient, we call them cupids or Ching Chong chickies. Ha!"

Mary is aghast.

"No, I will go. Sorry for your time, we go home now," she says.

"Home? You have no home. No land, no possessions. Oh, perhaps you could be useful. Your native knowledge could be very handy to trap renegade natives," he says.

Cold terror creeps up her back. Why did she come? Masters stands up with a gouty effort and walks over to the door. He closes and locks it with a large dark key. He hangs the key on his belt. Then he jumps, as if he's trying to skip over a rope. He takes silly little jumps toward Timmy and Mary, and she hides the child beneath her skirt.

"Oh, the bogeyman is coming to get you," he sneers at them.

Masters reaches for Timmy and Mary leans forward and bites his fingers until blood runs. The skin is thin and tastes of ink. She punches Masters on the nose and blood pours down his face.

"Oh, you cat! You wicked girl! I will have you flogged! Assaulting a magistrate! You try to murder me. Rodney! Come quickly! I have been attacked! I will have you put back in a place of incarceration and flogged! Or the pillory. They should never have released you!" screams Masters.

But Rodney does not come. Masters fumbles with the key and

plugs his nose with a handkerchief, as Mary climbs up onto the windowsill and heaves open the shutters. To leap or not to leap. She could hurt her child or even kill him.

She pulls Timmy onto her back and leaps down past a tall wall of climbing roses and stumbles into the flower beds. Timmy clings to her hip as the savage dogs of the estate are released. The boy screams in terror and climbs up her body, while the barking thunders all around. Mary and Timmy fly away out of the yard and then stop. The mastiff dogs are upon them. Mary turns, puts out her hand to the slavering dogs, and soothes them with her Darug language. "*Nallawalli, nallawalli mirri*, sit dog." They fall back and cringe.

She wants to protect Mercy too, but her friend has disappeared with no backward glance. Where on earth is she? Mary runs to the riverbank and puts Timmy in the boat under a blanket. He whimpers but she tells him to stay down and hide, *tuabilli*. Then she runs back to Masters's house, into the kitchen, past the dark-beamed rooms with stuffed heads of deer and a dusty fox stuck in a glass dome. But she can't find Mercy.

All the time, she can hear shouting behind her as the farmworkers search for her. She runs into the stables, past the tethered horses, and there she finds Mercy with Rodney, both near naked and lit by a beam of sunlight. They are panting, amidst joyful, lustful fornication. Mercy sits astride him with her rocking buttocks pinning him down. They turn their heads.

"Come, we have to go now!" Mary shouts, but Mercy is bouncing up and down, her dress bunched over her shoulders, ignoring Mary.

"I come later. I'm busy. Go. I can take care of myself," pants Mercy and she rocks forward in Rodney's arms.

One of Masters's servants takes Mary by the shoulder and hauls her out and across the lawn. She is dragged across to the rose garden and chained by her foot to a shed. She can hear them shouting out to find Timmy, who is discovered hiding in the canoe and is taken kicking to the cook to mind. Mary shouts and rattles the chain, but no one comes, not even Mercy. She tries to yank the chain from its hook, but come the damp morning, she is still a captive.

———

The next night, Masters hosts a dinner party to celebrate the governor's achievements, and he invites his old friends Captain Woodrow, Reverend Henry Smythe, and his wife. The old gang is back together. Mary watches their approach as they ride up to the grand house in a carriage. They are shocked to see a disheveled and wet Mary James, tied up in Masters's perfumed rose garden.

Masters walks down the stone steps and stands beside Mary, as if presenting her as an offering to the captain. Reverend Smythe is horrified but cannot speak. He looks away while his wife, Susan, titters.

Masters taps Mary's head and then wipes his hand on his waistcoat. He smirks at Smythe.

"Now, here you see our latest native specimen. You remember your feisty Mary. She ran away to the mountains, absconded from that excellent education with her native paramour, and stole food from your orphan school. Took fowls and a rooster, for pecuniary gain," says Masters.

"Henry, you used to think she was some virtuous, educated native person, but all these years may have changed your opinion of her, eh?" Masters asks.

"Not at all. She may be untrustworthy, but Mary is harmless. For God's sake, undo her bindings."

"Actually, she may be useful to me," says Woodrow. "She has lived with a native mountain tribe and has some tracking skills. Could I avail upon your generosity, Reverend Masters—may I take her on my expedition?"

"Be my guest. I have a surfeit of underlings," says Masters.

They move toward the house and no one looks back at Mary.

She huddles in the grass and works at undoing the shackle. She can see Masters smiling at Henry. Susan leans against her husband and strokes his cheek. Henry is mortified and carefully removes his wife's hand.

Mercy appears at the front door, dressed in full maid regalia with a starched, frilly white apron and a little hat. She signs to Mary across the lawn that she will help her, then darts inside with a tea tray.

"I will release that wretched woman and have her brought inside, so we can examine her for her usefulness," says Masters. "It can be like a party game."

A few minutes later, Mary is ushered into the house by Rodney, who wears full butler livery and stands in front of the assembly. He offers glasses of wine from a silver tray, while Mercy stands behind him.

"I believe that when you ran away from school, you found safe harbor with a wild mountain tribe? Oh, you are a brave girl. Weren't you scared of *myalls*?" asks Masters.

"She was of much help while engaged in our orphan institution, wasn't she, dear?" Henry asks his wife.

"No. She wasn't. I don't want this disgusting person in my sight," she replies.

"*N'aie pas peur*, Mary, don't be afraid. Did you miss your warm bed? Did you eat vermin, possum, and such?" Masters goes on and will not stop. "Perhaps your tainted virtue meant that you were no longer wanted by your own people? *Point de non-retour*? She will not be able to return, not really—not ever. Mother of two bastards. Mary, you are too much like us, then not like us at all. Quite spoiled, really. However, your actions banish you from all appropriate society. No doubt, you'll end up spending your days like those godless native wretches outside the hotel: in rags, begging for rum or a penny, or a bit of rumpity-tumpity. What is the going rate, Woodrow? A penny?"

"Wouldn't know, sir."

"Mercy will know," says Masters.

"Nothing, Reverend. Release her, kind sir," says Mercy and she curtsies.

"Nothing will come of nothing. Out you go," says Masters, and Mercy tiptoes out of the room.

"Enough of this talk!" says Smythe. "She is in distress. Either give her a position in your household or let her go free. I won't stand by and see her tormented by your un-Christian words."

"Ah, our lives are but a minute in time. We are insignificant. Perhaps I can tempt her. Would you like a shilling, Mary?" Masters reaches into his waistcoat pocket and flicks a coin. Susan giggles as it rolls to the carpet.

"Come, girl, give us some information on how to find the northern tribe Wonnaruah. Do I pronounce that correctly, Henry?" asks Masters. "Your grasp of native language is so much better than mine. Is it 'woo' as in 'who' or 'wo' as in 'won'? The tribe is wanted by British justice, either way. They have murdered shepherds in cold blood. You must lead Captain Woodrow and his soldiers to their lair. And you will be rewarded. A Queen plate around your neck?" says Masters.

Smythe urges Mary forward. "Speak up, don't be afraid," he says. She shivers, but no words come.

"We are but accessories of Christ. My life out here in the New World has been sacrificed to a great calling. I was summoned to take a great leap and save heathen souls," says Smythe. "Cut off from the virtuous world, Old England is now just a passing dream. Mary, you must agree to help. You must now choose sides."

"I cannot betray my countrymen," says Mary. She clenches her hands by her sides.

"Bring Mercy back in here. Perhaps she can talk sense to her companion," says Masters.

Rodney escorts Mercy into the room. Mary uses her eyes to implore her for help.

"Mercy, tell your friend of her duty to be chained and to lead the captain to the renegades," says Masters.

"She will not want to help a captain. She hates all soldiers. She might be better serving at table," says Mercy.

"The alternative is the Female Factory," says Masters.

"She won't like that. Too cruel," says Mercy.

Masters raises his hand to her and yells, "Silence!"

"Speak civil to us. We're grown-up women!" says Mercy.

"Help me, Mary, in my redemption. Please lead the captain on his search for miscreants," says Smythe. He tenderly takes her face and stares into it. Susan Smythe covers her scowling mouth with a fan and turns her back.

"Come, girl. You will be safe with me," says Woodrow.

Masters offers Woodrow a horse whip that hangs by his chair.

"Woodrow! Break her insolent spirit. You owe me a favor or two, the repayment of some debts," says Masters.

Captain Woodrow empties his wine glass and wipes the drips from his long, fair mustache.

"That will be unnecessary," says Woodrow.

"Beat her a little. A little harmless lash never hurt them. Or a taste of their quim. Their heads are tougher than ours. Come on, just a tickle," says Masters as he prods Mary's back. He has surely lost his mind.

But Henry Smythe can take no more.

"No, Reverend, I will not tolerate this. She wants to help us, don't you, Mary?" he asks as he touches her arm. "A little kindness can do wonders."

"You're useless," says Masters. "In God's name, girl, speak up and agree to go! Recalcitrant, *usque ad extremum*. To the very end." He lifts the whip over her, but Mary does not cringe. He whips her back, and Mercy rushes at him but is held back by Rodney. Mercy shakes with rage but is frozen to the spot.

Mary does not utter a sound. She is thinking about the way over the mountains. It shines like silver through the bush. The rocks that they sleep by, the teeming white waterfalls, and the high stone cliffs. The gray-green trees reaching tall into the mist. The cliffs that she leaps off in her sleep.

"You will follow the military directions and lead Captain Woodrow tomorrow morning north toward the mountain river or I will send your boy to grow up a servant in Van Dieman's Land. Bind her arms and throw her in the stable!" says Masters.

At last Henry has seen too much. He wrenches the whip out of Masters's hand. His face is red and he is struggling to keep control.

"You go too far, sir. You are an arrogant monster threatening this servant in my presence. You show me no respect! We have sworn holy oaths to take care of God's creatures. These young women and the child deserve such kindness and protection." Smythe is emphatic.

"Henry, don't get upset; she is just a native and she will have your guts for garters soon as look at you," says Susan. She continues, "You are a funny man to take it all so seriously. Your little Black pet will not be harmed."

"He is serious! He means to do her harm and I will not allow it!" Smythe screams.

"Reverend, you forget that I am your superior and you would do well to listen to your wife or be dismissed from this parish. I am a slave to this church and will be obeyed. Mary will be put in shackles and lead the party. I will not be defied!" says Masters.

Smythe is silenced.

Rodney drags Mary out to the yard while Smythe follows behind, a bundle of clothes in his hand.

"Give me your shift and apron. You must now wear the clothes of a felon. Mercy will have your child in her care," says Henry. "And

I am sorry, but you will have to wear shackles. Prepare yourself with prayer."

The word "shackles" clicks and terrifies. The sound of the word cuts her like a knife as she watches the captain put a pair in his saddlebag, next to his string of human ears.

———

Later, as Mary tries to sleep in a locked chicken shed, she can smell the hens and horses and the men smoking pungent tobacco. She can hear them laughing. Her chest trembles, her mouth is dry, and a creeping terror shows itself in her sweating hands. She imagines a knife in her fist, to work it into her prison wall. The straw pallet scratches with insects. It rains and the dirt floor turns to slush.

In this cold, terrible night, Mary looks through a chink in the clay wall and sees Henry walking in the mist toward the shed, carrying a jug of whiskey. A storm is growing and thunder erupts around her cell. Henry opens the door with a key, enters, then locks it from the inside. Squatting on the dirt, he swigs from the jug, his eyes never leaving her body. He hands the jug to Mary, but she shakes her head.

"You never drank before," she says.

"I do on occasion, and this is one such occasion," he says as his fingers run down her arm.

"I'll come back and burn down this house," she whispers angrily.

"No, you won't, because you would be hanged and then there would be no one to care for little Timmy," he slurs.

"Let me go, *naiya whu karndi*, you can be kind, Henry," whispers Mary.

"But not brave enough to disobey. I lack a steadfastness. I hope you are warm enough?" he asks, even though she has no cover, and it is obvious she is freezing. He hands her his coat.

"One must learn how to obey—that is what you must do for your whole existence. It is the consequence of thy servitude. Necessary but not evil. You see, people like myself are going to always control your life," says Henry. "I am, in truth, a terrible man. Cursed, if you will. I must confess, I can't trust myself. I want all the beautiful women I see. And I see you, dearest. My father spent all his time praying in the church. He ignored me and my suffering mother and I am eternally angry with him. But I am not like him. Save the Lord! I desire to be a good man. I sincerely pray for this. I want to be remembered by any children that God may grace me with as a moral man. What happened to our child? You must help us."

"She's lost. I don't have to listen to your rubbish talk. *Kaundi*, go on, get out!" Mary spits.

She turns away. She doesn't want to look at his earnest, lying face. Henry squats in his long black gown on the muddied floor and brushes the hair from her eyes; he strokes her cheek. She snaps at him with her teeth.

"Now, now. I'm sorry but I can't disobey my superior. I find I am in a position of subservience. I am so very, very sorry," he says.

He looks mournfully at Mary as she sits in the dirt, chains around her ankles and wrists.

Mary wonders how she could ever have felt anything for him. Henry takes once last look and shakes his head as he unlocks the door and stumbles out of the barn.

"I trusted you, for a long time!" Mary hisses.

CHAPTER TWENTY-THREE

1838: On the Mountain

King William IV of the United Kingdom of Great Britain and Ireland made a proclamation in 1836 but it is only reported now in the *Windsor Gazette*: The king recognizes the continued rights to land for Aboriginal people in South Australia in the "Letters Patent."

This promise of legal entitlement will not be kept.

A massacre of Aboriginal people occurs at Gravesend in New South Wales in 1837 with two hundred killed. Countless Aboriginal massacres happen everywhere, including in New South Wales. There have been fifty-five massacres since the arrival of Captain Phillip.

———

One early morning, the troopers march out of Windsor town. Yellow-tailed black cockatoos swoop overhead and a strong breeze blows the eucalypts in gray-green waves. Mary is ashamed of her subjugated position. Scores of people line the street waving small British flags as children hold their mothers' hands and point and cheer. In front are twenty soldiers on horseback, wearing red uniforms with gleaming silver buttons. Mary is tied behind the last brown horse and must run to keep up. She is sweating and miserable; the rope pulls at the metal chain and rings around her hands. She has never felt such unbearable humiliation and such rage.

They march for days along the rough roads and into the bush toward Wonnaruah country in the north, where she will be required to lead soldiers to kill the native people. White people from the small villages stand by the road, laughing and jeering.

Captain Woodrow stops his horse near a settlement and doubles back to stand near Mary. He unfurls a rough map.

"Mary. Use your wits to live. Where to from here?" he asks. She stands there with her manacled wrists; her throat is tight with bitter rage.

"The colonel tells me that I have not excelled in finding miscreant natives. I am no longer essential to the current authorities," says Woodrow. "But today is my last chance, the day I shall excel. You will escort us to find your countrymen."

"Don't force me! Let me go! I know nothing," hisses Mary.

"One last expedition into the wilderness and I shall return to the Indian hill station of Nainital to catch fish." He clips her backside with his riding crop, and they continue along a bush track.

After a few more hours, Captain Woodrow turns his mount around and rides back to Mary. He has a flash of pity and leans down to take her chin in his white-gloved hand. He gives her a sip from his water bottle, wipes the top, and then takes a drink himself.

"I have a pretty Indian cotton dress for you on our return. And you can play us some violin music and be rewarded with goods. Would you like that? Don't be afraid," he says.

Mary trembles at this unexpected kindness. She nods but cannot look at him. She will need his protection from the evil ways of the soldiers—the soldiers that jeer with pure lust at her. Mary can tell that they hate Captain Woodrow.

They stop for the night on a stone ridge in deep forest. The mist rises above miles of bird's-nest ferns and huge gum trees with girths so huge that ten men holding hands together cannot encircle them. The night is full of crickets and night birds. Making herself small, she curls up next to a thicket of bracken fern with a thin blanket.

"This chain hurts. Take it off. Give me water," she croaks to Woodrow. She can hardly speak.

Woodrow uncaps a water flask again and hands it to her. "Here, drink. Keep it. I have another," says Woodrow. "You have fallen, but don't despair; it's not your fault. Reverend Masters preaches about God's neglect. You are born to be Eve, the temptress. Are you a temptress?" he asks.

"I want to go back to Windsor, Captain. I cannot help," she whispers so faintly he can barely hear her.

"You have skills in tracking and, by Jove, you will help. You cooperate with us and we will do the same for you," says Woodrow. "You will explain to us about the tribes. We need to know more about the Awakabal in the northwest, the Worimi in the southeast, and here also the Wonnaruah. Your countryman Bowen is a Guringai, I believe."

"I'll tell you nothing," she says.

"We must follow native tracks to the Hunter region. You will show me the way. We need to punish them for some transgressions against settler families," he prattles on.

"I want food," she mouths.

"So be it, food in return for leading," he says.

"You are like little lost babies," she says, finding the strength to speak. "You don't know about this place where, behind every tree, native men are waiting to murder you. When you eat, when you piss, when you sleep. The mob have hook spears. When that spear goes into your body, you can't get it out. You must push the spear through muscle and skin. You have to saw the spear off. But a tiny bit of stone will stick in that wound and make poison."

"I have fought savages on the Indian frontier and I know that no honor exists among savages," he says.

"We fight for our country and, if we die, we go up into the sky, with Baiame. We are spirits. You just rot in the ground," she replies.

"We go to greet the Lord," says Woodrow. "You must prepare yourself, Mary. Pray to God that you find them before we are attacked because, believe me, I will shoot you if you betray us. I want this journey to be a success. I need this expedition to succeed to ensure my promotion and pension."

He takes hold of her shoulders and forces her to look at him.

"I will never help you!" she says.

"Well, be warned, I'm a man of my word. I will not hesitate to strip you naked, give you to my men for pleasure, and then leave you to bleed to death," he says as he strolls away.

"I will kill you first," she vows to herself.

They walk all day in terrible heat. She watches the soldiers eating, treacle dripping down from their mouths, and she drools. She looks at trees to climb or hang herself from. She imagines the rope, the knot, the crack of her neck. Squatting by a pool that is before a cascading waterfall, she can see her reflection and she is all haggard, dirty, and in rags.

Later, they give her a little salt beef and water.

As night falls the sky is full of ancestors. Mary lies back dreaming and hears her father telling her the stories of the beginning. The captain walks toward her and she sees that he is holding a pannikin of tea for her. For a moment she is happy.

In the cool, dark bush, Mary hears the sound of a cork popping. The captain drinks rum from a stone bottle with a young corporal. The young man scrapes mud from his long boots with a dagger and then cleans it against a tree. His hair shines red in the firelight.

"Don't drink too much, it has to last," says Woodrow.

"Much appreciated, sir. Doing me good," he says.

They laugh like old friends, and it makes her shiver. The red-haired corporal is whispering, and Mary can see his outline against the firelight. Red coats are pulled closer against the chilly air. Her teeth chatter.

"Let me have her, sir," says the corporal.

"Don't be a fool. Leave her be, on my orders," says Woodrow.

Her palms sweat and her breathing increases. A bird of prey hovers. A snowy owl. An omen.

Mary sees the corporal licking his lips and smirking at her. He even winks as though he has dibs on her, like he has won her in a game of dice. She imagines the laughter and clicking dice.

She watches to see where he keeps his pistol—wrapped in an oilskin in his saddlebags.

"Out here in the wilderness there's nothing but savages. We could have a taste. Just sneak her over the hill there. Tip her over and rumpity-tumpity," he says.

"She is our guide," says Woodrow. "Turn your mind to some useful thoughts, such as navigating our way back to Windsor at the end of this."

"Yes, sir. Just a joke, sir. Pulling yer leg. Wouldn't dream of it. Against regulations," replies the corporal.

Mary leads them on a native track in the morning light. She has no choice. The terrain is rough with sandstone, and she takes them down small ravines that will surely break a horse's leg. She stumbles over round stones near a creek surrounded by ferns, where they stop to drink the cool spring water and refill drinking flasks. She nibbles at sarsaparilla vine leaves and the sweetness slakes her thirst. The captain puts out his hand and she places one tender purple diamond-shaped leaf on his palm. She motions to him to eat it then spit. He chews with a smile and spits like her.

A while later, the captain brings her a blanket and some water to wash with. He even gives her some perfumed soap. Mary, however, waits for him to leave and she uses the soap to work on the metal manacles that bind her wrists. But the iron bolt is as thick as her finger and never loosens.

After the rest, Mary refuses to move on. She is pulled upright and stands rigid.

The captain takes her neck and chains it again. She is pulled along by a horse, its arse and its twitching black tail in her face. Flies flick from its tail to her mouth.

"Keep up!" the corporal shouts and giggles as they move on. His eyes are on the breast that peeks from her torn shift.

When they next stop for the night, she sits down on a grassy verge and sighs with an outflow of breath. The captain tips sugar from a cloth bag onto her hand and she eats it but does not look at him. He strolls away to lean against his mare, sipping tea.

The corporal walks up to her and whispers, "Black strumpet, fit for nothin' but fuckin'."

She can smell him—the stink of tobacco, blood, urine, shit, and semen. He scratches in the dust in front of her with his boot. Later, Mary hears men snoring and snuffling in their sleep; some cry out. She looks up in the gloom and sees the blue-eyed corporal over her, blowing kisses. She throws off her blanket and kicks his stomach with all her strength until he falls backward and lies in the dirt breathing hard. His face is pink and the blue veins in his neck are throbbing. She stands up and kicks him again. It feels so good.

She will fight rather than succumb to the *waibala* against her will. Her stolen country is somehow all bound up with this man who would try to rape her.

He kicks dirt at her face and she retaliates with another shove. The corporal swings his fist into her head, and she feels a lightning burst of pain in her temple. He has acne with yellow pus dotting his dirty face. His hair straggles to his shoulders, reddish and lank. He has bright blue eyes and white eyebrows. She sucks a tooth that is loose and lowers her head.

Mary lies back against the tree and feels her back aching from the punches. Her fingers are black, her nails caked with dirt, and she claws at the manacle as if sheer will can cut through the iron.

"Get it over with, you stupid fella, then I'll kill you!" she hisses.

His eyes widen as he hits her with the butt of his gun. The pain shoots through her head. She rolls on the ground and waits. She can hardly breathe. It hurts to move. She imagines she is turning to flame, like Satan in a picture in the Bible. Fire coming out of her eyes and mouth. If she were shot now, surely wild devils would pour out of the wounds. She hisses at her attacker and he walks away.

Sometime later, the captain returns to talk to Mary.

"That corporal bashed me, and you do nothing," she spits through swollen lips.

"He will be punished if indeed he has harmed you," he says, ignoring her obvious injuries.

"Where are you going? You're lost," she says.

"Come. Lead us again, Mary. The renegades seek our utter destruction. I do need and expect your cooperation. Do you sense where the renegades are camped?" he asks.

"You can follow me but please, Captain, take off the chain," she pleads.

The captain shakes his head, but there is a glimmer of kindness as he says, "I can't, because you might run."

As they continue and the track becomes rougher, she pictures herself as a child in her true country by the Deerubbin.

"Hey, Blackie, I'll shoot ya. That captain can't protect you if I've shot you while trying to escape. But I won't do that. I like you," leers the corporal.

Mary looks at this man, spit drooling from his curling lips.

He mimes kissing her with his musket.

Go on, she thinks, *shoot*.

She is fading.

"Which way? I can hear something ahead. Did you hear that shout? Quiet, everyone. Mary, can you follow their tracks?" asks Captain Woodrow.

"I'm not a tracker! Just woman," she says.

But she knows the telltale signs, the stone upturned, the broken twig, the bracken fern–brushed footprints. Boothuri taught her well. She sees a heel print. She knows that they are not far ahead, and panic rises in her. What can she do? She is at the end and can hardly see.

"She has tricked us! We have been puffing up this ridge, for what? The heathens are comin' and will surround us, tear us apart, and eat our livers," shouts the corporal.

The next day, Mary is manacled but no longer chained to a horse. She smells the smoke that draws the troopers onward to her people. The message beacons are lit and she can follow them. It might be the Wonnaruah people. But this is betrayal.

Suddenly, a thin warrior chief stands before her, and he recognizes her. Mary grits her teeth in a grin, and he sees her hands in their metal prison. He is silent and stands still in the shadows. Only she can see him. He whispers to her in his language and she can barely understand. She holds up her shackle and he nods because it is a commonplace thing.

"*Yalingen*, get captain, *barrao*," says the chief.

Mary uses her last breath to catch up to the captain's horse and reaches him on the edge of a fern-lined creek. His horse is drinking. He looks down at her with a grin.

"What is it, Mary?" he asks.

"The renegade chief, he's here. Come! Not soldiers, just you. He wants talk with you," she says.

He motions to the others to stay, then loads his musket, and walks his horse toward the dark trees. As he moves, the other soldiers load their rifles. An echoing click of powder and shot can be heard. The chief steps lightly onto the track. He is adorned with eagle feathers and a possum-skin cloak.

"Sir, you have come to surrender?" asks Woodrow. "We are well armed and you have your spears. Not a match at a distance for a Brown Bess with a range of six hundred feet. Hmm?" The two men eye each other, then the captain looks around the trees for signs of an ambush. Slowly, he takes tobacco from a pouch and offers it to the warrior. He fills a pipe, which the captain lights with a flint. The Aboriginal man inhales.

The captain pulls Mary in front of him and asks her to interpret the language of the warrior, but she is ashamed to face such an important man and shakes her head.

"Tell me what he says. You understand his lingo? I know you can do this," the captain implores Mary. She interprets as best she can.

"*Wirra* native? *Wirra? Burruberongal wah? Warmuli wah?* All finish? All about, no *bulla bingie.* No food. Talkem governor," he says.

"He wants to meet with the governor and talk peace. He wants coins for his land and for food. He wants you to give help for native people. They are starving. He wants land for his people. He asks why are native heads cut off and given to the king of England? He wants to know, is the king a cannibal?" she says.

The captain seems to be unable to speak but Mary keeps up the translation: "When will more white men come? What do you want from us? Why do you pour over the earth like locusts? Do you want to kill him, too?"

The chief motions to the captain and grins. He breaks a spear over his leg and throws it down. Mary stands with limp arms, and he laughs at her. She is dumbstruck at his audacity and courage because she knows he may be shot at any moment. The captain stares in disbelief.

Then this great warrior chief is gone; he disappears like a wisp of smoke. He evaporates, leaving only mist hanging in the place where he stood. The earth has no footprint on it. Currawongs sing out in garbling voices.

The broken spear is a challenge for war. The soldiers stay for a few minutes then resume the senseless walking, with Mary lurching from tree to tree to keep her balance. The air is thicker than blood. The terrible fear of sudden death is upon them all. Mary knows the warriors are now waiting for the soldiers, waiting to kill them all. It gets late and the party rests. Some guard the horses, terror prickling their bodies. The moon is nearly full and the night is bright. It seems that an ambush is possible now from any side.

The tribal men attack with *boondi* and spears. There is the stench of the horses' fear as they stampede into the oncoming spears. The chief throws a spear with deadly accuracy, and it slams into a soldier's chest. Another soldier tries to pull out the barbed point, but it causes agony for the dying man. The soft flesh rips on the spear and blood spurts forth. Then, all at once, the native men leap down the nearby cliff and, with clubs raised, begin to beat the soldiers. Skulls are split open, and brains spill out of their skulls like burst watermelons, while little white teeth lie scattered in red pools of gore.

Then the noise of death as people are pushed over a rugged cliff. The warriors are losing the battle, and Mary watches the fighting and hand-to-hand struggle at the edge of the precipice. It is pitiful and terrible.

Mary can hear the crows and the moaning of the wounded warriors and soldiers. She tries to give the wounded men water as their guts push out of the spear holes like little blind mice. Then suddenly, beside her, she sees an old native man who is dying, stretched across a dead soldier, with a gaping hole in his shoulder. Shock rushes through her.

The old man opens his eyes and is startled. He smiles; he is with her, now at this moment when he will meet his spirit. She sings to him, humming a half-remembered song, and touches his face, cleaning the clay from his eyes. Her eyes are close to his now, keeping him awake in his pain. If she can pull him away from the dead man under him, she thinks she might be able to save him. Mary cradles his head and slides on her backside, pulling the heavy weight with her. She rips her dress and pushes the material into the gaping wound. If she can stop the blood he might live. The man lifts his head; he wants to speak. He is like her dead father.

However, Captain Woodrow has nearly completed the slaughter and he sees Mary helping the warrior. He crashes through the bush toward him, his saber drawn. He seems intent on killing every Aboriginal warrior. Mary screams, trying to deflect the blow, but it is too late. The old man is dealt death's promise as the saber cuts through his neck. There is screaming now, and she bellows at the captain. She falls onto the man's chest and is soaked in his blood. His eyes flutter then close. There is nothing she can do. She crawls into a low cave to find some shelter and waits for the horror to stop. The end has come.

Captain Woodrow stands still above the carnage and is wracked by sobs. There are countless dead warriors. His face transforms as he takes in the enormity of the scene. He tosses his saber away and kneels on the stony ground and buries his face in his hands and prays.

===

An old man kangaroo—seven feet tall—sits in front of Mary's cave. He scratches his chest with black claws and leans back grandly on his huge, thick tail. He seems totally unafraid. His ears are erect and twitching. He might take Mary away, bouncing across the rocky escarpment. He watches her and then suddenly he is gone, leaping high over bushes.

In the evening, Woodrow lifts Mary out of the cave. She sits in desolation, but the captain is businesslike. He commands the remaining twelve men to dig graves.

By the setting sun, the moaning has stopped and the last young, wounded soldier has died. They press his eyelids closed and the others line up to pray. They dump the rest of the Aboriginal men's bodies over the cliff and watch them tumble into the abyss.

The troopers move on and camp by a tall stone face surrounded by dripping water and maidenhair ferns. The horses are tethered and the exhausted men crouch over small fires. Captain Woodrow is now in a dangerous, simmering rage, capable of anything. He grabs Mary's head and stares into her face. She is now chained by the neck all day with a hand-forged iron chain and hinged circular ring, its bolt strong but rusted.

"Which way do we go? Up or down?" demands Woodrow. "I think we must follow the creek and not the ridge, yes? Speak up!"

Mary does not reply.

———

At dawn, the captain is anxious to keep moving.

"Creek better. Horses walk better," says Mary. The captain looks at her with narrowed eyes.

"Spare me your lying prattle. You are trying to trick me," says Woodrow. "You're lying about the best way, aren't you? Trying to protect murderers? You're a savage and you want to help that murdering fiend!" He twists her arm and pushes her against the rocks.

"I hate you!" She spits as he throws her to the ground.

"You traitor!" he says and strikes her across the face. "We shall traverse that ridge, not along the creek to the valley. Watch that you don't break a horse's leg. Go now! Our liberty is to be had. For Christ's sake, be quiet."

"Let me go. You might get killed soon. Please, let me go," Mary whispers and her eyes beg.

"You will come and see your handiwork. Push her along, Corporal. Our guide has done her duty for the king and she will be given to you and your men to pleasure yourselves. I have protected her too long."

Mary wonders if she will have the power to stop an outrage on her body. The smell of these men is disgusting, and they have bloodied clothes and will probably kill her afterward. She imagines finding a sharp stick and hiding it.

Woodrow pushes her onto the track. She cries out "Cooee," again and again. She has warned her countrymen.

Suddenly there are screams and running, and a tumult of spears is thrown. They whistle through the air and slam into trees near the soldiers. The soldiers run and, with Mary dragged along beside them, keep moving until dusk. Mary sits by the trees and watches the fairy wrens in the grevillea bush. She can hear muttering curses. The air is thick with rage.

The corporal walks up to her and pulls back her hair, his fingers twisting the curls. He tugs as though he will pull the tendrils out. Mary's eyes are wild and she feels as strong as ten men. The corporal rips her dress from her upper body; Mary crawls along the ground and reaches out for a stick and with a ferocious force, she hits his head. He flinches and grins as she claws his flaying arms, like meat in her hands. Bloody and salty. He flinches and grabs his rifle, bashing the side of her head. Screeching pain and knives of lightning rush through her head. She slumps against a tree, and he ties her arms firmly with rope, wrapping it around the bark. She watches blankly as the captain walks off into a clearing, smoking a pipe. Laughter is behind her; she waits for the start of the terror. The soldier touches her and pulls her forward. A smack across her backside. Almost playful, then he pushes her face against the tree. The corporal whispers in her ear.

"My strumpet!"

They move toward her, wanting vengeance and retribution on her poor body. They are laughing.

"Heathen, savage!"

The men nearby watch and breathe hard, and the corporal whispers that he loves her. His sweet words trickle in her ear.

"I won't let them hurt you. I might take you away and marry you. I like black velvet ones. You want me, don't you?" The other men laugh. He nibbles her neck, and she turns and bites his lip hard. Blood spurts out and he belts her across the face with his pistol.

They beat her with sticks and chains. The misshapen iron hangs by her face. Her tongue lolls against it. The corporal jerks his pizzle over her belly. Another man leans in, with his breeches around his knees; his bad breath clings to her hair like something dead, and she knows that if they rape her, she will have to find each one and kill them.

The captain walks back to the clearing and sees the men standing over her limp form and curses, threatening them with his rifle. The men untie her and walk away, and the captain yells after them, "Give her the shift to cover herself and leave her be. Haven't we done enough?"

They laugh. Someone throws a water bottle at her feet. The captain smokes a pipe and will not look at her. His head hangs low.

———

The first morning light glistens through the trees and smoke whispers over the sleeping soldiers. She has a stick poking in her back and the blanket is wet with dew; she has not slept. The night has been punctuated by sudden cries and she wonders if they are her own. Men have been crying in their sleep and the cries of baby animals echo in the gullies.

She is numb.

As she pulls the blanket tighter around her, she spots the glinting of a broken blade. She stretches the chain as far as it can reach. Her hand quivers as she snatches the blade and hides it in the blanket.

Squatting on her haunches, she pees behind the tree. She examines the lock that fastens the two chains. With the blade she might click it open; she is good at locks. There is a satisfying click.

Later, the corporal approaches her again and untethers the chain. All the hatred and rage spill from her like vomit. She sticks the blade into his shoulder, and they are bathed in torrents of blood that is so warm and so clean. He tries to throttle Mary, but the neck manacle is in his way. Now she can see her freedom and her face grimaces as he lets her go with a groan as his eyes roll. His body slumps, and she presses the blade deeper into him and he screams.

She runs through the scrub as fast as she can, carrying the chain wrapped around her hand. She rushes through the bush, the tree branches tearing at her arms and legs as she stumbles and weeps and runs, running into the mist. Eaglehawks soar above her. They lift bits of human flesh into the blue sky. One drifts down to land beside her; the wedge of his tail is tipped in black; his head is smooth with pale, flecked feathers like a cap. She asks him where she can run, and he flies off on a rise of wind and she follows.

After a long rush through the undergrowth, Mary sees a rock shelter, and although she doesn't know how deep it is or where it ends, she goes inside. There are drawings by her people here. It feels safe, like a nest with wombat fur and bat droppings. Axe-grinding marks scar the sandstone at the back of the shelter, and she runs her finger in them, cleaning the grooves. She can lie down to rest. Some droplets of water collect in a trickle along the edge of the shelter, and she puts out her tongue to drink them.

She will hide now and seek cold vengeance when the moment comes. Her fingers caress the cuts and bruises on her body. She examines the grazing on her shoulders and knees and knows they will heal. She finds a tea tree bush and makes poultices of its leaves and presses them against the worst of her wounds. She falls into a deep, healing sleep.

The next morning is warm, and sunlight dapples through leaves;

honeyeaters dart through a grevillea bush. She can see the trail back to Windsor and her true country shining silver like a snail's tracing. Her instinct will lead her along that Blackfella path.

She scrapes wattle gum from a branch and stuffs gobs of it in her mouth. She eats raw tubers of daisy yams and sucks nectar from a waratah. She cups the water and slurps up the tadpoles from a small creek, then cleanses away the blood. A fig tree offers sweet sandpaper figs, and she gorges on them and saves some in a piece of paperbark that she fashions into a bag with string of a vine. She makes a skirt of bark, and for a moment she is happy; it is quite stylish. The creek ends in a pond of purple lilies, and she dives into the water to fetch lily bulbs to eat and chews on the crisp stems. She is full of food, but her bowels open in a sudden rush of stomach pain.

At sunset, crows sing out, but she will not watch them fly into the sun; she remembers that this is forbidden—but cannot recall why.

She will go back to find Timmy. There is no other path. Dead men hang stinking on trees behind her and she knows that is not her destiny. She must keep walking. She wills herself to see her children laughing. She sees smoke cleansing the land.

In the night she sleeps fitfully under a rock crevice and wakes up, after nightmares, with a wombat calmly nosing her side.

After walking for three days, Mary is released from the manacle by a farmer who gives her a salve for her wounds and offers her his dead wife's old housedress to wear. He sets a bowl of gruel in front of her and watches her eat. He is harmless and kindly. He waves her off with a supply of dry beef and damper, and she tramps on her own all the way to Windsor and collapses at the South Creek Aboriginal camp.

═══

On the return of Captain Woodrow from his expedition, Mary is not allowed to take back her son and is summoned from the Blacks' camp to the magistrate's court. She is led away by police constables and is placed in a cell to await her punishment. Her name is called and she enters the courtroom with trepidation.

The great wooden door opens and Captain Woodrow sits below the high bench of Reverend Masters. Her face falls and she expects to be taken back to prison. They look at her and say nothing. Woodrow begins to laugh, and he doubles over in mirth.

"What is amusing, Captain?" asks Masters.

"The look on Mary James's face. Like she is about to be drawn and quartered," says Woodrow. "I am exhausted by killing and do not want her charged," he continues.

Mary yells and points at the magistrate.

"I cannot be tried by him! He is a monster!"

Masters ignores the outburst.

"Most unexpected, be quiet! But this is your call, Captain. I will not stand in the way of your kindness; I am not a cruel man. Why, she did endeavor on this occasion to do her best, eh?" Masters also laughs.

"I wish to speak," says Mary.

"What is it?" asks Masters as he drinks a glass of brandy.

"Are there no other magistrates in Windsor? You look too old, sir. Why are you always here?" says Mary. "Why don't you just send me to the pillory now? You, who have taken my child. I have been assaulted by the men in that regiment. Hit and chained."

"Quite so. Members of the regiment who carnally knew you or ravished you are less than pious in their inclinations when engaged in battle. But are they scoundrels, Captain?" asks Masters.

"She was ill-used, sir."

"Mary, you wish to make complaint?" asks Masters.

"Yes. Most of all, I want my child back," she says.

"So, you want a reward for your service and silence," says Masters.

"Would it help me to make complaint?"

"No," says Masters.

He taps his gavel, drinks more brandy, and twitches his beard.

"You come hither and thither—I am at a loss," he says.

"The expedition was a success in its punitive endeavors but at considerable cost to my men. I regret the miserable events and I am weary of death. I would have her pardoned," says Woodrow.

"She can go? But your corporal has a wound inflicted by her, does he not?" asks Masters.

"He carnally knew her, and she fought back. He has but a scratch inflicted by a much-abused woman," says Woodrow.

"A scratch, a tiny scratch," adds Mary.

"Is that true, Captain?"

"Let her go, sir. I am nearly fifty. These proceedings are of little consequence in the greater world. Enough is enough," says Captain Woodrow.

Mary looks at the captain and he pulls at his collar. But he will not look into her eyes.

"Farewell, Mary. I hope your life will be better. The truth to tell, I admire your spirit, and I am too old to care too much what happens any longer to this colony. I am off to the subcontinent," says Woodrow.

Masters taps his gavel and clears his throat.

"Mary James, I have your son, little Timmy, nearby for you. He shall be the reward for your compliance, and your precious violin and bow as well," says Masters. "Now, let your sable friends know that we *waibalas* are not unkind. Captain Woodrow has been very benevolent toward you, even if you do not recognize it as such. We can see when a favor has been attempted and, although you failed to help with our total conquest of your brethren, we will give you back your child. You may go freely about your business."

Masters has Timmy brought into the courtroom. He runs tearfully to his mother and hugs her legs. He is healthy and at ease.

"You can take your sad little canoe and I will give you some supplies, clothes, and whatnot. I am not a cruel person. One wonders what will become of you. I feel that we shall meet again, and you may be doomed to one day face the gallows, for you are too rebellious," says Masters.

Woodrow unwraps a brown paper parcel and hands a toy bear to Timmy. The child laughs and holds it up to his mother. Woodrow then passes her a small purse of coins. She tucks it in her dress and turns her back on the captain, who leaves the room. She is free.

Mary pushes the thoughts around her head, wondering if people like Masters could change and become better or fairer and less ridiculous. Of course, she feels herself growing into a fiercer woman. She could stand up to a bully or shoot him. She knows a bit about muskets now, so having one might be useful. Her rage will keep. She dreams of revenge, simple payback for her torture.

＝＝＝＝

Over the coming months, Mary and Timmy make a living performing with her fiddle, playing some songs and jigs at town markets along the Deerubbin, the Hawkesbury River. Each week she travels from Gentleman's Halt to the small river settlement of Spencer, where she collects supplies.

One day when Mary is at Spencer, she sees the blue-eyed, red-haired corporal who has wandered into this tiny settlement and is buying bottled bung-head and rum at the makeshift store on the wooden wharf. It is him.

Mary has a reflection upon the consequences of actions, but she can recall her own resistance to the men's attack. She can almost taste the corporal's bloodied lip. She takes pride in that and how she stabbed the man's shoulder with a blade. It felt powerful. She has warrior ancestors.

She slips into the only store, with its sacks of flour and tins of Chinese tea, and asks about the purchase of a flintlock musket and cartridges. The storekeeper knows Mary well and is not inclined to offer her credit. She produces her violin and bow as payment. Her need is great.

"What would I bloody be doing with that?" He laughs and digs beneath the counter to lay out an old musket. He places the twists of paper cartridges beside it.

"For hunting kangaroo, to feed my little one," she says. He nods with a doubting expression but can see no harm.

"You know how to prime it? You take the paper cartridge with its musket ball and gunpowder and pour a little into the pan. See the touch hole? The hammer is half-cocked, but when you draw it back then you are ready to squeeze the trigger. You got that, lass?" he asks.

Mary nods and takes the heavy musket and ammunition wrapped in sacking.

"You got an old suit of men's clothes for me? I can pay later."

"Never knew a Blackfella who paid later—I don't know why I have such a soft heart for you lot. Take my worn-out coat and the bloody hat with it, for free!" He laughs. "Don't you go shooting your foot off!"

Next day, she covers Timmy with a blanket and creeps up the riverbank in her disguise. The sun is just rising and nobody is about except the sleeping corporal. Seagulls and cormorants fly over the wharf. Sandstone pillars are covered in old oyster shells, and yellow sun glints on the waves. It is a pretty scene. The corporal is snoring on a pile of blankets; he mumbles drunkenly alongside the trees by the empty Spencer wharf.

"You, Corporal! Wake up!" whispers Mary as she pokes the musket into his side. The man cries out in alarm and stumbles to his feet.

"What the hell?"

"Quiet now!" she says as she moves out of his reach.

He sits up, rubbing his head and, as he focuses on Mary, he whimpers and attempts to stand but staggers.

"Stand up and follow me. I have something for you," Mary hisses through tight teeth.

He stands and shakes. She cocks the hammer of the flintlock musket and without hesitation blasts him with the gun. The ball hits his hand. His fingers are smashed, and he screams as if he is about to die. Blood gushes down his arm but she thinks he is barely wounded. Mary lowers the weapon and throws it far out into the river and runs to her canoe, where Timmy sleeps. She must escape recognition. She will not return to the stone house on the riverbank.

Mary paddles ferociously down the river toward Marra Marra Creek. She has heard rumors of a settlement among orange groves and her cousin's home—a mythical world of peace and plenty. But she will still have to live in fear of arrest. Her home at Gentleman's Halt has to be forgotten.

CHAPTER TWENTY-FOUR

1839–43: Marra Marra Creek

Governor George Gipps served with the Duke of Wellington but missed the Battle of Waterloo. In Australia he helps set up the Protectorate of the Aborigines with the object of rescuing the Aboriginal tribes from misery and saving the whole race from extermination.

Mary hears the rumors of a rising up among the clans to the north, south, and west. The Myall Creek Massacre takes place when twelve heavily armed settlers round up and murder twenty-eight Aboriginal people at Henry Dangar's station at Myall Creek. The killers are caught and put on trial for the massacre of the Gammeray tribe near Terri Hie Hie in the far northern district. The colony is alive with the scandal of a court finding those men guilty of murder. There are good reasons for *waibala* to be silent about such things.

<hr>

Mary and Timmy take a day to reach the hidden valley of Marra Marra Creek, a tributary of the Deerubbin. It is a hidden meadow of rich soil and orange groves with small slab huts. Timmy is delighted to be on the river again for a long journey, and he lets his hand splash in the water. The river ripples with fish, and ducks dive beside the canoe.

Paddling along the side of the Deerubbin to escape detection from fisherfolk, Mary has a wallaby skin to keep warm, and she sings to Timmy to make him smile. She hides her growing fears of being followed.

The silvery water flows calmly around them and Mary watches the high cliffs of yellow sandstone with the dense green forest of gum trees. Mist wafts from the northern shore, streaming upward like spirit smoke. The river is peaceful now with pelicans lumbering overhead. Timmy feels droplets of rain and he holds out his hands to catch them.

"Don't put your *dhummar* hand in there. Lots of *eon*. Might bite you," she says.

Mary is not sure where the Marra Marra settlement hides and she waits near the shore for the ebb tide to turn. She waits for the current, and it takes her skimming across the expanse of the great river. She lands at Bar Point and makes a fire of driftwood on the oyster-covered rocks. She can see Coba Point and Berowra Creek in the distance and nearby Marra Marra Creek, where a woman wades with her *mootin* fish spear and cotton shawl, a dillybag of fish on her back. A small child wades next to her with a shark liver in her hand. It must be for lighting lamps.

She can make out eucalypt slab huts with bark roofs tucked under the hill, with tiny chimneys blowing wisps of smoke into the peaceful scene. Mary has heard the stories about this settlement, hidden among the mangroves.

Mary sees the river bend and she remembers coming here long ago with her father, to a place where piles of oyster shells heap on the riverbank and fires of lime are scattered among the trees. Mary follows the creek at high tide to the houses.

It is a fine summer's day and the wide Deerubbin dances in the sunlight as Mary paddles into the mangrove creek. Green seed pods float in the water and long tendrils of mangrove roots curl into gray mud. On the riverbank, crabs scuttle and the sandstone rocks are thick with *bittongi* oysters. Cormorants sit on branches drying their wings like flags.

With the sounds of singing children echoing in the morning sunlight, Mary has found this secret place, where the sheer distance from white men's towns protects the families. The children grow here, hidden from colonial authorities.

As she paddles across the oyster beds, she holds Timmy tightly.

A small sailing boat sits anchored near the riverbank, and Timmy calls when he sees other children dressed in worn cotton bonnets. The children run up and down calling to the newcomers.

At Marra Marra Creek, Mary greets Biddy, Bowen's sister, who has bought three acres of land for fifteen shillings at a public auction. The teeming group of children help Mary pull her canoe up on the riverbank and grab hold of their new playmate, Timmy.

"Welcome, Mary, we hear all about your troubles; you safe here. My children are Elizabeth, Mary Ann, James, Tom, Catherine, and Louisa Lewis," says Biddy.

The children cling to their mother as their names are called.

There are hugs for Mary, and the family immediately sets about finding a bed for her in a shack. They show her where to spear the best fish. She watches the men burning lime from oyster shell middens. Timmy runs after the older children and competes at gathering oranges and peaches from the orchard. Surely here she is safe.

A majestic old white man walks toward her, his hand out in welcome. He wears an old military jacket, braided and with tarnished buttons. At first Mary is unsure, but the many brown children and smiling women put her at ease, and she feels as if she has come home. John Ferdinand Lewis is an old Prussian ex-convict who was in a war against Napoleon Bonaparte. He has a long blond mustache, which he twirls with wax, and wears white shirts with lace collars. He smokes a Dutch pipe. The men in the Lewis family are shipbuilders. Biddy is a granddaughter of Chief Bungaree, who is now dead. When Ferdinand laughs, he tilts back his head and his teeth are yellow.

"Welcome, cousin. You can help with the children and protect the corn. *Ja?* I am shooting twenty crows every day. They are a plague. Another fifty hang from the trees," says Ferdinand.

Mary has never felt so happy. This sandstone country sings to her. The smell of eucalypt and wattle blossom summons the winter to end, as does the crackling noise of bush beneath their feet as they run through tracks and skip over black snakes. They gobble shellfish from the rocks and catch *wirriga*, goanna, to bake on driftwood fires. Mary plays with little Timmy and the children. With his bare brown feet he runs and plays wild games like jump-a-rope. Bickering squabbles erupt over knuckles, marbles, and string. Timmy is small, but he loves playing with these new cousins. Mary makes string games and creates bridges and boats and spears that tell stories about the ancestors—the eaglehawk and crow—and how they chased each other and made the great rivers in New South Wales.

The children sleep in the dark night, piled like puppies stretched over three old beds, top to toe. The adults talk beside a stove alight with hardwood. They drink endless tea and laugh at stories of the old times. The cracks in the slab hut walls are plastered with lime wash and old newspaper, and Mary stands in front of them reading news that is many years old. The old people are impressed with her ability to read and they ask her to read these stories from the *Sydney Gazette* aloud.

Some of the women knit or sew in the candlelight. Biddy makes a bone broth, with every bit of precious meat in the pot, like wombat, kangaroo, and echidna.

One night they hear the lone song of a piper across the mist-filled river, with a distant flute. Who can play like this? Mary longs for her lost violin.

Time passes in this contented existence and Mary thinks this quiet valley might remain her home. She could build a house and plant vegetables—raise seedlings in a box on the windowsill. They feed chickens with worms and collect eggs to make cakes, using the flour and sugar bought from the small village along the river.

The children shout that Mary's cousin Bowen has come by boat to trade flour for lime. He is a frequent visitor and makes camp by a clearing among gum trees behind the houses. He has his own fire and *gunyah*, complete with pots and pans and some guns that are cleaned and hung up high. He is well turned out in a government police uniform but does not bother with trousers. His hair is strung with fabric and feathers and ornaments of shells. Everyone rushes to see him in his blue military coat. The little ones touch his precious rifle and he demonstrates its firing. Mary knows about his great adventures, like that of his famous father. The men gather at his camp for long discussions about lime burning, boatbuilding, and catching runaway convicts. Mary, however, keeps her distance as he is, after all, now a police tracker.

Mary has some peace in this secluded creek community, but her feelings of loss for her daughter and father never leave. Each morning she takes *mootins* to spear little fish in the creek. Timmy and all the children squat by the fire while they cook them with salt on the coals.

One day, Ferdinand brings a letter from his brother that he has collected from Spencer. It is addressed to him but is about Mary James. She reads it aloud and is horrified. The letter asks Ferdinand to inform Mary that Masters is coming to collect her child to educate him. He offers to perform all sorts of Christian services for the inhabitants of Marra Marra Creek.

"We are pleased that a man of the church is coming. We have so many children unbaptized," says Biddy. She holds out her hand to Mary, but she looks away.

"I will run away if he comes here; he is a monster and not afraid of hell," says Mary.

"Don't you want us to be saved? Christened?" asks Biddy. "We have not been to a church for years and seven babies have been born. They will not be able to enter heaven. Your own boy—"

"Will not be taken by them. You see, there is no heaven," says Mary.

"Mary, you will be damned. Take care. I will not let you fall."

"You are ignorant about these fellas. I know them. They tell you sweet words but eat your heart. They will bring terror here," says Mary.

As she goes through the day, making tea, pouring water into flour for damper, Mary wonders where else she can go. It is becoming clear to her that she must leave and start yet again. She is scared that loneliness might kill her this time. If only she had both Timmy and Eleanor to share her life.

She packs a bag and folds and refolds Timmy's clothes. She presses their cleanliness to her face. But she is stalled. She realizes she does not have the strength to start again and will stay here with old Ferdinand to protect her. She goes to sleep thinking about Eleanor.

━━━

One morning, in the white spring mist, Mary thinks she hears a whispering from the river, the splash of waves and the sound of sea birds. She turns to the west, where smoke drifts on the breeze; then, a terrible vision appears on the river. A sailing boat is approaching on the high tide. On board are several *waibalas* and an Aboriginal woman. A boatman is in charge; a policeman and two ministers in black lean into the wind.

A sea eagle drifts on the wind, a warning to them, this clarion cry. The world is about to be turned inside out.

As the boat sails closer, Mary recognizes Masters. He is holding a huge wooden cross, like a skeleton. She can see him begin to stand up as he calls out. His piercing voice breaks the peace. Beside him is Henry Smythe and behind them both stands Mercy, in a red billowing dress. She cools herself with a Chinese fan.

The boatman hauls down the sails with the constable's help and they let the anchor out. It is shallow enough to wade ashore.

"Eve that hath tempted Adam. Behold, the Lord hath come!" Masters bellows out to the women and children on the shore. The men are busy lime-burning but come running through the smoke and mist to see who is causing the commotion. The ex-convicts are wary of visitors and look uneasily at each other, noting where the one shotgun sits behind a tank. Mary hides in the bedroom of Biddy's lean-to, among the bark shingles and old newspaper. She wants to grab Timmy but she cannot see him.

"What is it? Who is it? Why have they come here?" Biddy asks, babbling in joyful anticipation. Mary can't speak. She knows they can't hide all the children, who line up in their bonnets as their mothers wash their faces with spit. The women want to welcome him like the savior, this reverend from hell.

"He might christen them all, save them from whiteman's hell." Biddy is excited, tucking in children's shirts and sponging grubbiness from shifts.

Masters has aged considerably, and his girth is massive as he sits comfortably on the shore to catch his breath, the lanyard and cross poking from his crotch.

Biddy fears judgment by these men. Judgment of the dirt and poverty. The Ferdinand clan line up nonetheless, lambs to the slaughter. All the children stand along the muddy riverbank, while the men and women welcome this man of God, together with his hapless companions. Ferdinand smiles and bows to receive them.

The boatman helps Mercy step down onto makeshift stone steps near the beach. Mary watches her friend through a slit in the wooden window—she teeters in silk slippers.

"*Willkommen*, your highness majesty, to our house. We can make you a bed for the night," says Ferdinand. He bows, but his piercing blue eyes never leave Masters's face. Mary watches the women bobbing up and down like puppets.

"We have applied for permission to marry from the local reverend, but we hear nothing. You are so very welcome to baptize us all," says Biddy.

"Come, you must eat; come inside our house," says Ferdinand.

The river air billows around them. Seagulls dive. And the settlers dance like bags of bones.

Ferdinand holds out his hand to Reverend Masters, whose puffy body leans on the German's shoulder as he clambers into the house. The other men wade in from the boat, but Mary's eyes are on Henry Smythe. He has aged and has a full graying beard, but still there is that same bright face that first took her heart. Her mouth is dry with watching.

She must warn the others of the peril they face. These men will steal the children, steal them all. They will take them in the pretense of schooling, steal their peace, steal them away from families, and take all the love from their Aboriginal hearts. They will take her boy. Her panic rises like a storm, but it is too late—the family is excited as they bring the visitors into the house. Like a second coming.

Even though years have passed, Mary knows she will be recognized as the felon who stabbed a man and the woman who defied a magistrate. As memories of betrayals, beatings, and humiliation crowd Mary's mind, Biddy smiles at some joke by the reverend.

"How lovely to see you; what a nice surprise. Would you like tea? We got damper and we have oysters to eat, and fish. We are so honored," says Biddy.

They crowd into the house and Biddy wipes the chairs for the visitors to sit. She busily lays out china plates full of fish cakes and scones, and puts the kettle on the woodstove. Mercy sits primly on a box and watches the meal being laid out; she does not look at Mary.

"We have brought lovely gifts—some hymnbooks and pictures from the life of the Lord," Henry says. "Suffer the little children to come unto me. Do you know me? I am the Reverend Smythe," he continues.

"To assist in any Christian services that may be needed," says Masters, "we do weddings, christenings, funerals, whatever you require. We also come to see if you have drunk of the bitter broth called hell, and if children shrivel because of his dark presence." Masters pokes at the damper on a plate and there is an intake of fearful breath from Biddy.

"They know not when the Sabbath comes; forgive them," says Smythe.

"You know, Herr Ferdinand, I was not always a humble minister in a far-off colony. Oh no, I have visited the pilgrimage sites of Europe and I hear that you met Napoleon. Now, was that before you deserted?" asks Masters.

He continues. "No matter, I have seen the true Cross of Cong in Ireland and, today, I bring a new Bible. Will you swear on it that you will raise all these young ones out of the devil's reach and into the light of God? Come on, everyone, come and touch the Good Book and receive my blessings. Mercy tells me she has heard you all have many young ones in need of teaching and christening."

He holds the book above his head, as though he is Jesus himself.

Masters's pink hand flaps and the family members push each other away to touch the Bible and his gold ring. He sprinkles holy water and mumbles prayers. In a minute, he will recognize Mary. She will be shackled. She eyes the police sergeant. This is what betrayal looks like. The old father of her child, who strolled up the path with nonchalance, and her old friend, elegantly dressed as a lady, carrying a picnic basket, as though at a party. Panic bursts out like vomit. Is she so worthless that Mercy can throw away her love to run to whitefellas? Is Mercy someone's wife? Whose? No, surely she is a mistress to Masters. Has Mercy been bribed to bring them here? She would like to kill them. Her teeth clench.

Her head aches and she recalls Henry as a young man. She feels a miserable urge to hold him. This unbearable heaviness in her head. She must face them.

One of the farm dogs comes to her and waits for a pat. Mary strokes him and she is calmer.

The wooden step creaks, and Henry is in the next room of this poor wretched house, built of shingles, ironbark, mud, and desperation. It is a simple dwelling, with its earth floor and packing-case table. What once seemed like humble beauty is now in the visitors' eyes a sad display of poverty and oyster shells. She sees Henry through a chink in the wall. He takes off his cloak and folds it ever so carefully before giving out boiled lollies to the children. She shivers when she sees that even her own boy is crunching a sweet.

Biddy is smiling, her face whitened with powder newly applied to hide her brown skin; visitors are very rare. She wears her best lace collar and reaches for the precious china tea set with yellow and pink flowers, and a glint of gold on the rim, from up high on a shelf. She places scones and lilly pilly jam on a plate and puts out a plate of shucked oysters. Masters sits heavily before this repast, squeezes a lemon, and gorges on the oysters before she can offer him one stained and darned napkin. He burps and wipes his old chin with his hand.

Mercy stands nearby, apparently not wanting to belong to this untidy bunch. She brushes her dress and points her toes to show off her shiny red slippers. The children stare at her. Timmy recognizes her and calls out as he giggles and pushes up close to her. Mercy's face melts and her hand touches his curls with love. She smiles down at him and winks before she strolls into the bedroom and finds Mary.

"Don't touch Timmy. You betrayed us," whispers Mary.

"No, you're wrong. Masters finds out himself; there's lots of spies about. You're my sister; I came to find you. I can kill that fat one for you. I can do anything for you and Timmy," replies Mercy.

Mary understands that her friend has made a mistake. There is no malice in her, just the desire to survive and to take whatever is offered. She is babbling explanations about how she thought it would be helpful for Timmy to have the white men's protection, but Mary stops listening; she knows these men have hearts of stone. And she understands Mercy's desperation.

Mary sees now that Mercy is weak while Mary is strong. She loves Mercy and forgives her.

"Stay with me," says Mary.

Mercy nods and they embrace. Mercy motions for Mary to be quiet before returning to the main room.

Smythe eats nothing and surveys the room with apparent distaste. He has aged and his gray hair sticks out at an angle from his head. His nose is bigger and more hooked. Meanwhile, Masters tilts back his head and continues to tip the succulent oysters into his cavernous gob. Mary can see his purple tongue. His eyes are upon the children, as if they are dessert. He slurps his tea, then stands and strides about the house and into the bedroom, where Mary is. Smythe follows behind Masters and she sees his startled face, contorted with recognition. He has come to find her but looks away with a rush of emotion. He blots his face with his handkerchief and helps himself to his flask of brandy from his pocket. Mary walks with dignity into the kitchen.

"So, Mrs. Lewis," says Masters, ignoring Mary's entrance for now, "we have letters for you; we are your postman. Here, take them."

He hands out the letters while his eyes rest on Mary's face. He nods and looks quickly at Henry Smythe.

"Thank you, sir. We haven't had a letter for six months," Biddy says. She cannot stop curtsying.

"Yes, we are making the rounds with some letters from the old country," says Masters distractedly.

"Not my old country, sir. Prussia is very far away and no one can find me now," Ferdinand says.

"Perhaps for the best, seeing as you have been a convict. And I see you have another guest—a felon, no less," Masters says as he winks at Mary and sniggers.

"No sir, there are no such felons here. We are honorable," says Ferdinand.

Masters points to Mary in the corner and says, "Miss Mary James of Freeman's Reach; I wondered where you had got to. My dear, we are your friends and benefactors, are we not?"

She clenches her fists and holds his gaze. She will not be punished and mistreated again. Her eyes dart to the window and the bright blue sky and the call of magpies. Something has shifted. She thinks, without fear, of the policeman who stands guard outside.

Biddy leans slightly toward him while holding out her hand to Mary and says, "This is our dear cousin from Windsor town. She has been visiting us for a while."

"Careful what company you keep, Mrs. Lewis. We know her! Your Mary is notorious," says Masters. "Tut-tut. But your husband knows many ex-felons, I imagine. Consorting with escapees or bolters who run away from indenture. You could be charged for harboring such a person. Prison has not changed except we no longer employ thumbscrews," he continues.

"I am not a felon; I am a free person," says Mary. "We are not just servants to your kind! Your stock whip and pistol don't make us slaves. You're not wanted here. This land belongs to my cousin Biddy. She has deeds of sale!"

"Calm yourself; it's alright, Mary. We English have a privileged access to salvation. If we are unwanted, we will depart. Enough of the threatening talk, Reverend. Surely we come only on God's duty. To christen. Let us leave," says Henry.

"Really, Henry, I wonder what possessed you to want to come to this godforsaken place, anyway? They are all heathens!" says Masters.

"Get out of this house, or I will murder you," says Mary.

"Mary, stop this! They are guests. She is not in her right mind!" says Biddy.

"It is alright, my dear. I am ashamed of the violence in white men's hearts. This land is full of monsters of cruelty, violence, and lust," says Smythe. "We are all wounded by sin. As we sailed here, I saw the earth burdened and laid waste by cutting down trees. But I came out of duty, Mary. I thought I might inquire about your daughter, Eleanor? All grown now. Is she with you?"

"With me? She is gone; no one knows where she is. I lost her a long time past," says Mary.

"Oh, I see. A shame. I thought perhaps she might have a home here. I just wanted to know. I remember her, such a pretty child. It was foolish of me to ask; I did not think," he replies with sadness.

"You don't think? Reverend Henry Smythe. When you climbed on top of me all those nights. Did not think? Did not think when we had no money and no food?" Mary spits out.

Everyone is very quiet. Ferdinand coughs and sweeps up crumbs with his hand and lights his clay pipe. He is mildly amused by the events.

"We're not hiding in this place, sir. This is my land. My grant. We enjoy Mary's company. She's wonderful with children; she's teaching them to read," says Biddy.

"She may well corrupt their morals. Take care of their Bible teachings, no other material, mind you. No heathen naked dancing," says Masters.

"Oh, yes, we have a Bible. Husband, fetch it to show him," Biddy speaks eagerly.

"Mary cannot be a worthy teacher. She has spawned several illegitimate brats," says Masters.

"Oh no, sir, she is a good mother. Look at little Timmy," Biddy says, pushing Timmy forward.

"Stop it, cousin," pleads Mary. "Say nothing, for heaven's sake, nothing! All that comes out of your mouth condemns me."

"I do know this innocent child. But his mother has rejected the Good Book. She will burn. It is a shame. Pass the jam, my dear woman; is it local fruit?" asks Masters. "Do you have more oysters ready? I am partial to a good meal of seafood, aren't I, Mercy?"

"Mary reads to us," says Biddy.

"A Bible is defiled by her touching it. Put it away, madam. She is not allowed to touch this book. Defilement. Please, where are my prawns and oysters?"

Mercy enters the room with a plate of oysters and places them among the guests in silence. She uses sign language to ask Mary what is going on.

Mary surveys the room. Biddy can't speak for the shock and Henry hangs his head in shame.

Mary takes Timmy by the hand and starts to back out the door. But Masters grabs her arm in a wrenching grasp. The children's eyes grow huge as they stare.

"This, this wretch is an absconder! She has disgraced a member of the clergy. This temptress, this harlot!" cries Masters, as Biddy hustles the children out of the house.

Henry suddenly reaches forward and forces Masters to release her.

Mercy taps her fan on Masters's head. "Leave her alone, Reverend, or I will smash your head in," she says with a smile.

Masters laughs and slaps his thigh.

"Get out! They don't want your stupid prayers," shouts Mercy. "I don't want your tub of lard body on me. With your tiny *windji*. You disgusting old thing. Get out! You too, Henry. You no-good monster!"

Biddy places her hands on Mary's shoulders and pulls her against her breast. The possum cloak is between them, soft and warm. Mercy, who has been banging her fan against her palm, quickly moves to lean her whole body against Mary as well. The women protect their sister. Mary trembles and her legs shake—she is exultant.

"You should not have sheltered her, madam," continues Masters. "There are penalties."

But Ferdinand has heard enough. He jumps up from the table and is so agitated that his wife fears he may have an apoplexy of the brain.

"This is my home, sir, and my wife's! Mary is our sister and our guest. You will stop now or I ask you to leave, *unmittelbar*!" Ferdinand's agitated hand cuts the air as he speaks. Mary can see that he is braver than all of them.

"What is your full name again, sir? You are a Prussian, are you not? Ex-convict. You were assigned to old Chief Bungaree, am I correct? At his so-called farm?" says Masters. "An interesting experiment in social welfare that the old governor sought to undertake. Oh, the Russian expedition liked it enough. They also visited the Native School. They are everywhere, those Russkies." Masters picks his teeth and examines the toothpick. Ferdinand is silent.

Timmy runs in and strikes at Masters with a stick and twists himself around his mother's legs. Masters's face lights up, ignoring Ferdinand's demands that they leave. He pulls Timmy forward, grips the boy's little hand in his white fist, and removes the stick.

"I know this naughty fair child. Has he been christened? Little man, would you like to accept the Lord as your savior?" Masters asks. Timmy's face is upturned to the reverend, his large blue eyes gazing.

Biddy stammers, "This is Timmy, Mary's boy." Mary silently implores her to say nothing.

"Yes, I recognize him. Mary's bastard," says Masters and continues. "Who is the father? Come, let me sprinkle holy water on him. Let me examine him. You should have let me have him a while ago to train him up."

"Leave him alone," Mary hisses.

"Perhaps she doesn't know who the father might be, eh, Ferdinand? Let me look at the child's skin. Blue eyes. Ah, yes, it would be another white man, perhaps German?" says Masters. "Well, Mary? Speak up, girl, are you a concubine again? Pay well, does it? Easy work I have always thought, just open your legs. Jiggety jiggety."

Ferdinand takes Timmy from Masters's arms, gives the magistrate a shove, then deposits Timmy out the door.

"Mind the child," says Ferdinand to Mary.

"You can't hide the truth from me. What is this place, anyway? A nest of illegitimate vipers?" challenges Masters.

"Are you making insults, sir? Watch what you speak," says Ferdinand.

"Timmy is my son and you will never get him," Mary says from the doorway. Steady and strong.

"Who said I would take him? Oh, but now you mention it, he would make a good servant on my new estate. Like you were, Mary," says Masters. "Very docile, I think not! Do you remember your Tahitian dance with Mercy here, for the governor? Oh dear, how can we forget? And, Henry, surely you remember pretty Mary back then? Do you find her much changed?"

"It was long ago," says Henry.

"That estate of yours is near the South Creek. It's my father's country," says Mary.

"Your country! You, a servant girl? Wake up, lass, we have a new world order. We have conquered you," says Masters. "Your native people are dying out and we can soothe their pillow. Let's make a deal. If you hand the child over, I will forget to tell the policeman outside that you are an escaped felon. The clergy is here to protect you. I hope to be elevated to the position of bishop; isn't that so, Henry? I want to be remembered for having done something extraordinary for you pathetic, impoverished people. We do not discriminate. One person may be Black, another brown, another an ex-convict. All are the same in God's eyes. But, oh dear, you're all so filthy."

"Excuse me, Reverend, why do all your speeches sound so rehearsed and smell of such pride? This is not the place to lecture," Smythe asks.

"We are here to save souls. To give christening and save lives from Satan's grasp," says the deluded reverend.

"You deny their right to live as they wish," says Smythe. "Mrs. Lewis has her own land grant! And a respectable husband—if not by a marriage certificate, then in God's eyes. Perhaps God doesn't need their souls. Mary is having a good influence here; she has redeemed herself. I do know her, so very well. And I am ashamed to have betrayed her."

Mary is astounded at Henry's confession.

"She is kindness and gentleness and does not deserve more ill treatment. I will defy you, sir, if you attempt to take her child!" says a red-faced Henry.

"Oh, defy, is it? You are my inferior, so mind your manners. You have no power here," says Masters. "I had heard about this secret valley on the Deerubbin. A nest of half-caste children hidden away from our colonial administration. But we have the authority to take the children, to place them in the orphan school, at our church's expense. I care about them. I only want what is best for them!" He surveys the children who have crept inside again. They tremble at the words "take the children."

"No. We care for them here. They learn to read. Tell them, Herr Ferdinand Lewis," says Mary. She stands in front of the children, a lioness.

The children scatter, jumping out windows and doors. Mary takes Timmy and they run into the bush. The police sergeant tries to catch them, and Ferdinand laughs as the little ones scatter and kick the boatman.

"Go, children, run! *Schnell, schnell!*" Ferdinand cries out.

Masters and Henry hurry outside the hut. A spear thuds at their feet and out steps Bowen, his grace and presence impressive. In one fist he holds a bundle of war spears; his woomera is in the other, poised and raised above his head with a sharp hook spear in place. It shakes, begging to fly free into the air.

"Leave them! We kill you! *Whu karndi kurung*! Run," shouts Bowen.

He stands erect and fearless, his breastplate gleaming over his military uniform. The older boys stand in motley dress behind him. They all have spears held high. Masters and Henry stand terrified. The policeman runs to hide in the boat.

"*Nea dullai bunggawurra*, friend! *Yuin, jumna yanna in bunnia*, the sun, us together friendships! My good man, we are all friends here," says Smythe with a nervous shudder. "We come to help. Put down the weapons, your *karmai*. Why, someone might get hurt."

Bowen looks amused at Henry's use of Darug language. Everyone is surprised that this curate knows these words.

"*Naiya* not your good man. *Naiya paialla, mujar paialla, harabundi* not *yella bi daialong*. You don't talk for us. We belong this place, not *waibala*." Bowen laughs as he speaks, then holds up his spear and carefully places it in the woomera. He aims it at Masters. It shakes and whirs.

Ferdinand is horrified at how things are turning out. Mary hides behind a wall, where she sees a chamber pot full of piss and shit.

"Put down that spear, young fella. Easy now, we can work this out. You would like some trading goods? We are all friends here, aren't we, Herr Ferdinand?"

The Prussian turns away in disgust.

"Dear Henry, can you speak that native language? Make them understand!" Masters says. He is shivering.

"I am no friend of yours," Ferdinand hisses.

"We callim Masters *gorai jagara*, fat flea," Bowen says.

The crowd begins to laugh.

"Be warned, I shall return with a letter from the governor about these children. The law shall win. It is written! We have English justice," says Masters.

Now Biddy finds her voice. "Get out of our home, *yan yan* you fiend! Haven't we lost enough? *Whu karndi?*"

She comes at Masters with her hand raised, ready to strike. He ducks, but at that moment Mary, alive with rage, rushes up to Masters and empties the sloshing chamber pot over his head. *Goona* runs down his face. Shit clings to his hair.

Bowen motions to the boat and shouts, "Before the tide, go now! *Whu karndi!*"

Masters is angry and shouts at the laughing crowd as they stand watching the tide ebb away. His face is full of fury; he clutches his chest. Henry holds him up and they walk slowly to the boat, but Masters must have the last word. He stops and summons up a scrap of dignity.

"Don't speak unless spoken to! You all must learn to show respect! I represent not only the governor but God himself," says Masters. "Who knows why I have been called to this wretched outpost. Look at yourselves, you white ex-convicts marrying Blacks. You are a disgrace to your race! The new world has only brought heartbreak for England. The Americas have been lost and now fester with rebellion and tomahawking Indians. You allow your native concubines to befoul my person, my clothes. You won't win, you know. We know where you and your half-breeds are hiding. You can't escape British law! The children of Cain must accept their place in the hierarchy of the Lord's kingdom. They are placed here to serve us—and you, Mary James, are the worst!"

He coughs and chokes and all those watching are a little alarmed at his purple face, which looks as if it might burst. Henry Smythe speaks up:

"Listen to yourself, Reverend. I fear that you are outnumbered here," says Smythe. "You are wrong, sir, terribly wrong to threaten them. Let us leave these good folk to their own devices. I see such kindness here, and love of freedom. We must not disturb their small paradise. Come, sir, leave dear Mary and her family alone!" Henry nods at Mary and she smiles. He registers that smile as a small act of forgiveness. He walks toward the boat with heavy feet. Just before he reaches it, he takes out a package wrapped in brown paper from his carpetbag. He looks at Mary, and the teeming children, and places it on the ground.

Mary kneels down, her hand shaking. Henry watches her from a distance. She removes the violin and bow, and tears of laughter fill her eyes. She throws back her head, tucks the instrument under her chin, and begins to play. Mercy smiles and dances with the children, swinging them around and around with her gown flying in the wind.

As Mary plays, Masters lumbers down the beach behind Smythe, to where the boatman and policeman are hoisting the sail. A squall is coming, with black clouds moving quickly up the river valley. Lightning flashes—the storm is about to break.

The tide is going out quickly and the boat will be stranded on mudflats at any minute. The boatman pushes the vessel off the mud, and the policeman helps as the tide swirls around them. They use oars to steady the craft and yell for the reverends to hurry.

Masters staggers down the oyster-covered rocks like a hunted animal and wades into the river with Henry beside him. Rain has begun to fall. The family on the bank begin to laugh—all twenty of them standing in the gray rain and howling. Henry makes it to the boat, but Masters staggers under the weight of a soaked cassock and cannot lift himself up to the stern. Henry reaches out and tries to catch the old man, but the rain and the mud have made his hand slippery. The elder man's pale, fat, trembling fingers reach out. There is a terrible moment of realization—Henry does not want to save him. Masters's hand hovers but Henry pulls his away and stands stiffly, watching the man claw the air.

Masters howls and attempts to swim, but he is purple now and is going under. Perhaps those mythical monsters the bunyips pull him under the rippling waves. His tongue turns white, and there is the gurgling, spitting, gulping sound of death. Henry leans far out over the boat's stern, but he will not grasp Masters's hand. He holds on to the boat's rail and watches as Masters sinks into the gray swirling river.

The men on the boat have not moved to help; they can't swim. They just stare and raise the sail. The boat takes the wind, the sail fills, and they are away, heading back to Windsor. Mary watches Henry. He shouts out, but his voice is lost in the howl of the storm. Henry is hunched over the rail and seems to be crying; he is black against the swirling gray clouds.

The family watch Masters rise and sink again in the brownish water, and Ferdinand yells for the children to save him. The oldest boy dives into the water and swims fast toward the bubbling figure. Masters sinks again, then he rises and sinks again with a gurgling cry. A pale, clawlike hand reaches out of gray waves and shakes; a gold ring with a black cross flashes, and then he disappears. Bubbles break the surface, then stop.

Above them, a sea eagle weaves and drifts in the rising gale. Mary swims out, and she and the oldest boy dive to try to find Masters. They dive again and again, but he is gone. The rain and wind burst upon the surface of the river, and they swim back to shore, exhausted and cold. Ferdinand holds out his arms and embraces them both while Mercy places a blanket around them.

"You try good, but death he come. The will of God. *Ja*," says Ferdinand.

They walk back to the house and drink tea. No one speaks.

What if the soldiers come to ask after the reverend? The policeman watched him drown. He did nothing, mind, but the Lewis family will surely be blamed. The boat has sailed and they are now left to watch for the body to be washed up on the beach.

"We will be in trouble. Masters will be missed; they will come for us," says Mercy. "But I will explain. We cannot fret about him; he was real cruel, but he kept me in employ and fed me for many years so I will not curse him, but I am free, free as a bird."

The next morning, the children come running. They have seen the huge white form of Masters washed up on the beach at high tide. Mary walks down to look at him. His eyes are open, white globes, and his hands are claws of terror. Gray-helmeted soldier crabs eat his face as it lies sideways in the mud. Seaweed and mangrove pods cling to his hair and his black cassock is hitched up to reveal his white buttocks. Death is never pretty.

She looks but can hardly believe he has gone; she keeps expecting him to stand up. One child prods his body with a mangrove stick and Mary tells him to stop.

"Show respect! That man spirit now. *Goong*," she says to the child.

He is food for the fish and crabs. Bluebottle flies begin to buzz around the corpse. She cannot look away from this shape festering on the beach, thinking that he would not have wanted to die in this strange, wild, exotic place, away from his homeland, his green England. Mary takes a blanket from the house and places it gently over him.

Mercy walks out of the house. She twirls her parasol, showing her fondness for this newfound freedom. "Poor old fella, gone to hell now," she says, looking down at the body. "He was going to give me his wife's pearls, but I don't care for things now. I just want to live here, build a little house of slabs for myself with a hob and a white clay wall." She speaks with a newfound seriousness and Ferdinand listens and nods. He can find her a spot to build.

"The corpse won't keep. By the time the authorities arrive, he will stink to high hell," says Ferdinand.

"We must bury him. You can say a few prayers," says Mary.

"No, we will cremate him our way. Make a fire," says Biddy.

Ferdinand begins to pick up logs and sticks, and he and the

children work together to gather a huge pile of wood on the beach. The men carry the body and set it alight to become the pyre.

Ferdinand reads from his Bible and they stand with lowered heads. A burning man, a funeral of sorts, and mumbled prayers.

As he burns, the heat causes the body to flex, and Masters sits up, amidst the flames, making all the children scream and run away. Mercy watches with a grim face.

The body burns for many hours, after which the women wash smoke over themselves and the children with branches of gum leaves and sing and dance in mourning for this man. This cleansing ritual gets rid of his ghost, and his ashes are gathered and buried under a stone. He will be remembered, but not kindly. The family hope that the truth will be told by Smythe and the death of Masters declared an accident.

———

Bowen is going back to Palm Beach. He holds his spear in its woomera and shows Mary where she must row, for one day, toward the ocean, along Deerubbin River to Broken Bay and Barrenjoey. He tells her she will see *gawura* whales, dolphins, and soaring gulls.

"You go *warawara* find lion head on that bay and look way over south side to other headland, long thin beach white *marang* sand— that home. *Kabu*, by and by, look see us mob. You come! Lot of crayfish to eat!" he yells.

He nods at Mary to follow his government boat, but she is frozen. She wants this home with Ferdinand's family and the journey seems daunting. Ferdinand is not frightened of the police who will surely come to investigate the death, but Mary is. The next day, she decides to row her canoe to Palm Beach.

CHAPTER TWENTY-FIVE

1843: Barrenjoey, Palm Beach

Riots over terrible conditions break out at the Female Factory in Parramatta after the women's sugar and bread ration is cut. The rioting women say they will shave the governor's head. They march on Parramatta town. Troopers are sent to quell the rioters, and eighty women are arrested. The ringleaders are placed in stocks. It is pitiful.

Thirty thousand European people now live in Sydney Town while the camps at Woolloomooloo, Botany, Kirribilli, Manly, and Narrabeen have only about thirty Aboriginal survivors each.

═══════

Mary paddles downriver, east toward the rising sun. She continues all day under fluffy clouds as Timmy sits in the bottom of the canoe, which slowly fills with water. The child bails happily with a tin mug, but Mary is anxious. It might sink at any moment, and she sees the dark shadows of bull sharks. Her heart pounds. Dolphins nose the boat with curiosity. She smiles at Timmy and sings to him. She does not show fear, but the green waves lash the small craft and the water continues to pour into the canoe. Gray clouds gather and the wind picks up, and Mary fears she will be blown out to sea.

She has no idea how far it is to the beach but she sees Lion Island ahead. She is unsure how the Guringai Blackfellas will greet her. Even though she is related to Bowen, they might see her as a traitor after her journey with the military. What if they know about the killings? Her lips are pinched, her skin is drenched, and her arms ache. Fear builds as she takes the pannikin from Timmy and bails out water faster. The canoe is sinking and she fears the dark sea will drown them.

Suddenly, she looks up to see an English whaleboat near Lion Island, with one headsail and a single mast. It quickly tacks toward her. It is too late to escape detection.

There are three half-naked white men on board and they are rounding up into the breeze. They will be upon her soon. One waves to her. She looks over at Patonga Beach, but it is too far to reach. They are gaining on her, and she panics and paddles faster. The whaler noses into the wind and the sail flaps; the boom is let loose, and the boat stops next to her sinking craft. A sailor leans over the side and smiles. He holds out hairy blond arms and nods at the child, while another man dives into the water and swims toward her, his long pale frame cutting the water until he is beside her sinking canoe. She wonders if she should hit him with the paddle, but it is all happening too quickly and Timmy is crying. To her great alarm, the captain leans from the ship and beckons to her.

"Hey, Miss, you heading to the Americas?" he calls. "Want a lift to shore?"

"My boat's sinking," she calls back, and a wave crashes over her.

"Like feeding sharks, do you? You better come on board," he yells against the sound of gulls and wind.

She is exposed on the deep river with the Barrenjoey headland looming ahead. The swimming man puts out his arms for Timmy and the child screams and kicks, but she soothes him and hands him to the Englishman in the water. She takes one last look at her canoe, jumps in the water, and swims to the side of the whaler. Mother and child are hauled aboard, and the child huddles near baskets of fish. Mary collapses against the stern of the boat. She watches as her canoe, with her precious violin, fills with water and slowly submerges.

"Your boat is sinking, all the way down to Neptune's realm. Nothing to save, darlin'," says a sailor.

"My *naoi!*" sighs Mary.

"Just bark," says the sailor.

Mary sits on the boat and touches her pocket, where she keeps the parting gift from Ferdinand, a sharp dagger in a leather sheath. She sees the two sailors nudge each other and she covers her breasts with her apron. Her eyes are on the broad-chested young captain because he will determine her fate. Breathing in and out, she slows her breath as her hand runs along the wooden seat. She cannot look at the men with their yellowed teeth and fair hair. Mary holds tightly to Timmy and he searches her face for guidance. They are both calming.

The men are surrounded by baskets of fish from their expedition. They have caught bream, whiting, and snapper, and piles of mud crabs in the inlets of Pittwater. They offer Timmy water and bread and as he chews, he smiles. The captain says he is heading to Palm Beach Customs House, as he has business with the customs officer about a certain barrel of grog.

"The new governor, George Gipps, has gone and established a ruddy customhouse at Barrenjoey on Palm Beach for the government. That customs officer must catch smugglers and bushrangers. So you watch out over there," says the captain.

"You can get any booze, smudge, wine, gin, grog, whiskey, *bool*, spirits, and liquor all brewed at McCarrs Creek," says a sailor.

Timmy is allowed to sit next to the good-looking captain, and he helps the boy to steer. His chubby hands grip the tiller. The man points out a line of gray kangaroos jumping along the clifftop. One of the men produces a boiled sweet from a tin. Timmy chews the sweet and the men are not threatening. Mary tells them about Bowen and how she has come to join him.

After beaching the whaler in the small bay of Station Beach, the captain makes sure the woman and child are safe near Bowen's camp. The sailors all know Bowen, the famous and admired police tracker, and they point out his camp to Mary. They walk along the gray sandy shore to the custom shack, and she is forgotten.

Bowen looks up in surprise and calls out as he strides from his camp to greet Mary with a pannikin of water. She licks her lips, swallowing the water, and stares at the beach where a huge white shell midden stretches along the back of the camp. Children run along the shore to welcome Timmy, and they sit down in a huddle on the sand. Little stingrays scatter in the seaweed. She has arrived.

Bowen walks next to the new arrivals, looking up to Barrenjoey headland covered in golden wattle and gum trees. Mary is relieved and she hugs and kisses her son. She sees Bowen's mother, grand old Queen Cora Gooseberry, sitting near her *gunyah* of paperbark with a mob of the Guringai clan. They are busy roasting a sheep. The smell is delicious.

"You want *patama?*" asks Bowen, knowing the answer.

He laughs and pats a place on a blanket next to Gooseberry— children pile on her lap. The old dame has her trademark white kerchief tied around her hair and a white clay pipe in her mouth. Mary thinks about the offer she once had to live with this old lady and wonders how different her life might have been had she taken up this offer. But Mary knows that to live here, deep into the country of the Guringai of Broken Bay, is a last resort and she is still drawn to her true country upriver near Windsor.

The old lady holds up her bronze breastplate for Mary to read: "Cora Gooseberry: Queen of Sydney and Botany."

There is happiness here among the *gunyahs* made of paperbark, timber, and tin—and there are chickens and a cow for milk.

She can see back along the great sacred Deerubbin. It is the

shining silver track that binds and links her people from the Blue
Mountains to Freeman's Reach, from South Creek to Marra Marra
Creek, and then to Barrenjoey. The vision is clear with intercon-
nected lines of marriage, kinship, and a cluster of mixed-up clans.

"*Mingangun pittuma*? Muraging, you see my *duruninang*, my
daughter Biddy?" asks Queen Gooseberry. The old aunty flashes a
smile and inclines her head up the long river, past Lion Island, to
where her extended family lives.

"*Dullai, wirawi guirgurang*, mob happy," says Mary.

"Give Muraging more water," says Gooseberry.

Mary cries at being called by her tribal name.

The river glistens behind them on what is now called the Pittwater
by settlers, after Mr. Pitt the Younger. The immense gray-green gum
forest, with bursts of yellow wattle, leans in the wind. Some canoes are
on the water with people fishing. Men and women stand with *mootins*, spearing fish in the clear shallows. A black-and-white sea eagle
soars overhead. Mary sees distant *waibala* sailing ships, setting sail for
England. She wishes them good riddance.

Timmy runs back and forth, and she hears the laughter and giggling of children playing along the shore. "*Pittuma jumna bulbi,
bado*, family," says Mary.

Mary strolls over the midden to the ocean, where she can see
whales spouting out to sea, and dolphins playing in the white foam.
The long curve of Palm Beach glistens; the white sand is fringed
with cabbage-tree palms.

As she watches, Mary sees a golden-skinned toddler on the beach
with her family. There is something familiar in the little girl's body and
hair. She is like her lost daughter, Eleanor. The family is sitting now
and the child lounges in the arms of a golden-haired young mother.
They see Mary and watch her with curiosity, nudging each other.

The mother is dressed in a dirty blue bustled dress with long
necklaces of tiny silver shells. A sweet song rings out over the sand
hills, and Mary has tears in her eyes.

The young woman sees Mary and walks toward her with growing curiosity. Mary holds out her hand as tears stream down her face. It is Eleanor.

She is here, alive and thriving in the Guringai camp, and Mary has a granddaughter.

"*Waiana?*" asks Eleanor.

Mary runs and takes her in her arms.

"I'm *waiana*, mother, Muraging. I look for you!"

"*Waiana?*"

Eleanor is unsure, sad, and angry. She stands back and throws a stick at Mary, then walks away up the beach. Mary cannot catch her breath. Her daughter's back is bent over, sobbing. Eleanor turns and runs back to her mother.

"You left me! You left me! Awful people, *waibala*! I looked for you, looked and looked. And cried and you just gone," says Eleanor.

"Eleanor, I'm sorry. *Ngubuty kurung*. We were starving," says Mary. "I wanted you; I looked for you. But you were gone," says Mary.

Eleanor walks toward her mother. At last they embrace with Eleanor's child pressed between them. Timmy runs to them and takes hold of Mary's legs, laughing. She lifts him to meet his sister and niece.

"Sister. Timmy, this is your sister. She is all grown up. A *wirawi* woman."

Bowen walks along the track and hangs his musket carefully on a tree. He smooths his feathered topknot and strolls with his mother toward Mary, and they squat near the fire. Gooseberry hands Mary a lump of roast mutton and she shares it with her son and granddaughter. They chew the meat and spit gristle on the sand.

"Fat sheep good," says Bowen.

"You have a good life here, all the *dyins* and *dullai* are happy." Mary smiles.

"That right, real *budjery*," says Bowen.

"Where did you find her?" asks Mary.

"A farmer at Prospect give us Eleanor and that baby for present. He say take her to her people," says Bowen.

He is proud that they are all together. This family is strong and now they might live in peace.

"Eleanor *budjery* safe now," says Queen Gooseberry.

Mary sleeps in a pile of wallaby pelts by the fire. She is with Timmy, Eleanor, and her granddaughter. She strokes the children's hair and curls it in her fingers. Timmy lies in her lap and Mary whispers his totem, magpie, *wibbung*.

In the morning, Mary breathes the fresh sea air and looks down the river. She is free. She joins the women dressed for a welcome corroboree. She strips off the *waibala* clothes and paints up in white ocher. Mary wears a possum skirt and has white feathers and shells in her hair. She sits with the children and women to celebrate the dancing of "shake a leg," which goes on all day. Near the men's circle sits a young man with golden skin; he looks a little like a *waibala* in English dress, but also one of the tribe. It is curious to see him tie up a tall horse near the camp and bring bags of flour to share with the camp. This man is a possible *mulamang* husband for her daughter. They both have *waibala* blood.

———

The family fills its days diving for crayfish and gathering shellfish in dillybags. The oysters are as big as a hand. Mary fishes from the rocks with the children for bream, whiting, flounder, blackfish, jewfish, and flathead. She cooks the fish and adds bones to the midden that runs the length of Palm Beach. She collects pandanus nuts and cuts the hearts from cabbage tree palms for roasting; she grinds lomandra seeds and bakes dampers. Only sometimes do they eat *waibala* bread and mutton, for the land teems with wallabies, bandicoots, wombats, goannas, and possums.

One bird-filled dawn, Mary wakes and swims in the salt water with her curly hair streaming out behind her. She looks across the bay toward Lion Island and imagines Deerubbin weaving the Rainbow Serpent in and out of inlets. She speaks aloud her Darug language, mouthing a chant for the trees, *bunda, dirrabari, mambara, yarra, muggargru, kwigan, budjor.* The sounds are from her childhood, before the *waibala* took her.

Her words are also a prayer. Across Broken Bay, convicts and settlers are burning immense forests of trees to make way for cattle and sheep. The crack of many axes rings out along the river. Great trees fall and burn, and plumes of dense smoke waft across the green water. They are different from the small native message fires dotting the escarpment. The smoke is eucalypt-blue and ominous. She can feel the land shifting and changing. The smoke fills the sky with a gray haze; it drifts along the river, transforming the blue to mist, like a haunting, like the death of forests. Some huge trees blaze long into the night and a red glow ripples on the horizon.

For now, she is safe at Bowen's camp, in the shadow of Barrenjoey, its cliffs towering over the beach, protecting and hugging the clan that lives here. She thinks of the solitude of Marra Marra Creek and worries that police will come to arrest Ferdinand.

She will always be seen as a traitor to the English authorities, a turncoat who didn't appreciate their education, their God—their benevolence.

She uses a stick to draw a map in the wet sand and marks the lands of the Darug, Gaimariagal, Garigal, Gundungurra, Darkinjung, Guringai, Awakabal, Wonnaruah, Worimi, and Biripai.

AFTERWORD

Benevolence is a work of fiction based on historical events of the early years of British invasion and settlement around the Hawkesbury River in Western Sydney, New South Wales, Australia.

The characters derive from Darug, Gundungurra, Guringai, and Wonnaruah Aboriginal people who defended their lands, culture, and society. Muraging is based on my great-great-grandmother, Mary Ann Thomas, who was a servant on colonial estates in the Hawkesbury area. The other characters in the novel are inspired by historical figures and my imagination—except the governors, who are based on historical documents.

The Parramatta Native Institution existed, and some of the characters and events are inspired by research on that school.

I was able to research information about the Darug Nation while working as a senior researcher for Professor Peter Read on the University of Sydney project that led to the creation of the website www .historyofaboriginalsydney.edu.au. This website includes a rich multimedia collection of more than 800 images, 30,000 words of analysis and commentary, and 400 digital videos of oral history interviews. The website is now hosted by the Western Sydney University.

While researching, I was able to find stories about the Darug and Gundungurra Nations' survival and resistance in the early days of British colonization.

Over five years, I interviewed Aboriginal Elders from Darug, Gundungurra, Guringai, Gaimariagal, and Wonnaruah Nations and others from as far north as Newcastle to as far south as Botany Bay. During these interviews I developed a passion for finding out about my own Burruberongal clan of Darug Nation and my Aboriginal and English convict history. I carried out in-depth research on the family history of my father, Neville Walter Janson. Some family members dispute my account of this history.

I discovered that the dark old lady who sat in the sun and watched us children play at the rented family house in View Street, Chatswood, in the 1950s was my great-grandmother, Mary Reynolds (née Bartle). Some twenty-five family members lived in that house and my dad, Neville, rode a horse bareback down to the Lane Cove River in the 1940s and 1950s to shoot rabbits and collect oysters.

Great-grandma Mary was the daughter of Mary Ann Thomas, born at Freeman's Reach on Black Town Road, near Windsor on the Hawkesbury River. Mary Ann was a servant who relinquished three children to the Benevolent Society in order to marry the ex-convict Henry Bartle. She gave birth to four more children, one of whom was my great-grandmother, Mary Bartle.

I have some early birth, death, and marriage certificates that reveal a story of illiteracy, constant movement, poverty, and occasional employment as servants and log splitters along the Hawkesbury River from 1810 to the 1900s. There are also successful family butchers and landowners, such as the Reynolds family in Wilberforce.

Mary Ann Thomas was difficult to find. She seemed to have no birth certificate. Then one day I stumbled upon a certificate from 1832 that named a certain reverend of the Church of England in Windsor as her possible father and her mother as Maria Byrnes. This fascinating tale grew into *Benevolence*. Some names have been changed to protect me from accusations of historical error.

THANK YOU

Thank you to the Australia Council for the Arts for all the grants and my residency at the B. R. Whiting Rome Studio, where I worked on earlier novels.

Thank you to Magabala Books and their wonderful staff who believed in this novel.

I would like to thank friends and relatives who encouraged and read my manuscript over a five-year period.

I give heartfelt gratitude for reading and commenting on the manuscript and showing support to: Michael Fay, Virginia Fay, Byron Fay, Jovanna Janson, Zoey Allan, Morgan Kurrajong, Lesley Giovanelli, Rose Pickard, Peter Read, Geraldine Starr and the Celestial Writers Group, and Writing NSW.

I also give thanks to my literary agent, Sarah McKenzie, at Hindsight, for believing in the novel. Many thanks to the numerous editors, including Brigitte Staples, Bruce Sims, and Margaret Whiskin, and publisher Rachel Bin Salleh at Magabala.

I acknowledge the support of the First Nations Australian Writers Network and the FNAWN Workshop 2018, and especially the much-loved Aunty Kerry Reed-Gilbert (dec.).

The historical details and anecdotes portrayed in this work of fiction are derived in part from the sharing of information of a number of valued sources. Protocols in relation to First Nations' permissions were given during the recording of interviews for the project that led to the creation of the website: www.historyofaboriginalsydney.edu.au.

I give thanks to Aunty Val Aurisch (dec.), Elder of Darug Nation from Katoomba, who contributed many memories of growing up with traditional Darug knowledge.

Uncle Colin Lock, Darug Elder, contributed his stories to the website of childhood visits to the Darug and Gundungurra camp in the Gully in Katoomba.

I pay tribute to the descendants of Queen Matora, Queen Gooseberry, and Chief Bungaree, who shared their family history about Marra Marra Creek. My great-aunt Louisa Bartle (née Lewis) was born at Marra Marra Creek. She was descended from one of the children living with their Prussian father, Ferdinand Lewis, and Aboriginal mother, Biddy (daughter of Matora).

I especially thank Bungaree descendant Uncle Bob Waterer (dec.), who was my father's friend in the army after World War II. I thank Neil Evers and Laurie Bimson, the Garigal cousins and descendants of Bungaree, who contributed to the imagined events on the Hawkesbury River.

I pay tribute to the Lewis descendant Muffy Hedges, who shared stories and photographs from Marra Marra Creek. I thank architect legend Col James (dec.), who shared his house at Gentleman's Halt with us drama students in the 1970s. From this grand ruined stone house, I paddled a canoe along the Hawkesbury to Spencer with my small child.

I owe a special debt of gratitude for stories of childhood and cultural knowledge from Aunty Robyn Williams (dec.), Wiradjuri and Gundungurra heritage.

I thank my friend Sue Pinckham at Walanga Muru, Macquarie University, and my friend Aunty Clair Jackson for their generous support.

I thank my cousin Shane Smithers, who contributed Darug male knowledge relating to our Aboriginal family history.

Many of the extended Darug families live today in Parramatta, Plumpton, Riverstone, Liverpool, Katoomba, Northern Beaches, and Blacktown. They are related to the families who lived at reserves such as the Gully in Katoomba, Sackville Reach Aboriginal Reserve, Freemans Reach Blacks' Camp, La Perouse Aboriginal Reserve, Redfern community, and Narrabeen Lake Reserve. We did not die out.

Many members of these families and Elders shared stories of their lives in oral history videos for www.historyofaboriginalsydney.edu.au. I pay respect to their knowledge and culture and thank them for allowing me to learn about our history and celebrate fragments of these stories in historical fiction.

Readings:

Barkley-Jack, Jan. *Hawkesbury Settlement Revealed: A New Look at Australia's Third Mainland Settlement, 1793–1802.* Kenthurst: Rosenberg Publishing, 2009.

Brook, Jack, and James Kohen. *The Parramatta Native Institution and the Black Town: A History.* Sydney: UNSW Press, 1991.

Gapps, Stephen. *The Sydney Wars.* Sydney: NewSouth, 2018.

Gilbert, Kevin J. *Because a White Man'll Never Do It.* Sydney: Angus & Robertson, 1973.

Kohen, James L. *Daruganora: Darug Country—The Place and the People.* Sydney: Darug Tribal Aboriginal Corporation, 2009.

Karskens, Grace. *The Colony: A History of Early Sydney.* Sydney: Allen & Unwin, 2009.

Website: historyofaboriginalsydney.edu.au 2009–2013

ABOUT THE AUTHOR

Julie Janson is a Burruberongal woman of Darug Aboriginal Nation. Her career as a playwright began when she wrote and directed plays in remote Australian Northern Territory Aboriginal communities. She is now a novelist and award-winning poet. She was winner of the 2016 Oodgeroo Noonuccal Poetry Prize and the 2019 Judith Wright Poetry Prize.

Julie's novels include *The Crocodile Hotel* (2015), *The Light Horse Ghost* (2018), and *This River of Bones* (2022).

She has written and produced plays, including two at Belvoir St Theatre in Sydney NSW, *Black Mary* and *Gunjies Two Plays*, published by Aboriginal Studies Press, 1996.

Here ends Julie Janson's
Benevolence.

The first edition of the book was printed and
bound at LSC Communications
in Harrisonburg, Virginia, July 2022.

A NOTE ON THE TYPE

The text of this novel was set in Adobe Caslon Pro, a typeface designed by Carol Twombly in 1990. She studied specimen pages printed by William Caslon (designer of the original Caslon) from the mid-eighteenth century. The original Caslon enjoyed great popularity; it was used for the American Declaration of Independence in 1976. Elegant yet dependable, Adobe Caslon Pro shares many of Caslon's best qualities, making it an excellent choice for magazines, journals, book publishing, and corporate communications.

HARPERVIA

An imprint dedicated to publishing international voices,
offering readers a chance to encounter other lives and other
points of view via the language of the imagination.